## SCEPTER OF DEATH

Doc threw a punch. The Wraith blinked. Doc's fist passed through the thing's jaw, unresisting.

Suddenly, the long-bearded apparition began to weave the murky air with his scepter, making passes and circles that threatened the bronze man with terrible punishment.

Slowly, Doc was backed around a corner. He stopped. The Wraith faded back. Doc eased forward, peering around the turn.

Some intuition must have seized the bronze man then. There was no warning sound, but Doc whirled.

And the bejeweled scepter was plunged into his chest!

This time, his whole muscle-cabled body shot with pain . . .

The New Adventures of Doc Savage
Ask your bookseller for the books you have missed.

ESCAPE FROM LOKI by Philip José Farmer
PYTHON ISLE
WHITE EYES
THE FRIGHTENED FISH
THE JADE OGRE
FLIGHT INTO FEAR
THE WHISTLING WRAITH

(*Don't miss another original Doc Savage adventure*, THE FORGOTTEN REALM, *coming in November 1993*)

# THE WHISTLING WRAITH

## by Kenneth Robeson

BANTAM BOOKS
NEW YORK • TORONTO • LONDON • SYDNEY • AUCKLAND

THE WHISTLING WRAITH

*A Bantam Spectra Book / July 1993*

*SPECTRA and the portrayal of a boxed "s" are trademarks of
Bantam Books,
a division of Bantam Doubleday Dell Publishing Group, Inc.*

*Doc Savage is a registered trademark of Condé Nast
Publications, Inc. Registered in U.S. Patent and Trademark
Office and elsewhere.*

*Interior art by Joe DeVito.*

ISBN 0-553-29554-3

*Published simultaneously in the United States and Canada*

*Bantam Books are published by Bantam Books, a division of Bantam
Doubleday Dell Publishing Group, Inc. Its trademark, consisting of the
words "Bantam Books" and the portrayal of a rooster, is Registered in
U.S. Patent and Trademark Office and in other countries. Marca
Registrada. Bantam Books, 1540 Broadway, New York, New York 10036.*

PRINTED IN THE UNITED STATES OF AMERICA

OPM      0 9 8 7 6 5 4 3 2 1

## DOC

Unique among men is Doc Savage, man of amazing abilities, and of but one goal in life—to do good. His bronzed features, his flake-gold eyes, are symbols of power and mercy. There is strength unknown in the mighty thews of his body, and knowledge unfathomable in the brain of this remarkable man. Where others are experts in one line, he is a superman in many. Doc—Clark Savage, Jr.—was raised from infancy for his work of going from one end of the world to the other, righting wrongs, helping the underdog, and liberating the innocent.

## HAM

Ham Brooks, whose mind, whetted by careful legal training, was clever enough to save a whole division in the war, was not able to overcome the weighty evidence piled up against him in a case of stealing hams from the commissary. Monk still reminds Ham of that incident, which is about the only thing that can upset the impeccable, waspish Theodore Marley Brooks, and his great legal mind. Ham's wit is as sharp as the point of the sword cane he invariably carries.

## MONK

Monk, whose looks are described by his nickname, is Andrew
Blodgett Mayfair. He's the world's foremost chemist, super-
seded only by Doc, whose knowledge is greater than any of his
companions. Monk has a fortune in his own name: could make a
dozen fortunes by sticking to his profession. But as an aide of
Doc, he too gives his life so that innocent victims may not suffer,
and would rather fight than eat.

**RENNY**

Renny, or Colonel John Renwick, is a giant of a man who towers four inches over six feet. He weighs fully two hundred and fifty. His face is severe, his mouth thin and grim, and compressed tightly as though he is just finishing a disapproving *"tsk! tsk!"* sound. Altogether, his features have a puritanical look.

But despite his odd looks, Renny is noted for his engineering accomplishments. His favorite act is to slam his great fists—bony monstrosities—through the solid panel of a heavy door. It is his boast that there is no wooden panel which he cannot destroy with his huge hamlike hands.

## LONG TOM

Long Tom—Thomas J. Roberts—known as the wizard of the juice—is the electrical expert of Doc Savage's band of intrepid fighters. Small in stature, his brain holds an enormous amount of learning. It is he who furnishes the electrical equipment and radio devices that have done much to further the success of Doc Savage's triumphs over his enemies—men who wish to further their own ends at the expense and suffering of mankind.

## JOHNNY

Johnny—William Harper Littlejohn, one of the world's greatest archaeologists—is the man who assists Doc Savage when knowledge of ancient countries and ruins is an absolute essential to the success of any expedition undertaken. Johnny is frail-looking, but underneath his gaunt appearance burns a strength and fire unbelievable—a strength equal to that of the strongest man. No hardship is too much for Johnny to endure: his long, lanky frame is capable of assimilating much punishment.

## PAT

Patricia Savage, better known as Pat, is the beautiful and talented cousin of Doc Savage, and is well known to the bronze man's aides, having accompanied them on several of their trips.

Trying to keep Pat from coming along on these expeditions and subjecting herself to dangers that might result in her death has long been Doc's aim—but all to no avail. For Pat, like the other members of Doc's little band, is instilled with the love of adventure.

# Contents

| | | |
|---|---|---|
| I | ONE MISSING KING | 1 |
| II | SWORD SWALLOWER | 13 |
| III | THE PERSISTENT MOUSE | 27 |
| IV | MAN FLASH | 35 |
| V | FAR-FETCHED YARN | 47 |
| VI | CASPAR | 58 |
| VII | GOLD-LEAF TRAIL | 65 |
| VIII | GRIEF FOR PAT | 76 |
| IX | SNOW-BEARDED SPECTER | 82 |
| X | MISSING MOGUL | 93 |
| XI | THE EMPIRE MAKER | 107 |
| XII | THE DISPIRITED | 117 |
| XIII | INFERNAL DEVICE | 124 |
| XIV | THE STRANGENESS | 133 |
| XV | GRIEF AND MORE GRIEF | 143 |
| XVI | THE WORST KINDS OF LUCK | 153 |
| XVII | REIGN OF TERROR | 160 |
| XVIII | TESTIMONY | 170 |
| XIX | VOID! | 178 |
| XX | ANOTHER SWORD SWALLOWER | 190 |
| XXI | SKY SEARCH | 196 |
| XXII | DEAD MAN DYING | 203 |
| XXIII | HARRIED | 216 |
| XXIV | "GRIM SEAS" | 227 |
| XXV | MONARCH OF MYSTIFICATION | 236 |
| XXVI | DOWNFALL | 246 |
| XXVII | CROWN OF GUILT | 258 |

# I

## ONE MISSING KING

The King of Merida vanished before the eyes of the entire world.

In truth, there were perhaps fewer than three hundred witnesses to the king's actual vanishment, but one of them happened to be a newsreel cameraman, and the inexplicable event wound up being repeated in movie theaters all over the world in subsequent weeks. So, there was more truth in the statement than falsehood, technically.

The king—his royal name was Egil Goz the First—had come to Washington, District of Columbia, for one of those elegant soirees known as a state dinner. The king was to dine with the President of the United States and other dignitaries. His homespun steak and baked potato repast was never consumed.

King Goz's motorcade pulled up to the White House at a little past five in the afternoon. The machine was heavy, its sides armor-plated, glass bulletproofed, and tonneau windows curtained to protect His Highness from the stares of commoners. The king had enemies. Particularly in a neighboring state.

The official car was driven by a liveried chauffeur. When the car pulled up, a footman in a uniform more appropriate to an opera than a state affair stepped smartly from the front seat, where he had been riding beside the chauffeur, and opened the back door.

The footman stood with his back ramrod straight, his head thrown back and his eyes looking—seemingly—at nothing, while he waited for King Goz to step forth, resplendent in his bemedaled official uniform. Although King Goz had started out on the road of life as a war chieftain, he was a thoroughly modern king. No regal robes or showy crowns for him.

King Goz did not step out. Minutes crawled past. Overeager newshounds wasted flashbulbs. The lone newsreel cameraman cursed to himself as he wasted expensive film. The President of the United States looked at his watch with polite interest.

Finally, the footman was forced to unbend his military posture and look inside the limousine tonneau.

He gave a squeak in his native tongue and suddenly there was pandemonium.

King Goz could not be found!

Excitement boiled around the limousine. The seat cushions were thrown about. The floorboards examined. Dignified aids suffered the indignity of getting down on hand and knee to look under the chassis. They even checked the trunk, even though witnesses—and there were many—clearly recollected the king entering the limousine outside Blair House, where visiting dignitaries enjoyed American hospitality.

When questioned by District of Columbia police, the other passengers of the limousine—the chauffeur and the befuddled footman—insisted that at no time did the limousine stop to deposit a passenger. Of this, they were quite certain, even vociferous.

One, however, did recall stopping at a light. This was the stiff-faced chauffeur.

"Notice anything suspicious?" a cop inquired.

The chauffeur considered this a moment. Then he remarked in a remarkably unaccented voice, "I do recall a whistling."

"Whistling?"

"Yes, it was rather a melancholy air."

The footman, too, suddenly recalled hearing the whistling. He could not tell from whence it had originated. But he, too, remembered a whistled refrain that was infinitely sad in its strains.

The police next asked for an official photograph, with the idea of manufacturing missing posters for telephotoing purposes.

They received an unpleasant surprise: There were no photographs of King Goz. The point was pressed and a member of the king's anxious retinue remembered a solitary snapshot, which was speedily dispatched to Washington by air mail.

It proved to have been taken when King Goz was a mere lad—a beardless mountain youth dressed in flowing native clothes. It was quite a handsome photograph, showing that the future monarch possessed a certain warrior flair even then.

Unfortunately, it was useless for the purpose required.

That was on Tuesday.

Doc Savage arrived in Washington the following Thursday to look into the matter.

His arrival was quiet. This was necessary, because everybody, almost, knew who Doc Savage was.

It did not stay quiet for long.

Doc Savage arrived by passenger plane at the Washington airport. Normally, Clark Savage, Jr.—to use his given name—seldom resorted to public conveyance. By repute, he owned a fleet of airplanes, and was an expert pilot. The fact that he himself had designed the fleet—which were bronze-painted marvels of aeronautical engineering and instantly recognizable to anyone familiar with his reputation—probably had something to do with his choice of transportation. Doc Savage was the stuff that newspaper copy was made out of.

Doc Savage was spotted by an eagle-eyed newshawk as he deplaned. The airport was awash in reporters. Some had staked out the place in hope of ambushing arriving dignitaries come to the nation's capitol to gather firsthand accounts of the inexplicable regal evanishment. Others were themselves just arriving. The disappearance of King Goz was hot copy.

"Is *that* who I think it is?" gulped a surprised scribe.

"Is who?"

"The tall chap coming down the air stairs."

The other man emitted a bleat of surprise. "I'll be!" he said with the enthusiasm of a man who smells a story. "The Man of Mystery himself."

A third individual joined them, and asked, "Who?"

"The man they claim is a human scientific product," the first scribe explained. "The one who was trained from the cradle by the great scientists of the world until he was greater than any of them—a kind of superman. And he was trained so as to be a kind of a modern knight in an armor of science to go around over the world helping people and righting wrongs."

The second observer whistled. "So *that's* the fellow they claim is probably the most remarkable living human being," he muttered.

"Yeah," said the first. "Blazes! I thought he'd be an old guy. He's ten years younger'n I am, bet you."

"Who are you talking about?" asked the exasperated third journalist.

"Doc Savage."

"Oh." The befuddled scribe had heard of Doc Savage.

Presently, the object of their attention entered the terminal building.

He was a tall man bundled in a tan gabardine coat, who towered over his fellow passengers. A gray hat was pulled low, the snap brim throwing shadow over his face, in an attempt to mask the distinctiveness of his features. It was a futile gesture.

Even bundled up as he was, the amazing nature of his muscular development was evident. The sinews stood in great bars under the fine-textured skin of his neck. Huge cables sprang out in his hands as he walked along. They indicated fabulous physical strength.

Long exposure to tropical suns, coupled with the use of a solar health radiator which he himself had perfected and which had all the beneficial qualities of natural sunlight, had given Doc Savage's skin a bronze hue which caused him frequently to be called the Man of Bronze.

This distinctive bronze coloration all but shouted his identity.

The scribes plucked copy pencils and note pads from about their persons and made a bee line for the big bronze man.

They were blocked by a sudden wall of men.

"One side, pal," invited the first newspaperman in an indignant voice. "We're the Fourth Estate."

The blocking wall of men did not move. They were

polite, but very firm about their not moving. They looked tough. Not in the gangster manner, but tough nevertheless.

"Please step away," one invited in a no-nonsense tone of voice. But for his crisp suitcoat, he might have been a Marine.

"Press, see?" the anxious scribe insisted. Press cards in hatbands were indicated with stabbing fingers.

One of the blocking men removed his billfold and offered it open, for the belligerent newshound to see.

He got a gander at an ornate badge, stepped back, and croaked, "G-men!"

Thereafter, the press contingent became as polite as the human wall of what were obviously government agents. They made room as the agents approached the big bronze fellow and, after exchanging low words, surrounded him protectively.

Doc Savage was efficiently escorted from the building.

A few newspapermen were so bold as to shout questions to the departing bronze man. No answers were forthcoming. No one seemed surprised.

"Well, for the love of Mike!" said one of the press men. "Doc Savage is working with the Feds on this thing."

"So what are we waiting for? Let's hotfoot it after them."

The reporters charged through the busy terminal to the taxi line outside. They spilled out, heads turned every which way. One spied the big bronze man ducking into a nondescript sedan in a line of nondescript sedans.

"There!"

They rushed the line of machines.

One of the Federal men, seeing them approach, flashed his badge and growled, "Any man found to interfere with Uncle Sam's business will find his pants clapped in the local pokey."

That seemed to settle that. The reporters, wearing disappointed faces, watched the line of sedans bear the mystery man, Doc Savage, away.

The scribes then found a bar and began swapping yarns about Doc Savage, hoping to bring to light something new and unpublished which they could give their city editors in lieu of the story they had not gotten.

Doc Savage, their talk disclosed, was quite a remarkable fellow, being something, in fact, of a combination of mental wizard, physical superman, and inventive genius. Concocting wild stories about Doc Savage's fabulous feats, it developed, was a favorite pastime with the tabloid quota of the gathering.

Doc Savage, they all agreed, was a strange fellow who went to the far corners of the world on the rather thankless business of helping other people out of trouble, righting wrongs, aiding the oppressed, and punishing evildoers. It might have been noted that several reporters did not believe that this muddlesome matter of the missing King of Merida was really Doc Savage's business at all. The king was hardly oppressed. In fact, he was something of a benign tyrant, having been elected president in a popular vote and, after a suitable interval, declaring himself king. But all present admitted Doc Savage was a man of mystery, and that anything was possible where he was concerned.

One thing was noteworthy about the confab: No one spoke deprecatingly of Doc Savage. They all seemed to agree that he was a personage of great ability.

One person who was an avid listener was a woman, or girl—if girls are still girls in their early twenties.

She was a little mouse of a girl. She wore a mousy coat and a mousy hat, and her stringy hair was remindful of a rodent that had been washed until all the color had leeched out of its fur. She had followed them out of the airport terminal and been privy to their reaction to the unexpected arrival of Doc Savage. No one had paid her any mind, and now she was listening intently.

A reporter was yarning enthusiastically now. "I heard that this Doc Savage was once offered the crown of a Balkan country, not far from Merida, but turned it down cold. And there was a princess gonna be thrown in with the deal, too."*

"Imagine! Jilting a princess!"

"How thrilling—if true," the girl murmured. She was

---

*The King Maker

noticed then. Not many looked at her twice. She was that plain. But reporters are afflicted by an innate curiosity and, noticing the press card affixed to the lapel of her spring coat, asked after her identity.

Her name, she said, was Barbara Bland. With the Denver *Globe*. Everyone had heard of the *Globe*. No one had heard of her.

The conversation veered back to the subject at hand. Some one remembered that a magazine had just published an extensive article on Doc Savage and one of the journalists went to fetch a copy off a news stand.

The magazine—it was of the sensational true-crime variety—rapidly became dog-eared as it was passed around, reporters taking turns reading the most interesting portions aloud. More than one scribbled notes for later use.

After the young woman reporter had absorbed her fill of the topic at hand, she slipped away and found a telephone booth, where she fed a nickel into the slot and whispered a number to the answering operator.

She continued to whisper after she had reached her party. Her manner was clipped. She might have been dictating copy to a rewrite man on the other end.

"Doc Savage has just arrived." She paused while that sunk in. "Federal agents met him at the airport and took him away. There is no doubt but why he is in town."

The voice on the other end of the line was firm, cultured, and masculine.

"If anyone can find the king," said the voice, "it is this man, Savage. He may represent the opportunity we have been waiting for. Attempt to learn all that can be learned."

"Understood," the girl said, and terminated the connection.

On her way out the door, she passed the reporters. They were still engaged in the swapping of yarns about Doc Savage. If anything, their talk was wilder than it had been.

The girl reporter, Barbara Bland, gave a tiny snort of disbelief as she walked by. It was plain she took the reportorial tall tales with a very large grain of sodium.

\* \* \*

The Federal agents who had taken charge of Doc Savage were respectful. He might have been their superior. In a way, he was. Doc Savage held an honorary rank of special agent with the Justice Department's Bureau of Investigation, in return for certain assistances rendered in the past.

They first took him to the scene of the disappearance—or rather to the spot where it had been discovered, in front of the White House door.

From there, the bronze man backtracked to the intersection where the eerie whistling had been heard, according to the chauffeur and footman. It was an open intersection, literally around the corner from the White House. The circuitous route the kingly motorcade had taken was evidently for purposes of making a dramatic entrance and impressing the cameras. The king could have walked to his assignation in less time than it took to be driven.

At the intersection, there were no objects or buildings which might have produced a whistling sound, whether mechanically or through the action of wind. There was not even a whistle-blowing traffic cop stationed at any corner.

If the bronze man made any discoveries, he gave no outward indication.

"Take me to the king's limousine," he requested.

The vehicle was garaged in the Department of Justice Building. It was a short walk from Blair House to the Justice Building—virtually everything in official Washington is within walking distance of everything else—but they drove, anyway.

There, the bronze man examined the machine. The hood and boot had been thrown up and the doors all lay open. Additionally, fenders had been removed for inspection of the wheels and chassis.

After a cursory examination of these cavities, the bronze man fell to investigating the tonneau into which the King of Merida had stepped, not to be seen again. He lifted cushions, pried up the floor coverings, and conducted what appeared to be a very thorough search.

He rolled the windows up and down, examining the thick, bulletproof glass. There was a glass partition between tonneau and driver's compartment. This, he cranked up and down as well. The speaking tube came in for scrutiny, too.

The Federal men watched in silence. Their orders were not to interfere with the bronze man who was Doc Savage. This had come from the Director himself.

When he was finished in the back, Doc Savage fell to examining the driver's compartment. He was not at this long when an unexpected sound permeated the garage confines.

It was a trilling, low and melodious. Tuneless, it roved the scale, sounding in the confines of the garage like the sound of a small breeze in a chill Arctic ice pack. It hardly seemed to be a product of human vocal cords, but there was no other possible source. The Federal agents found themselves looking at one another doubtfully as if suspecting one of their number to be the author of the elusive sound.

Doc Savage suddenly emerged from his study, and the sound trailed off. Only then did it occur to the agents that the strange bronze man might have been responsible for the nebulous tremolo.

Doc straightened, holding something between metallic thumb and forefinger.

An agent was so bold as to ask, "Have you found something, Mr. Savage?"

"Hairs."

"Eh?"

"Red hairs."

The agents exchanged blank looks. The royal car had been examined for fingerprints, blood, and other forensic clues. No one had thought to look for hairs, or if they happened upon any, attached great importance to them. Hairs fall out of perfectly healthy heads all the time.

But the mysterious bronze man evidently thought the hairs he discovered had significance. The G-men looked at the hairs. They were short and thick and definitely reddish. Almost like copper wire.

"Must belong the the chauffeur," said an agent promptly. "He was a redhead, by reports."

Doc reached into his coat and from somewhere produced a metal phial with a screw cap. He unscrewed the cap and let the metallic red hairs drop into the phial. Recapping it, he stowed it back on his person.

Then Doc Savage said, "There were numerous press

photographers and a newsreel cameraman present when the king's limousine stopped before the White House."

"There were," an agent admitted.

"I would like to see their pictures," Doc said.

"All of them?" gulped the agent.

"All."

It was not as difficult an undertaking as the Federal agents expected. They had already confiscated several sample photographs, and when none proved illuminating, further requests were abandoned. It was assumed that the king had disappeared en route to the state dinner and that no clues were to be found among the photographic record, any more than a snapshot of a patch of sky where lightning had appeared a day before would reveal any trace of the flash.

Too, the name of Doc Savage opened many doors. The photos began arriving at the Department of Justice Building, along with requests for interviews. The photographs were accepted. The interview requests were not.

A few magazines and newspapers, hearing of this lack of reciprocity, made noises about withholding their photos.

The editors in question received personal telephone calls from no less than the Director of the Bureau of Investigation of the Department of Justice. The photographs were sheepishly surrendered.

In a projection room in the Justice Department, Doc Savage was studying the photographs. Oddly enough, he had not removed his hat and his fine-textured features were not readily visible to onlookers. A person familiar with the bronze man's methods would have found this behavior uncharacteristic. Doc Savage seldom wore a hat.

"The newsreel is here," announced a government clerk.

The bronze man left off his examination. The reel was loaded and the room darkened.

They watched intently.

The so-called raw footage was brief. Ragged. It depicted the king's limousine arriving, the chauffeur and footman visible through the windscreen. The film darkened and brightened again, this time showing a different angle.

The footman emerged from the ostentatious machine,

went to the rear door, and threw it open. The footage dwelt on the open door for what seemed an interminable interval until the footman, impatient, bent and looked within.

The rest was chaos. Milling reporters and police. A shot of the waiting president and other dignitaries. It was difficult to imagine how the footage had been spliced into anything coherent, but it had, and was already packing in theatergoers around the civilized world.

After the lights had come on again, Doc Savage stood up and said, "I think the chauffeur might help clear up the mystery."

"Don't you want to see the film again, Mr. Savage?"

"Not necessary," replied Doc.

They went to the dignified hostelry where the chauffeur—and the rest of the king's retinue—were ensconced and asked for him. The Merida party had long since departed the official hospitality of Blair House, to await the results of the official investigation.

There they were met by a stern-faced white-haired man in an ostentatious crimson uniform and carrying about him a very dignified air. The medals on his chest were many.

"I am General Graul Frontenac," he said by way of introduction. Even his voice had a stiffness.

"This is Doc Savage," one of the G-men said, indicating the bronze giant.

The general was burdened by the stiff-backed carriage of the European military man to whom soldiering is a point of family honor.

At the mention of the name Doc Savage, he lost some of his stiff-necked bearing.

He was wearing a monocle in one eye and it popped out, saved from extinction only by a long black cord anchored to his gold uniform braid, which was profuse. The general clamped the monocle back into his eye and employed it to give Doc Savage a thorough going-over. He was very bold in the manner in which he did this.

"The Director personally asked that Mr. Savage enter the investigation," one of the Federal men said, hoping to dispel the awkwardness of the moment.

General Frontenac clicked his heels together and executed a stiff bow.

"I am honored to meet the great *Domnule* Savage," he purred.

If the bronze man was impressed by this morsel of flattery, he did not acknowledge it. Instead, he said, "We would like to question the chauffeur who was driving the limousine on the night the king vanished."

"But he has already been questioned thoroughly."

"We would like to question him further, please."

Behind the monocle, the weaker eye of General Frontenac of Merida swam blearily.

"As you wish," he said, snapping his fingers at two courtiers who rushed ahead to pave the way. "Let us go to him now."

They were led to a suite elsewhere on the same floor. The courtiers had thrown open the door and stood waiting impassively.

They entered. The room was unoccupied. General Frontenac pointed his monocle at the two trembling courtiers.

"Where is he?" he snapped.

"W-we do not kn-know, General," one stammered.

"W-we have not seen him today," the other gulped.

Red-faced, General Frontenac demanded of the courtiers, "When was he last seen?"

The courtiers looked blank. Neither, it turned out, could recall when they had last laid eyes on the missing chauffeur to the missing king.

"*Find him!*" General Frontenac thundered, his face crimsoning until it threatened to rival the blood hue of his sumptuous uniform.

The chauffeur was nowhere to be found. It was not surprising. In the land from which the chauffeur had come, men had lost their heads for less offense than misplacing a head of state.

"*Ce plictistor!* How vexing!" said General Frontenac, after a complete search had turned up no trace of the man. "This is very strange." He turned his monocled eye in the bronze man's direction. "Tell me, Savage, do you suppose the strange fate that befell our glorious monarch might have taken the chauffeur, as well?"

The bronze man did not answer. Indeed, he seemed to not have heard the question. His eyes were questing about the chauffeur's room. It was quite lavish.

He turned abruptly, and said, "The footman, if you do not mind."

Again, General Frontenac snapped his fingers and courtiers rushed ahead to, presumably, announce them.

Why they would have to be announced to a flunky of the low status of a footman no one thought to ask. Or if they did, the question was never put forth.

The courtiers came rushing back, white-faced and winded. They talked over one another in a violent effort to be the first to break the news.

Finally, the plainly exasperated general demanded of one, simultaneously hushing the other with a curt chop of his hand, "*Cum?* What is it? Speak!"

"The footman," gasped the courtier who had been given leave to speak, "is dead."

"Dead?"

"Murdered."

# II

## SWORD SWALLOWER

The footman had indeed been murdered.

They found him, ironically enough considering his occupation, impaled to a footstool in his own room. It was an expensive room, but not as lavish as that which had formerly been occupied by the chauffeur who had evaporated.

No one was paying attention to the surroundings, however. All eyes rested on the bejeweled sword which had been used to skewer the unfortunate footman where he knelt. It had been thrust into his mouth with great force and driven downward through his vitals. The begored point had exited the victim's back and penetrated the footstool's cushion.

Seeing the sword hilt protruding from the dead face, General Graul Frontenac swore profusely in his native tongue.

"Tha-that sword!" he choked, lapsing back into English and pointing at the bizarre sight.

They waited for him to get it out.

"It-it is the king's own ceremonial sword!" he managed.

This much might have been guessed by the expensive baubles which encrusted the golden hilt which filled the footman's mouth so grotesquely. The next statement the general made gave a twist to the mystery that shocked even the hardened G-men.

"Good King Goz," the general said in a hollow voice, "was wearing that very sword the night he entered the limousine from which he never emerged."

No one had anything to say to that.

The coroner was called, the corpse photographed from all angles and covered with a sheet pending removal by hearse. There was a knot of hard-faced police detectives, and after some consultation with the government men, it was agreed that this was a Federal matter. The detectives went away. They looked glad to be shed of the responsibility.

After the death scene had been completely scrutinized by all present, General Frontenac put forth a theory.

"It is clear to me," he announced in an important voice, "that the poor footman has been done away with by the missing chauffeur."

The government agents began nodding their heads in silent agreement. It was a reasonable theory. They looked to the bronze man, who was deep in the study of the dead man's awkward posture. He had removed the sheet.

"Do you not agree, *Domnule* Savage?" he pressed.

Doc said absently, "There is no evidence pointing to the chauffeur."

"But," sputtered the general, "it is so obvious. The chauffeur is somehow responsible for the disappearance of our beloved monarch, and has now murdered the footman. Perhaps they were accomplices in this act of extreme treason."

Restoring the sheet, Doc Savage straightened. "One thing is clear," he imparted.

"And that is?" inquired General Frontenac interestedly.

"Once we locate the chauffeur, we will locate King Goz."

"You sound very confident of this," the general murmured. "As if you have already plumbed this unfathomable mystery."

"I would," Doc said calmly, "be very much surprised if my theory were to be eventually disproved."

"Which is?" the general prompted.

"That the missing chauffeur is the key to this particular mystery."

General Frontenac lost his monocle again. This time, he did not seem to notice. The crimson was coming back into his features. He opened his mouth to speak, sputtered something unintelligible, cleared his throat noisily—and decided in the end to say nothing.

It was clear that the manner in which this big bronze American fellow had swept into the puzzle of his ruler's uncanny evanishment had bowled the Balkan general over to the point of speechlessness. The fame of the U.S. Bureau of Investigation's G-men had spread even to his tiny nation. Yet they had accomplished nothing.

Less than an hour in Washington, Doc Savage had all but solved the mystery—if his unspoken theory were proved correct.

"I wonder," ventured the general slowly, "if you have a thought as to the meaning of the strange whistling that was heard prior to His Highness's disappearance?"

"Not as yet," Doc admitted

"I have hesitated to mention this before, but the whistling may have significance."

"How so?"

"I myself did not hear this sound, of course, but the footman and the chauffeur both claimed that they did. They repeated it to me, and I was quite astonished by what I heard."

"Go on."

"It matched exactly the folk lament known in my country as 'The Funeral March of Old King Fausto.' Perhaps you know the story."

"I have heard a version," Doc admitted.

"This was during one of the periods of political strife in my country, many, many years ago," related General Frontenac. "King Fausto was a wicked ruler, who burdened the good Meridan people with unjust laws and unfair taxes. In time, there was a popular revolt and King Fausto seized. As punishment for his wickedness, Fausto was sentenced to death, and the manner of his execution was to be chained in the lowermost dungeon of the royal castle as, brick by brick, a confining wall was constructed before his unrepentant eyes. Do you understand what I am saying?"

Doc nodded. "He was entombed, still living."

The general shrugged. "Those were crueler times, of course. At any rate, the bricks sealed him in a small space and death was expected to be slow. Yet, a day later when the people went down into the dungeon to tap at the brick wall for signs of life, they were astonished to hear a whistling refrain emerging from behind the bricks."

At this point, General Frontenac pursed his thin lips and essayed a tune. It was, for a whistle, very close to a dirge. A Scotsman would probably have enjoyed it. The patient Federal men, hearing it, developed long faces. It had that effect.

At length, the general stifled the melancholy refrain.

He continued his tale. "For days, whenever the people ventured down into the castle dungeon, the king's sad whistling mocked them—taunted them with the bitter knowledge that the hated Fausto yet lived. There were those who called for the wall to be broken down and the despot put to the sword. Others insisted that the slow, lingering death by asphyxiation or starvation had been the sentence meted out, and it must stand. Still others claimed that the king was already departed, and it was his shade which whistled."

* * *

The general drew in a ragged breath.

"For seven days they argued, and for seven days the people stood at the brick wall and listened to the maddening whistling. On the eighth, the wall was ordered taken down."

The general paused, obviously for dramatic effect. He went on in a low, doubtful tone. "When the brick and mortar had been set aside, they discovered the limp, dangling chains in which Old King Fausto had been hung. But of the king, there was no sign."

One of the listeners gasped.

"No body was even found," General Frontenac went on. "Although the entire dungeon was taken apart, brick by brick, no secret doors or panels, or possible escape route, ever came to light. All that remained was the memory of the whistling defiance of the despot, Fausto."

"Huh!" a G-man grunted. "Another missing king."

"Since those days, there have been tales told of Old King Fausto—or his ghost—roaming the royal castle. Whenever a calamity befell the kingdom of Merida, always someone—a chambermaid or page—would later claim to have seen the dead king's shadow, or heard his dreadful whistle."

"Superstition," Doc said.

The general adjusted his monocle, and his eyebrow took hold of it again. "So, too, did I think. But of late, King Fausto's ghost has been seen about our royal palace. Many have reported the sad, bittersweet sound of his whistling."

"Anyone can imitate a whistle," Doc stated. "You yourself have just demonstrated this."

"Ah," said General Frontenac quickly. "But no less than His Highness has confided to me that with his own eyes he beheld King Fausto—or his shade—roaming the palace halls, attired in kingly robes and fingering his long white beard as he made his rounds. His Highness, although a brave man, was so shocked by this sight that he retreated to his bedchamber until the whistling could no longer be heard. What do you think of this, *Domnule* Savage?"

"A fanciful story," Doc stated mildly.

"*Intr'adevar*. Indeed. But the whistle was heard before

His Highness vanished. And it is a popular belief in my country that the shade of Old King Fausto exists only to bring harm to the royal line. It suggests a threat to the ruling family of my country, does it not?"

"Possibly."

"And we have but one enemy in the entire world. And that is the territorially-ambitious president of our Balkan neighbor, Carrullana."

"With whom you have been having border disputes."

"Correct."

"Perhaps this suggests a line of investigation?" General Frontenac said pointedly.

"It does," agreed Doc.

The general clicked his heels elaborately, taking his monocle from his eye and executing a reserved bow. "*Ma bucar*. Good. If I can be of service in any way, I shall be most grateful for the opportunity."

"Thank you," said Doc, and without a word left the death room, the Federal agents in tow.

Outside the hotel, Doc Savage was met by an entourage of the Fourth Estate. Every police station has a reporter assigned to it, and the call for a hearse and detectives naturally brought curious scribes, who had stationed themselves outside the hotel in ghoulish anticipation of a body.

The Federal men flashed their badges and formed a flying wedge about the bronze man. They bulled their way through the crowd of reporters. Doc Savage ignored the questions shouted at him.

"Is it true that the king has been found murdered?" one newsman demanded, evidently giving voice to a popular rumor.

He was ignored.

At one point, a mousy-looking young woman pushed her way to the edge of the swarm of scribblers. She was a very determined woman, if the manner in which she employed her elbows to knock huskier rivals out of her path was any measure of singlemindedness.

"Mr. Savage! Mr. Savage!" she cried, waving a stenographer's pad. "I'm Barbara Bland of the Denver *Globe*. I would like an interview, please."

This brought an outburst of laughter from the others.

Wry smiles quirked the otherwise stolid faces of some of the G-men.

"No interviews," Doc said firmly.

"Haw!" said a reporter unkindly. "What a she-cub! Doesn't even know the bronze guy never gives interviews."

"Darn!" said the woman calling herself Barbara Bland angrily.

The Federal men made it to the cars and got the doors closed. The autos were surrounded, but that lasted only long enough for the sheeted body to be brought out. Reporters surged for the hearse. They were too late. The back door was clapped shut and the hearse took off, the government cars in close pursuit.

The body was taken to the District of Columbia morgue and separated from the blood-soaked footstool and ceremonial sword worn—according to reports—by King Egil the First just before his eerie disappearance. The autopsy was brief; it turned up no cause of death other than the obvious one—impalement. Doc Savage assisted. Of all his specialties, he was foremost a surgeon.

The body was then wrapped in a sheet and rolled into a refrigerated drawer. The sword was wrapped in oilskin and laid to one side, with a tag on it. It was evidence, and so would not be returned to the Meridan government until the matter was concluded.

No one could venture of a guess as to when that would be.

The next day, with the headlines still dominated by the matter of the missing monarch, Doc Savage did a strange thing. He visited a museum.

Before he did so, he called his New York headquarters, which was situated on the eighty-sixth floor of Manhattan's most impressive skyscraper.

The voice that answered the phone was distinctly female.

"Hello, cousin," it said. It was a very buoyant voice.

"Pat," said Doc with a distinct lack of enthusiasm.

"The very same," Pat said cheerfully. "And don't sound so darned delighted to hear my voice; you'll give me a complex or something."

"I had thought," Doc said dryly, "that you had already left for Canada. And your fishing vacation."

"I did. I came back. Forgot my fishing tackle. Can't catch fish without tackle, now can I?"

"It is not like you to be so forgetful. This does not have anything to do with this Washington matter I am presently investigating, does it?"

"Exactly what are you trying to accuse me of?" Pat demanded.

"Exactly what might be expected." Doc Savage sounded weary. "You think you scent some excitement. So you have forgotten all about your vacation."

Pat's voice became conspiratorial. "Find the mislaid monarch yet?"

"No."

"Swell! I have me some solving notions. I'll be right down."

"Not for a minute!" Doc said swiftly. "You started a vacation. Go ahead and take it."

"But, Doc, you know I dote on excitement—"

"Pat, there is a difference between excitement and danger. My objection applies to the latter. Catching a game salmon can be just as exciting—"

"As Renny would say, 'Holy cow!' "

"We have been over these arguments before, Pat."

"Yes, and—"

Doc cut Pat's protestations off. "Are Monk and Ham at hand?"

"Haven't seen hide nor hair of them. Renny, Johnny, or Long Tom either. It's positively spooky up here all by my lonesome."

"Renny, Johnny, and Long Tom are absent from New York," Doc stated.

"I stand ready to serve in their stead," Pat said jauntily.

The men named were Doc's five assistants. An unusual group, the five. Each a skilled master in his particular profession. Each a lover of adventure, of excitement. Each, above all, an admirer of the amazing Man of Bronze. They had been with Doc some time—whether because they had such an admiration for him, or whether they liked the excitement the association got them, was difficult to say.

Doc considered. "Perhaps there is something you might do to help out," he said at last.

"What's that?"

"Contact the Denver *Globe*. Give a fake name. Do not let them know you are asking on my behalf."

"Sounds mysterious."

"Ask after a reporter named Barbara Bland."

"Who is she? Some *femme fatale* after your scalp?"

"Claims to be on the *Globe* staff."

"And you don't believe her?" Pat questioned.

"There is reason not to," Doc admitted.

"I'll get right on it."

Doc terminated the connection and, after donning his gray hat and drawing the collar of his tan topcoat up to the level of his ears, went down to the hotel lobby and claimed a waiting taxi. Although he was bundled up to avoid recognition, his passage through the lobby did not go unnoticed.

The door to a telephone booth popped open and a mousy young woman stepped out. She slipped up to the great revolving doors and overhead Doc give instructions to the hack driver.

"The museum, please."

In Washington, there is really only one museum of consequence. The National Museum, popularly known as the Smithsonian. The mousy girl—the airport reporters would have identified her as Barbara Bland—jumped into the next cab in line and rapped, "Smithsonian. Please hurry."

It was a short distance to the sprawling museum, and the hackman had his work cut out for him beating the first cab. But he managed it.

He pulled up and deposited the young lady, who tipped him excessively and disappeared into the great entrance.

The National Museum is located on the west side of the Mall, the broad strip of park which is situated in the center of Washington, between the grandeur of the Capitol dome and the masonry finger that is the Washington Monument. Starting at the entrance and going completely through the museum so as to observe all the exhibits and read the cards stating what they were, might very easily take up a week's time.

Various wings of the museum were given over to archæology, geology, anthropology, and other branches of scientific knowledge.

Doc Savage arrived, paid the admission fee, and went directly to the Mayan exhibit. This was dominated by cases containing artifacts pertaining to the Mayan Indians of Central America, a tribe that as far as its once-advanced civilization was concerned, had fallen into decline centuries before Columbus came. They had never built more than a handful of cities, and these ruins were subsequently covered over by jungle. The Mayan people had all but vanished from their haunts. It was exceedingly difficult to find traces that they had ever existed. Archæologists therefore considered them very important.

Doc Savage moved among these exhibits, pausing every so often. There were life-sized wax replicas of Mayan people in their habitats. Dioramas. Everything looked astoundingly lifelike.

It was not a busy time for the museum. Few patrons were inside. In fact, there came a moment when the Mayan room was empty, except for a single, rather bored-looking guard.

Soon, several men percolated into the room. Most were nondescript. One, however, stood out. He was a big man, not in the way of Doc Savage, whose size was evident only when he was near something to which he could be compared. This man was a human hulk. His shoulders were round, as was his chest. His head had a roundness to it, too. Not that the newcomer was fat. He was not. The way he rolled into the room, making soft sounds with his feet, told that. If anything, he had something of the aspect of a football player. A linebacker, perhaps. He moved to a case containing a broken tablet of some sort and began studying it.

The men distributed themselves about the room, and gave their attention to various exhibits. From time to time, they stole quick, furtive glances in the direction of Doc Savage and the guard.

One man sidled up to the big hulk of a fellow and whispered, "That's him, Hike. Tan topcoat and gray hat. Just like the chief said."

"O.K. Get set," said the one addressed as Hike. The first man moved off and joined the other two.

The bronze man seemed oblivious to all this furtive activity. He was gazing intently at a display case containing an array of Mayan weapons—stone-handled knives with wicked blades shaped from obsidian, a black volcanic glass which when chipped to a smoky brown edge has the cutting ability of a modern straight razor. A prominent bronze plaque named Clark Savage, Sr. as the donor.

Clark Savage, Sr. was Doc's father, now deceased, and the man who had placed Doc in the hands of scientists for the work he now pursued. Few knew it, but Clark Savage, Sr. had discovered a tribe of Mayans still holding sway over a valley deep in Central America, and in repayment for certain kindnesses, the leader of the tribe had promised to supply the son with a limitless supply of Mayan gold to help finance his remarkable career. Doc, in turn, kept the secret of their existence from an intruding world, and was fabulously wealthy as a result.

The hulk named Hike remained at the case which held the tablet covered with Mayan hieroglyphics. He coughed softly. The other two ripped blackjacks from under their clothing, and applied them to the head of the unsuspecting guard.

The use of force was excessive under the circumstances. If it had been intended to silence the guard before he could give outcry, the raiders were very much mistaken, for the guard emitted a bleat of shock—perhaps reflexive—before crumpling to the polished floor.

This, in turn, captured the attention of the bronze man.

He turned. The others—there were now four, led by the hulking Hike—were advancing on him with grim purpose.

Obviously preparing for a fight, the big bronze man shucked off his topcoat and let his gray hat fall to the floor.

He stood revealed now. The bronze of his hair was a little darker than the bronze of his features. The hair was straight and fitted so close as to give the impression of a metal skullcap. Not the least thing were the incredible tendons visible under the bronze skin and hair.

Most arresting of all were his eyes—uncanny eyes,

like pools of flake gold, always in motion. In the dim illumination of the museum, they seemed to scintillate faintly.

Doc stood his ground, and did not look particularly perturbed at the prospect of imminent violence. Neither did he register, as far as appearances went, any great excitement over what he was doing. This was one of his peculiar traits. Only on the rarest occasions did he show any undue excitement.

The same could not be said for his would-be assailants. Spreading his arms to hold back his fellows, the hulking Hike stopped short, a flabbergasted look making his face roundly incredulous.

Had he been confronted with a large and obviously hungry lion, the hulking Hike could not have looked more shocked.

He said suddenly, "Careful, boys! Careful! We're standin' right in the open door of hell!"

His companions did not all agree with him. Two of them sniffed and drew weapons which seemed to be ordinary children's water pistols.

Doc Savage showed he was not recklessly brave then. He faded back, mere inches ahead of twin streams of some pungent chemical. His keen sense of smell identified it in an instant. Hospital chloroform! A potent knock-out solution—if the fumes were inhaled deeply for several seconds.

Still moving away from the splashing streams, the bronze man held his breath. The water pistols were of the cylindrical type. Their capacity was not great. This fact was demonstrated a moment later when the tiny nozzles ceased discharging.

"We're outta gas!" a man complained. "And he ain't down for the count yet."

Hike growled, "Need a job done right, a man's gotta do it himself!" And the hulking bruiser rushed the bronze giant, arms out, ready to grab his foe. He made a confident clutch, and got armfuls of air.

Hike gaped at the empty space where the bronze man had stood. Off balance, he teetered. He did not see the hand that sent him sliding on his face, to mash his nose up against a rude stone idol. He recovered enough to get himself organized.

Hike yelled, "Sic 'im, boys! If you lick 'im, your names will go down in history!"

The others produced additional weapons. Tiny flat automatics, easily concealable and, at close quarters, as deadly as heavy-caliber army automatics.

"Nix!" Hike barked. "This guy won't bluff and you've only got blank cartridges in your guns!"

The next instant, the bronze man had grabbed the gun. He pointed it at the hard marble floor, snapped it, and it roared, but no bullet hit the floor. Blanks, right enough.

The fact that the men should have blank cartridges in their guns was surprising enough to cause the bronze man's unusual flake-gold eyes to widen.

Doc flung the weapon aside and began treating his attackers in a similarly careless fashion. A man would attempt to grasp his coat, only to find himself bouncing off walls and other hard surfaces. It soon became clear that the unexpected was about to transpire. The amazing bronze giant, who had a fabulous set of muscles, was going to whip his several foes.

*Had* them whipped, in fact! He crowded them back, bruised, panting, into a corner. Each man who tried to rush past him, he drove back with blunt, awful blows.

"Our mothers'll sure be proud of us for this!" Hike puffed. He turned, yanked a stone-bladed hatchet off the wall at his back, and let fly.

It was neatly dodged by the giant man of bronze.

Hike now demonstrated he was not the halfwit his laughable operations had made him appear.

Hike seized the unconscious guard and bore him back up the hallway, obviously intending to use him as a shield against the mighty bronze giant's wrath.

The bronze man, as soon as he could tear himself away from his foes, wheeled and pursued Hike.

Hike had gained a few yards. He turned as he ran, saw the Herculean bronze man was pursuing him alone.

"Run!" Hike howled at his men. "Get yourselves clear! I'll handle the rest!"

The men obediently turned and ran for the nearest exit. Hike had an unusual set of muscles himself. He made time, bulky as he was. But he was not a rabbit, which he needed to be to escape. The bronze giant overhauled him.

Hike suddenly hurled the limp guard back against the bronze man. This delayed the latter slightly. Doc caught the man as if he were no more substantial than a feather pillow. Mindful of the guard's injured skull, he kept the man from falling to the hard floor.

Hike wrenched open a door, popped through it, slammed it. There was a bolt on the inside. He threw it. He did not stop there to get his breath, but dashed away.

It was evident that Hike knew every recess of the great museum, because he scuttled through remote passages, occasionally hunching over to knock aside a shouting guard, and left by a side door.

He found his men grouped anxiously on a side street.

"Run!" Hike gasped. "If we get outta this, we'd all better go to church Sunday."

"We gonna let *one* guy put the kibosh on us?" a man snarled.

"Yep," Hike told him. "Because that one guy happens to be Doc Savage."

"Doc Savage?"

"The Man of Miracles himself," Hike puffed. "Come on!"

They ran.

In the meantime, Doc Savage had lowered the insensate guard to the floor, made sure he was alive, and ascertained that dynamite or a cutting torch was the only way of opening the door immediately.

He whipped back out of the museum through the same exit employed by Hike's gang just moments before, and immediately observed Hike and his erstwhile kidnapers legging it down a side street.

A few yards to the left stood a young woman. A rather plainly attired young woman whose gray eyes were wide with amazement at the goings-on.

The bronze man ignored her, and raced after Hike and his men. But the latter had two large automobiles waiting, and leaping into the machines, they took off.

Doc Savage, observing a taxi cab parked down another side street, whipped toward it. The cab was a mossy-green thing, ancient. The driver stuck his head out.

The driver had his cap yanked down over a somewhat thin face. In the back of the car sat another man, but his figure was indistinct. A bulky fellow, though.

Doc Savage stopped. He shouted. His words were not English; they were in a tongue that would not be understood by more than a dozen men in the so-called civilized world—ancient Mayan, the pure strain.

The car instantly left. Its speed was surprising for such a ramshackle-looking old vehicle.

Doc Savage seemed to lose interest in the two cars in which Hike's gang had fled. He did, however, repeat the license numbers, once forward and once backward, which was enough to fix them almost permanently in his trained mind.

A newsboy, unaware of what had happened, stood on a nearby corner, waved a paper, and yelled the headlines.

"All about phantom potentate!" he shouted. "Goz still gone! Extra!"

## III

### THE PERSISTENT MOUSE

After the ancient green taxi had departed the vicinity, Doc Savage turned back into the museum.

He was accosted by the young woman he had passed.

"Mr. Savage," she said anxiously. "Perhaps you remember me. I'm Barbara Bland. With the *Globe*?"

Her eyes were a sparkling gray and her lips were probably all that could be asked for—when they were not held in such a grim line. Seen up close, her lack of make-up did not detract from her natural beauty so much.

"You followed me here," said Doc. It was not a question, but a statement. It was not challenged by the girl calling herself Barbara Bland.

"I really, really must have an interview for my paper,"

she said in a wheedling tone. She actually wrung her hands together, and brushed at an eye as if to intercept a tear.

"It is not my policy to give interviews," Doc said flatly, reentering the museum. He moved briskly toward the spot where he had left the unconscious guard.

"Let me explain," Barbara Bland said breathlessly, running a little in an effort to keep up. "The *Globe* hired me on a trial basis. I need this job very badly. The editor—he's an old meanie, I guess—promised that if I could furnish some good copy on this missing king matter, he would make me a permanent part of his staff. So you see, I'm in a fix. Oh, won't you take pity on me?"

"Sorry."

This was not the answer the young woman reporter expected. "In heaven's name, why not?"

"In our line of work," Doc explained, "publicity is bad business. Enemies could learn useful items that could be turned against us. As a matter of fact, for the past several months, we have been keeping our pictures out of the newspapers, and have been buying up all copies of magazines and newspapers containing our pictures, all over the country. We have managed to have the radio commentators cease mentioning us. It seemed to be getting results."

Barbara Bland was carrying a hand bag. She pulled a rolled-up magazine—it was of the true-crime variety—from within. "Then how," she challenged, "do you explain *this?*"

Doc's flake-gold eyes flicked to the cover. A nearly imperceptible frown darkened his metallic features. It was the magazine which had cover-featured him.

"A regrettable event," he said. "And the chief reason I have been forced to try solving this mystery incognito."

They reached the guard. He was no longer alone. A fellow guard had found him. The latter looked up, seemed about to reach for his sidearm, then recognized the approaching Man of Bronze.

"Mr. Savage!" he said. "What do you know about this?"

Doc dropped to one knee, moved his strong metallic fingers about the back of the guard's skull, seemed satisfied by what he learned, and wiped a tiny amount of crimson off his fingertips onto a handkerchief.

"No fracture," he pronounced, coming erect. "This

man should be hospitalized at once, in case there is concussion."

"An ambulance is on its way. But what happened here?"

"He ran afoul of an attempted kidnaping," Doc explained.

"Yeah? Who'd they try to kidnap?"

"Myself, it would appear."

The guard looked dumfounded. "What kind of ignoramuses would try to snatch *you*, sir?"

"That remains to be determined," said Doc. "Has anything been stolen?"

"Not that anybody's found."

Barbara Bland inserted herself into this conversation. "Do you believe these kidnapers are the same ones who spirited away the King of Merida?" she queried.

The young woman might have been expecting any kind of an answer, but the one she got surprised her. It was silence. The giant bronze man seemed simply not to hear the question, just as he had missed General Frontenac's interrogatives earlier in the day. That was a strange trait of this remarkable Man of Bronze, frequently an aggravating one. When there was something he did not want to discuss, he became suddenly deaf to all queries on the point.

"I asked if you thought those men you were chasing had anything to do with the king's disappearance," Barbara Bland persisted.

Doc Savage continued to ignore her. He went to the display case that had been donated by his father and, satisfied it had not been damaged in the fracas, moved away, his weirdly active eyes questing about the Mayan room.

The other guard went into the next room, to check on the exhibits.

Barbara Bland tapped a shoe on the floor angrily and said, "Well?" But that did no good.

At last she changed her tactics and tried cajoling. "Please, can't you tell me something? Anything? I am terribly desperate."

Before the bronze man could reply, there came an interruption. From somewhere about Doc Savage's person a voice emerged.

"Calling Doc. Renny calling Doc."

From under his coat, the bronze man extracted a small case equipped with knobs and a grille. It would have filled out his inner coat pocket completely. He spoke into the grille.

"Go ahead, Renny."

"We trailed those birds to an apartment house across from the Capitol Building. It's in a rat hole called Dingman Alley. The name on the door says 'Hike Ewing.' "

"Hike is the large fellow," Doc advised.

"Fits him," grunted Renny.

The girl, gazing wide-eyed at the case, said nothing.

Renny's voice came out of the compact case again. "This Hike made a telephone call a few minutes ago. Long Tom was unable to get his electrical listening-in device close to the right telephone wire in time to catch the conversation, though."

The girl made surprised shapes with her colorless mouth. "That thing is a radio receiver!" she gasped. "And so small." She added, "Renny and Long Tom are two of your assistants. I have just been reading about them. You had them at the museum, and they had their work assigned to them. You certainly do not overlook any bets, do you?"

Doc Savage seemed not to hear her.

Renny asked, "What do you want us to do about this, Doc?"

"Sit tight," the bronze man advised. "I am on my way."

Doc put away the case, and a contingent of District of Columbia bluecoats arrived. They asked many questions. They were deferential in the manner in which they questioned the bronze man.

After Doc had explained that the hulking Hike and his men had escaped—Doc left out the fact that his own men had trailed them to Dingman Alley—the police turned their attention to Barbara Bland.

"And what's your role in this?" one demanded.

"I can vouch for her," Doc said unexpectedly. And the men in blue calmed down as if oil had been poured on their troubled waters.

Barbara Bland looked at the bronze man, and for the first time seemed to become aware that he might be more than a big fellow named Doc Savage. He was strikingly handsome, and furthermore apparently not aware that a very attractive young woman stood at his side. An intriguing combination, to the young woman concerned.

"If no one minds," Doc said, "I must continue my investigation."

No one minded. In fact, the police all but curtseyed the bronze man out of the museum.

Barbara Bland hurried after him, saying, "You owe me a favor."

"How so?"

"You neglected some items back there. Like the minor fact that your two aids followed those men to a house."

"My aids and I prefer to work unencumbered," the bronze man explained as they stepped out into the cool air of the day.

"Mind if I tag along?"

"It would not be advisable. There could be danger."

"I'll chance it. I simply must return to Denver with a story, or my poor mother and I will be thrown out of our home."

Doc Savage seemed to give the notion—unappealing as it was from the standpoint of danger to the earnest girl reporter—further thought.

Before he could reply, Barbara Bland interjected, "And you'll have to admit, it would be better than my going back to those policemen and telling them exactly where to find those crooks."

The bronze man agreed that it would, but the lack of gratitude in his tone was something the young lady seemed to find vaguely aggravating.

Doc signaled a taxi and it bore them toward the nearby dome of the Capitol Building.

"Have you made any progress in locating King Goz?" the girl wondered after several silent moments had passed.

"None so far," Doc admitted.

"Then you cannot explain how he vanished from a moving car traveling along Pennsylvania Avenue?"

"I have a theory."

Barbara Bland raised a plain eyebrow. "What is it?"

"It is best not to say at this time," Doc stated.

When the bronze man did not elaborate on that, in fact
did not say anything more, the young woman nipped her
lips in an exasperated manner. She had decided that this
bronze giant—who as far as personal appearance and ability went, had everything—was one of the driest conversation wells she had ever tried to pump.

While she sat there and gently sharpened her teeth on
the emerald setting of a ring which was not on her engage-
ment finger, she pondered. Could it be that he was scared
of pretty girls? She was half tempted to ask him.

In the shadow of the Capitol dome, two men hunkered
down on an apartment house rooftop.

One was a tall, gloomy fellow with a face that was
long and pleased. Conversely, this meant that Colonel John
Renwick was unhappy. As an engineer, Renny—to use the
form of address he preferred—was without peer. Bridges,
railroads, and dams from Texas to Egypt bore his stamp.

He was bending over a boxy bit of apparatus which
had been set near the roof combing. A telephonic headset
was clamped about his ears, and he tapped one earpiece ex-
perimentally.

The second man came scuttling up, moving low so as
not to be seen. His physical build was nothing to brag about
and his complexion always started people worrying about
his health. It was the color of mushrooms. In actuality,
Major Thomas J. Roberts—Long Tom, oddly enough,
given his lack of stature—could whip most men he chanced
to encounter and give those he couldn't a memorable work-
out. He was an electrician by trade—tops in the field, by
reputation.

"What's wrong?" Long Tom asked sourly.

"Dunno," thumped Renny, in a whisper that startled a
robin off a nearby magnolia bough. He transferred his tap-
ping to the amplifier box.

"You'd better not have broken my listener, you big
oaf," Long Tom complained.

"Hold your durn horses," said Renny, getting up.

He glanced over the edge of the roof. A pickup mike
dangled by an electrical cord before an open window
below. It was hardly likely the occupants of the apartment

below had seen the microphone. But no sound was coming from the supersensitive listening-in device.

Hands with which Renny made the adjustments were incredibly huge; either fist would more than fill a quart pail. Both fists obviously had been mistreated in the past. Their scarred appearance and anvillike texture lent considerable credence to Renny's favorite boast that he could knock the wooden panel out of any door with either fist.

He turned up the volume control.

A fly buzzing near the microphone made an airplane noise. Renny had to cut the volume briefly. Then he turned it up after the fly had moved on.

He heard certain very small shuffling sounds.

"It's working," the big-fisted engineer said at last.

"It should," huffed Long Tom, who took great pride in his devices and disliked anyone other than himself working them. But he had a separate apparatus to tend to, with which he had tapped into the apartment house phone connection—too late, as it turned out, to pick up anything other than the close of a cryptic conversation. The missed opportunity rankled the undersized electrical wizard.

Renny, listening, asked, "Seen anything of Johnny?"

Johnny was another of Doc Savage's little coterie of assistants, and a renowned geologist and archæologist.

"Not yet," Long Tom admitted. "But the long string of bones said he'd be here about now."

"He'll be here," murmured Renny. His voice was not made for murmuring. The robin had just alighted once more on his favorite branch and now he took wing again. This time he did not return.

Suddenly, Renny raised a shushing finger.

Long Tom crowded close. "Got something?"

Renny clamped the headset more tightly to his big head.

Long Tom, frustrated, grabbed one headphone loose of the giant engineer's ear and put his own ear close to it. It was a big ear, designed for capturing sounds.

A rumbling voice was saying, *"Boys, this is bad. This is real bad."*

"Sounds like Hike," Renny said.

"How would you know? We haven't identified his voice yet!"

"Pipe down," Renny rumbled. The conversation continued.

*"Damn that Elvern D. Kastellantz. Why'd he put us up to this? That's what I wanna know."*

*"Relax, Hike,"* came another voice. *"We shook Savage. We're in the clear."*

*"You don't get it, do you? Guys what mix with that bronze guy ain't ever in the clear. He'll remember us. He'll hunt us down. We gotta blow town."*

A rustling sound like a newspaper being picked up filled the receiver.

*"That King Goz business is still all over the front pages,"* a new voice said, evidently attempting to change the trend of the uncomfortable confabulation.

*"They find the old boy yet?"* the second voice wondered.

*"Nope,"* said the other. *"It's got everybody mystified."*

*"Mystified, hell,"* snorted bull-voiced Hike. *"What mystifies me is why this Kastellantz character hired us to snatch Savage—without even tellin' us who the guy was. Dumb clucks that we are, we actually went after the guy armed only with trick water pistols."*

*"Maybe it had something to do with this missin' king,"* a fourth man interjected.

A finger-snapping sound broke in. It was quite loud. Big hands had made that sound.

*"Hey! You got an idea! I hadn't thought of that. Maybe it does, at that."*

*"But how does this Kastellantz hook up with a king?"*

*"Dunno,"* Hike said meaningly. *"But the minute that egg gets here, we're gonna shake it out of him. Get me?"*

Renny and Long Tom exchanged wide-eyed glances.

"The guy behind this is coming here!" Long Tom hissed.

"Holy cow!" rumbled Renny, using a pet expression. "If this Elvern D. Kastellantz they're talking about is involved in the king mystery, then we can land on the whole gang once he gets here."

"Right. And won't Doc be pleased," agreed Long Tom.

An unexpected voice, quite friendly actually, piped up directly behind them.

"That," he said, "I rather doubt."

Renny and Long Tom started. They were too practiced in the risky work of trouble-busting to make any unnecessary moves. So they did not jump, evade, turn around, or otherwise give the man who had slipped up behind them any excuse to shoot.

"In case you are wondering about your rather skeletal comrade," the voice added pleasantly, "he is sleeping off a headache in his car, where I found him."

"Holy cow!" Renny said thickly.

# IV

# MAN FLASH

"Stand up!"

Gloomy Renny and pale Long Tom obeyed the harsh command from their unknown captor.

"Turn around."

They turned.

They were not surprised to find a pistol pointed in their general direction. It was a revolver. The blunt lead noses of the bullets resting in the cylinder openings looked ugly.

The first thing that they noticed about their captor was that he was nattily attired. His clothes were not by any means spectacular. It was just that they were elegantly cut and he filled them out without an ounce of adipose tissue.

The fellow had a long nose which came to a sharp point, eyes which looked as if they were made of black glass, and his bluish cheeks bore traces of powder, as if he had shaved recently.

His hair was a distinctive red. Not bright; more of the color of dully glowing copper.

Neither Renny nor Long Tom had ever seen him before in their lives.

"Now," the copper-haired individual invited, "slowly raise your hands—and take that rig off your ears, long and unhappy."

Renny lifted his monster paws and let the headphones drop to the roof.

"It is well-known that you gentlemen carry certain frightful weapons," said their captor. "I would like them taken out and set at your feet," he added. His voice was very smooth.

Renny and Long Tom took infinite care in spading their hands under their coats. They came out holding intricate pistols not much larger than oversized automatics. They were fitted with curled magazines.

These were examples of a machine pistol which Doc Savage had perfected and constructed. The only samples of this gun ever fabricated were in the hands of his five aids, although the design would likely have brought a fortune from any one of several war departments. Doc Savage had no intention of adding to the array of devices which man has made to kill man.

In fact, they were usually charged with so-called "mercy" bullets—hollow shells which broke upon contact with human flesh and containing a fast-acting anæsthetic potion.

"I shall take those," said their captor, putting out a hand.

The faces of Renny and Long Tom fell. But having no choice in the matter, they complied.

The weapons made a quite a handful and the other dipped his knees when one of the tiny weapons started to tumble from his grasp. He caught it, simultaneously jutting his revolver at Renny, who was in the process of lowering his massive hands for a quick grab.

"Not so fast!" the gunman snarled.

Renny subsided. His big paws lifted once more.

"Very good," said the copper-haired man, regaining his composure. "Now we will join my followers below."

Renny and Long Tom were marched along to a roof trap, and urged down this.

Moments later, hands still lifted ceilingward, they stood to one side while their red-headed captor used one of the machine pistols to rap on an apartment door.

"Who is it?" a bellowing voice demanded. Hike Ewing.

"You know my voice!"

"Just the guy I wanna see," gritted Hike Ewing, throwing the door violently open and shoving out his roundish face. He saw the man, then his eyes shifted to the helpless Renny and Long Tom.

Hike Ewing's mouth dropped like the jaw of a flummoxed steam shovel.

"Mother of men!" he croaked. "Where'd you find these two?"

"Inside—quickly!"

Hike motioned to the captives, saying, "C'mon. In there!"

Renny and Long Tom were hustled in.

Hike Ewing's men came out of the chairs in which they had been sitting. There were more of them than either Renny or Long Tom expected. A full seven. Toughs. With hard faces. They looked as if they should, from force of habit, line up and do the prison lockstep, once they started moving.

"Who're those characters?" one demanded.

"Don't you guys know nothin'?" Hike groaned. "Those are two of Doc Savage's boys."

This brought quiet, thoughtful expressions to Hike Ewing's underlings.

The copperhead bushwhacker then answered the question that was on every mind.

"I found them on the roof, eavesdropping," he explained. "They tapped your phone and stationed a microphone outside a window."

"Lotta good it done them," Hike grunted. "They couldn't have heard nothin' from us. Because we don't know nothin' to start with."

"Precisely," returned the other, motioning Renny and Long Tom to take seats on a long, threadbare divan. Several gunmen moved out of the way. Renny Renwick weighed in excess of 250 pounds and had the general build of an elephant. No one seemed eager to be caught in grab-bing range of his knobby paws.

When the big-fisted engineer sat on his end of the divan, Long Tom's end actually lifted off the floor notice-ably.

The redhead with the machine gun turned to his hire-lings—for that is what they were—and complained, "Not only have you failed to carry out my instructions, but you allowed two of Doc Savage's men to trail you here. This was stupid. I cannot have stupid men working for me."

The air seemed to have leaked out of big Hike Ewing's ire at being sent out to abduct the legendary Doc Savage unawares. He swallowed his retort. He could not explain away the embarrassing presence of Doc's men.

"We were sure nobody followed us," Hike mumbled contritely.

"It is fortunate that it was only these two, and not Sav-age himself who got on your trail—otherwise you would not now be standing here making weak explanations," the redhead said bitingly.

"You made your point," Hike muttered. "Now answer us this: What's this all about? Why do you want Doc Sav-age snatched? Don't you know he's poison?"

"Don't ask me any questions," the other snapped. "You might give something away to Savage's pals, here."

"Sure, Elvern," Hike said, thoroughly cowed now.

"That," the redhead snarled, "is going to cost you a week's pay!"

"What?"

"Mentioning my name."

"Gosh, Elvern. I'm sorry!" Hike exploded.

The man who was apparently Elvern D. Kastellantz said, "The other one, Littlejohn, is down in a car parked around the corner."

Hike began, "But—"

"Don't ask questions, you fool!" Kastellantz ripped. "We'll see if we can use Littlejohn for bait to decoy Doc Savage into our hands."

Hike motioned for two of his gang to go and fetch the third of Doc's aids.

"What about these two here?" Hike asked after they had shut the door behind them.

Kastellantz swore.

"Tie them and gag them," he ordered.

This was done. Renny and Long Tom continued to sit on the divan, looking abashed and angry by turns.

"We can get them out by the alley without anybody seeing them," Kastellantz said. "We'll take them to a place I have set up and burn them in the furnace."

Through his tight gag, Renny Renwick expelled a polysyllabic grunt that was probably his pet expression again.

"I thought you didn't want any killin'," Hike protested.

"It is Doc Savage I did not wish killed," said the smooth Elvern D. Kastellantz. "And even that rule is subject to revision once I learn what he knows about the disappearance of the Chief of the Sons of the Falcon."

"Which?" blinked Hike.

"King Egil Goz the First," returned Elvern D. Kastellantz. "He is a descendant of the Turkish Mohammedans who conquered medieval Merida during the Crusades. That is the title given him by the warrior tribe of his birth."

"So this *does* have something to do with that king fella!" Hike blurted. "Listen, this may be too big for us. We're strictly second-story men by trade."

"Nonsense. You men have only to follow my orders and you will be handsomely rewarded."

At that moment, the tramping of feet rattled on the stairs. It sounded like two men walking awkwardly, as if sharing a burden.

"That must be Hank and Cy, with Savage's man," Hike said, going to the door. He threw it open—and was yanked from sight by a pair of metallic bronze hands.

Stunned silence greeted this feat of legerdemain. And while all eyes ogled the empty doorway, Renny Renwick lurched up from his seat and tore his bonds asunder. One big paw swiped off his gag. The other grasped Long Tom's bonds, gave a wrench, and the puny electrical wizard bounded off the cushion and socked the nearest Hike Ewing underling flat.

The room became a boil of fighting men.

Pulling his gag loose, Long Tom Roberts fell upon another gunman. The man misjudged his seemingly undernourished assailant and hauled off to deliver a roundhouse right. It never landed. The pale electrical wizard was all over him like a human flailing machine.

Face bloodied, the gunman was pummeled up against a wall.

Renny was surrounded by three men. They looked like terriers nipping at a rhinoceros.

One fellow started a haymaker, was lucky, and connected. Renny only blinked reproachfully. The man began to moan, and pinch and knead his hand, trying to make the knuckles look natural again.

They had not used their guns, so it was evident that the weapons they flourished remained unloaded from their earlier effort to run a bluff on Doc Savage.

A man whacked Renny's head with a gun. Renny knocked him down.

"Creeps!" another gunman choked. "They're rock men!"

Using his fist like a circus maul, Renny brought it up over and down on the gunman's head. The unprepared man's knees knocked together, then twisted as he fell to the floor.

Doc Savage was in the room now, a flash of metal. The mighty bronze man confronted the last remaining member of Hike Ewing's crew. He had snatched up one of Doc's own supermachine pistols, which he tried to use. Doc twisted the weapon out of his hand and shoved the man toward Renny.

Doc was driving toward the open window, through which red-headed Elvern D. Kastellantz was endeavoring to squeeze his natty form.

Seeing the bronze man, Kastellantz whipped out a purloined supermachine pistol and pointed it at the bronze man's head.

"I don't know if this thing is charged with real lead or

one of those trick bullets you use," he growled, "but either way, a burst in your face will stop you in your tracks."

The bronze man was brought up short. The man spoke the truth. Although he and his men habitually wore chain-mail undergarments that would turn lead, they were vulnerable to a head shot.

"I know who you are," Doc said pointedly.

Elvern D. Kastellantz blinked. His eyes rolled upward to his forehead, where a disordered lock of copper-red hair dangled.

"I must remember to dye my hair," he returned. And then eeled through the window. The sound of his feet hitting the alley below was a single click.

Scooping up the remaining superfirer, Renny lunged for the window.

"No!" Doc warned.

Renny was well-trained. He managed to drop into a slide—just as the window shivered into pieces as a flurry of bullets ripped it apart.

"Durn!" Renny moaned. "Musta been Long Tom's cannon. Mine was charged with mercy bullets."

"That was an ordinary pistol report," Doc hazarded. "He had no time to figure out our special safety latches."

"Teach Renny to stick his neck out without looking first," Long Tom gritted. He was in a corner, still beating on the gunman who had raised his dander.

"Stay with Hike's men," Doc rapped, surging out the door.

The bronze man took the stairs three at a time, gained the lowermost landing, flung himself outside.

Across the alley was another apartment house. A door was slipping closed.

Doc Savage knew better than to tempt fate. It was easy enough for a fleeing person to push a door open and move along, creating the illusion that he had entered. On the other hand, the wily Kastellantz might indeed have entered and be lying in ambush.

The bronze man circled the dwelling. It was a decrepit thing of cracked brick and loose, crumbling mortar. He saw no sign of the fleeing Elvern D. Kastellantz.

Doc Savage noted a door on the opposite side of the building. A reasonable exit opportunity to a fleeing man. It was unlocked. He got through it in time to make room for at least five bullets to come down the hallway. The shot sounds were dull, might have been hard blows on a big drum which had been left out in the rain all night.

It was not the sound of one of his supermachine pistols.

Doc waited. He never carried a gun. He believed that carrying one led to too much dependence being placed on it. A gunman without a gun is a helpless creature.

The bronze man pulled out of a pocket a case containing little glass capsules which were filled with his special anæsthetic gas. He flung some of them down the corridor. Then he held his breath. The gas would produce quick, harmless unconsciousness, but was ineffective after mingling with the air approximately a minute.

A minute crawled past.

Came furtive sounds of movement. Cautious shufflings. The bronze man knew then that the foe was acquainted with the anæsthetic gas. Not strange. Doc had used it for a long time.

Some one somewhere barked at him to put up his hands. Some one else barked at the first man not to be a fool and shoot, that the sound would draw the police. This was evidently a well-known criminal hangout. None of the voices resembled the smooth tones of Elvern D. Kastellantz.

Doc palmed more gas capsules and pegged them at long intervals. He was taking a chance. Although his ability to hold his breath was prodigious, it was not infinite. Still, he had learned the skill from the masters of the art—the pearl divers of the South Seas.

A figure collapsed in the gloom. Doc waited. His keen hearing apprised him of steady breathing. A tense person could not have duplicated that relaxed rhythm.

Cautiously, Doc moved forward.

He found Barbara Bland crumpled behind a hallway door.

His trilling noise, the small fantastic note which he had made in the Department of Justice Building garage upon discovering red human hairs in the Meridan king's limousine, came into being briefly. The sound was a tiny thing which he did unconsciously in moments of mental turbulence, or upon making a surprising discovery, as he had now. Doc throttled it.

Wordlessly, the metallic giant gathered the mousy girl reporter into his strong, corded arms and bore her out of the apartment building.

A few heads poked out of windows and cracked open doors enough to permit viewing. They were hastily clapped shut. Doc Savage was instantly recognizable, now that he was hatless.

Doc went to a sedate sedan where three men slumbered. Two, in the back, were the Hike Ewing henchmen who had gone for Johnny Littlejohn. They had fallen victim to the bronze man's might.

The one seated behind the steering wheel was that august personage himself.

William Harper Littlejohn craned his long neck out of the window. He was a tall and wonderfully bony individual blessed with a high forehead and a shaggy mop of hair cut at what is politely called scholastic length. In the vernacular, he resembled a musician of the longhair variety.

"I'll be superamalgamated, Doc! Who is she?" The tall string bean sounded groggy. It was evident he had just awoken.

"No time," Doc said. "Seen anything of a well-dressed man with red hair?"

"No," said Johnny. The lanky archæologist was addicted to the most amazing words on most occasions—jawbreakers beyond the comprehension of the average man—but when he was alone with the bronze man, he did not use them. It was suspected that this affectation was a way of showing off, and Johnny understood that Doc Savage's command of esoteric vocabulary exceeded his own arcane knowledge.

Noticing the pair in the back seat, Johnny asked, "Who are they?"

"Hike Ewing's men. Come on. There is a lot to do."

Johnny unfolded himself from behind the wheel. The

term beanpole might have been coined to describe his general physiology. He came near to standing seven feet tall.

William Harper Littlejohn, in the days before he had won the cognomen of Johnny, had been an eminent professor in a great university. He usually maintained some of his professorial dignity, except for his clothing, which probably always had looked, and always would look, as if it had been contributed by a cornfield scarecrow.

Additionally, he wore a monocle on his lapel, but did not bring it to his eyes. It was, in fact, a magnifying glass, not an eyepiece, and handy in his work.

Doc left Barbara Bland in Johnny's place, and locked the car. It would not do to be seen carrying an unconscious woman about in broad daylight.

In Hike Ewing's apartment, there was shambles.

"No luck?" Long Tom asked sourly, when Doc and Johnny entered.

Doc shook his head.

"Holy cow!" said Renny, knobbing and unknobbing his fists. "Who was that guy, Doc? From what we overheard, he hired this Hike to snatch you."

"He fits," Doc Savage said, "the description of the chauffeur who drove King Goz's limousine to the White House gate on the night the king vanished."

"Holy cow!" Renny boomed. "So it all ties in!"

"Just how, we do not know," Doc said, bending over the groggy form of Hike Ewing. The big bruiser probably weighed no less than 275 pounds, but Doc Savage yanked him up to a seated position by his coat lapels with no visible exertion.

Hike was not unconscious exactly. He was as loose and lifeless as a marionette, but his eyes were wide open. Wide and staring.

Doc reached out to his neck and with metallic fingers began to perform certain spinal manipulations. Hike shivered and his arms and legs began to shake as if palsied.

He gave his round head a last shake and looked up at the towering form of Doc Savage with sick eyes.

"Wha—what'd you do to me?" he asked thickly.

Doc said nothing. Terror grew on bulldog Hike's face.

"Talk," rapped Doc.

"What'd ya wanna know?"

"Everything. Or the paralysis you just suffered *could* become permanent." Doc's golden eyes were cold, remorseless.

The big man wet his lips, stuttered, "Then I'm in a huh-hell of a j-jam, because all I know is that a guy named Elvern D. Kastellantz hired me."

"What is your business?"

The man hesitated. "I'm a gug-gunman."

"At least you are frank enough to admit it," Doc said. "Who is this man, Kastellantz?"

"No clue. He called us up and offered a bundle to do his dirty work for him. We didn't know it was you he wanted snatched, Savage. Honest."

"How did you know to go to the National Museum?"

"Kastellantz called a second time. I got the idea he greased a hotel doorman to keep tabs on you for him."

Doc was an excellent judge of character. He knew that the frightened gunman was speaking the unvarnished truth. The bronze man's cabled fingers reached out again and went to work. Hike went limp, and his eyes started jerking about in his skull. The eerie spell had returned.

Doc moved among the others. Some were out cold and needed no further attentions. Others were subjected to the same weird chiropractic manipulation that produced helplessness. It was the result of long study, that trick. Doc had merely applied pressure to certain nerve centers and volition departed. Consciousness did not. Inasmuch as they would be awake and acutely aware of their helplessness, the crooks were suffering a well-deserved scare.

Doc went to the telephone and put in a call. He spoke quick orders, then hung up.

"They going to college?" Renny asked.

The bronze man nodded. "They can tell us no more."

"Too bad," Long Tom offered, tugging on a big ear. "You had the right idea, Doc. Going to a public place, figuring it would draw out whoever's behind this mess into trying to get you out of the way, so we could nail them."

"It has worked before," Doc agreed somberly.

Doc Savage next placed another call, this one to his skyscraper headquarters.

"Pat, have you had any luck digging up the facts on Barbara Bland?"

In a voice so shrill it filled the room with its terrified vibrations, the voice of Pat Savage came.

*"Doc! Never mind that phony—I found your missing king! He's here! In your reception room! I got him cornered in the office safe! Come running!"*

The connection terminated with a click.

Doc Savage turned to his men. His words were clipped.

"Renny, is our plane still parked at the Washington airport?"

"Yeah, Doc. Just what you wanted."

"I must return to New York immediately."

"Holy cow!"

"You three carry on without me," said Doc. "These prisoners should keep until collected. Endeavor to find Elvern D. Kastellantz."

Renny boomed, "Where do we start? He could be anywhere."

"Remember—Kastellantz has one of our machine pistols."

Long Tom snapped his fingers. "Of course! It should be a snap. I got everything we need in my equipment case. We'll get right on it, Doc."

Johnny reminded, "What about that she-reporter, Barbara Bland?"

"See if she won't accompany you."

Johnny quirked an eyebrow. "Is that smart?"

"Her role in this affair may prove larger than hitherto suspected."

With that, the bronze man left the room. His departure was as silent as a passing cloud.

## V

## FAR-FETCHED YARN

Doc Savage disliked publicity. This did not mean that he was not exactly human, as some individuals had concluded on certain occasions. Fame is a wine, which even the modest find pleasant. But, with Doc Savage, it was a question of whether or not he remained in the world of the living. The bronze man had enemies—even he knew not how many—and any publicity connected with his movements was likely to lead to traps.

Doc Savage had not given the monthly true-detective magazine an interview for the basis of its article. As a matter of fact, there had been no interview. The writing staff had gone on its imagination, and on rumor. The result, if not fact, had been pleasant reading, and interesting, not to say sensational. It had also boosted the circulation over the million mark.

There was a crowd in the lobby of the skyscraper which held Doc Savage's headquarters. Readers of the magazine, autograph bugs, and probably some individuals, perfectly normal, who had nothing better to do than to stand around and watch for a glimpse of a famous person.

The crowd knew what it was looking for. The magazine had carried a picture of Doc Savage, snapped without his permission. An artist had colored the photograph to show Doc Savage's unusual metallic coloring. The throng was keeping its collective eye peeled for such a personage.

Not even a second glance did anyone give to a stooped figure in a shiny, threadbare black overcoat which hobbled into the lobby of the magnificent building. This individual wore a derby hat which looked as old as some of the observers. He had a hooked nose, and black whiskers which could have stood a good combing. His old shoes were out at the toes, and he assisted himself along with a cheap cane.

If this person had started mumbling that he bought old clothes, no one would have been surprised.

The shabby, stooped figure entered an express elevator.

"Eighty-sixth," he said in a quavering voice.

He was carried up and deposited in a corridor which was very plain and seemed to have only one office door. This bore a legend in small bronze letters:

*CLARK SAVAGE, JR.*

When the stooped figure approached this door, it opened as if by magic. Out of the room beyond came two voices engaged in a furious altercation. One of the voices sounded as if its source might be a small child. The other was suave, well-modulated. One obviously accustomed to much public speaking.

"You're nuts, Ham," affirmed the childish voice.

"Monk, you thick-headed missing link," said the other voice. "You not only have the voice of a child, but the mind of one, too. Believing in such things!"

The newcomer with the derby, the whiskers, and the old overcoat walked into a reception room which was equipped with luxurious rugs, a massive inlaid table that was undoubtedly costly, numerous expensive comfortable chairs, and an old-fashioned safe of which a bank would have been proud.

Abruptly, the pair broke off their argument. They made quite a picture.

One—he had been addressed as Monk—was not very tall, almost as wide as he was high, and his arms, remarkably enough, seemed thicker than his legs. His neck was negligible, and so was his forehead, but his mouth wasn't. The mouth looked as if it were fashioned for taking an entire grapefruit at a bite. He was scarred in places, and the hair growing out of his leathery hide very much resembled rusty wires.

His resemblance to a fullgrown gorilla was marked. His full name—which was Lieutenant Colonel Andrew Blodgett Mayfair—was such a mouthful that few ever called him anything other than Monk.

The other was slender and wasp-waisted and attired in faultless evening dress. It was said that Brigadier General Theodore Marley Brooks, who was called Ham by those who were not afraid to, was often followed down the street by tailors enraptured by his sartorial splendor and Ham's ability to wear clothes as they should be worn. His face was sharp, his dark eyes intelligent. He was waving about a lean, dark cane, as if on the verge of braining the seemingly brainless Monk.

These two looked at the newcomer with the derby, the beard, and the old overcoat.

The dapper Ham indicated his apish companion. "If you're buying old clothes, you might make a deal for those he's wearing. They are ready for the rag barrel."

The simian Monk looked indignant.

"Beat it," he told the fellow who had just arrived. "I'm gonna slaughter this fashion plate and you might be gored."

The newcomer now spoke. His voice was entirely different from the one he had used on the elevator operator. Its modulations, its unmistakable suppressed power, its pleasantness, were little short of startling.

"What are you two arguing about now?" he asked.

The two dissenters—Monk and Ham—jumped as if they had suddenly found their feet in cold water.

"Doc Savage!" Ham exclaimed.

Monk recovered from his surprise, and emitted several squeaks of mirth. "What's the idea of the disguise, Doc?"

Doc Savage straightened, removed the derby, the black whiskers, and the old overcoat. He became a bronze giant of unusual stature, but with a good deal more than size to make him striking. He seemed to have grown in height and stature. That was impossible, of course, the apparent phenomenon being due to his having carried himself previously so as to seem not only less tall, but less conspicuous.

"That magazine article seems to have stirred me up a public," he explained. "They looked friendly enough, but there might have been an exception among them."

Monk scratched his nubbin of a head. He did not look the part, his dwarfed skull seeming to afford no room for brains, but he was admittedly one of the greatest of industrial chemists.

"I know the guy what owns that magazine," he said. "He might fire the editor who printed that story."

"They have to make a living," Doc Savage told him quietly. "And it did not contain enough facts to do us harm. It might conceivably do some good, because it certainly bears down on the moral that crime does not pay. However, it has undone our recent efforts to downplay our unfortunate notoriety."

Monk nodded, seemed to dismiss that matter, and turned on the nattily clad Ham.

"Listen, shyster. If Pat says it's so, then it's so."

"Only a superstitious ape such as yourself would believe such a ridiculous yarn," Ham sniffed. "There are no such beings as ghosts, spooks, phantoms, shades, revenants, apparitions, or specters!"

"Tell it to Harvard!"

Doc Savage studied the pair as he finished removing his disguise. They were the remaining two of his aids, assistants in the strange work to which he devoted his life. They were experts in their particular professions, and invaluable. Ham was one of the most astute lawyers Harvard had ever turned out. Each of these two had, on occasion, risked his life to save the other. But a stranger would never imagine it to watch them. They squabbled continuously—on anything.

Doc asked, "Where is Pat?"

"In the library," replied Ham.

"Lock her in?"

"Naw," offered Monk. "Pat's trying to prove that what she saw wasn't no hallucination. Said your library was probably the only room in the joint that wasn't haunted."

"Something was said about the safe," Doc reminded.

Monk squeaked, "We ain't tried to open it, Doc."

"No reason to," added Ham. "Even if Pat is your cousin, Doc, her story is just too preposterous. She told it to us when we got back from kenneling our pets, and then flew into a huff when I expressed disbelief."

Doc asked, "Kennel?"

"We," Monk announced proudly, "have turned over a new leaf."

Doc, after a cursory glance at the big office safe, went into the next room. It was filled with substantial bookcases crammed with thousands of tomes, all ponderous-looking, on shelves and in cases. The books were on technical scientific subjects, erudite things which would never be found in an ordinary library. *Incidence Lines of the Neutron* was a typical title.

Light was slanting in through a tall bank of windows, illuminating spirals of dust motes like fading galaxies.

Doc saw his cousin.

"What took you so long!" asked Pat, leaping from a leather divan. A thick book she had been consulting clapped shut as it was tossed onto the cushions.

"Difficulties," said Doc, without elaborating.

Pat marched up to the big bronze man. She was a striking, outdoorsy-looking girl. Her frock was tasteful yet fetching. She had a wealth of bronze hair, much the color of Doc's, and her eyes were a golden tint. They were snapping now.

"That—that fashion plate, Ham, had the nerve to question my story," Pat said excitedly. "I came in here to see if one of your reference books could explain it."

"Something was said about a king in my safe," Doc reminded.

"Something!" Pat huffed. She seized the bronze man's arm and marched him back into the reception room. The bronze man did not resist. He knew better than to stir up the vivacious Pat. She could be a tigress when aroused.

Monk and Ham wisely made way as Pat piloted Doc Savage to the massive safe. It was as tall as Doc himself, which was to say that it was not short. It was of laminated construction, and elderly.

"Open it," Pat insisted.

"First, your story," Doc said.

"I've been waiting hours to see this box cracked," Pat snapped. "And I won't wait any longer!"

"If there is something inside the safe, it is not going anywhere," Doc said reasonably.

"Not some *thing*! Some *one*! Your missing king! The

monarch they're turning Washington upside down to locate! I saw him with my own eyes!"

"Describe this person," Doc requested.

Pat looked odd. Her face settled into calmer lines. It was quite pretty, that face. She could have been a magazine cover girl, or a movie queen.

"What do you expect! He looked like a king!" she said exasperatedly.

"Details, Pat."

Pat sighed and the tension went out of her voice. One golden eye on the imposing safe, she began rattling off description.

"He was dressed in a red robe with an ermine-trimmed cloak, for starters. He had the biggest gold crown you ever saw perched on his head. And hanging off his face was a long white beard Old King Cole would have envied."

"Old?"

Pat reflected. "I didn't see his face clearly. I was in that wizard's workshop you call a laboratory, and I thought I heard a noise. I raced right into the library. That's when I spied him coming through that door." Pat pointed to the connecting door. "In this direction."

"Go on," Doc prompted.

"I caught up with him right here," Pat said, scuffing the spot on which she stood. "He was looking about, curiously, and playing with that silky beard of his. I yelled at him and he didn't seem to hear me." Pat swallowed some air, as if getting her second wind.

"This is the part that gets goofy," Ham interjected.

"You stay out of this, you—you skeptic!" Pat snapped.

Ham clutched his dark cane tightly and said nothing.

"As I was sneaking up behind his back," Pat resumed, "he walked into the safe."

"It was open?" Doc asked sharply.

"No," said Pat in a suddenly small voice.

Doc Savage rarely betrayed emotion. He gave a slight lift to one eyebrow, which Pat took for an expression of extreme skepticism—which it was.

"Don't you go looking at me like that!" she flared. "I saw what I saw! He walked right up to the safe door—and *through* it."

"Through?"

"Yes!"

"You are certain?"

"*Yes!*"

Doc regarded his attractive cousin at length. Pat made a grim face back.

"What do you think, Doc?" Monk asked in his small voice.

"I think," the bronze man stated, "it is high time the safe was opened."

The big safe—the much-faded floral design on its door attested to its great age—bore a combination lock and Doc Savage gave the dial a preliminary spin.

Strangely, he ignored the dial thereafter. Instead, he placed the tip of one metallic finger against certain petals and leaves of the floral design, in which an enameled red rose predominated.

Doc yanked down the handle. The safe door rolled ponderously open.

The explanation was quite simple. The steel door concealed a sensitive thermostatic device. Warmth from Doc's fingertip, touching the proper spots in a certain sequence, unlocked the safe. The combination dial was a dummy.

The safe interior proved quite spacious. It was possible for an average-sized man to enter it without having to bend. Doc nevertheless was forced to stoop as he stepped inside.

Doc had out a spring-generator flashlight of his own devising and he speared the narrow beam into the gloomy interior. The quarter-sized light disk roved about, showing shelves, cubicles, and other cubby-holes.

But no king. No living being at all. And no sign one had ever dwelt within.

"I waited at the door with my six-gun ready," Pat said unhappily, "and he never came out."

Doc Savage said nothing.

Pat whirled on Monk and Ham. "Unless—unless these two fell asleep on me!"

"Not us," squeaked hairy Monk. "Nothin' came out of the safe while we were here."

"That is because nothing went in," Ham said. "It is not possible. No living being could enter a locked safe without first opening it."

"That's the part that gets me," Pat muttered uncertainly. "What if he *wasn't* living. What if he was a—" She swallowed. "A ghost?" The word sounded weak.

Ham snorted.

Monk scratched his nubbin of a head and looked dubious.

Doc Savage, his examination concluded, stepped out of the safe. He closed it.

His next words were unnecessary, but he spoke them anyway.

"There is no one in the safe, Pat."

Pat stamped a well-shod foot. "I know that!" she blazed. "But I tell you, some one went in. He was rigged up like a fairy-tale emperor. In a red robe, ermine-trimmed cloak, gold crown, orb, and bejeweled scepter. The whole regal works."

"He could not have entered a closed safe," Doc pointed out.

"He *melted* in!" Pat insisted. "After that, I put my ear to the door. And I could hear him whistling some infernally morose tune!"

Doc Savage's trilling came briefly. It sounded this time like a forlorn and lost soul in search of its own grave.

"What is it, Doc?" Ham inquired.

"Pat," the bronze man said in a level voice, "you have just described Old King Fausto."

"Who?"

"A monarch of medieval Merida. Long dead."

That so stunned the bronze-haired girl that she vouchsafed no immediate reply.

"Then the mystery monarch hasn't been found, after all?" she muttered.

"Unfortunately, no," said Doc.

Pat squirmed her exquisite eyebrows thoughtfully. Her tanned face brightened.

"Swell!" she said cheerfully. "That means there's still something for me to horn in on."

"You don't—" The Man of Bronze looked vaguely indignant. "Now, Pat, you know you cannot get mixed up in—"

"Can't I!" Pat stamped a foot. "I'm already in it!"

They stared at each other, tight-lipped, in a struggle of wills. Neither weakened.

"Match you," Pat offered.

"I do not gamble," the bronze man said.

"All virtues and no vices!" Pat said indignantly. "Such a guy! You're not human."

"You started off on your Canadian vacation," Doc said firmly. "There is still time to reach your destination if you leave now."

Pat folded her pretty arms stubbornly. "Aren't you going to ask me about your Barbara Bland?"

"Not if there is a price tag attached."

"Could be important, you know," Pat said in an enticing tone.

"I already know she is a fake," Doc advised.

"How'd you find that out?" Pat exploded.

"From you. You blurted out the fact that she is an impostor during our last telephone conversation."

"Hah!" Ham said gleefully. "That's one time you outfoxed yourself, Pat."

Doc Savage stepped up to the reception room door. It valved open again, without him touching it. This was easily explained. The bronze man carried a radioactive coin on his person, the emanations of which tripped an electroscope relay, which in turn operated the door-opening mechanism.

The bronze man made room for Pat to depart.

"Out you go," he invited.

"You haven't heard the last of me!" said Pat, grabbing a capacious metallic hand bag off the inlaid table and flouncing out.

In the past, pretty Pat had aided Doc Savage in some of the often fantastic adventures which frequently befell the bronze man as he pursued his strange Galahadian life career of righting wrongs, aiding the oppressed, and battling evildoers too clever for ordinary justice. Pat had aided just often enough to get the fever.

They all knew her departing promise was not an idle one.

Doc Savage turned to his remaining aids.

"I have left Renny, Long Tom, and Johnny to pursue the Washington angles of the matter," he explained.

Ham's dark eyes gleamed in anticipation. "Anything for us?"

Doc quickly recounted his recent experiences. Then he said, "Pat's story, wild as it sounds, cannot be discounted. It is plain that she saw something. What, we cannot adequately explain. I suggest we conduct a thorough search of our headquarters."

They started with the reception room, found nothing out of place, and passed into the scientific library, which was equaled for completeness by possibly only one other—one which Doc Savage maintained in the mysterious spot known only to himself and designated as his Fortress of Solitude, to which he retired periodically to experiment and study.

The only thing out of place, they found after some investigation, was the heavy book Pat had dropped. It was a dictionary. Doc lifted it up and consulted the still-open pages.

"Find anything?" dapper Ham asked.

Doc set the book open on its stand. "Pat was evidently looking up the definition of a word."

"What word?" wondered hairy Monk.

A bronze finger came to rest on a specific definition. "At a guess, the word ghost."

"Ghost!" Monk said, ambling up to the book. His gimlet eyes narrowed as he read along. "Says here a ghost is the spirit or soul of a person which manifests itself after death."

"Bosh!" Ham snapped. "Such phantasmagoria cannot be."

"Yeah, shyster? Then why do they got the word in a dictionary? You don't see them puttin' in words for things that don't exist, do you?"

"I am certain that dictionary is full of words for nonexistent items," the dapper lawyer returned in a superior tone of voice.

"Oh, yeah?" said Monk, riffling through the wide pages. He looked up. "Nope. It's not here."

"What?" Ham inquired.

Monk grinned. "There is no such word as lawyer-honest. Proves my point."

Ham purpled. But he could think of no retort.

Crossing the library, the bronze man next entered a laboratory-workshop, also of unusual completeness.

Pat Savage had dubbed it a wizard's workshop. It was certainly that. It was by far the largest room of the headquarters setup. Glass-topped benches held apparatus and cases of rare chemicals and metals. Strange machines crouched in corners, devices that only one of Doc's fabulous scientific learning could fathom.

They gave this room the most attention, even though Pat had not seen the superannuated apparition in this laboratory. Doc Savage overlooked few bets.

They examined every nook and cranny of the big room. Their operations revealed numerous runways within the walls and secret passages between rooms. It was evident the floor was a labyrinth of mechanical secrets.

At the end, Monk and Ham expressed a disheartening lack of result.

"Looks like nothin's been touched," was the way Monk put it.

Doc Savage was examining a bank of instruments set in a black Bakelite board. These consisted of rolls of graphed paper, on which a stylus would ink a line if any of the many guarded approaches to the headquarters were disturbed. They were part of the elaborate monitoring system that honeycombed the 86th floor.

Noting the absence of wriggling lines, Doc Savage said, "There is no indication that an intruder has entered the headquarters."

"That settles it, then," Ham said firmly. "That means there was no ghost."

"On the contrary," said Doc Savage. "It means there was."

Ham goggled and separated his cane—revealing it to be a sword cane, of the finest steel.

"Huh?" Monk blurted.

Doc turned from the instrument bank. Vague, disturbed eddies troubled his weirdly active flake-gold eyes.

"We all know Pat," he said. "She is a very excitable

young woman. But she is not subject to hallucinations. If Pat said she saw something, then she did. The fact that the indicators show no sign of intrusion means that Pat clearly did encounter a phantom presence of some sort."

"Blazes!" Monk squeaked.

Ham sheathed his sword cane with a sound like a skull's jaws clicking shut.

## VI

## CASPAR

Pat Savage had absolutely no doubt that she had seen a ghost.

She repeated her conviction as she took Doc's private speed elevator to the skyscraper lobby.

"I don't know what I saw, I just know that I saw it," she muttered under her breath. "And I'm going to prove it!"

Unlike the elevator which Doc had taken up while in disguise, this one was fully automatic. There was no operator.

It dropped like a dornick off a bluff, literally lifting Pat's heels off the floor. She grabbed the rail to steady herself for the expected sudden stop. The elevator had not been designed with feminine footgear in mind. Pat had broken more than one heel riding in the thing.

The elevator stopped abruptly, and Pat was all but thrown to her knees.

"Darn this overactive dumb-waiter!" she fumed.

Straightening, she checked her heels. They were intact. Then, donning a pair of colored glasses and wrapping an unflattering kerchief about her trademark bronze hair, she stepped out into the modernistic lobby.

The autograph hounds were still there. But their eyes were on the main bank of lifts. Pat had stepped from a blank panel in a secluded corner of the spacious lobby, out of their sight.

She crossed to the entrance, all but unnoticed.

A tall, sandy-haired young man loitering by a cigar stand happened to catch sight of her, folded a magazine under one arm, and followed Pat out onto the busy avenue.

Pat hailed a taxi and directed the driver to take her to Pennsylvania Station. She was sufficiently upset by her unsettling experience that her voice carried.

The sandy-haired individual who was following her overheard, and rushed around a corner, where he climbed behind the wheel of a roadster of moderate price.

The machine scooted out into traffic and began wending its way downtown. The driver showed good judgment and made no attempt to follow Pat's cab. Manhattan is literally awash in cabs, and trying to follow a specific one can be folly.

Pat was fulminating in the back of hers. She had, as she had informed Doc, departed on her Canadian fishing vacation. She had not forgotten her tackle. Not all of it, anyway; that much was a fib. She had learned of the news that Doc had been reported in Washington during a Montreal refueling stop, and abruptly decided that hunting a king would be more interesting than catching salmon.

Pat had immediately flown back in her seaplane. She was not returning to it now. She had intentions of taking the next train to Washington, where Renny, Johnny, and Long Tom were pursuing clues, and elbowing her way into the growing mystery.

"If I can't nab one king, I'll find another," she said aloud.

"What say, miss?" asked the cabby.

"Mind your driving," sniffed Pat.

At Pennsylvania Station, Pat alighted and went to a ticket counter. She paid no attention to the bustle around her and was oblivious to the sandy-haired young man who had taken up a position behind her in line.

After Pat had asked the agent for a round-trip ticket to Washington's Union Station, the tall man made a pretense of having misplaced his wallet and stepped out of line, patting down his pockets noisily.

He followed Pat to her track, got in front of her without warning.

"Excuse me, mystery maiden," he said grandly, doffing his hat.

Pat stopped. She was still swathed in her dark glasses and kerchief, which hardly concealed her undeniable beauty.

"Do I know you?" Pat asked suspiciously.

"No. But I know you," the man said gallantly. "You see, I've seen you when you were your true self."

"Do tell."

The tall man bathed Pat in the pearly luster of his smile. "Honestly, after I first saw you, I went home and put my clothes to bed and almost hung myself in the closet."

"And beat your wife, I'll bet," returned Pat snappily. "Listen, you never saw me before. My name is Enola Emmel."

Pat tried to step around him, but the smiling young man was too quick. He waved a magazine which had been folded back to an inside page. It showed a photograph of Pat in all her glory. It was the same true-crime magazine which had caused Doc Savage such inconvenience.

"Your name is Patricia Savage," he said, "Pat for short, cousin of that amazing man of mystery, Doc Savage." Grinning, he folded the magazine and added, "I could be a wife beater if I had someone as ravishing as you to beat. How about it?"

"Scat!" Pat directed. "I have a temper."

"You also have lots of money, which makes you even better. I always wanted to marry a rich girl. It's outrageous the prices you charge in that place you call a beauty parlor and gymnasium for ladies. Say, did you know a sinister-looking man has been trailing you?"

Pat looked him up and down. "Not until this moment."

The man grinned disarmingly. "Thanks. But you're wrong. I mean a tall, stoop-shouldered old lad with long white Father Christmas whiskers. Listen, I'm not kidding. Oh yes, my name is Prestowitz. Caspar Prestowitz."

Pat studied him. He was tall, athletic-looking, and possessed a face with character rather than handsomeness. His eyes were a faded blue, as if he had overworked them. He seemed a brazen zany, but she thought she detected some earnestness in his manner.

"Were you kidding about the whiskers, my suitor?" she asked him.

"Thanks. No. Honest."

Pat made a thoughtful face. Moments before, she had been in a rush to reach Washington, where a swell mystery awaited. Just now, however, this young swain promised at least a measure of intrigue. She decided to draw the man out.

"It is going to take some selling to make your story take effect," Pat said, fibbing again. "Right now, I don't believe it."

"He trailed you here. I followed him—and you. But I lost him on the street. I think he's still there."

"I'll look," Pat agreed. "But seeing an elderly man with whiskers does not necessarily prove anything. Lots of old gentlemen in New York wear white beards."

"Granted," said Caspar Prestowitz. His smooth brow gave a pucker. "I don't know whether I care for a wife who thinks I'm a confirmed liar. I'll have to reconsider my matrimonial intentions. Come."

Pat decided to go along. It was very strange, she realized suddenly. The last time she had tried to go on vacation, only weeks before, she had stumbled upon a fantastic international plot during a tour of the Orient.* By the time it was all over, Pat had ended up in more trouble than she had ever planned. Her Canadian fishing vacation had started out as a real one, but the trouble bug had bitten her again, despite her purest intentions.

"Coincidence," she murmured as they mounted the stairs.

Prestowitz asked, "What say?"

"This white-bearded gent," Pat wondered. "By chance was he tricked out like Old King Cole?"

"Not unless Old King Cole wore blue serge. Did he?"

"Not in my girlhood storybooks," Pat replied.

There were not many persons on the street at this late hour, and no man, young or old, with a beard—garbed in blue serge or otherwise. Prestowitz was not abashed.

"He's around somewhere," he declared, unfazed.

---

*The Motion Menace

"We'll take a ride in my car. He'll follow us. We'll seize him."

"I have a train to catch," Pat pointed out.

"Not a good idea. If the old duffer with the whiskers is after you, a train is not a good place to be found. No place to run to."

The suggestion made sense. One of the clocks on the Paramount Building tower near Times Square was visible from where Pat stood. She had nearly an hour before her train left. Time enough to see if the white-whiskered one was skulking about.

"My coach awaits, princess," said Caspar Prestowitz. He didn't exactly bow. But he came close. Pat decided he had a vaguely Continental flavor to him, which she found appealing.

She took his arm and allowed him to escort her around the corner. The arm-taking served a dual purpose. It gave her one less male arm to worry about and she could still get to her commodious metallic purse—in which reposed a huge single-action six-shooter Pat had long ago learned to wield to excellent effect.

The gallant if impulsive Caspar Prestowitz escorted her to a nice-looking roadster, the top down and in a boot. It was polished as if new.

Pat's opinion of the man went up a notch. And then another when he opened the passenger door for her and shut it carefully before taking the wheel.

The clutch, however, needed fixing. The car gave a jump when it started off. After that, it ran well enough.

"Watch behind for the old gink with the beard," he suggested.

Instead of looking around, Pat turned the rear-vision mirror so it would serve the purpose.

In the next half mile, she saw no one.

"I thought so," she said.

The young man's next words gave her a start.

"I lied about the gent with the Father Christmas beard," he said casually enough.

Pat took off her colored glasses. Her golden eyes narrowed suspiciously.

"Just tell me this—who are you?" she demanded thinly.

"Some one who happens to share your abiding interest in royalty," he returned.

"Royalty?"

"Don't play coy. Although I must admit, it becomes you," he gushed. "Wonderfully."

Pat shared a number of her famous cousin's peculiar qualities. His love of excitement, his apparent fearlessness. One trait Pat had never managed to master was Doc's habitual poker face.

Try as she might to resemble a bronze-skinned sphinx, Pat looked surprised. But only for a moment. She forced herself to frown, hoping to cover the betraying lapse.

Was the young man merely doing some guessing? she wondered. He might be a journalist on the trail of a hoped-for story.

"Does the name H. Startland Drago mean anything to you?" he asked abruptly.

It didn't. Pat shook her bronze-haired head.

"Not surprising. He operates Drago & Company, the bond house. I work for him. Or did. Until he vanished."

This statement piqued Pat's interest.

"Vanished?"

"Mysteriously. Oh, not as mysteriously as King Goz the First, but mysteriously nevertheless."

"Any connection that you know of?" Pat wanted to know.

"One: H. Startland Drago was King Goz's investment banker."

"Hmm," said Pat.

"Is that a hmm of interest, prithee?"

"Just a hmm, thank you."

"How very disappointing."

"Sorry," Pat sniffed. "I believe in long engagements."

"You're old-fashioned," Caspar Prestowitz said. "What say we leave the bustle of the city behind us. Then we'll have a heart-to-heart talk. I think I'm going to interest you."

"Don't let your hopes run away with you," Pat suggested dryly.

Caspar Prestowitz sent the big machine through the Holland vehicular tunnel and into New Jersey. After many minutes of driving, they came to a more rural portion of the state. Roads narrowed, lost their coating of macadam. Farms and barns became visible along the sides of the road.

Eventually they turned into an even more desolate area.

There were no fences. The road had never been graded. Wheels had beaten it down, and had pounded plenty of ruts. Every so often the car jumped like a jack rabbit. Pat looked at the speedometer. Too much. Fifty.

"Where are you taking me?" she demanded.

"No questions. We're almost there." His voice was now cold, remote. The sudden change was so abrupt, it prompted Pat to announce, "I have changed my mind. I prefer to catch my train, after all."

"Too late," the other clipped.

Pat drew in a double lungful of shouting air. "Help!" she screeched. "Murder!"

It couldn't do any harm, she thought. It nearly did, though. Caspar Prestowitz's suddenly rattled driving left some fender paint on a tree.

"Please, Miss Savage," he admonished mildly.

At that point, Pat decided she had had enough of the forward young man and drove a hand into her big metallic purse.

The man was ready for the move. Keeping one hand on the steering wheel, he reached across and grabbed at the bag. He had a long reach, and Pat's weapon was no derringer. It was heavy as an anvil, and very long of barrel. Too, it boasted a fanning spur in lieu of a trigger. Getting all that assembled hardware out of the closed bag was no simple operation.

The bag, gun and all, was snatched out of her hand. The drawstring opening loosened and the ivory grips popped out.

Pat tried to recapture the weapon, but Prestowitz gave the wheel a savage jerk to the left—throwing Pat hard against the right-hand door. She had to grab the hanging strap.

By the time she got herself organized, the maw of the old-fashioned frontier six-shooter was pointed in her direction.

"You wouldn't shoot a woman," she said confidently.

But he did. Once. In the upper arm. The pistol roared! Pat grabbed her bare shoulder, saw a trickle of blood leaking between pretty bronze fingers.

Pat Savage stared at him very much as if he were a mother dog that had been caught eating her own young.

Then the air went breathily out of her parted mouth and she slumped against the cushions.

Caspar Prestowitz noticed the smoke curling up from the long barrel and gave it a nonchalant puff.

"So much for Calamity Jane," he said, sounding very pleased with himself.

# VII

# GOLD-LEAF TRAIL

"An interminable tedium," muttered scholarly-sounding Johnny Littlejohn as he watched the landmarks of Washington, D.C., fly past his car window.

"Say it in English, Professor," Renny thumped, holding the steering wheel steady in his monster hands.

"A crashing bore," grumbled Johnny.

"Pipe down, you two," Long Tom called from the back seat. His pale eyes were fixed on a boxy object in his thin lap, which housed a bell jar. From time to time, the car took a corner, forcing the limp form of Barbara Bland up against his puny shoulders. Long Tom, scowling, nudged her back into place each time. Long Tom ordinarily had little to do with the gentler sex, so-called. In this case, he was positively exasperated by the annoying feminine presence.

"Any chirping yet?" Renny called back.

Long Tom was staring at the bell jar, particularly at two strips of gold leaf affixed to electrical contacts. They were touching, like hands in prayer.

"Not so far. Try driving south."

Renny complied. They were cruising along Constitution Avenue now. Passers-by continually hailed them, not noticing—or perhaps not caring—that the taxi's flag was down. It was a warm summer's day and the tourist sights were soaked in sunlight.

"What if he ditched the superfirer?" Renny wondered in his bear-in-a-cave voice.

"At least we'll recover the thing. It won't do to have one of Doc's pistols in bad hands."

"Not much good to him unless he figures out all the safety catches," Renny pointed out. The intricate little weapons were equipped with cunning concealed latches, the disengagement of which was necessary to allow them to be discharged.

A low moan filled the cab's interior.

"A resurrection," Johnny said suddenly.

"Which?" asked Renny.

Johnny turned in his seat and indicated Barbara Bland in the rear. Her eyelids were fluttering. Fingers, held tight, loosened.

"Coming out of it," Renny opined.

"Rats!" muttered Long Tom unhappily.

Barbara Bland came to wakefulness in slow stages. Her body constricted itself more tightly, as if the nerves were gathering themselves. Her mouth compressed and she made thick tasting noises with her tongue.

The flutter in her eyes died, picked up, and died again. Then they came open, showing a clear, intelligent gray color.

Focus was slow in coming. She looked about the car bewilderedly.

"Who—who are you men?" There was no detectable fear in her tone. Just a muted curiosity. The woman had nerve.

"We are associates of Doc Savage," Johnny told her, using small words.

"W-where is Mr. Savage?"

"He had to return to New York very suddenly," Johnny related. "He asked us to keep an eye on you."

This sunk in. "The last thing I remember was seeing a man run from the apartment house and into another," Barbara Bland said slowly. "He had a gun. I realized he must be one of the gunmen. I—I chased him into it."

"That took guts," grunted Renny.

"Very foolish," sniffed Long Tom sourly. "You could have gotten killed."

"I had a gun," she said. "Normally, I carry it for my own protection. In this case, I thought I could do Mr. Savage a favor and he would agree to sit for an interview in return."

This brought a trio of differently pitched snorts from Doc Savage's three men. They sounded for a moment like a distinctly unmusical barnyard symphony.

"Doc isn't much on interviews, miss," Renny offered.

"So I gather." She eyed the bell jar on Long Tom's lap.

"Isn't that an electroscope?" she inquired.

Long Tom blinked. He looked up and over to Barbara Bland as if seeing her for the first time. His usually sour expression lost a dash of vinegar. But not too much.

"Yes. How do you know?"

Barbara Bland pointed at the praying leaves. "Those gold strips. Tinfoil of gold leaf, aren't they?"

Long Tom grunted.

"Why are you carrying it like that?"

"We're chasing that red-headed guy you fumbled," Renny explained.

"I'll tell it!" Long Tom snapped. And everyone was surprised. The puny electrical wizard rarely took notice of any woman. He seemed to be taking a marked interest in plain, gray-eyed Barbara Bland.

"The guy lifted one of Doc's supermachine pistols, see?"

"Yes?"

"We've always been worried about that happening, so we took precautions. In the handle of every one is a small fragment of radium. You know what radium is?"

"Yes. Of course. A substance that gives off certain radio emanations."

"Yeah. Right. Exactly."

Barbara Bland's voice grew softer. "Ah, I understand now. We're driving around hoping to detect those emanations with this electroscope. When the leaves fly apart, we shall have found the gun."

Long Tom was so taken aback by the girl reporter's understanding of his specialty that his jaw hung slack with wonder.

"But isn't that dangerous?" she wondered. "People have been known to die of radio poisoning."

"The quantity is too small to cause harm," Long Tom said in a thin voice.

Some moments passed as they circumnavigated the city without any hint of a stir from the silent electroscope. They were on the outskirts of the nation's capital now, near the U.S. Soldiers Home.

Presently, Barbara Bland broke the protracted silence with a question.

"This man whom we are seeking. Who is he exactly?"

"Calls himself Elvern D. Kastellantz,'" Long Tom offered.

"And who is Elvern D. Kastellantz?"

"You ask a lot of questions, lady," Renny put in.

"I'm a reporter," she said smartly. "It is my job to ask questions."

Pallid Long Tom added in a voice that could have almost sweetened cream, "Doc thinks Elvern D. Kastellantz—if that is his real name—is the chauffeur who was driving King Goz's car when he up and evaporated."

Barbara Bland's pale, mousy eyebrows shot upward. "Oh," she said. "Oh."

"We find him and maybe we'll get a line on the missing king."

"I just remembered something," the girl reporter said abruptly.

"Yeah?"

"I must call my mother, back in Denver. She worries about me so."

"I dunno," Renny said slowly.

"Look, you're not getting anywhere, and it will only take a minute," Barbara Bland said pleadingly.

The big engineer hesitated.

And Long Tom said, "Give her a break. She's been through a lot."

Barbara Bland reached over and patted the puny electrical wizard on the hand. "Thank you. You are very kind to a working girl."

Grumbling, big-fisted Renny pulled up to a filling station where there was a coin telephone.

"I shan't be a moment," Barbara said, getting out.

Watching the girl journalist enter the booth, Long Tom was heard to remark, "Isn't she something?"

"Kinda plain," Renny thumped.

"Symptomatologically androgynous," inserted Johnny.

"You two watch your language!" Long Tom said hotly. "Don't forget, Doc told us to keep an eye on her."

"That *could* mean she's a bad apple," Renny said pointedly.

Long Tom's face regained its normal sourness. His bulging forehead gathered in wrinkles, and he said after some cogitation, "One way to find out."

"How's that?"

"By listening in."

Long Tom reached down to the floorboards, where various apparatus reposed. He had a case of electric equipment that he took on adventures. It was remarkably varied, for all its compactness. The inactive electroscope was one component of its array.

The electrical wizard brought out a contrivance with a reflector attachment.

"Pickup mike," he said, clapping earphones to his big, saillike ears. He cranked down the taxi window and pointed the parabolic reflector in the direction of the phone booth, and tripped a switch.

Barbara Bland was speaking. "They say his name is Elvern D. Kastellantz. They believe him to be the missing chauffeur, who is in turn suspected of complicity in the murder of the king's footman, the only other person in the limousine at the time of the king's disappearance."

"That is all?" asked a detached male voice.

"Holy cow, that thing is picking up what's coming out of the telephone diaphragm, too!" Renny exploded.

"What do you expect?" said Long Tom. "Now shut your trap."

"What should I do?" asked Barbara Bland anxiously.

"The chauffeur is the only lead anyone has. Follow it."

"And if Doc Savage's men find the missing king?"

"Perhaps," said the voice who was definitely not Barbara Bland's mother, "you will be famous, after the fashion of Joan of Arc."

"I'll take my fame some other way," retorted the girl. "They cut her head off or something, didn't they?"

"Nothing like that is apt to happen to you. Report as needed."

Barbara Bland hung up and Long Tom hastily packed away his listening device.

As Barbara Bland reemerged and walked back to the waiting taxi, Johnny was heard to remark, "A maternal impossibility."

"Huh?"

"He means," Renny said, low-voiced, "that Bland gal wasn't talking to her mother just now."

Long Tom said, "Musta been her editor, then."

Then the girl's return put a damper on further conversation.

"How's your mother?" asked Renny, with a straight face.

Barbara Bland slipped inside. "Fine. She's such a dear to worry about me so. I am her only daughter."

Renny grunted skeptically.

Long Tom covered the sound by complaining, "This electroscope isn't reacting at all."

"Could it be broken?" Barbara asked innocently.

"Not a chance; I put it together myself," said Long Tom, as if the fact was the last word on the subject. Which it was.

"Have you gentlemen considered returning to the place where you lost the trail of this man, Kastellantz?" the girl suggested.

"What do you mean?" Long Tom asked.

"Surely you have heard that famous saying that criminals return to the scene of their criminal activities?"

"Yeah?"

"Might not this man return to that awful alley?"

"What makes you say that?" Renny asked suspiciously.

"I assume the men who attempted to seize Doc Savage are in police hands by now?"

No one said anything to that. An uneasy silence followed.

Some time ago, Doc Savage had established, in upstate New York, in a region that was remote and mountainous, an institution that was rather unique. The patients of this place underwent a delicate brain operation which wiped out all knowledge of their past life. There they were taught a trade, and schooled to hate crime and criminals, and to be good citizens. Then they were released, often to be given a job in one of the many industrial institutions which Doc Savage controlled.

No crook, however bad an actor he had been previously, had ever gone back to crime after being graduated from Doc Savage's unique scientific "college."

It was to this college that Hike Ewing and his gang had been spirited.

Existence of this place was one of the bronze man's deepest secrets, so no one disabused Barbara Bland of her assumption.

"This Elvern D. Kastellantz may not know this," she continued. "He might think he can contact his men again."

"Unlikely," Johnny said.

"Or recruit new ones," Barbara added.

Long Tom brightened. "A possibility."

"A dubious one," Johnny said flatly, polishing his monocle magnifier elaborately.

"I don't see any rushing progress being made otherwise," Long Tom pointed out.

That settled the argument. Renny muscled the wheel around and the taxi—they continued to be hailed despite the flag being down—whined back in the direction of Dingman Alley.

"This is quite a machine for its looks," Barbara noted.

"This is one of Doc's special jobs," Long Tom offered helpfully. "There's a sixteen-cylinder motor under that hood and the sides and glass are bulletproof. Doc keeps a few of these garaged in larger cities, in case we need one."

"Doc Savage is quite a remarkable fellow," Barbara Bland said approvingly.

"You don't know the half of it," said Long Tom proudly, and began to regale the mousy girl with stories of the bronze man's exploits.

Up front, Renny and Johnny looked violently unhappy.

They would have missed the electroscope leaves flying apart except that Long Tom had the leaves set to trip a contact, which started a buzzer buzzing noisily.

Everyone's attention flew to the electroscope then.

"We're gettin' close to Dingman Alley," Renny warned.

"You were right!" Long Tom said loudly.

Barbara Bland bestowed upon the puny electrical wizard a smile that was radiant with approval.

There was no way to determine how close they were to the radioactive element embedded in the stolen supermachine pistol. The electroscope registered only the nearness of the isotope, not the direction or its exact proximity.

They parked the cab a short distance from the disreputable alley and got out.

"You should stay here," Long Tom told Barbara Bland.

"Nothing doing! I'm here for a story, and I'm going to get it."

There was a short interval during which Renny, Long Tom, and Johnny debated the wisdom of allowing this.

"She has spunk," Long Tom insisted earnestly. "And I say she tags along."

Renny and Johnny exchanged doubtful glances. In the end, they caved in. Long Tom had a temper. It was legendary. Although he was, perhaps, the least physically imposing of the Doc Savage outfit, Long Tom Roberts was crossed at the offender's peril.

"Stay behind us at all times," Renny warned as they approached.

They entered the alley. It was dark now. Window shades were pulled down—where windows had shades, that is.

"Maybe we should split up," Renny suggested.

"A tactical convenience," big-worded Johnny agreed.

Long Tom turned to Barbara Bland. "You can stay with me," he offered gallantly.

Which suited the other two perfectly fine.

As they moved off in different directions, Renny had a final mutter for Johnny.

"My money says she bops him on his head and teaches him a lesson in trust," he thumped.

"Indubitably," Johnny assented.

They selected separate doors in the apartment house and entered them.

It was not Long Tom or even the careful Renny who fell into difficulty, but scholarly Johnny Littlejohn.

Johnny had selected the apartment of the would-be kidnaper of Doc Savage, Hike Ewing, as the first place to be searched.

The door was closed, but not locked. It had been left that way by the attendants who had picked up Ewing and his underlings.

Johnny entered and began reaching for a light.

"Hold it!" a voice advised.

The lanky archæologist felt the pressure of a hard barrel in his skeletal ribs, and made an accurate deduction.

Since the man evidently had a gun, Johnny decided to take the advice.

The light switch clicked on.

Johnny possessed excellent eyesight, despite the foppish monocle affixed to his lapel. He had good peripheral vision. He did not have to turn around to recognize redheaded Elvern D. Kastellantz.

"Don't do anything fatal," Kastellantz cautioned.

"An univocular recapitulation," Johnny murmured.

"Eh?" growled Elvern D. Kastellantz.

"Your last word describes your intentions," Johnny translated grimly.

"One word describes what's going to happen to you if you don't obey me to the letter," Kastellantz ripped.

"What?" Johnny demanded.

"Scragged," Kastellantz returned. "In case you don't know that one, it means something a bullet or a knife does to you."

Neither man said anything for a while.

* * *

Presently, Elvern D. Kastellantz ordered, "Call your friends."

"Eh?"

"You heard me. Get them in here. I came back here to hire more men to locate you and your chief, but it seems you saved me the trouble. I assume Doc Savage is somewhere in the vicinity."

"A distinct negativity."

"My English isn't the same brand as yours," warned Kastellantz, poking Johnny's lathelike ribs again.

"Doc has returned to New York," Johnny volunteered.

"The truth?"

"The truth," Johnny said quietly.

Elvern D. Kastellantz seemed to consider this turn of events. "Call your friends, anyway."

Johnny was prodded to the window and threw it up. He leaned out.

Before he could speak, the muzzle gouged the hard bumps of his spinal column along his back painfully.

"No tricks!" Kastellantz warned suddenly.

Johnny hesitated. He had been planning to insert a few words of ancient Mayan, the language to which Doc and his aids often resorted when they wished to communicate without fear of being understood by outsiders. Doc had used just that trick back at the National Museum, to instruct Renny and Long Tom to follow the fleeing Hike and his men, but here it was too risky.

"Long Tom! Renny! Come to Hike's room," Johnny shouted, and was quickly yanked back from the window.

Renny Renwick was the first to arrive. He lunged in through the door and tripped over a small table that Elvern D. Kastellantz had placed in the way. He went down on all fours and when he looked up, the sad-faced engineer decided to remain where he had landed.

"Crawl over to one side," Elvern D. Kastellantz warned.

Renny did so, looking ridiculous, like a crippled bear.

"Some prognosticator you are," he muttered at Johnny. The gaunt geologist offered no reply. The expression on his face was indignant.

Long Tom came next, with Barbara Bland in tow.

He managed to avoid taking a tumble, but still barked one shin on the edge of the obstacle. He grabbed a place under his knee painfully.

"Hold on to that knee," ordered Elvern D. Kastellantz.

Barbara Bland popped in next, stopped, and her mouth became thin and more colorless than usual. She neither shouted nor complained, which raised Renny's and Long Tom's estimation of her instantly.

This newfound respect took a wild twist as she was walking over to join Long Tom and the others, impelled by a wagging gun.

Abruptly, she got wobbly at the knees. One hand flew to her mousy hair. "Oh, I think I'm going to faint."

"Go ahead. I've got you all now," Elvern D. Kastellantz gloated, keeping his captured weapon trained on the others.

"I don't care what you've got," snapped Barbara Bland suddenly. "I've got a gun! It's a little gun, but it will kill a man. It was hidden in my hair. Look at it!"

Everyone looked. It was indeed a gun. A derringer, to be exact. The gray-eyed girl cocked the hammer. She had the drop on her captor, and this was reflected in the latter's face.

Slowly, Elvern D. Kastellantz lowered the supermachine pistol.

"Good work," said Long Tom fervently. "You saved our bacon!"

Barbara Bland whirled, stepping away from them.

"Stay back! You're my prisoners, too. All of you! And we're going for a little ride!"

Long Tom Roberts gaped at the tiny pistol. It was pointed at his underfed midsection. His pale face became crimson.

"You sure can pick 'em, Long Tom," Renny rumbled.

# VIII

## GRIEF FOR PAT

"I am deeply sorry it was necessary for me to shoot you, my dear Miss Savage," said the voice of the man who had wounded Pat Savage.

The voice seemed far away. As if the person were speaking at the other end of a long tunnel.

Pat Savage roused, murmured something under her breath, and then her sparkling golden eyes snapped open. She looked at her hands. They were looped together at the wrist by strong hempen cord.

It all came back to her then.

She was still seated in the nice roadster. It had stopped. They were in a patch of murk on a field. The moon was high, and very bright, like a Chinese lantern hung against a black curtain stitched with stars.

Zany Caspar Prestowitz was still sitting behind the wheel. He looked relaxed, confident, untroubled by the fact that he had just shot a young woman with her own six-gun.

"You—you could have killed me!" Pat accused.

"I aimed at your arm."

"And if there had been lead in that cannon instead of one of Doc's mercy bullets, I could have bled to death!" Pat retorted hotly.

"I figured that you had probably taken to carrying them in your gun," Prestowitz said unconcernedly.

Pat's eyes grew suspicious. "That's mighty clever figuring."

"Thank you," returned the young gallant. "But not really. You see, I'm very aware of Doc Savage's policy against taking human life, and the mercy bullets his men are compelled to use. Since you have developed a penchant for joining him in his escapades, it was only reasonable to

76

assume that the bronze man had cooked up a supply for your rather charming antique."

"How long was I out?"

"Oh, about a half hour. I have whiled away the last few minutes observing the endearing way your face wrinkles in slumber. Did you know that you snored?"

Pat grew indignant. "I do not!"

"More of a hum, actually. But a nice hum. Musical."

"Humph," Pat said, testing her bonds. There was no give. She looked out through the windscreen for the first time and saw the plane.

It was an amphibian, a late model. But it was not a racer like Pat's personal seaplane. And it was hardly in the class with Doc Savage's private armada of planes. Still, it was no crate. It had cost money. Rather like the roadster.

"What are we waiting on?" Pat asked.

"For you to wake up."

"Eh?"

"I really didn't care to carry you to the plane. Not when you can walk under your own power."

"I'm not getting in that thing," Pat said flatly.

Caspar Prestowitz lost his faint smile. He took up Pat's long-barreled six-shooter from the door pocket and pointed it in her direction.

"On the other hand," he said, "I can put you out again and carry you, after all. I just prefer to do it this way."

Pat considered. She had not completely shed her initial impression that this young man was a harmless if impulsive whelp. She received no strong sense of danger in his presence. And he represented excitement of a sort.

Pat had a weakness for exciting situations, even if they did involve a salting of peril.

"Lead on, Macduff," she said grudgingly.

At this, Caspar Prestowitz laughed. It was a healthy laugh. He then got out of the car and went around to assist Pat out.

Pat's legs were linked by a short stretch of hemp. Not enough to impede walking totally, but running was out of the question. She would trip over her own feet.

Getting to the plane was a matter of a short walk through the warm, summery night. Prestowitz carried a bulky package under one arm that was tied with common twine.

Pat allowed herself to be helped onto the float and into a door. She took a seat. There were only two.

Stowing the package, Caspar Prestowitz got the engine cans going. He fed juice to the throttle, and the wheels began bumping along, gathering speed and lift.

The plane took off. Pat herself had learned flying from a master of that art. The remarkable man who was her cousin—Doc Savage. She had to admit this zany aviator knew what he was doing. The ship climbed beautifully. It headed north.

"Maybe I'll get my fishing done after all," she said.

"That reminds me," said Caspar Prestowitz. And he took a cloth roll of some kind and gave it a shake. It proved to be a sack. Burlap. It settled over Pat's kerchiefed head like a scratchy shroud.

"I can't see," Pat complained.

"The very idea," returned Prestowitz in good humor.

Then the plane began to undergo some very elaborate gyrations, looping, banking, and the like.

"What's happening?" Pat asked in an unsettled voice.

"Turbulence."

Pat said nothing to that. She was not fooled in one respect. They had started north. But after she was blind-folded, the plane made several turns, with the idea of confusing her. It did. She had not the slightest idea in which direction they flew.

Pat settled down for a possibly extended flight.

In that respect, she was fooled. After no more than an hour and one half possibly, the plane slanted down and the hissing of water cascading along either side of the floats came to her ears. Water drummed and spattered along the side cabin windows.

The plane coasted some distance, settled, and the floats bumped something. Propeller clicking, the motor died.

"Here we are," Prestowitz said, pleased with himself.

Pat was taken by the arm and helped out of the plane. Only when she was standing was her sack blindfold removed.

It was quite dark. Pat looked around. Trees stood about like dark giants. They were at the end of a small lake or large pond. There was insufficient moonlight to tell.

The plane had been tied to a solid rock shore. Ropes to hold it had been looped about boulders. Caspar Prestowitz gave these a testing hitch and, satisfied, took her by the elbow. He had his package under one arm.

"They have laws against this sort of thing," Pat pointed out.

"Laws don't concern me."

"And then there is my cousin," Pat added pointedly. "Doc Savage will take you to the cleaners so fast your head will swim—swing, I should say."

Caspar Prestowitz only laughed at that as they walked along.

Pat thought about that laugh for a moment. It had not sounded forced. Caspar Prestowitz, as he called himself, really did not seem afraid of Doc. Yet Doc had a reputation that often caused habitual criminals to take sudden vacations when Doc came to town.

They walked for a time in a forest of some sort along a path that was horny with worn stones. Pat nearly fell once. And then pretended to a second time.

"You could," she suggested, "lead the way for a lady."

"Won't run away, will you?"

"Cross my heart, and hope to marry a rich prince one day," said Pat, in the darkness crossing her fingers.

Caspar Prestowitz took the lead. He glanced back a time or two, seemed reassured by Pat's easy compliance, and concentrated on his own feet.

Pat Savage was a very strong young woman, thanks to the hours daily spent demonstrating reducing exercises to fat, wealthy lady matrons in her New York establishment. She made her brown right hand into a fist that was much harder than anyone would have expected. She picked out a spot behind the young man's right ear and let him have it.

Caspar Prestowitz's head rocked forward, taking the rest of him along for the ride.

He must have hit his head on a stone, because he didn't get up immediately.

Quickly, Pat knelt beside him and started going through his pockets. She found a clasp knife, fought it open, and began sawing at her wrist bonds. She worked furiously. This was no place to be caught trying to escape.

The ropes parted and, hands free now, she attacked her ankle bonds.

When Pat stood up, she was holding her six-shooter, which Caspar Prestowitz had been carrying tucked into his belt.

Holding the big bore trained on the man, she hauled him over. He was out cold. A trickle of blood had run down out of his scalp.

Pat resisted an urge to wipe it clean. He had been such a charming rogue, she now felt a pang of pity for him.

It was clear that Prestowitz would enjoy a long period of unconsciousness, so Pat decided to reconnoiter the vicinity. The mysterious package could wait, she decided. It looked rather ordinary—too much so to arouse much curiosity.

She stepped off the path, where footprints would not show.

It was quite dark now. The moon had ghosted behind a cloud and somewhere an owl hooted.

Pat walked as far as she felt confident in one direction and abruptly changed course. It was her idea to walk in a box, always keeping the path and Caspar Prestowitz fixed in her mind. If nothing in the box proved interesting, she would switch to another approach.

Pat was walking in a line that corresponded to the second side of the imaginary box when she heard a snarl. She froze. It came again. Low, guttural. Unhuman.

"Uh-oh," she said, eyes darting about.

Standing in one place, Pat tramped her feet about, slowly sweeping her six-gun about her, ready to fend off any danger.

She saw the eyes then. They were greenish-gold. Small. But high. The eyes belonged to a low-crouching shape with tufted ears in a nearby tree branch. They were looking at her. Once, they winked. It was a creepy wink. Patient. Unafraid.

The bronze-haired girl knew what it was then. Her "Oh" was very small in the darkness.

The bobcat was not a dozen feet distant, and bobcats are not customers to meet at that range, not even with a high-powered rifle. Pat's earlier days had been spent in western Canada—her entire life, in truth, until a series of incredible and amazing adventures had taken the life of her father, and might have resulted in her own end, except for the intervention of that unusual man, her cousin, Doc Savage. Wildcats aplenty had been in her part of Canada. They were man-killers.

The thoughts that lashed Pat's brain the next instant were chaotic. She did not think about her past. She thought how deceptive looks can be. A bobcat is not a large animal, all told. But its ferocity more than makes up for its lack of muscular bulk.

The thing was a crouching shape in the darkness, and Pat began to sense the shifting outlines of its fur. It was gathering itself now, ready to pounce.

Pat steeled herself. She lifted her six-shooter and took careful aim, wishing that this was one time she was packing solid lead, not mercy bullets. Big-game hunters often used mercies to bring down large animals humanely. But the tiny shells Doc had perfected contained an anæsthetic designed to leave no lasting effect on a human target. How effective they would be against a live bobcat was a question.

There was no time for more than the thought of failure to flick through her mind. The bobcat sprang; Pat fired! Two shots, then she threw herself off to one side, feeling the harsh fur graze one arm.

The bronze-haired girl rolled, came up in a crouch, and got off another shot. It was wild. There was no aim involved. She was making noise in an effort to frighten off the bobcat.

It was a wasted effort, she found when she got herself organized.

The bobcat lay on its side, fangs bared in a stiff snarl. Its lambent eyes were open. But it was out cold. There was a smear of crimson on one spotted, tawny shoulder.

More cautious now, Pat resumed her trek.

* * *

The house appeared through a break in a stand of trees as if a curtain had been drawn aside. The moonlight helped that effect.

It was a big house. Rustic. But no log cabin. From a distance, it reminded Pat Savage of a hunting lodge. Not quite so large, but built along those same substantial lines.

There were lights on in windows, so Pat began walking toward the house. The closer she got, the larger it loomed. It began taking on the look of a hunting lodge after all. There was a circular driveway in front, paved in crushed stone, surrounding a rather generous ornamental pool edged in marble.

A plain dirt road led to this.

And coming up the road, so suddenly that Pat dropped to the grass before she was quite certain it was the proper course of action, were twin funnels of light that were busy with gnats.

Headlamps of an auto! The machine came into view a moment later. A taxi, green and somewhat dilapidated.

Pat watched it wheel around the circular driveway, tires making gritty noises, and stop. The headlamps were doused.

The bronze-haired girl crept up for a closer look. Doors opened. Darksome figures began stepping out.

One towered over the others by a rather large head. He looked familiar, threw up monster hands.

A deep booming voice said, "Holy cow! A hunting lodge!"

# IX

# SNOW-BEARDED SPECTER

At the sound of Renny Renwick's foghorn voice—for the booming voice without question belonged to the gloomy-faced engineer—Pat Savage shed all her caution.

She popped up out of concealment, waving her six-shooter over her head. She lifted her voice.

"I am going to count to three, and then start cutting loose with this shooting iron!" she announced. "Anyone still on their feet at three is bound to lose ears, noses, and assorted fingers!"

A slow counter could have counted to twenty in the silence that followed her words sinking in.

Pat began counting off. "*One!*"

No reaction.

"*Two!*"

Pat never got to three. Instantly, the dark knot of forms beside the taxi became a frantic boil.

A voice—unmistakably Renny's—shouted, "She's a madwoman when her dander is up like that!" and leaped into the pool.

In short order, Johnny and Long Tom followed.

Pat started shooting then. She picked the handiest form. Her pistol roared! And the figure dropped from sight. With her muzzle, Pat followed the remaining figure on his feet. She got off a shot. It struck the car body as the runner reached it, but did no harm. Mercy bullets have little penetration power. Besides, the cab was armored.

The fifth figure got behind the wheel and the starter ground noisily.

Headlamps blazed into brilliance as the taxi swung around, roaring in Pat's direction.

The bronze-haired girl ran smack into its path, hoping to run a bluff.

She took dead aim at the shadowy face behind the wheel.

The driver stomped on the gas. The taxi surged ahead. He—or she—held to his—or her—course.

Pat flung herself out of the way just in time.

She sent a spiteful bullet snarling after the whining machine, knowing that it would do no good. But it made her feel a little better.

Still, she assayed a pungent "Darn!" in the darkness.

Pat Savage walked up to the marble pool, where Renny and the others were lying flat on their backs, making bubbles.

Pat gave the marble rim a hard tap with the butt of her six-gun. Three dripping and unhappy faces surfaced and blinked at her reproachfully.

"You boys do this thing often?" she asked cheerfully.

"What?" Renny demanded, blowing moisture off his puritanical mouth.

"Go swimming after midnight with all your clothes on?"

"We are hunting a mermaid," Johnny retorted.

"That," Pat said, "lets *me* out. Anyway, mermaids are found on the bottom of the sea, not swimming around on top. You fellows had better go down on the bottom—"

"Rats!" said Long Tom.

They clambered out and began wringing their clothes free of moisture.

"One got away," Pat said unhappily.

"Elvern D. Kastellantz," Renny rumbled.

"Who's he?" Pat wondered, pretty brow crinkling.

"We think he's the guy who drove King Goz into the afterlife—or wherever he ended up."

"Too bad he got away, then," Pat said, striding over to the fallen figure she had brought down with her well-placed mercy bullet. It was a girl.

Noticing the plain-looking form lying in the driveway, Pat remarked dryly, "She could stand a little sprucing up at my beauty shop."

"That's Barbara Bland," Long Tom said sourly.

"Do I detect a note of extra disdain in your voice, my soured-on-life friend?" Pat asked.

Renny piped up, "Long Tom took a shine to her and she up and glommed us."

"*Tisk, tisk,*" Pat said. "Didn't anyone ever tell you never to trust women, my son?"

Long Tom's neck turned red. He grunted finally, "Listen, Pat—how'd you happen to be way out here?"

"I'm taking a hand in this!" Pat said emphatically.

"Does Doc know about it?" the electrical wizard asked.

"Knowing me," Pat said, "Doc probably won't be surprised when he finds out."

"Probably not," Long Tom agreed dryly.

"Doc will not be pleased, of course," Johnny interjected.

"Does he think he's got a corner on the excitement in this world?" Pat flung back. "Does he think nobody but him gets a kick out of a little trouble? Just who does he think he is, anyway? And who are you to be telling me—"

Renny interjected at that point, "Listen, let us settle this later. This Bland gal has a story to tell."

"If that is her name," Pat sniffed.

"What do you mean?" Long Tom asked.

Pat indicated the slumbering girl with the muzzle of her six-shooter. "Doc asked me to check her story," she explained. "It didn't pan out. They never heard of her at the *Globe*."

Renny grunted. "A phony, huh?"

"Be a while before she comes to," Long Tom said thickly.

"In the meantime," Pat invited sweetly, "you strapping fellows can do a gal a favor and collect my traveling companion, Prestowitz."

"Who?"

"Caspar Prestowitz. A rascal of recent acquaintance. He flew me down here—wherever here is. I left him back up the trail—after I conked him one on the noggin."

"He kidnap you?" Long Tom grunted.

"He," Pat said airily, "underestimated me. Like some others I know," she added tartly.

"Let's fetch him," Renny said, starting off.

Pat led the way. She was listening to their story of being captured when, without any preliminary warning, a sound filled the spruce woods.

It was a whistling. It had a harmonic, inexpressible sadness to it. It seemed all around them, saturating the woods, tugging at the heartstrings, and making them look in all directions at once in an effort to ascertain the source of the morose melody.

"What's that?" Renny rumbled.

"A spectral evanescence," Johnny muttered, bringing his monocle magnifier up to one eye.

"It's that spook!" Pat gasped. "Here!"

"Spook!" Long Tom exploded.

"Old King Mysterious!"

"Huh?"

"If I tell you," Pat sighed, "you're not going to believe me. But watch out for an old goat straight out of the Brothers Grimm."

Keeping together, they continued down the unlit path. The woods pressed close to them. Johnny brought out one of Doc's tiny spring-generator flashlights and speared light into the trees. An owl hooted in annoyance and swiveled its head away from the intruding blaze of illumination.

They saw no one who might be the author of the unearthly melody.

The whistling seemed to invade their brains, depressing their spirits. It played on the nerves, like an unending dead march.

They trudged on.

Eventually, they came to the pond or modest lake where the sporty seaplane lay at anchor.

"Something's wrong!" Pat hissed urgently.

"What?"

"I left that Prestowitz on the path! We should have stumbled across him before now!"

"Well, we didn't," Long Tom pointed out.

Pat started back. "Come on, let's find him."

"What is producing this infernal whistling?" Johnny wondered, digging at an ear.

"The other phantom king," Pat shot back.

"Huh?"

"Or maybe it's the same one, I don't know," Pat said distractedly. "Just come on!"

A scream—high and shrill—pierced the night.

"Barbara!" Long Tom exclaimed, starting.

"Nope," Pat puffed. "Unless I miss my guess, that's my bobcat."

"Your what?"

"Ran into a bobcat and brought him down with a mercy bullet. Guess he woke up."

The scream came again, short and ferocious. This time, it sounded distinctly feral to their ears. Bobcat. There was no doubt. They veered off the trail, in the direction of the sound. As they ran, the mournful whistling, which had not abated in the least, grew—not louder so much as clearer.

"We're coming up on Pat's spook," Renny ventured.

"Don't remind me!" Pat hurled back.

Sometimes in life timing is all-important. They had been tearing through the dark woods, avoiding low-hanging boughs, obstructing tree boles, and inconvenient rocks in their path, not quite certain why they should be so anxious to meet up with a loose bobcat. Perhaps it was the bobcat's screech. It was a warning sound, as if it were about to pounce on prey.

Knowledge that Barbara Bland or Caspar Prestowitz might be the prey impelled them to run their hardest.

What they expected to find when they came upon the bobcat none of them could rightly put into words. What they saw was another matter entirely.

Renny—the tallest of the tiny band—saw it first.

"There's the cat!" he thumped, leveling a knobby forefinger.

All eyes followed the monster digit. The cat was a dark hump in the high bough of a hickory tree. Johnny brought his light up, and it washed the crouching feline in calcium brightness. Its coloration was yellow-brown and mottled with dark spots.

As if the light were a thorn in its hide, it sprang downward.

Johnny jumped the light down. So they saw it clearly.

A tall, slightly stooped figure, all in scarlet, and draped in an ermine-trimmed red cloak. Bony hands clutched a heavy gold sphere surmounted by a filigreed device like the back end of an old-fashioned dungeon key, and a bejeweled scepter, also of gold.

Atop the apparition's head was a heavy golden crown, ostentatious with emeralds, rubies, and other brilliants. It was fantastically large and ornate and made the head below it seem ridiculously small in comparison.

The crown was tilted back and the face of the apparition stared up, unafraid, at the snarling bobcat. It was an old face, like a gnarled-with-age tree carved along human lines, with a knothole for a mouth. The whistling was coming from the dried orifice, they knew.

It stood as if rooted, long Rip Van Winkle beard hanging like an icy waterfall.

"Pat's spook!" Renny grunted, sounding very surprised.

There was too much distance between them and the snow-bearded specter to affect the outcome. The bobcat, foreclaws outstretched, went for the revenant's thin, wrinkled face.

The claws struck the unflinching countenance—*and passed on through!*

It happened in the blink of an eye. Had they not been looking squarely at the scene, they would have missed it entirely.

What happened next confirmed the impossible tableau as no trick of the eye.

The bobcat landed behind the kingly vision in a spitting ball of fur. It rolled furiously, and found its paws.

Snarling, it slunk back. The apparition turned, slowly, gracefully. Its face, etched in the bony archæologist's light, was a mask of benign power. Its profile was somehow eaglelike, predatory, the dark eyes unwinking.

The ermine trim of the regal scarlet cloak settled back as the bobcat leaped for its wearer.

One bony hand made passes in the air with the scepter, as if writing cabalistic signs in the murk. The ceaseless whistling continued, unabated and depressing to hear.

Again, the bobcat passed through the unflinching form, to land, sprawling, among the pine needles.

The witnesses to this eerie tableau found their voices then.

"Holy cow!"

"I'll be superamalgamated!"

"It can't be!"

"You three are witnesses!" Pat said, and brought up her six-shooter.

Renny clamped a titanic paw on the cylinder, inhibiting the weapon's mechanical action.

"What are you doing!" he thumped.

"I'm going to bag me a spook!" Pat retorted.

Renny thought about that a moment. Then, releasing the weapon, he growled, "Be my guest."

"Thanks." Pat shut one golden eye, gave her delectable lips a precautionary moistening, and drew a bead. She fired once. Then gun thunder and a saffron lance of ignited powder split the night.

The wraith of a vision turned at the sound, saw them, and its wizened face split in a cracked grin of some sort. The morose whistling ceased. Then it pursued its lips again, and the sound resumed. It was distressingly glum.

"You missed," Long Tom said.

"My eye!" Pat snapped. "I plugged him dead center! He just refuses to go down!"

Renny fetched up a fallen hickory branch, gave it a whirl, and it went sailing toward the apparition's snowy head.

They all saw it go clean through and carom off a spruce, directly behind. It struck the bewildered bobcat, who promptly lit off for parts unknown.

They got very, very quiet after that. Even the disconsolate dirge grew thin and spectral.

Looking at the queer old fellow began to make them feel as if some one were pouring a trickle of something cold down the middle of their backs.

Then, abruptly, the whistling specter presented the rear of its scarlet cloak to them and floated off down a hickory corridor.

The sound of its going was not discernible to the ear. In fact, there seemed to be no attendant sound at all. The whistling had abated entirely.

"Come on!" Pat urged. "He's getting away!"

They trotted after it, noting that for a spook, it betrayed none of the usual phenomena associated with ghostliness. True, it was unsettlingly silent. But it did not shine, appear transparent to the eye, rattle chain, or moan, as the popular conception of roaming spirits of the dead are reputed to do.

Although they had to admit that the unceasing whistling dirge was as nerve-wracking as any ghostly moan a fiction writer might conjure up. It seemed to hang in their minds even now, after it had left the air.

Big-worded Johnny was using his flashlight to keep it in sight. It was not very quick on its feet, and they were overhauling it by degrees.

"Are my eyes playing tricks on me," Long Tom muttered uneasily, "or is that thing walking *through* some of these trees?"

"I was hoping it was *my* eyes playing tricks," Pat puffed.

There was no question of it now. The regal vision didn't exactly walk through the trees, but it certainly seemed unconcerned by the obstacle they presented to its departure.

The trailing cloak and sometimes its arms and elbows simply brushed through inhibiting tree boles. This enabled it to move in a straight line, where its pursuers had to wend their way through the wild woods.

"An incorporality," Johnny said at one point.

"A which?" Renny rumbled.

"An ectoplasmic enigma."

"I should've settled for the first choice," Renny muttered.

The light began to fade. Johnny gave the flashlight crank a hasty spin, and the light strengthened. A little farther along, he had to repeat the operation.

That was when they lost sight of the uncanny apparition.

When they caught up to the spot where they had last seen it, they found no trace. Not even footprints.

"Lost him!" Long Tom murmured. "Better backtrack to the prints."

"I have a news flash for you boys," said Pat. "I've been watching the ground, and there *aren't* any footprints."

"Hah!" Renny snorted skeptically.

But when they retraced their steps, it was true. The only prints they discovered were their own.

"We all saw it," Renny said aloud. "How could it be there and not leave prints? This ground is pretty durn soft."

"How could it be there and be bobcat-proof?" Pat returned.

No one had an answer to that. So they fanned out and sought any sign of the lamenting liege.

It took some time before they gave it up.

"Goose eggs," Long Tom reported.

"Ditto," said Johnny, at a loss for a word more jaw-breaking.

"Let's find my pal, Prestowitz," Pat said fiercely.

Retracing their steps, they found the path and worked along it.

Soon, they came to the spot where Pat had brained the unpredictable Prestowitz. There was no sign of him or the package he had been carrying. Pat knelt and found a trace of blood where he had hit his head on a bald stone.

Footsteps led up to the spot. None led away—save their own. To be certain, they pressed their shoe soles into assorted footprints until all prints were accounted for.

Except for Caspar Prestowitz's footprints, which led up to the stone but did not lead away again.

"He might have walked backward, stepping into his own prints," Renny opined. "You know, using the old Indian trick."

"Wouldn't he be in the plane then?" Pat pointed out, reasonably enough.

"We can look."

They looked. There was no one in the tiny seaplane.

"Baffling," Long Tom said.

"Suppose that spooky old gink lit off with this Prestowitz character?" Renny wondered aloud.

"On a night like this," Pat said in exasperation, "*anything* is possible." She took stock of her surroundings, blew into the palm of her right hand, and then made it into a fist. She blew into the palm of her other hand and made that into a fist.

Then, fists tight, she strode purposefully back up the path in the direction of the hunting lodge.

"Where are you going?" Long Tom called after her.

"If I can't snag me a spook, then I'm going to spook me a fake," Pat said meaningly.

Everybody understood exactly what the determined Pat meant by that. They all but tripped over one another in their haste to get out in front of the grim-faced young thrill-seeker.

"Barbara Bland is *our* prisoner," Johnny pointed out.

Pat snapped, "Hah! You lads were *her* prisoner until I stepped in! And lucky for you that I did, too. Not that anybody here is in a mad rush to give a gal proper credit."

"We got nothing against you mixing in with our troubles, Pat," Renny said plaintively. "You know that. But if anything happened to you, Doc would have our hides—salted, cured, and skinned."

Pat stopped suddenly. "Cut a deal?"

The others looked doubtful.

"What?"

"Put in a good word for me with Doc."

"Sure," Renny allowed suddenly. "We can do that."

Pat resumed her mad march. "I," she said, "shall hold you gentlemen to that promise."

Barbara Bland, when they found her, could no longer be numbered among the unconscious.

She wasn't exactly the most clear-eyed person they had ever encountered, either. She sat in the crushed stone drive, her gray eyes dazed.

The girl got up, apparently, just to see if she could stand. Then she sat down again. "How long have I been out?" she murmured weakly.

"Half an hour, approximately," Long Tom said in a subdued voice.

"You," Pat Savage said grimly, "have a passel of explaining to do. Starting with the rank falsehoods you've been feeding everyone. Reporter for the Denver *Globe*, my sweet foot!"

Barbara Bland's eyes seemed to clear a little then. She struggled to her feet, took a moment to spank the dust off her plain frock, and swallowed a time or two.

"I am afraid that I have been going about this all wrong," she admitted in a soft, contrite voice.

"What do you mean?"

"I am not Barbara Bland. There is no such person."

"Hah!" Pat crowed. "The truth will out!"

They regarded the erstwhile Barbara Bland expectantly.

"My actual name is Joan Manville," she explained.

"And I am the niece of H. Startland Drago—if he is still among the living."

# X

## MISSING MOGUL

Pat Savage was not a girl who could be accused of being unnecessarily demure. In fact, if polled on the matter, those who were numbered among her small circle of friends would have been unanimous in saying that the beautiful cousin of Doc Savage could probably have stood a strong dose of demureness in her mental make-up, if such a thing could be injected by needle.

Pat blinked speechlessly at the mousy bogus reporter who had called herself Barbara Bland and was now claiming to be Joan Manville. Her mouth went round, her eyes became golden slits, and her brown fists turned pale at the knuckles.

"Something wrong with her story?" Renny wondered.

"H. Startland Drago!" Pat burst out, startling the others.

"Y-yes," stuttered the erstwhile Barbara Bland.

"H. Startland Drago, of Drago & Company?"

"That is correct."

"The international bond broker?" Pat persisted.

"That is his profession."

"Who is also the personal banker to King Goz?"

This time, it was the turn of the others to lose their composure.

"Holy cow, Pat!" Renny boomed. "Where'd you dig that up?"

"My missing chum, Prestowitz. He claimed to be working for Drago. Said he vanished."

Mousy Joan Manville—if that was her true name—brought colorless nails to her colorless mouth and squeaked, "Vanished!"

"That," Pat said, eyeing her coolly, "was his story."

"Where—where did you meet Caspar?"

"So you know him, eh?" Pat clucked.

"For years. He is in my uncle's—Uncle Startland's—employ. He has been looking into the matter of the recent threats against Uncle Startland's life."

Renny inserted his imposing bulk into the conversation at this point.

"Let me get this straight," he rumbled. "The mug that drug Pat clear down here at gunpoint is a friend of yours?"

"Caspar would never do that," Joan Manville protested.

"Why not?" Pat snapped at her. "You pulled the same stunt on Renny and the others. You even tried to vamp poor Long Tom in the bargain!"

Joan Manville colored. The color rose from her slim throat and made burn spots on her cheeks. Suddenly, as if a magic wand had been waved, she looked easily threefold more attractive than before.

"As I said," she offered, weak-voiced, "I have been going about this all wrong. My uncle asked me to come to Washington to look into the matter of King Goz's disappearance. That is why I undertook the imposture of being Barbara Bland of Denver, a nonexistent person."

"Doesn't explain kidnaping us," Renny thumped.

"I can explain that."

"We're listening," Long Tom growled.

"Uncle Startland was afraid to leave his home because of the threats," Joan Manville continued.

"Threats?"

"Uncle Startland had reason to believe that the person threatening him was—is—responsible for the weird thing that happened to King Goz of Merida," Joan Manville explained. "When I learned that Doc Savage had entered the investigation, I reasoned that he might lead me to the person responsible, who seems to be named Kastellantz.

"I—I guess I was overwrought by anxiety, but I thought that by bringing you all here, I could get to the bottom of it." Her tone shrank. "Now, if what you say is true, Uncle Startland has disappeared, too."

"Add Caspar Prestowitz to the growing list," Pat said tartly.

The effect of this sudden statement was to make Joan Manville—they were still thinking of her as Barbara Bland—flinch and leak slow tears from her eyes. Her lower lip quivered. Choking, she was forced to turn away.

"Th-this is Caspar's home," she sobbed. "It—it was where we were to l-live after our muh-marriage."

"Humph!" Pat sniffed unsympathetically. "If that's the case, you haven't lost much, sister. That masher spent half his time proposing to *me*. I finally took my fist to the back of his thick skull and put an end to that!"

Joan Manville only sobbed more loudly at Pat's uncaring words.

Long Tom sidled up and whispered in Pat's ear, "What's the point of rubbing it in?"

"Gone soft on us, eh?" Pat sniffed.

Long Tom colored and subsided.

"Look," Renny said suddenly. "We're not getting anywhere standing here jawing."

"Then make a suggestion, Mr. Big Fists," Pat snapped.

"It's gonna be light soon. Let's stick around and hunt up that spook in the Old King Cole getup."

"You wouldn't find him!" Pat retorted hotly.

"And why not?" Johnny demanded in his precise voice.

"I had him locked in Doc's office safe and he still managed to give me the slip!"

The gawking she got after that admission slipped out prompted Pat to explain the events that had transpired at Doc Savage's 86th-floor headquarters.

"Go ahead and bray, if you donkeys want," Pat said after she had concluded her account. "Just remember that you saw him, too."

No one so much as smirked. It was a fact. Their minds were still wrestling with the impossibility of it all.

Finally, Johnny said, "Expediency is mandatory."

Which not only communicated the need for haste in searching the woods, but demonstrated that the scholarly archæologist had recovered his words.

* * *

The dawn came up like smoldering fingers through the thick woods, and they began their search. It was careful and methodical.

And it proved of no value whatsoever.

They did find the bobcat, shivering in a hollow tree trunk.

Renny called them all to it with his big bellow of a voice. And they stood about looking at the frightened feline in thoughtful silence. Its tufted ears were laid back, close to its tapered skull, in defeat.

"The sole fruit of our endeavors," Renny stated morosely.

After that, they made plans.

"We still have to find this bird, Kastellantz," Renny pointed out.

"Yeah, and now he has one of Doc's armored machines and all three of our superfirers," Long Tom said, sour-voiced.

"Someone should escort Miss Manville to Doc," Johnny suggested. "Doc will want to interview her."

Everyone looked to Pat at that point.

But Pat wasn't buying. "Nothing doing!" she said huffily. "I'm staying here with you all! This is where the mystery is!"

"Sounds to me," Renny interposed, "that there's a whole different branch of the mystery taking shape up in New York."

"You boys just don't want to face Doc about the mess you've made of your end of this," Pat sniffed.

The silence that greeted Pat's accusation said it all.

There was some foot-scuffing, a little throat-clearing, and such a general air of little-lost-boyness about the three Doc Savage aids that the bronze-haired girl caved in.

"All right, all right," Pat relented. "I'll go. But at least one of you could volunteer to accompany a gal, to put in that good word with Doc."

"No room," Long Tom said quickly. "That crate seats two."

Which settled that.

Joan Manville was surprisingly docile about the whole

thing. She evinced no great liking for the spectacular Pat, but offered no protest when the plan was outlined for her.

They trekked down to the seaplane, and it was at that juncture that Pat snapped slim fingers and asked, "Say! Where are we, anyway?"

"Virginia," Renny grunted.

"Near Manassas," added Joan Manville.

"Picturesque, isn't it?" Pat said darkly.

As Pat clambered into the tiny plane, she called out, "How are you all going to get back to Washington?"

Bony Johnny lifted a narrow ankle, pointed at it, and said, "Shanks' mayor."

Which immediately brightened Pat's spirits. It would be a long, long walk back.

Pat got the prop ticking over. Renny cast off for her, and she sent the tiny bus scooting along the placid water. Giving the stick a short push and pull, she sent the craft climbing. It got altitude, and moaned northward.

Two hours later, Pat set the little ship on the Hudson River, within sight of the dazzling spire that housed Doc Savage's headquarters.

She throttled down the motor and sent the craft racing toward a sloping apron of concrete that led from the water up to the big doors of a long pier that was of ancient, sooty brick and bore a faded sign that said:

HIDALGO TRADING COMPANY

It was Pat's hope to anchor the seaplane at the foot of the ramp and step out on dry concrete.

But as the wheeled floats bumped the apron, the high doors rolled aside as if by magic, revealing a gaping, man-made cavern.

Pat raced the throttle and the seaplane bucked and surged up the top of apron, came level, and trundled into the dim cavernous space within.

Behind her, the doors rolled back again.

Up to this point, Joan Manville had been a quiet passenger, no doubt immersed in her own downcast thoughts. But now she asked, "Where is this?"

"Never you mind," said Pat, throwing open the cockpit door. She poked her bronze-haired head out and as quickly withdrew it, mouth suddenly thin and tight.

"What is it?" Joan gasped.

"My day of reckoning—too soon," Pat clipped.

A voice said, "You may come out whenever you wish."

"Doc Savage!" Joan exclaimed, throwing open the door on her side, and stepping out eagerly.

"Might as well face the funeral music," Pat muttered, and followed suit.

The big bronze man stood by himself in the vast length of the warehouse. Behind him, an amazing armada of airplanes, ranging from a bronze-painted trimotored amphibian to spidery autogyros, rested. Fast speedboats and even a large cruiser reposed in slips. An ungainly submarine sat in dry dock. And farther along, visible through an open door, seeming to bump the rafters of the great establishment, a dirigible of modest size—for a dirigible—hung in silence.

"Waiting for me, cousin of mine?" Pat inquired.

"Yes."

"Looks like somebody squealed."

"Never mind that. I know everything that transpired."

"In that case," Pat said archly, "I needn't introduce you to your former Barbara Bland, now passing for Miss Joan Manville, which, if you ask me, is a name not to be taken on faith alone."

"I can explain everything," said Joan Manville hastily.

"And you will," Doc stated calmly. "After I have had a word with my cousin."

Doc motioned Pat to step over to one side.

"Listen, Doc," Pat began breathlessly. "Did Renny tell you that he saw the royal spook with his own eyes?"

"Something was said about that," the bronze man admitted.

"And it couldn't be shot, caught, or fought?"

"It *is* puzzling," Doc admitted.

"It's darned frustrating is what it is! Good thing for me that I followed my nose. I saved Renny and the others from some dire fate at the hands of this female falsehood."

"If there is not an old Chinese proverb that she who follows her nose runs the risk of having it chopped off," Doc said dryly, "there should be."

"I earned my salt!"

Doc's eyes seemed to twinkle briefly.

"Now you can go home, wash it off, and get on with your well-deserved vacation," he said.

"You're not throwing me out now!"

"Of course not," Doc agreed.

Pat relaxed. She began to smile.

"You are going to leave under your own power."

"Listen, master of men, this is bald-faced discrimination against the fair sex, and I won't stand for it!"

"Out, please," Doc ordered, his voice now very stern.

"You haven't heard the last of me," Pat said, storming off.

Her hard heels *tap-tapped* away as if she were using them to drive railroad spikes into press board.

Joan Manville drew close to the bronze man after Pat Savage had left the building. The look in her eyes was nothing if not deep. During the flight, she had donned her war paint—rouge and some tasteful lipstick. The change was remarkable.

"You were very hard on her," she said.

"With Pat, there is no other way to be. She is very headstrong."

"I hope you will not hold it against me that I have misrepresented myself to you and your men."

Doc did not reply directly. Instead, he said, "According to my associates, you are the niece of H. Startland Drago."

Barbara Bland nodded. "This is true. You know of him?"

"Drago & Company is one of the most important brokers in international bonds. Your uncle is a power in European affairs. In fact, he has quite a reputation."

"Yes, I understand they call him the Empire Maker. And now I am given to believe he has vanished, just as he had feared."

Joan Manville seemed to lose all of her composure then. The tears flowed anew. She pressed herself close to the bronze giant, as if drawing comfort from the strength of his presence.

Doc, it might be seen, shrank slightly from the gesture. He had long ago formed a policy of no feminine entanglements, knowing enemies would strike at him through any woman in whom he became interested.

"I have been making inquiries," Doc said without visible emotion. "And understand your uncle has been under police guard for some time."

Joan Manville managed to nod. "Yes. At his home."

"Let us go there now," the bronze man invited.

Joan Manville plainly approved of the size and discreetly subdued paint job of the sedan to which the bronze man led her, and it passed through the landward end of the big warehouse, the doors opening magically before it and closing after the machine had rolled out into the street.

Like the trick headquarters door, this occurrence had a simple explanation. A radio signal from a hidden car transmitter actuated the automatic doors.

Joan Manville seemed too preoccupied to note the phenomenon, nor did she remark at the big warehouse that was in fact a concealed combination airplane hangar and boathouse. Its existence was unknown to the general public. There was an elevated express highway passing by the Hudson River waterfront, and it was unlikely that the motorists who used it daily realized that the Hidalgo Trading Company structure was anything other than an old, disused steamship pier warehouse.

In reality, there was no such concern. Doc was the Hidalgo Trading Company.

Doc piloted the sedan north, to the residential reaches of upper Manhattan and the fashionable West Side.

He broke the silence with a question.

"Have you any inkling what is behind your uncle's apparent disappearance?" he asked.

Joan Manville shook her head. "Merely that he was being threatened, for no reason that he could think of," she offered. "If it had not been H. Startland Drago, I doubt that the police would have assigned detectives on such a thin story, but Uncle Startland contributes heavily to the police pension fund."

Doc nodded. He did not pursue that line of questioning further, nor did he reprove the young woman for her earlier imposture.

He drove directly to the palatial home of financial titan H. Startland Drago on the upper West Side, as if he had made the trip often.

An acre of ground surrounded the old heirloom, which was fortunate because of the modern fifteen-story apartment houses all around. Several gardeners were busy on the grounds, trimming shrubbery and looking for the liquor bottles and trash which the apartment house tenants would throw out of their windows.

One out-of-place touch was a gigantic oak tree, growing very close to the rear, whose spreading branches threw the place into its shade.

The entrance was guarded by men in blue. They put on intimidating expressions as Doc's sedan rolled up to the gate. These melted when they got a clear look at the big bronze man.

"Mr. Savage!" one exclaimed. "How can we help you, sir?"

Doc indicated Joan Manville.

"This is Joan Manville, niece of H. Startland Drago, the missing man."

"Missing?"

"I have information that he has disappeared," Doc revealed.

"Not that we've heard. He's just been holed up in his digs, for three days now."

"Mind if we have a look?"

Mind? The guard detail not only did not mind, but they decided to accompany the bronze man to the front door and to shower him with their opinions on the situation.

"Mr. Drago claimed the threats were just telephoned to him," one guard muttered as they strode along. "He says he can't imagine who or why. That sounds kinda phony to me."

"Nothing about H. Startland Drago is phony," growled another guard, a policeman assigned by Centre Street to the job. "Drago is a deacon in his church, chairman of the biggest committees to raise money for the orphans, and an upstanding fellow. Everybody knows it. Some nut is threatening him."

"That's my guess," agreed a third. "Some mental moron. A goof. Nobody but a goof would threaten such an upstanding citizen."

At the door, they were met by a butler.

The butler was a middle-aged fellow who looked as tough as sagebrush roots and was about the same color. He was bowlegged, as if he had once been a cowboy, and he wore rimless eyeglasses at the end of an impressively sharp nose.

"Miss Manville!" he said. "Where have you been, miss? I have been frightfully worried about you!"

"Washington," said Joan Manville, suddenly shedding her mousy demeanor. She stepped in and demanded, "Where is my uncle at this minute?"

"I do not know."

"We have reason to believe he is missing," Doc said.

"Hardly," the butler drawled. "He is merely in seclusion."

Joan Manville inquired, "When did you see him last?"

The butler thought. "Yesterday. But it is the master's habit to spend long periods alone in study—as you know, being his favorite niece."

"Take us to him," Doc directed.

The butler hesitated.

"*Now*, Seymour," said Joan Manville sharply.

The butler took on a new attitude. He led the way, walking in his peculiar bowlegged fashion, as if his legs had been rubbed raw by chaps. The old house creaked strangely. The noise grew as they approached the back, and it soon became evident the sound emanated from the unpruned oak, whose branches were rubbing against gutters with a sound like bones rasping together.

They were taken to a study that was closed by two ornate doors. Very heavy, and quite solid. The sound of the butler's knuckles rapping on these might have been the click of cat's claws on a marble floor. Receiving no answer, he began to pound, timidly at first, and then loudly. The massive doors hardly shook under his compact fist.

Doc Savage stepped in and threw the doors open with both hands as if they were made of paper. The others followed him into a library that was large yet somehow cozy and walled with books and mementos of a rich man's comfortable life.

A radio broadcast receiver was on. It was a console model and tuned to a station that was broadcasting an orchestra recital. That was all they found in the way of activity in the old study.

H. Startland Drago was a nonexistent personage, as far as the immediate vicinity was concerned.

They searched the next room. Then the master bedroom. The cellar. Virtually every room in the house, except the attic, which was padlocked and according to the butler—Seymour Holman by name—unopened in years.

There was no doubt about it. H. Startland Drago, noted financial power, had departed the hoary dwelling.

Doc checked with the guards, who had remained outside. They nearly had fits when they heard the news.

"Impossible!" one insisted. "No one came or went in the last, oh, three days or so."

"Since about the time of King Goz's disappearance," Doc said.

"If that's how you look at it," a detective replied. "Shall I call Headquarters?"

"Not as yet," said Doc.

The bronze man returned to the study, where Joan Manville was looking puzzled, yet somehow determined. The radio was still playing. Dance music now.

She called in the bowlegged, bespectacled butler. "Did my uncle say anything was wrong?"

"No, miss," replied the flunky. "He said you were not to worry."

"There must be an explanation!" she insisted. "Tell me, when you last saw him, what was he doing?"

The old butler made faces as he summoned up his recollective powers.

"I believe," he said at last, "he was about his safe."

"Maybe there's some clue in the safe," Joan said swiftly.

She moved to a corner of the study, where two bookcases joined. She fiddled with the left-hand case and it swung out, exposing a safe of squat but substantial portions resting on bird-claw legs in a large cubby-hole.

"My uncle kept his most important papers here," she said.

Doc asked, "You have the combination?"

"No. Only Uncle Startland knew it. He was very protective of its contents." She turned. "Oh, could you perhaps open it for us?"

Doc said, "I will try," and knelt at the safe. He gave the dial a test spin, put an ear to the door beside the dial, and his bronze fingers went to work.

The old butler put in his oar. "Your uncle might not approve, miss."

"Uncle Startland always approves of what I do," the young woman said confidently.

Doc Savage continued to work with the safe knob.

"The master will not like that," said the bowlegged butler.

The girl asked anxiously, "Do you think this is in the best interests of my uncle, Mr. Savage?"

"In my opinion, yes," returned Doc.

"Go ahead, then."

The old butler sighed, then craned his neck to inspect the safe door. Apparently he knew something about safes, because he looked relieved and said, "Begging your pardon, but you will never be able to open that without the combination."

Then the safe immediately fell open.

The bowlegged butler broke the somewhat strained silence which followed. He had been goggling at the safe. Now he pointed at it.

"Begging pardon, sir!" he exploded. "But how in—I mean, how could you open that safe so easily?"

"This is Doc Savage," Joan Manville explained. "His business is helping people out of trouble. He has mastered many professions by intensive study, and uses them in his work. I presume he has made a study of safes."

The old butler swallowed several times.

"Doc—Savage," he said in much the same tone a

farmer would use to tell his wife the lightning had just struck the milklot and killed all the cows.

Doc reached a cabled hand into the safe, and withdrew sheafs of paper and other memoranda. He took these to a walnut desk and began going through them under the watchful eyes of Joan Manville and the sagebrush-colored butler.

Doc quickly separated the papers into piles, seeming only to glance at the writing on each sheet. When he was done with this sorting, he took up the smaller of the two piles.

"Have you discovered something, Mr. Savage?" Joan asked plaintively.

Doc Savage looked up, his metallic face expressionless. "According to these notes," he imparted, "your uncle has been gathering evidence on a financial operator known as Laurence Kingsley Goldwill."

"Yes, I know the name. He and my uncle have had dealings in the past. He has been a guest in this very home. That was before his crooked dealings came to light, and Goldwill and my uncle had a falling-out."

"Goldwill, according to your uncle's notes, has had his hand in many a shady venture," Doc stated. "He lost a young fortune in the recent business depression, speculating in silver stocks, and has been attempting to recoup by promoting doubtful mergers and stock flotations."

Joan Manville nodded grimly. "When these things came out, Uncle Startland refused to have anything more to do with this man."

Doc went on, "These papers hint at a scheme more audacious than any Goldwill had been hitherto accused of. But there are no details given."

"Do you—do you think that this horrid man is behind my uncle's disappearance?" Joan Manville gasped.

Doc Savage lifted a sheet of paper on which there was extensive writing.

"Is this your uncle's handwriting?" he asked.

Joan Manville accepted the sheet, looked over the crabbed tracks of ink, and nodded. "Yes."

Then she read the close lines.

Joan Manville's fingers dug into the bronze man's

arm. "Oh! According to this, Uncle Startland believed that Laurence Kingsley Goldwill in some manner engineered King Goz's disappearance, and that he himself was the next target of the man's crooked machinations. Why, this is beyond belief!"

"It is peculiar, to say the least," Doc said, and was acutely conscious of the hand on his arm.

At that point, the dance music ended and a news commentator came on and said, "Greetings, folks, greetings. The New York grand jury today failed to indict Laurence Kingsley Goldwill on a charge of swindling investors. It seems the wily Goldwill skated in and out through the technicalities of the law, and did not once let the ice break under him. The district attorney said that in his opinion justice miscarried through the inability of the law to—"

Doc shut the radio off.

"You probably prefer not to hear that," Doc stated.

"Thank you," Joan said.

Doc gathered up the papers and returned those not pertaining to Laurence Kingsley Goldwill to the safe, and then locked it. The others he kept.

Joan Manville asked meekly, "What can we do?"

"First, we might inform the police of your uncle's disappearance. Then, a confrontation with Goldwill is in order."

"He should be hung!" Joan burst out.

The bronze man said grimly, "Goldwill has been jailed twice, but there was not enough evidence to hold him. He is clever."

The police wore unhappy faces when they put in their appearance not many minutes later. The girl had called them. They insisted on a complete search of the house being undertaken, despite having it pointed out to them that this had already been done.

"Something might have been overlooked," one blustered.

The girl, Joan Manville, had a sharp tongue when necessary, and this she proved by the verbal pitchforking she gave the police. The latter sailed about like a flock of jaybirds which had just found an owl in their favorite tree, but it did no good in the end. They agreed to skip any further searching.

"Which isn't to say we won't do one later," one warned.

The bluecoats departed, vowing to issue a pickup order for the missing H. Startland Drago.

After they had taken their leave, Joan Manville turned to Doc Savage and murmured appreciatively, "I want to thank you for not mentioning my uncle's past connections with Laurence Kingsley Goldwill. It would do his business reputation terrible harm if it got out just now."

"We do not wish police interference in our own investigation," Doc said, gently but firmly disentangling his arm from her grasp.

# XI

## THE EMPIRE MAKER

On the way to the Wall Street office of Laurence Kingsley Goldwill, Doc Savage stopped at a news stand kiosk and purchased a bulldog edition of a morning newspaper.

The matter of Laurence Kingsley Goldwill had pushed the disappearance of King Egil Goz of Merida off the front pages. The sheets had already exhausted every angle in the case, it seemed. The Japanese and Russians were not having frontier incidents, and the Republicans had stopped for a breather, so news was slack, anyway.

The main streamer was big and black. It read:

GOLDWILL ELUDES INDICTMENT
Accused Stock Manipulator Goes Free

There was a photo of Laurence Kingsley Goldwill emblazoned on the front page. It showed a rather self-important man with the general demeanor of a pouter pigeon, a pince-nez perched on a thin-bridged nose. The photo seemed to have been selected with an eye toward drumming up reader antipathy for the accused financier.

The accompanying article was brief.

An issue of common stock had been sold the public, it explained. High-pressure methods and enticing phraseology had been used, and as a result poor people, small buyers, had been the majority purchasers. An unloading on the widows and orphans, in effect. Then, by a bit of fast but perfectly legal work, the common stock had become practically worthless, and the promoter of the scheme— Laurence Kingsley Goldwill—had made four million dollars. The four million was legal fees, salary, reorganization counsel fees, and so on.

It was evident from the article that Laurence Kingsley Goldwill was a Wall Street money hog of the kind which gives the Street a bad reputation from time to time.

"The man is a thorough rascal," Joan Manville fumed as she read along. "He would stop at nothing to line his pockets."

Doc was driving down Broadway, the thoroughfare that runs the length of the city. They were moving through lower Manhattan now, where the rattle and slam of the elevated was a constant racket.

The building which housed the brokerage office of Goldwill & Son—Laurence Kingsley Goldwill, the newspaper article had indicated, was the son, the elder Goldwill long since having departed this mortal vale—was not actually situated on Wall Street, home of the world's money troubles, but it was adjacent enough that, if it upset, part of it would fall on the Street.

The structure was a grimy edifice, and old enough that it might well have overlooked the Curb—as Wall Street is sometimes still called—in the days long past when traders actually operated at curbside, shouting orders to persons in office windows and banging on a swill bucket to denote the closing bell.

Still, it had an elevator, albeit a creaking one. They took this up to the office of Goldwill & Son.

It was a dingy place and they were met by a rather obsequious individual who offered profuse apologies, but

Laurence Kingsley Goldwill was not present and further was not expected back at the office until Monday, at the earliest.

He was very polite. In fact, a number of officials came to meet with them and all were polite. Excessively.

It was evident their politeness didn't mean anything. They acted exactly like what they were—a bunch of old stockbrokers bowing and scraping to a customer whom they were hopeful of relieving of his shirt.

"Where does Mr. Goldwill live?" Joan Manville demanded.

"And you are?" the first obsequious one inquired.

"H. Startland Drago's niece, I'll have you know!"

The old stockbroker looked startled. The name of H. Startland Drago was one to conjure with. He actually paled as he wrestled with a horny dilemma.

Finally, he said, "I am deeply, deeply sorry, Miss Manville. But Laurence Kingsley Goldwill prefers to keep his home life separate from his business dealings. However, I will be pleased to convey any message you care to leave."

"Not necessary," said Doc, abruptly piloting Miss Manville out of the rather gloomy office confines.

As they rode down in the rickety cage, the elevator operator seemed to be staring with frank admiration at Doc Savage. Doc took a great deal of pains not to notice this, himself looking intently at the floors as they dropped past.

Once more in the sedan, Doc Savage fired up a short-wave transmitter and receiver set clamped under the dash and reached his headquarters.

"Monk here."

"Monk. I would like the home address of Laurence Kingsley Goldwill, the stockbroker."

"You mean Laurence Kingsley Goldwill, the slippery crook, don't you?" Monk countered.

"He has been convicted of nothing to date," Doc pointed out.

"Humph," said Joan Manville.

"And the devil ain't been brought up on charges, either," Monk squeaked. "But that don't mean he ain't guilty. I'll get right on it."

Doc drove north on the theory that a rich man like

Goldwill would live in upper Manhattan, or possibly on Long Island, which could be reached from midtown Gotham.

His surmise was correct, as Monk Mayfair reported moments later.

"Tudor City, Doc." He gave an address, then asked, "Want me to meet you there?"

"You might do that," Doc related.

The doorman failed to rouse any answer from the occupant of Laurence Kingsley Goldwill's apartment, and at first refused them entry beyond the vestibule. This building was an exclusive one. There was nothing so coarse as a doorbell to be rung. One had to receive permission to pass beyond the vestibule area.

Doc Savage solved this impasse in a simple manner. He made a telephone call, and soon the superintendent of the building bustled up, shooing the doorman off and offering all sorts of assistance.

Doc, as it turned out, owned a part interest in the fashionable apartment building.

Still, the bronze man's request to gain admittance to the private apartment of the shadowy stockbroker was unusual. What tipped the scales in Doc's favor was a simple fact.

"That Goldwill always rubbed me wrong," the superintendent said. "If you are investigating that man, it can only be to the good."

As a precaution, they buzzed the apartment once more. When no answer was forthcoming, they ascended.

The superintendent opened the door with a master key. Doc asked him to remain outside, which he agreed to, although a trace of disappointment flickered across his eager features.

Doc pushed the door open with a hand. His flake-gold eyes seemed to whirl more quickly as he took in the parlor. Red leather chairs predominated. Heavy as they were, they had been crowded into one corner. A wall tapestry hung askew. Taboret drawers were out of their receptacles, they and their contents scattered about the rug.

The others peered past him. Joan Manville gasped.

"The place has been ransacked!" the superintendent exclaimed.

Doc was already inside then. He took in the disorder of the parlor. There had been a struggle, or perhaps the apartment had been searched by uncaring persons.

There was a room beyond. A sitting room. The curtains were drawn. And tied to a modernistic chromium chair sat a man. Dark eyes started at sight of the bronze man.

Ignoring the man, Doc moved through the remaining rooms, discovered no other persons, and returned to the bound individual.

The bonds were ordinary hemp. Thick, tough, and the knots would have done a sailor proud. Doc Savage's corded fingers made short work of them, however. His fingers seemed no more than to touch the various knots and they sprang apart.

The man lifted hands to his gag and pulled it down. A wadded handkerchief fell out of his mouth.

"Whoever you are, I owe you a great debt," he said fervently.

Joan Manville rushed into the room a moment later, and threw her arms about his neck.

"Uncle Startland! I knew that was your voice! Oh, thank heavens you are safe!"

"Yes, no thanks to that rascal, Goldwill."

Doc asked, "You have been held here by Laurence Kingsley Goldwill?"

The popular conception of a plutocrat is of a portly fellow, possibly affecting a pince-nez, with an ample belly and the jowls of a swine.

H. Startland Drago was a plutocrat. Of that, there was no doubt. He was a millionaire many times over—if not a billionaire.

He did not fit the public conception, however.

He was a lean, cadaverous fellow. His eyes brought to mind a raven's acquisitive gaze. His hair was likewise jet black, and combed straight back. He possessed good posture and carried himself with an erect, aristocratic air. Altogether, he was a striking individual—if somewhat saturnine of feature—and cut a figure that sartorially-conscious Ham Brooks would have envied.

He bore little enough of a resemblance to attractive Joan Manville.

Straightening very correct clothing, H. Startland Drago got around to answering Doc's question.

"It is merely surmise on my part. I never got a look at my abductor. I was at work in my study when I heard a strange noise."

"Noise?"

"A whistling. I had believed it was the radio at first. I enjoy listening to music as I do my work, but it quickly became clear that the whistling did not emanate from the radio set. I was in the act of turning around to investigate the sound when a curtain fell before my eyes."

"Curtain?"

Drago hesitated. His voice grew uncomfortable. "Well, that is how I recall it. A darkness came over my vision, and that was the last I knew until I awoke here, bound and gagged, I do not know how many hours ago."

"If you did not see your supposed abductor," Doc Savage questioned, "then why do you assume it was Goldwill?"

"Laurence Kingsley Goldwill," said H. Startland Drago, "is the only enemy I have in the entire world."

"Uncle!" Joan Manville exclaimed. "This is Goldwill's apartment!"

"That would seem to settle that matter." Drago turned his intensely black gaze upon his bronze rescuer. "And you, sir—to whom do I owe my rescue?"

Joan Manville burst out, "Don't you recognize him, Uncle Startland? This is Doc Savage! Simply one of the most amazing of living men!"

H. Startland Drago did not look like a man who was ordinarily impressed by very much. He was impressed by Doc Savage. It showed in tiny ways. The nearly imperceptible straightening of his spine. A flicker of interest that came into his black, birdlike eyes. And the momentary pause that inhibited his reply.

At last he murmured, "I have heard a great many things about you, of course."

Doc cut through the soap. "You have been assembling facts that point to Laurence Kingsley Goldwill's complicity in the disappearance of King Goz. What are your conclusions?"

This time, Drago actually started.

"How did you know that?" he demanded.

Joan Manville laid reassuring hands on the plutocrat's arm. "When I discovered that you were missing, Uncle Startland, I invited Mr. Savage to investigate. He gained access to your safe and learned of your suspicions."

"Amazing. I would have thought that safe was impregnable."

Doc said, "Let me see if I have a clear picture. You are King Goz's personal banker?"

"Not only personal, but official."

"Explain, please."

H. Startland Drago did not seem to be a man who was free with information. He hesitated and then, evidently recalling the debt he owed to the big bronze man, launched into a recital.

"I own a bond house," he related. "International bonds, to be precise. Much of the holdings of Drago & Company consist of various government bonds, which as you know are promissory notes offered by governments to borrow funds to perform certain functions—to build railroads, bridges, or in some cases to pay off war debts."

Doc nodded.

"King Goz of Merida, despite his background as a war chieftain, was a forward-thinking monarch. His country is poor, even by the standards of the Balkans. Too poor to issue bonds—or at least bonds that anyone would be likely to purchase in significant quantities. On the other hand, as you know, money can be raised through the speculation on the bonds of other governments. Currently, for instance, the American Liberty, the British Consul, and the French Rente are considered worthy securities."

H. Startland Drago paused, then continued, "As King Goz's banker, I have been buying and selling bonds on behalf of the government of Merida. Through this, His Highness hoped to acquire capital to modernize his beleaguered nation."

"It has been suggested that King Goz has been quietly amassing munitions and conscripts, evidently fearing that one of his neighbors might attempt a land grab," Doc stated.

"His Highness was very concerned with the border disputes that the League of Nations is attempting to negotiate," Drago allowed. "But you will recall that a number of years ago, the king turned to Santa Bellanca for protection. Santa Bellanca is a very strong power in Europe, and there is a treaty calling for that nation's army to come to the defense of Merida should a neighbor—say, Carrullana—attempt mischief."

"Santa Bellanca has gotten into mischief of its own in Africa," Doc pointed out.

H. Startland Drago shrugged. "I concern myself with finances, not politics," he said diplomatically.

Doc abruptly changed the subject. "How does Laurence Kingsley Goldwill fit into this picture?"

"Goldwill recently made certain business overtures to me," Startland said, "overtures of a preposterous illegal nature, having to do with the forming of an investment syndicate for the purpose of improper speculations. Naturally, I threw him out of my office, thereby incurring his enmity. Although he was cagy enough not to give away his entire plans, I learned enough that I am certain I could recognize his scheme once it is implemented. Knowing this, Goldwill has attempted to silence me."

"By holding you prisoner?"

"I imagine a ransom would have been involved."

"That is an unusual approach to silencing an enemy," Doc pointed out.

"Goldwill may be a scoundrel, but I do not think he is capable of murder. I could be mistaken, however."

"How does the vanishment of King Goz tie into this?"

"That," H. Startland Drago admitted, "baffles me, frankly. At a guess, the disappearance may be the first move in Goldwill's cunning game, and my abduction the second. What comes next, or how the scheme works, I have as yet no clear idea. I do know it involves speculation with bonds on a scale never before attempted. I regret I do not know which bonds are involved."

Doc Savage said nothing.

Joan Manville spoke up. "What matters, Uncle, is that you are safe. And now we have proof that Goldwill is as crooked as they come, don't we, Mr. Savage?"

"Your uncle's presence would seem to point an accusing finger in Laurence Kingsley Goldwill's direction," Doc admitted. "But there are a number of questions still to be settled."

"Name them," said Drago.

"A man named Caspar Prestowitz has become embroiled in this affair. Know him?"

In the excitement of the moment, Joan Manville had evidently forgotten the man who was her fiancé. Her slim hands came off her uncle's arm and covered her mouth.

"Caspar! I had almost forgotten him. Oh, Uncle! He has disappeared, too! What can it mean?"

H. Startland Drago's rather forbidding face darkened.

"Caspar Prestowitz is a close friend and business associate, Mr. Savage," he explained. "He is very loyal to me. And when I informed him of these threats against my person, he offered to look into the matter."

"As did I," Joan Manville said proudly.

"Yes. Joan and Caspar thought that the disappearance of His Highness was a portent of things to come. Each looked into the matter—Joan in Washington, and Caspar here in New York."

"And the nature of Prestowitz's employment?"

H. Startland Drago hesitated. "In my field," he said slowly, "it is sometimes necessary to gather facts regarding the economic well-being of nations who float bonds. These facts are jealously guarded and not easily uncovered."

"In other words," Doc prompted. "Prestowitz is a private investigator?"

"Nothing so common," Drago said with a trace of indignation. "He is a financial fact-gatherer, and a superlative operator."

"He took my cousin, Pat, prisoner at gunpoint," Doc said.

"Overzealousness. He knew that you were looking into the mystery and perhaps thought that he could learn something from her."

"Perhaps," said Doc.

"I imagine the authorities should be brought into this now," H. Startland Drago said.

"It might be advisable not to," Doc stated.

H. Startland Drago cocked an ebony eyebrow, making gullies in his tall forehead.

"A police search might only drive Goldwill into hiding," Doc explained. "I would like to station some of my associates at this building, and others to stand guard over you at your home, if this is acceptable to you."

"I would be very grateful for any protection you can extend. Obviously New York's Finest were not up to snuff on this occasion."

Joan Manville puckered eyebrows together. "I still don't see how you were spirited out of your home under the very noses of the police, Uncle Startland." She turned to Doc. "What do you think, Mr. Savage?"

"The whistling heard before your uncle lost consciousness might explain it," Doc said.

"How so?"

Doc said nothing. They waited for him to speak, thinking that he perhaps was gathering his thoughts. Instead, the bronze man turned on his heel and passed from the room.

They found him outside in the hall, speaking in a low voice with the building superintendent. Evidently an understanding was reached, because without comment the man ran them down to the lobby in the building elevator.

Outside, a gaudy roadster had pulled up. Monk.

At sight of presentable Joan Manville, his homely features split into a wide grin.

"Who's the number, Doc?" he asked unabashedly.

Doc Savage made quick introductions and said, "Monk, please convey Miss Manville and her uncle home. Remain with them. I will have Ham relieve you in a few hours."

"I left that overdressed ambulance chaser at headquarters, like you told me to," Monk grinned, plainly relishing the idea of beating the dapper lawyer to a potential conquest.

"He understands that he is to keep an eye on things?" Doc Savage asked.

"Yeah, the shyster."

Doc started for his own machine.

Monk called out, "Say, where are you going, Doc?"

"To look into another angle of this mystery," said Doc Savage, easing behind the wheel of his sedate sedan.

## XII

## THE DISPIRITED

In a room on the top floor of one of the more sumptuous hostelries in Washington, District of Columbia, three dejected men settled into comfortable chairs.

They immediately took off their shoes.

"Are my dogs killing me," Long Tom grumbled.

Renny, massaging feet as preposterously huge as his knobby fists, said, "Holy cow! My *corns* have corns now."

Oddly, lanky Johnny seemed the least drained by their long walk out of the Virginia woods after their nocturnal encounter with the phantasm that whistled. The skeletal archæologist was blessed with the freakish endurance of a marathon runner. Too, there seemed insufficient meat on his bony feet to support blisters.

The uncanny experience of the preceding night had preyed on their minds all during the long trek, which ended only when they chanced upon a helpful farmer driving an old flivver. They hitched a ride to a modest Virginia town, and from thence arranged for transportation to this very establishment, which like many in the nation's capital, was named after a deceased president.

As they tended to their aching feet, the big-fisted engineer, happening to glance out a window, noticed a plane buzzing the city. He went to the window, threw the pane up.

"Something?" Long Tom asked.

"Plane," Renny said, squinting.

"You never see a plane before?" Long Tom groused.

"This one's just flyin' aimlessly. Can't make it out from here, but it's not a passenger job."

"In trouble?"

"Not that I can see."

Turning suddenly from the window, Renny walked gingerly to the connecting door, hauled off, and practically demolished the panel with one blow of his huge right fist. This fabulous feat did no appreciable damage to his fist.

"Holy cow!" he rumbled. "What breaks we get! We could've cleaned up on that blamed chauffeur, Kastellantz, made him talk, and maybe cracked this whole mystery wide open. Instead, we let him get away. We should've piled on him first chance."

"Intriguistic exercitation approaches indefectibility," Johnny said.

"Some day you're gonna die in the middle of one of them words," Renny predicted gloomily. "What'd you say?"

Long Tom offered, "He thinks using our heads was much better."

"Thanks," Renny grunted. "How'd you know what he meant?"

The pale electrical wizard sighed. "It was either slaughter Johnny or take up the study of the dictionary. I'm against bloodshed."

Gloom settled over the trio, and they returned to administrating to their smarting feet.

Not long after, a crisp knocking came to their door.

"Now who could *that* be?" Renny thumped.

Johnny hazarded, "A revenant of our nocturnal perambulations, possibly."

"If you mean that spook of the sad song," Renny grumbled, going to the door, "I'm kinda leaning toward the idea that he never existed." The big-fisted engineer threw open the door.

In walked vivacious Pat Savage.

"Greetings!" she said brightly.

Consternation seized the three Doc Savage aids.

"More grief!" Johnny exclaimed, shock for once knocking the big words out of him.

"I thought you were in New York!" Renny accused.

Pat stuck up her chin. "I was chased off! So I thought I'd see if there was any action left over from last night."

The bronze-haired girl stopped, noticed the unhappy trio lounging about in their stocking feet.

"We just blew in," Renny said by way of explanation.

Pat smiled sweetly. "Now I don't feel so bad," she said tartly. "I take it there have been no interesting developments?"

"That depends on how interesting you consider blisters," Long Tom complained.

"Still smarting from your collision with true love?" Pat inquired archly.

Coloring, Long Tom put more effort into rubbing his feet.

"I tried to tell Doc about that whistling spirit we encountered last night, but he wasn't in a listening mood," Pat offered.

"We," Renny said flatly, "have decided there was no such entity."

Pat's pretty mouth came open. She shook a firm finger in their faces. "Don't you go all skeptical on me! You saw that whiskered old goat, the same as me!"

"We're prize suckers," Long Tom opined. "I'll bet that thing last night was some kind of night mirage!"

"Night mirage!" Pat exploded. "Now see here—"

"I never heard of a night mirage," Johnny said slowly, "but there's no reason why there couldn't be one, maybe."

Renny harbored similar opinions. "Last night, chasing that spook, I was beginning to feel as if we were hunting for the foot of the rainbow," he said thoughtfully. "I did that once when I was a kid. The rainbow get bigger as you go toward it, but it always keeps just ahead of you, and finally it disappears, leaving you feeling like a goop."

"Goop," Pat said snippily, "about describes the three of you! Some Sorry Sams you all turned out to be."

That sassy opinion was met with no particular retort, so Pat changed the subject.

"What about that chauffeur, Kastellantz? Any luck tracking him down?"

"With what?" Renny grunted. "The guy run off with Long Tom's only electroscope."

"So, get another."

"Where? You can't exactly walk into a drug store and buy one on time."

"So you're going to just sit here and do nothing?" Pat said, aghast.

"Right now," Long Tom said bitterly, "it's all I can do to work the knots out of my toes."

"Me, too,'" Renny chimed in. "I couldn't walk to the door if there was a fire."

"A triumvirate of unanimity," Johnny added.

But when the telephone jangled less than a minute later, all three leaped from their seats in an effort to beat the others to the instrument.

Pat, the nearest to the telephone, won handily. Her cheery "Hello!" was triumphant.

Abruptly, her face went as white as the proverbial ghost, and without another word she passed the instrument to Renny.

Clapping a big paw over the mouthpiece, Renny asked, "You O.K.?"

Pat's mouth made speaking shapes. Only one word emerged.

"Doc," she squeaked, pointing to the telephone as if it were a rattlesnake in disguise.

"Serves you right for being so quick on the draw," Renny grumbled. Uncovering the mouthpiece, he said, "That was exactly who you thought it was, Doc. The pest just barged in."

Renny listened a moment. He lowered the phone and told Pat, "Doc said to barge right out again."

"Nothing doing!" Pat said vehemently.

Renny listened some more. The others crowded about to catch what they could. All except Pat, who was looking a little green of face. She had not expected to be found out so soon.

"On our way!" said Renny exuberantly, hanging up. He turned to the others, his face gloomy—which indicated profound good humor. "Grab your kicks, everybody. We're going places!"

Instantly, the three shed all traces of fatigue and yanked on assorted footgear.

"What's up?" Pat asked breathlessly.

Renny ignored her, said to the others, "That plane I saw earlier? That was Doc, using a radio locator to scour for that slippery Kastellantz. Says he's got a fix on him."

"Where?" Pat asked.

"In that hotel where the king's retinue are holed up. Doc's at the airport now, and said he'd meet us there."

Pat brightened. "Goodness! Progress!"

They made a bee line for the door. Pat, taking up the rear, suddenly found a big inhibiting paw in her face. Renny's.

"Nothing doing!" he rapped. "Doc told you to take your vacation! Now vacate!"

Pat set fists on hips and struck a defiant pose.

"Need I remind you of our little understanding?" she said pointedly.

Renny scowled. The feisty girl had him there. A promise had been made.

"I can't let you tag along," he rumbled slowly. "Doc would dislocate my fists."

"But you won't stop me from following you, eh?"

"After I shut this door in your face," Renny said unhappily, "you are on your own."

The door clapped shut, forcing Pat to hastily withdraw her perfect nose.

"Men!" fumed Pat.

The hotel where the retinue of King Egil Goz was ensconced was the Grant. It was one of the better hotels in the city, which meant that it often catered to diplomats and other foreign dignitaries. It was a very conservative establishment, so a great deal of effort was expended on the part of the management to maintain a genteel decorum conducive to the peace of mind of its clientele.

So when Renny, Long Tom, and Johnny piled into the lobby like a trio of race horses just out of the starting gate, the deskman looked up from his duties, acquired a displeased demeanor, and signaled to two men quietly distributed among the lobby chairs, reading newspapers.

They came up from their stations and sauntered in the direction of the unusual trio. They were swathed in gabardine topcoats, despite the warmth of the season.

"Something we can do for you?" one asked in a less-than-welcoming tone of voice.

"Hotel dicks," Long Tom sniffed disdainfully.

"We're looking for Doc Savage," Renny thumped.

From behind the desk, the clerk offered a snooty comment. "We have no Doc Savages registered at this hotel."

"You heard the man," the second hotel detective said.

"How about an Elvern D. Kastellantz?" Renny countered. "Got one of them?"

To their surprise, the deskman hesitated.

"Well?"

"What is your business with Mr. Kastellantz?" the deskman asked grudgingly.

"Man oh man!" Renny whooped, surging for the desk. "Now we're getting somewhere!"

The hotel detectives hastily got out of the big engineer's way, like row boats beating away from an oncoming ocean liner.

"What's his room number?" Renny demanded.

The deskman hesitated, so Renny gave the register a spin until it faced his side of the counter. He flipped through the pages, stabbed a spot with a thick forefinger, and crowed, "Room 14-C!"

They made a dash for the elevators.

"Wait for me!" an anxious voice called after them.

It was Pat. The pretty young girl was hotfooting it through the lobby, having just stepped from a taxi.

There was a uniformed elevator starter. Renny dropped a huge paw on his shoulder and hissed, "There's a fiver in it if you run the doors shut in her face."

"I heard that!" Pat shouted, just as the cage closed.

The other elevators were in use and Pat could only fume and pace as she waited for a free cage.

At one point, the two hotel detectives made to approach her.

Casually, the bronze-haired girl extracted her antique six-shooter from her commodious hand bag, gave the cylinder a rattlesnake spin, and remarked to no one in particular, "My father made this by hand to shoot grizzly bears with. In our neck of the woods, there was so much brush that you never saw a grizzly until you were right on him, or her, as the case may be."

The hotel detectives swapped uncomfortable looks, and resumed their seats, pointedly burying their blank faces in morning editions.

During one restless tour of the lobby, Pat's head came up and she saw her famous cousin emerging from a cab.

"My darned luck!" she muttered. Abruptly deciding to take the bull by the horns, Pat hurried up to meet the bronze man as he came through the revolving doors.

"Doc! You're just in time!" she said excitedly. "Renny and the others have tracked that sneaky Kastellantz. He's registered in Room 14-C. In this very hotel! Brazen, huh?"

"Brazen," Doc said, his flake-gold eyes chilly, "describes all manner of inexplicable behavior."

"Now, Doc—"

"Since you are here," the bronze man said in a brittle tone of voice, "you may guard the lobby."

Pat flared up like Vesuvius. "My foot! I want in!"

Doc continued on without breaking stride. "The lobby or the door. The choice is yours."

It was rare that the big bronze man showed his displeasure so openly. The frostiness of his metallic tone told Pat that she had overstepped her unwelcome, as it were.

Seeming to shrink, she stopped, her buoyant mood diminished as if cold water had been dashed in her entrancing face.

Doc Savage disappeared into the elevator.

One of the hotel detectives jeered, "Looks like you met a grizzly of another color!"

Pat directed the maw of her cannon in his direction

and said, "My eyesight isn't so hot. Sometimes, I just aim at any old growl."

An instant later, there came a sound far above.

It was a racket remindful of the bass string of a titanic bullfiddle being plucked violently. The noise was ear-splitting.

Pat, hearing the familiar sound of one of the bronze man's supermachine pistols discharging, made a face and said, "Darn! How do I always get left out?"

Then, suddenly realizing that neither Renny, Long Tom, nor Johnny were in possession of their superfirers—and knowing her cousin never carried one—she went very wide of eye.

"Oh! *Oh!*"

# XIII

## INFERNAL DEVICE

On the 14th floor of the Hotel Grant, Doc Savage, mighty Man of Bronze, plunged from the elevator cage, one of his anæsthetic grenades in hand. He knew that the bullfiddle bellow coming from this floor had not been triggered by any of his aids, in all likelihood.

He came out into the corridor, veered around a corner, flake-gold eyes taking in the numbers on the closed doors. Moving stealthily, he came to the door numbered 14-C.

The portal lay open. A foot protruded from the gaping opening. Doc recognized it by the hole on the bottom of the well-worn sole. Long Tom. The puny electrical wizard—notoriously penurious—was wont to wear out his shoe leather to the thickness of vellum before having his footgear resoled.

Doc eased up to the door with the soundlessness of a great tawny tiger.

Glass bomb readied for throwing, he stuck his head in the door, then withdrew it with blurring speed.

No bullets sought the bronze blur that was his head. If any had, they would surely have missed. The bronze man was as fast as verichrome.

He threw the bomb. It made only a brief tinkle breaking. Doc waited, breath pent, ears alert. He heard no movement, no fall of a body overcome by the quick-acting gas.

When it was safe to inhale, Doc entered the room and examined Long Tom, who lay on his stomach. He turned the puny electrician over.

Long Tom breathed. In fact, he was actually snoring now that Doc had shifted him.

His unhealthy-looking face was unmarked. A row of tiny rips showed along his coat front. No blood seeped through, however.

Examining the pallid hands, Doc found a modest wound on the palm of one. It had barely broken the skin. Mercy bullet.

Getting erect, the bronze man slipped into the room. Johnny lay asprawl on an ottoman. His coat front, too, sported a stitchery of moist rents.

The mercy bullet that got him had scraped a red line along the side of his bony skull.

Farther in, he found no one. And no trace of Renny.

Doc went to a telephone and got the front desk.

"Connect me with General Graul Frontenac," Doc clipped.

A moment later, the Meridan general's stiff voice came.

"*Da?*"

"This is Doc Savage."

Silence. Doc was about to repeat his statement when General Frontenac said, "You catch me at an inopportune time, *Domnule* Savage. I am in the throes of packing, having sent the king's retinue on ahead."

"Ahead?"

"There are difficulties in my homeland. The forces of Carrullana are even now massing on Merida's western border. As deeply as it wounds me to do so, I must return to take command of the Royal Army. It is my duty."

"You should be advised that Elvern D. Kastellantz is loose in this hotel, and is possibly on his way to you."

"And who is this Kastellantz person?"

"That is the name by which the missing chauffeur is going," Doc explained. "And he is armed with one of my supermachine pistols. It might be a good idea to lock all your doors until I arrive."

"Of course. Of course. Thank you for calling. I await your arrival, *Domnule* Savage," said General Frontenac, terminating the conversation.

The bronze man next made for the elevator bank, eerie golden eyes alert. As he moved, a bronze shadow, he began humming under his breath. The humming became louder, and turned into words—words of some exotic, guttural song in a foreign language.

Surprisingly, it brought no curious faces to doors. The habitués of the Grant were evidently respectful of other persons' affairs, no matter how noisy.

Doc listened. No answer to his urgent musical questionings came. He had been singing in the Mayan tongue, hoping that the missing Renny could and would answer.

Abandoning that tack, Doc took the elevator to the topmost floor, where the retinue of King Goz had set up housekeeping.

Stepping off, he launched once more into his guttural song, with no discernible result.

Going to the door of the Meridian suite, Doc paused, seemed about to knock, and instead grasped the knob. He gave it a turn. The door opened easily.

The bronze man found himself in an antechamber dominated by an antique table resting on a vermilion rug. On the table reposed an envelope, propped against a silver candelabra.

Doc's sharp eyes easily read the inked legend on the envelope face. It was addressed to him.

Doc's trilling came then. The exotic vibrations were very low this time, so ethereal that they could not be heard at a distance greater than a few feet.

Often, this sound came unbidden. This was one of those times. Doc sometimes worried that it would one day give away his presence to enemies and result in a calamity.

This was one instance when the bronze man's unconscious habit possibly saved his life.

His trilling had only begun roving the musical scale—and the antique table abruptly became a geyser of white-hot liquid!

Doc jumped back, impelled by trained reflexes. He brought the door shut with him. Still, some of the liquid heat splashed out into the corridor, igniting the nap in several spots.

There was a chemical extinguisher mounted in a fire cabinet. Doc seized this, returned to the blaze. Pumping the handle furiously, he directed the fire-retarding chemicals at the burning spots in the corridor carpet.

He might as well have been attempting to water an oil fire. The chemical hissed and sputtered and the blaze only burned up anew. Doc seemed not at all surprised by this.

Redirecting the spray, he coated both hands with the foamy chemical retardant until his fingers were a powdery white. This bizarre behavior made sense in the frantic moments that followed.

Seizing one corner of the nap, Doc exerted his mighty muscles. A rip like canvas tearing came, and the burning section of carpet came loose in metallic hands.

Dragging this to the smoking door, Doc tossed it into the room, now blazing like the pit of Tartarus itself. It could do no harm—adding the carpet section to the roaring conflagration—and might possibly help contain the spread of the blaze.

Slamming the door, the bronze man raced to the elevator and commandeered a cage. He stopped on the 14th floor and collected insensate Johnny and Long Tom.

Pat Savage met him in the lobby, her six-gun in hand.

She saw the limp figures of the puny electrical wizard and the bony archæologist, one slung over each of the bronze man's broad shoulders, and asked, "Where's Renny?"

Doc Savage said nothing.

Horror twisting her features, Pat brought a hand up to her face. "No," she choked, "Not Renny!"

"Watch for Kastellantz, or any other suspicious person," Doc said, sweeping past her like a grim presentiment.

Doc got the flustered hotel staff organized. A fire alarm was tripped. Anxious guests flooded down the stairwells and poured off the elevators like skim from a stew, to collect in the street outside.

In the confusion, it was no wonder that Pat Savage was unable to recognize Elvern D. Kastellantz, whom she had never clearly seen. Her grief did not assist alertness.

The fire department was the first to arrive. By the time they reached the top floor, the fire had mostly burned itself out. Not that they would have accomplished much. They dragged hoses that were too short to reach the twenty stories to the top floor, and the city water pressure was insufficient to direct streams of water into smoke-discharging windows. Besides which, they realized when they saw the fierceness with which the blaze had gutted the top-floor anteroom and surroundings, mere water would have accomplished no useful purpose. It was a chemical fire, unquenchable by any means at their disposal, and would have to be left to burn itself out.

They could tell this by the blackened skeleton in the ashes. The person caught in the blaze had been all but cremated.

Doc and Pat, along with Long Tom and Johnny—both of whom were now ambulatory, thanks to a counteractant Doc had administered from a syringe carried in his equipment vest—stared at the vitreous remains.

They poked at the charcoal thing for any signs that it represented their comrade in adventure, Renny Renwick.

One item turned up. It was mostly slag now, but some freak effect had allowed the snout of one of Doc's unique supermachine pistols to survive the inferno intact.

This discovery had a pronounced dampening effect on their hopes.

"I can't tell," Long Tom said thickly. "Are—are the finger bones big enough for—for—" Words failed him.

"An imponderability," Johnny muttered.

Pat looked away.

The Washington police arrived next. In force. The importance of the persons who typically inhabited the Grant required this. The contingent was led by no less than the captain of the District of Columbia police, a red-faced man with a flavorful brogue.

They conducted a brief tour of the blackened suite, and satisfied themselves that there was only one body—although the incredible heat did not preclude the possibility that some portions of the warm ashes collecting their tracks might not have once been human.

"It is very clear what it was," announced the police captain grimly.

Pat Savage looked curious. "Yes?"

"Some one set a bomb made of that—what do you call it—Thermit stuff."

"Thermit!" Long Tom exclaimed. They all knew the awful properties of the deadly stuff; often, they used it in their work. Additionally, the puny electrical wizard—who had fought in the Great War—had seen firsthand the damage created by incendiary bombs made of the chemical, which burned with a terrific heat. The room had much of that aspect now.

"Musta been a wire laid somewheres," the captain mumbled.

"More likely copper filings sprinkled in the nap of the rug so as to make a contact with concealed electrodes on the bottom of the table legs," Doc Savage interposed. "The filings could have been connected by wires through the floor to the room below."

"Glory be!" gulped the policeman. "I never thought of that."

"It would be the simplest way of doing it," Doc told him. "Wires from the table would be discovered when the table was used. The rug has a reddish color, and copper filings sprinkled in it would hardly be noticed. A thin layer of them, deep in the nap of the rug, would be invisible to the casual eye. No doubt a person hiding on this floor or the one below triggered the infernal device at the sound of my approach—too soon, as it happened."

"How—how can you be so cold-blooded about this!" Pat choked. "Renny may be dead!"

"No," said Doc calmly. "That is not Renny's remains."

"No?"

"The skull is too narrow. Further, the femurs—the leg

bones that provide much of the stature of a given individual—are too short for this person to be Renny."

Relief washed over the faces of Doc's associates. If the bronze man had satisfied himself on that score, it was more than good enough for them.

"And who are you thinkin' it might be, Mr. Savage?" the captain inquired.

"I had spoken with General Graul Frontenac just moments before the explosion. In fact, was on my way to meet with him. He claimed to have been alone in the suite."

"You think that's the general?"

Doc let the question slide. He had a habit of not hearing questions when they concerned some point about which he was not absolutely clear. The bronze man was not given to casually broaching theories, no matter how plausible.

He said nothing about the elusive Elvern D. Kastellantz. The police seemed reluctant to press the matter.

"So where's Renny?" Pat wanted to know, a bit of natural timbre creeping back into her voice.

"If you did not see him leave the building," the bronze man stated, "then he must be on the premises. A search is in order."

So they went hunting for Renny.

They found him, but the big-fisted engineer was only located after a protracted search.

Renny lay on his back in a seldom-used stairwell and was quite senseless.

"It was an ashtray," Renny rumbled, when they revived him.

"Talk sense," suggested puny Long Tom.

"A glass ashtray," Renny repeated. "Kastellantz picked it up and popped me."

Doc Savage murmured, without particular emotion, "So Elvern D. Kastellantz knocked you out, then disappeared."

"That makes a long story short," Renny said sheepishly.

A thorough search was conducted for Elvern D. Kastellantz, but no one seemed unduly surprised when they failed to find him. Nor did any indication that it was not

General Frontenac who had been consumed by the Thermit death trap come to light.

They did, however, find evidence that the old green taxi that Kastellantz had commandeered back at the Virginia hunting lodge of Caspar Prestowitz had been parked briefly in the hotel garage.

A few of the hotel patrons still milling about the sidewalk awaiting word that it was safe to return to their rooms, attested to that intriguing fact. Close questioning brought out the fact that no one had caught so much as a glimpse of the driver. The hack was noticed only because of the high rate of speed at which it had quitted the area—which had occasioned some comment.

After all search possibilities had been exhausted, Doc Savage collected his men together and got their story.

They had attempted to barge in on Elvern D. Kastellantz in his room, when the latter, caught by surprise, had opened up on them with one of the stolen supermachine pistols.

Johnny and Long Tom, themselves bereft of weaponry, went down despite their bulletproof undergarments. The rapid-firers boasted a rate of fire that was withering.

"I got clear, and faded back to lay for the guy," Renny said, taking up the story. "After a while, he slid out, and went for the stairs. I followed him. Guy musta heard me or something, because as I was climbing them steps, he jumped out of the shadows and conked me one."

"Humph, " Pat sniffed. "So much for the superiority of the male sex."

"Your presence here, young lady, should have an explanation attached to it," Doc Savage said firmly. He was looking, however, not at Pat, but at long-faced Renny Renwick.

"Gosh, Doc," Renny said mournfully. "We did try to run her off. Honest. But you know Pat. What can a guy do? What can *three* guys do? After all, Pat is no ordinary gal."

"Yeah," Long Tom said. "It's easy enough to *tell* her that around us is no place for a woman, but that's all the good it does."

"Indubitably," Johnny chorused.

Pat said cheerfully, "You're really being the best old grandpas to me."

Doc said, "Kastellantz—assuming it was he driving our machine—may still have possession of at least one superfirer. Our best course of action is to get up in our plane and attempt to trail him with our locator device."

"If you ask me," Pat said sassily, "it's your *only* course of action."

Saying nothing, Doc Savage led them from the hotel.

As they followed in his wake, Renny muttered to Pat, "If I was you, I'd sort of keep my yip shut until Doc kinda gets used to you being around."

"You," snapped Pat, "were going to persuade Doc to let me in on this excitement."

"Well, you're here, ain't you?" Renny demanded.

"Through my own efforts, young man!" Pat assured him. "Through my own efforts!"

They taxied to the Washington airport and boarded the big bronze speed plane in which Doc Savage had come from New York.

In the air, Renny flew while Doc, assisted by Long Tom Roberts, manipulated the locator device, which functioned on the order of an electroscope, but on a much more sensitive scale.

The locator was a cumbersome knot of wires, coils, and vacuum tubes surmounted by an ordinary radio loudspeaker. It was suspended over a great lense of glass inset in the floor of the plane cabin on a swiveling mount.

Often in the past, the device had filled a tremendous need. Doc Savage, in his career of righting wrongs and punishing evildoers, had as his enemies all men outside of the law. These foes often sought to strike at him through his five aids. There had been occasions when the need was urgent that Doc find one of his associates in order to remove him from peril. Hence, the radium in their supermachine pistols and the locator device.

This present usage, however, was unique, for no one had ever before come into possession of one of the bronze man's superfirers. It was a worrisome development, and this was written over the faces of Doc's assistants.

They circled the District of Columbia and environs for

better than two frustrating hours. Once, they got a reaction—a brief wailing—but it proved to be a sample of radium in a Maryland hospital.

"Now what, Doc?" Renny asked from the cockpit.

"We are wasting time here," Doc said, shutting off the locator.

"Land?"

Doc shook his head. "Home."

A silence descended upon the soundproof cabin of the great plane. It was rare that Doc Savage admitted defeat, much less abandoned a chase. But he was doing so now.

They flew northward in a depressing silence. Not even the normally irrepressible Pat Savage vouchsafed any of her usual unbridled optimism.

## XIV

## THE STRANGENESS

Sword cane tucked under one natty arm, Brigadier General Theodore Marley Brooks presented himself at the door of the estate of H. Startland Drago at three o'clock in the afternoon.

"My good man," he told the butler who answered, "I am here to relieve that infamous ape, Monk Mayfair."

"You must be the lawyer."

"The very same," Ham drawled in a self-important voice.

"The one with the wife and thirteen half-wit kids."

"What has that insect been saying about me now!" Ham exploded, losing his dignity and for a moment his cane. He snatched it up in one gray-gloved hand before it could clatter to the hard bricks of the walk. He entered the vestibule in a huff.

Monk appeared then. His grin was broad.

"Hiyah, shyster," he said. "I see you made my pal, Seymour's, acquaintance."

Tucked under Monk's arm was the afternoon newspaper, with a front-page editorial lambasting the inability of grand juries to indict persons who had perpetrated notorious swindles. Laurence Kingsley Goldwill's name was not mentioned, but there was not much doubt as to whom the item referred.

Calmly, the dapper lawyer picked a heavy sculpture off a decorative table and without a word used it to brain the hairy chemist. Monk sat down hard.

"That," said Ham, replacing the sculpture in an unruffled manner, "is for telling tall tales about your betters."

Monk got up and blew on his fists. Ham grabbed for his sword cane, separating it. They squared off. Violence appeared imminent.

"I've been waiting to test this new batch of dope I use on the end of this!" Ham said, flourishing the blade, the tip of which was sticky with some brown substance. "I'm afraid it's strong enough to kill my victims."

"Get set for a new set of teeth!" Monk raged.

The bowlegged butler, Seymour, hastily beat a retreat into the confines of the big house. He returned moments later with cadaverous H. Startland Drago and presentable Joan Manville.

"See here. What is the meaning of this?" Drago demanded.

Instantly, Monk and Ham subsided. Ham put on his best demeanor while Monk glared and rubbed his bristled head absently.

Ham informed everyone of Washington events and the apparent death of General Graul Frontenac.

Saturnine H. Startland Drago started. "General Frontenac—dead! You are certain of this?"

"The remains have yet to be conclusively identified," Ham admitted.

The bond broker's eyes grew sad. "I knew him well," he uttered. His gaze abruptly sharpened. "And King Goz? Nothing of his whereabouts have been learned?"

"Not as yet."

"Has—has there been any word of Caspar?" Joan Manville asked.

"I am sorry, but no," Ham said gallantly.

"I cannot understand what came over Caspar," Drago offered. "It is not like him to be so uncommunicative. And this business of him abducting Doc Savage's cousin. It simply does not sound like the Caspar Prestowitz I know."

"If Pat said he tried to kidnap her," Ham said firmly, "it is so. I admit Pat has her moments, but she would not lie about a matter of such gravity."

A silence settled over the bond broker and his niece. At length, Joan Manville murmured. "I wonder: Could Laurence Kingsley Goldwill be responsible for all this? He is obviously attempting to strike at my uncle through his business associates."

"Perhaps," H. Startland Drago said slowly, "too many have suffered due to Goldwill's enmity. It might be better if he was allowed to finish what he has begun."

"Oh, Uncle! No!"

"Allow me a moment with this furry lunk," Ham stated.

Monk and Ham withdrew just out of hearing.

"He would do as an uncle-in-law," the homely chemist grinned, careful that the presentable young woman and her uncle did not hear him.

Ham made gargling sounds of startled rage.

"You haven't proposed to her already, have you?" he demanded.

"Wel-l-l," Monk said evasively. "That happens to come under the heading of my own personal business."

"What did she say?" Ham demanded anxiously.

Monk sounded as if the discussion had become abruptly painful.

"She said she wouldn't have a husband who went around with somebody always trying to kill him," grumbled the homely chemist.

"Then you'll be leaving Doc's gang for matrimony?" the dapper lawyer queried—still anxiously.

"Heck, no," snorted Monk. "I'll do my fighting out of wedlock."

Ham purpled.

This discussion—Monk had probably never proposed to the young lady in question at all—was carried on quite seriously and with utter disregard for the appearance of clownishness it lent them. Monk and Ham were a pair who seemed unable to get along. If buried side by side, they would argue in their coffins.

Monk suddenly remembered something. "Say, shyster. What's the idea of showin' up early? You know Doc don't want our headquarters left unguarded after what Pat saw that time."

"Pat," Ham drawled, "saw only a figment of the feminine imagination. Such an experience could not possibly happen to me."

Monk snorted. "Yeah? That's on account of you got no imagination, feminine or otherwise."

At that moment, a remarkable animal strode into the foyer, hooves clicking happily.

It was a pig, the equal of which probably did not occur in the porker strain once in an age. He possessed the long legs of a dog, a snout built for inquiring into deep holes of small diameter, and a body that was negligible.

"Hey, Habeas," Monk called over to the pig. "This shyster left our headquarters unguarded. Can you figure it?"

The pig stopped, sat down, and lifted phenomenally long ears ceilingward.

"Then phooey on him," he seemed to say.

At this, Ham emitted words in such a violent rush, he fairly hissed.

"What is that—that *hog* doing here!" he howled.

"Habeas, he's just keeping me and Joan—I mean, Miss Manville—company," Monk said nonchalantly.

"But—but you were to keep that beast in his wallow," Ham sputtered. "In return, I was to keep Chemistry out of your sight. It was to have been a trade."

Ham had a peculiar fixation against pigs, and pork in general. This dated back to an incident in the Great War, when Ham had taught Monk certain awful French words, telling him they were polite terms, fit for flattering a French general, a practical joke which put Monk in the guardhouse. A bit later, the dignified and highly touted brigadier general had found himself framed on a charge of stealing pork from the army larder. He stood court-martial on it. After that, he had been known as Ham, a name he detested.

To this day, he had never proved that Monk had framed him.

It was to further bedevil Ham, the dapper lawyer strongly suspected, that Monk had adopted the ungainly shoat.

For Habeas was Monk's pet, and the homely chemist had spent enough time training the porker to educate several college students. Owing to a very tough youth, Habeas would probably never grow any larger.

In turn, Ham had acquired the runt ape he had dubbed Chemistry in South America on a recent adventure.* Chemistry was as remarkable a specimen of the simian race as Monk's pig, Habeas Corpus, was of the porker family. No one quite knew what Chemistry was. A baboon of some new tailless variety was the most popular theory.

For his part, Monk referred to Chemistry as the "What-is-it." Monk ordinarily loved every little living thing, but Chemistry was an exception. Chemistry bore a distressing resemblance, in miniature, to the hairy chemist himself. It was that simple.

After interminable months of a four-sided feud, which had climaxed with all participants having gotten a bad case of fleas, and each owner blaming the other's pet, the hairy chemist and the dapper lawyer had come to an agreement to leave their pets at their respective homes for a while.

"If you hadn't showed up early," Monk countered, absently scratching a knee without having to stoop much, "this mightn't've happened."

"Then you should be getting on your way," the dapper lawyer said pointedly.

Monk stooped and picked up the ungainly porker. He turned to the others. "Unless Doc says otherwise, you're stuck with this lilac-water tort."

H. Startland Drago composed his rather forbidding countenance.

"If no one objects," he stated, "I shall repair to my study. Fortunately, I am able to run the affairs of Drago & Company by telephonic communication from here."

Drago withdrew.

---

*Dust of Death

On his way out the door, Monk hissed to Ham, "Keep an eye on that little clunk, Seymour. I don't like his looks."

Monk stopped at his Wall Street penthouse on the way to Doc Savage headquarters.

It was one of the flashiest in the city, with a goodly portion devoted to an enormous chemical laboratory, where the simian fellow had perfected numerous discoveries which had garnered him his reputation and his fortune, both.

In one room had been installed a marble-and-silver wallowing place for his unusual pig, filled with perfumed mud and equipped with health-ray lamps and other creature comforts designed to promote the ultra in porcine contentment.

The public had read about this wallow in the newspapers and thought it a scandalous extravagance, a waste of money which could have been devoted to relieving some of the suffering in the world. But the hairy chemist didn't care. He doted on Habeas.

"In you go, Habeas," said Monk, depositing the ungainly shoat beside the wallow. With a piggy squeal, Habeas leapt into the mud. Soon, only his long, rabbitlike ears were visible.

"That's your reward for playin' along with my little ventriloquism trick," Monk said approvingly. "It gets under that shyster's thin skin every time."

Since it was quicker than driving, Monk took the subway to Doc Savage headquarters, and was soon sauntering through the modernistic lobby. Autograph hounds, hopeful of an encounter with the bronze man, descended upon him. The hairy chemist, no great believer in modesty, false or otherwise, obliged all comers.

Then they began to follow him to the concealed speed elevator. Monk foiled this by pointing to a tall individual exiting the building through a revolving door and exclaiming, "Hey! Ain't that Doc there?"

Human nature is a funny thing. The person the apish chemist had pointed out resembled Doc Savage not in the slightest. But there was an immediate exodus on the part of the autograph seekers. Outside, they caught up with the hapless man, surrounding him.

"Sometimes," Monk muttered to himself as he thumbed the elevator call button, "I think we'd be better off operatin' from a cave somewheres."

The door opened instantly.

Doc Savage's speed elevator was a private conveyance, unknown to the general public. Only Doc and his five aids, and his cousin Pat, enjoyed free use of the cage.

So when the door opened, showing the cage to be occupied, Monk Mayfair would have naturally raised an eyebrow.

But the sight of a white-bearded figure caparisoned in ermine-trimmed scarlet silk, burdensome gold crown, empty belt scabbard, and other kingly regalia, brought his jaw dropping to his chest.

"The spook!" he squeaked.

The superannuated monarch said nothing. Avid black eyes—like opals set in a gnarled tree branch—regarded Monk with faint amusement.

Hastily, the hairy chemist stepped aboard.

Monk reached inside his coat. That garment had no conspicuous bulge. Yet Monk produced one of Doc's compact supermachine pistols, which could put out bullets with only a little less speed than buckshot could be poured out of a cup.

"No funny business, you phantasm," Monk advised.

Inasmuch as the apparition clutched an ornate scepter in one withered hand and balanced a heavy golden orb in the other, there was not a lot of business it could do, funny or otherwise.

Except whistle. It knotted its dryish lips and filled the cage with an ineffably doleful air.

The hairy chemist reached for the elevator control, threw it.

What transpired next happened so fast that the remainder of his natural life, Monk Mayfair was never quite certain it had happened at all.

The cage shot up, taking Monk with it.

The regal apparition did not ascend, however.

The floor of the speed elevator seemed to rear up and

swallow him. Or perhaps it was that he simply dropped through the apparently solid floor.

With an abruptness that took the breath away, Monk Mayfair suddenly found himself the sole occupant of the rapidly moving elevator.

The simian chemist, seeing the weighty crown drop through the floor, immediately discharged his tiny weapon. It moaned, sending a stream of smoking brass cartridges rattling around the floor. The hollow shells splashed along the opposite wall, low to the floor.

The lift was so speedy it traversed the height of the shaft before Monk could do anything more than stare at the spot on the floor into which the regal crown had seemingly melted. His eyes were bugging from his head, and he had been thrown to his knees by the speed of the ascent—a sensation he normally enjoyed.

"Blazes!" Monk gulped weakly. "Blazes!"

Clambering to his feet, he gave the control a downward bat. This time, the hairy chemist seemed to lift off the floor as if weightless.

He kept the muzzle of his superfirer trained on the exact spot where the crown had vanished, and one hairy finger on the trigger, as if in expectation of the phenomenon reproducing itself in reverse.

When the cage settled, no king had appeared. There was no one else in the elevator at all. The cage door opened and a lone autograph hound offered a piece of paper and a pen.

"Nix! Nix!" Monk said, shutting the door. He sent the cage back up, a peculiar expression on his unlovely features.

He was still wearing that expression when he stormed into the reception room of the 86th-floor headquarters. He took care, even in his agitation, to step over a cork mat set immediately inside the bronze portal.

The room proved to be deserted. Monk made a circuit of the layout, and found nothing amiss. But the presence of the revenant in the speed elevator could only mean the uncanny being had lately been prowling about the floor.

Face wrinkling, Monk went to the big office safe and placed a bullet-scarred ear to it. He heard nothing. Not that he expected to; the laminated walls were all but sound-proof.

There was a short-wave broadcast transmitter in the laboratory, kept always warmed up and tuned to the wavelength used by Doc and his men, for instantaneous use. Monk hunkered down before it and attempted to contact Doc Savage, en route from Washington.

Doc Savage's well-modulated voice came soon. "Yes, Monk?"

"Doc, I'm at headquarters," Monk said excitedly. "That musical monarch was here again!"

"What!"

"I think I chased him off, though."

Renny's voice cut in, "And you didn't grab him!?"

"He wasn't grabbable."

"What do you mean, Monk?" Doc asked.

"I was just returning from Drago's digs," Monk recited. "I go to step on the speed elevator, and when the door opens, there he stands, big as life. I pull my superfirer on him and hit the control. The elevator goes up. I go up. But the king don't. He slips clean through the floor, or something."

"What did I tell you!" Pat interjected. "It was a ghost! A certifiable ghost!"

"I don't know what it was," Monk said in a small voice. "But it's got me buffaloed like nothin's ever buffaloed me before."

"We shall," Doc said quietly, "be there directly."

They arrived by elevator not long after. Doc entered first, assisting Pat Savage over the same cork mat that Monk had earlier taken pains not to trod.

The others, seeing this, gingerly stepped over the mat, too.

Monk crinkled an eye at pretty Pat Savage and remarked, "I thought you was on vacation."

"Don't give anybody ideas!" Pat hissed.

Doc, moving with long space-eating strides, passed from the reception room to the library and on to the great laboratory, stopping to check on the monitoring devices scattered about.

Meanwhile, Renny, Long Tom, and Johnny opened cubby-holes, wall runways, and other hiding places, performing much the same investigation Doc had after the regal apparition's first foray into their preserves.

"You won't find nothin'," Monk offered good-naturedly.

"Says you," Renny grumbled.

But it was true. The indicators plainly showed that no one had entered the setup, except for themselves. The radioactive token required to open the doors made that conclusion an apparent undeniability.

When that was ascertained, Doc announced, "No one has tripped any of the alarms in our absence."

"Maybe I caught him going up, not coming down," Monk pondered, worrying an ear.

Pat ran slim fingers through her hair and murmured, "This is all becoming more baffling every minute." She looked at Doc Savage. "Do you think Old King Mysterious has any connection with the disappearance of King Goz down in Washington?"

Renny snorted. "That tall tale about King Fausto's ghost is nothing but a bunch of hooey."

Doc said nothing.

"Does anybody," Pat said suddenly, "care to check the safe?"

The thought seemed not to have occurred to anyone, but Doc Savage, without acknowledging Pat in any other way, walked up to the big safe and repeated the fingertip-on-rose-petals operation and unlocked the ponderous door. He pulled it open.

No one, perhaps not even Pat, had actually thought that the safe would disgorge anything unusual, so they had not approached the big depository.

Doc's trilling, sounding furiously shocked, brought them running. They crowded around the bronze man.

"What is it? What is it?" anxiously asked Pat, who had been caught by surprise and was now attempting to see over the heads of the others by standing on tiptoe. "I can't see!"

Doc stepped in, knelt to examine something crumpled on the safe floor.

It was a corpse.

There was no doubt but that it was a corpse because of the quantity of blood that pooled on the safe floor. A bit of it, seeping over the edge, began to dribble to the rug.

The cause of death was apparent to all.

It was a sword, quite long and ornate, which had been driven into the dead man's open mouth to exit out the small of his back.

Renny boomed, "Holy cow!"

"I'll be superamalgamated!" Johnny gulped.

"Anybody know who that is?" Long Tom, more nervy than the others, asked.

No one seemed to. Until they realized Pat Savage had had nothing to say for nearly a full minute.

As one, they turned.

The bronze-haired girl was slowly backing away, having finally gotten a good look at the dead man's face and the hideous thing filling his mouth. Her golden eyes were stark. Her tanned hands showed white around the knuckles.

"Now do you understand why Doc don't want you seeing such sights?" Renny rumbled.

"I—I—I—" Closing her eyes, Pat swallowed, tried again. "I know him!"

"Huh!"

*"That—that's Caspar Prestowitz!"*


# XV

# GRIEF AND MORE GRIEF

It would have been difficult to calculate which was the more astounding revelation: the fact that—despite all evidence to the contrary—there was a body in Doc Savage's private safe, or that the dead man would be the missing Caspar Prestowitz.

Assorted expressions of amazement and perplexity crawled over the faces of Doc Savage's present aides. They groped for words, some theory to offer, anything that would explain the impossibility that there should be a corpse in a safe whose combination was known only to Doc Savage.

This was modern New York—radio, television, subway trains, and airplanes—and people knew all about hobgoblins and sea monsters and ghosts. Science had proved they didn't exist, except in fertile imaginations.

But there he was, looking for all the world like some gluttonous sword swallower.

"This is all that fashion plate's fault!" Monk gritted. "He wasn't supposed to spell me till you guys got back from Washington!"

A chime went *do-re-mi* with a beautiful tone. Doc went over to the inlaid table and leaned over it, absently resting his hands upon the ornate surface. An inlay that looked like ancient ivory became a picture of the hall outside the door, telephotoed by some mechanical device. A rare frown crossed Doc's metallic features for an instant.

"That spook come back?" Monk asked.

"Police," Doc rapped, moving to the safe with a speed that showed the urgency of the situation. He pushed the ponderous door shut, locking it.

A buzzer shrilled. The doorbell. At a nod from the bronze man, Monk answered the door.

"Police," a man announced unnecessarily. He possessed a big frog voice—it sounded like the sailor in the movie cartoons—and was short and wide and dressed in a shiny serge suit.

On either side of him stood two uniformed patrolmen wearing the sheepish expressions of sinners entering a church after a protracted bout of waywardness.

Without another word, they started in.

"Watch the mat," Monk said hastily. "Some careless person spilled a little acid."

A plain-clothes individual who had harness bull written all over his square face and the two police officers took pains to step over the mat. Once inside, they looked around wordlessly.

The square-faced man addressed the bronze man.

"We got a call about a body," he said in his hoarse, croaking voice.

"What body?" Doc asked quietly.

"The caller didn't say. He just said to come up to this place and we'd find a body."

"You see any body?" Monk inquired in an innocent voice.

"Who the hell are you?" the square-faced one demanded.

"Monk Mayfair."

"You said it like it means something," was the sarcastic reply.

"Oh, yeah?" retorted Monk, cocking a thumb toward the silent figure of Doc Savage. "That there's Doc Savage. Put that in your corncob and smoke it."

"I don't give a damn if he's Santa Claus with a coat of tan," snapped the plain-clothes man. "This is police business."

"Doc Savage holds an honorary commission as inspector on the New York police force," Johnny Littlejohn put in.

The other snorted. "Did you know that the new commissioner has canceled all of them fancy honorary commissions?"

The way Johnny clipped his lips together showed that he did. He fumbled with his monocle.

"I've heard all about you, bronze guy," growled the plain-clothes man. "And I don't like you horning in on my pasture. You got your men guarding that Drago; don't think I don't know about it." He scowled at Doc. "And I'm going to have a look around this fancy joint, like it or not."

"Be my guest," invited Doc, touching an inlay on the big table. The doors to the library and the one to the lab beyond valved open.

The frog-voiced man strode through, looking not at all impressed by the minor display of scientific magic.

"Watch them, you two," he instructed the two patrolmen.

The pair remained, shifting their feet and looking uncomfortable.

Doc Savage asked them, "Who is that gentleman?"

"Saul Sampson," sighed one. "He's the new inspector in charge of Manhattan Island. They call him 'Push 'em Down' Sampson, on account of he likes stepping on the backs of necks belonging to people who get in his way."

From the library, Inspector Sampson's bullfrog voice called back.

"If I find so much as one of these big books is overdue from the library, there'll be trouble. You may have amounted to something in this town in the past, Savage, but from now on you don't draw any more water than the next guy."

"Old Push 'em Down is honest and tough," the second officer breathed. "He's just getting off on the wrong foot. He's a right guy once you get to know him. You'll see."

"Where did he come from?" Doc questioned. "I thought I knew most of the New York police officials, but Sampson is a stranger."

"He's been pounding a backwoods beat on Gravesend for the last three years," chuckled the first cop. "Got himself promoted at last. I guess he pushed down on the right necks for a change."

While this exchange was going on, Pat Savage retired to a corner to compose herself. The others stood about with various poker expressions making their faces look blankly guilty.

Monk Mayfair, noticing the seepage of gore dripping down from the lip of the closed safe door, stationed himself in front of it. He planted his wide feet on the stains and made soft scuffing sounds, endeavoring to rub the seepage into the colorful Oriental rug.

Not long after, Inspector Sampson stamped back in.

"I didn't see any body," he announced.

"Do tell," Long Tom muttered.

"But that don't mean there ain't one," Sampson added.

He marched up to the bronze man, who towered above him. Inspector Saul Sampson gave the impression of being constructed of great building blocks. His square head sat on squarish shoulders, which in turn were part of the rectangle that was his body. His legs were short and ended in feet like leather barges; squared fists resembled bricks that had been chipped by careless hammers.

"Know a bird named Caspar Prestowitz?" he demanded.

"I have never met any individual by that name," Doc stated truthfully. "Why do you ask?"

Instead of answering, Inspector Sampson turned on Monk, Long Tom, Renny, and Johnny and roared, "What about you misfits? Know this Prestowitz?"

"Never met the gent," Monk offered.

"That goes double," Long Tom said.

"Me neither," added Renny.

Noticing pretty Pat Savage, Sampson demanded, "What about you, girlie?"

"You have not answered my question," Doc interposed quietly.

Push 'em Down Sampson gave the bronze man a flinty look. "The voice that called in the complaint said I'd find Prestowitz's body up here."

"As you can see, there is no body on the premises."

"Something was said about the safe," muttered Sampson meaningly. "I neglected to mention that earlier," he added in a voice that indicated otherwise.

And to the astonishment of all present, Doc told him, "You may examine the safe if you wish."

"If I wish!" Sampson grunted, bearing down on the ponderous object. "Hell's fire!"

Monk, stationed in front of the safe, gave a final surreptitious scuff, and stepped aside.

Sampson looked at the safe, noticed its age and air of antiquity, and put out a truculent lower lip.

"Who's got the combination?" he growled.

"The dial," Doc said coolly, "has not been operable in some time."

"Prove it!"

Doc went over to the safe and gave the dial a spin. It spun freely, without any of the resistance or clicking of a working combination dial.

"As you can see," he repeated, "it has not functioned in some time. It belonged to my father and is something in the nature of an heirloom."

"One side," Sampson rapped. He ran the dial back and forth, one ear clapped to the floral pattern. He made various faces, and not liking what he heard, gave the handle a hard yank. The stubborn door refused to budge.

"When was the last time this safe was opened?" Sampson demanded, whirling.

Doc said, "That, I shall not answer."

"You mean you can't answer—or you won't?" Sampson barked.

"Won't, if you prefer," the bronze man told him.

"We'll damned well see about that! I'm going to be back with a court order to have this box cracked!"

He stormed for the door.

"Watch the mat," Long Tom said sourly. "You don't want acid eating at your bunions."

"And another thing," Sampson threw back. "I don't want your men guarding Drago. Something fishy's going on, and I got an idea who might be in back of it."

Inspector Sampson would have slammed the door shut behind him except that it closed on its own, forcing him to scoot to avoid it.

"That spook planted that body, wantin' to frame us!" Monk said fiercely. He looked down at the rug before the safe door. As it happened, it was fairly red where the nap ran up against the safe. His scuffing had been successful.

"What makes you say that?" Renny wanted to know.

"He had a scabbard at his belt," Monk explained. "It was just long enough to carry a sword big as that one in the dead guy's back—and it was empty, to boot!"

Long Tom demanded, "Doc, what's this all about?"

Instead of replying, the bronze man strode over to a locker and got from it a device resembling a folding box camera, except the lense was quite black. There was a switch on the side, which he turned on.

No light came forth. Nevertheless, he fell to directing the lense about the floor.

"New ultra-violet lantern you've got there, isn't it, Doc?" Pat asked hopefully.

The bronze man seemed not to hear.

Pat continued. "And I suppose you fellows all still carry that chalk which leaves an invisible writing that can be brought out by that ultra-violet projector. How do you carry the chalk now? Buttons on your clothes?"

"Yes," Renny admitted, glancing at Doc, who had his back turned, and then shaking his head admonishingly at Pat. A moment later, he got his chance and whispered at her, "Quit riding Doc! You know he's right about wanting to keep you out of danger. If you had a man's gumption, you'd know that!"

Pat declared, "If I had a man's gumption, I wouldn't consider I had any to speak of."

If Doc Savage heard this exchange, he gave no sign. He was preoccupied in the seemingly pointless activity of directing the nonexistent light on the rug.

He paid particular attention to the area surrounding the big safe.

"I don't get it," Pat whispered.

Monk indicated the cork mat which everyone had been studiously avoiding.

"Coated with grains of that fluorescent powder we use," he explained. "Anybody stepping on it will track the stuff all over the rug. Doc set it up earlier."

"I don't see any glow," Pat said slowly.

There was none. Only when Doc backtracked to the mat, did anything glow. The mat. It became a square of ghostly blue light.

Doc went back to the safe, opened it, and directed the invisible, so-called black light on the contorted body of the late Caspar Prestowitz. He gave particular attention to the soles of the man's feet. No glow sprang up.

"Well," Pat said. "That proves my ghost *was* a ghost."

"Not necessarily," Johnny said. "The body could have been carried in."

"By who?" Renny wanted to know. "A person would have to give a little jump to clear that mat. Prestowitz is no child. It would take a spry man to jump it with that kind of burden."

"Or a spry spook," Pat insisted.

"That black-eyed phantasm," Monk grunted, "was no spring chicken."

"And *you* should invest in some spectacles," Pat retorted. "He had *blue* eyes."

"I stood nose-to-nose with him, and I say they were black," the homely chemist insisted.

Doc Savage's trilling began, quickly died. His strange golden eyes took in the quarreling pair.

"You are certain of his eye color?" he demanded.

"Natch," said Monk.

"Sure," frowned Pat, suddenly sounding unsure.

"A polychromatic chimera," Johnny inserted thoughtfully. "Identification preponderately suggests dualism."

Everyone looked at him.

"Perhaps there are *two* phantom potentates," he explained.

"That don't explain how either of them got up here without leaving tracks," Renny rumbled.

They were stumped. Flummoxed might not have been too strong a word for their collective state of mind.

"Hey!" Monk exploded suddenly. "Maybe he snuck up from the floor below, somehow."

"How?"

"Why don't we take a look?"

"Waste of time," Renny snorted.

"Don't you ever get tired of packin' them fists around?" Monk wanted to know.

Renny said, "You start riding me like you ride Ham and the first thing you know, you won't know anything!"

Monk grinned. "O.K. I got the habit. But what about Old King Fausto, or whoever he was?"

"The floor below," Doc said quietly, shutting off his lantern, "would be an excellent place to store the body until this matter is cleared up."

"Gotcha, Doc," said Monk, entering the safe to gather up the grotesquely impaled figure of Caspar Prestowitz.

Pat averted her eyes as Monk reemerged with his unpleasant burden.

The floor below had for a time been tenanted by an insurance company, but so much violence had occurred around the bronze man's layout that the office employees of the insurance company had become unnerved. At any time of the day, they might hear shots and screams and other manifestations of grim happenings. The employees had come to the point where they could not do their work properly, so the insurance company had vacated. The floor was now empty.

Doc Savage was paying the rent on this floor as a matter of kindness to the owner of the building. But that was beside the point. The operators of the building would have preferred to get rid of a tenant who drew as much violence as did Doc Savage, but it happened that Doc owned a large slice of the building, and they couldn't throw him out.

"Want me to take the secret way down?" Monk asked Doc.

There was a concealed stair in the great laboratory, that terminated inside a fire cabinet on the floor below.

The bronze man nodded. "There may be police lurking in the stairways and elevators."

Monk carried the body, sword and all, from the room as if it were no more than an inconvenient sack of flour.

After the simian chemist had gone, Pat Savage was heard to say, "There's only one explanation."

Everyone looked at her.

"That king's spook must have snatched Prestowitz from where I left him down in Virginia and brought him here."

"Brought him here how?" Renny demanded.

Pat threw up her hands. "How do I know? By broomstick, or however spooks travel!"

"What I would like to know," Johnny murmured in his scholarly voice, "is how that sword came to be here."

"Simple," Long Tom snorted. "It's not the same sword that did for King Goz's footman down in Washington. It's a duplicate."

But it was the same sword. Doc Savage proved this with a long-distance telephone call to the District of Columbia morgue.

The coroner at first did not wish to volunteer the embarrassing truth, but Doc identified himself as a Federal operative, which cut through the man's reluctance.

"As you know, Mr. Savage," he said uncomfortably,

"we removed the sword from the body of the murdered footman. It was being stored here."

"The sword's present whereabouts, please," Doc prompted.

"It showed up missing this morning. That is, during an inventory of the dead man's effects. It was no longer with the rest of his possessions."

Silence.

"I personally spoke with the guards," the coroner added hastily. "None of them had seen the sword or any suspicious persons. Except for the whistling."

"Whistling?"

"Yes. Two of the guards swear that just before the sword was discovered missing—last night—they heard a mournful whistling in the property room. When they went to investigate, they found no one. And no source for the whistling, which faded before they entered. The sword was not discovered gone until later." His voice grew abashed. "I-I cannot explain it."

"Thank you," said Doc, hanging up.

The bronze man had been speaking on an instrument with a loud-speaker attachment that reproduced both sides of the conversation, and his aids had heard everything.

"Now what?" Pat asked in a small voice.

Doc ignored the question and said instead, "Caspar Prestowitz is Joan Manville's fiancé. Under the circumstances, it will be best if she learns nothing of his death at this time. Nor should H. Startland Drago be informed. Instead, we will take turns guarding the two of them and keeping a close watch for the missing Laurence Kingsley Goldwill."

"Anything we can do in the meantime?" Renny asked.

"Yes," said Doc. "Put Pat on the next passenger flight to Canada."

"With pleasure," Renny said with enthusiasm.

"Wait a minute!" Pat protested. "Isn't this kidnaping?"

"Maybe," Renny whispered. "But judging from the look in Doc's eye, going along would be a darn sight better than the alternative."

"Which is?"

The gloomy-faced engineer cocked a thumb like an

uncooked sausage. "Being locked in that there safe for the next hundred years."

Swallowing hard, Pat went without further argument.

# XVI

## THE WORST KINDS OF LUCK

The next two days were relatively uneventful.

Inspector Saul "Push 'em Down" Sampson had returned, but was met by Ham Brooks, whom Doc had recalled for the express purpose of fending off an examination of the office safe, which had been chemically scoured of all traces of the late Caspar Prestowitz.

Stymied, Sampson had stamped off, vowing to be back with a court order proof against the dapper lawyer. Thus far, he had not.

There had been no progress on the dragnet for Laurence Kingsley Goldwill.

There had been no sign of the missing Balkan king, Egil Goz, who was fast becoming the most celebrated missing person since Judge Crater vanished. In fact, the Goldwill matter had pretty much pushed the other off the front pages, except for dispatches from Europe, reporting border friction between the kingdom of Merida and its Balkan neighbor, Carrullana.

In Geneva, the League of Nations Council was meeting over the matter, in the hope of averting a land grab. Ominous noises were emanating from the dictator of the European nation of Santa Bellanca, which considered itself the patron and protector of Merida. The two nations, which faced one another across the Adriatic Sea, were bound by treaty to come to one another's aid in the event of hostilities.

For its part, there was much silence from the capital of Merida. Rumors of General Graul Frontenac's disappearance had been reported, and possibly his death as the result of fire, but Washington had ordered the matter hushed up, lest heads of other nations fear to visit the U.S.

Quietly, Doc Savage had performed an autopsy on the body of Caspar Prestowitz. Autopsy was not quite the term for the grisly process, inasmuch as there was no doubt as to the cause of death. Separating the victim from the death weapon—the traditional sword of Meridan royalty—was the real purpose of Doc's efforts.

The sword went in Doc's safe. The body was sealed in an air-tight trunk and returned to a closet on the vacant 85th floor.

The only noteworthy event occurred when an express package came to the 86th floor, addressed to Doc Savage, on the second day following the advent of Caspar Prestowitz's body in a place where it could not be.

As was his custom, the bronze man gave the package a thorough examination before opening it. He put a stethoscope to it, to detect suspicious ticking. He sprayed it with a chemical designed to change color in the presence of deadly gases, no matter how minute. Finally, he put the thing under a fluoroscopic screen.

Doc Savage had many enemies. Such precautions were routine with him and had saved his life many times in the past.

Monk happened to be on hand and sidled up to the screen as Doc operated the controls.

Doc's trilling came, low and puzzled.

"Bomb?" Monk asked.

"Pat," Doc said, indicating the screen.

Monk peered at what the screen revealed. Bones. Rows and rows of them. Quite small.

When Doc opened the crate, the smell was disagreeable enough to cause the ordinarily imperturbable bronze man to back away hastily.

"Phew!" Monk said, grabbing his pug nose. He looked into the box. There lay a dozen salmon, neither wrapped nor in ice. In fact, no effort had been made to delay decomposition.

There was a note. It read:

HERE IS A BUNCH OF STINKERS FOR A BUNCH OF STINKERS.

LOVE, PAT

P.S. YOU JOKERS FIND ANY KINGS LATELY?


"Pat," Doc said, reclosing the box and placing it in a locker, "is obviously having a successful fishing vacation."

"Next time," Monk muttered, "tell her to send posies."

Doc suggested, "It is about time for you to spell Johnny at the Drago estate."

"Hurrah! Powder River!" Monk enthused. "Am I glad that Long Tom had a bad time with Miss Manville. He keeps refusing his turn to guard her and her uncle." Monk wrinkled his low brow. "Where is that runt, anyway?"

"With Renny," Doc replied. "Watching the Wall Street offices of Goldwill & Son."

"You ask me," Monk opined, heading for the door, "that Goldwill would have to be pretty dumb to show his face by now. He might get himself strung up."


Two of Doc's men, Renny and Long Tom, were discussing that very possibility, seated in a coupe not a block away from the Goldwill building. The auto belonged to Long Tom. In fact, he had recently purchased it. Faint on a rear window was a legend, "Special Value: $375." Long Tom had kicked about the price, even though he had knocked the dealer down from an even four hundred dollars.

A young news vendor stepped out from a corner drug store and began hawking his wares.

"Extra! All about the Goldwill financial squabble!" the urchin proclaimed. "Extra!"

"There goes any chance that Goldwill mug will show up," Long Tom said sourly.

"You said it!"

Renny and Long Tom listened with interest as the cries continued.

"Investors threatened with nervous breakdown!" shouted the newsboy. "Say there is no justice in world! Wall Street has new jitters!"

Big-fisted Renny rumbled softly, "Holy cow! Laurence Kingsley Goldwill sure laid it on Wall Street!"

"It has raised a mess," Long Tom agreed.

"I'll say. If Goldwill had stolen the White House, he couldn't have stirred up more of a stew. People want to boil him in oil."

"And I think the feeling is the result of a public trend."

"What kind of trend?"

"Against the methods of certain financial sharpers who legally relieve people of their money," Long Tom explained. "America is getting tired of the way big business as a whole has turned into a skin-the-other-fellow-if-you-can game. I mean, of course, certain financial moneybags who follow that policy, and not the American businessman in general. I think the public is sick of it. I think that is why Goldwill is sure to get lynched—if he ever turns up."

"Probably," Renny agreed. "Which means he won't."

The wait had been a boring one, and to kill time while the big-fisted Renny watched the building entrance, the feeble-looking electrical wizard was sorting through his equipment case, swapping tubes. Long Tom sometimes bought his tubes secondhand to save money, despite the knowledge that certain species of storefront crooks had taken to giving old tubes just enough juice to warm them up, only to die after a few hour's usage.

Long Tom had once purchased an entire gross of bad secondhand tubes, with the result that a piece of equipment failed at an inopportune time. It was enough to teach him a lesson, but not to cure him of his penny-pinching.

Long Tom had just replaced a worn tube in a spare electroscope and had turned it on when the gold leaves flew apart and the contrivance buzzed angrily.

"Works," Long Tom muttered.

"So far," Renny grumbled.

"It picked up the radium in your superfirer right away, didn't it?" Long Tom said indignantly.

"My superfirer is in the glove compartment, which is lined with lead," Renny rumbled. "It must be reacting to yours."

Long Tom blinked. "Mine's there, too."

Renny turned around, his mournful face comical with surprise.

Then the buzzer stopped.

"You thinking what I'm thinking?" Renny muttered.

"Don't just sit there, you overgrown oaf! Drive around!"

Renny got the car into traffic. They made a hasty tour of the Wall Street sector. The coupe showed symptoms of carbon knock. Once, the electroscope buzzed briefly. Then it cut out again.

"Go back!" Long Tom urged.

Renny doubled back. The buzzing returned anew.

Soon, they narrowed it down to a car. It was a rather ostentatious town car, a well-known model nicknamed a "Ten Thousand" because that was the purchase price of the machine, when new. It was a dazzling white hue, polished to perfection.

It was wending its way south.

"Try to get alongside of it," Long Tom urged.

"Think it's one of our missing superfirers?" Renny rumbled, jockeying in and out of traffic.

"Radium doesn't exactly come two for a penny," Long Tom shot back. "And I'm registering a good-sized chunk."

Eventually, they came to a traffic cop, and Renny was able to pull up beside the expensive town car.

They peered into the driver's seat, trying not to be obvious about it.

At first, they did not recognize the man. They had never seen him before, they thought. Then it hit them.

His coppery red hair was now as black as jet and as shiny as patent leather, but the powdered profile was unmistakable.

Elvern D. Kastellantz!

"Holy cow!" Renny exploded.

It was an unfortunate outburst.

Kastellantz heard it, turned his head, saw them, and sent the long supercharged machine into the hum of cross-traffic.

The move caught Renny flat-footed. Literally. One big brogan came off the brake pedal and tramped the other. He fed the machine gas and gears. It lurched into the honking, screeching tangle created by the lunging town car.

With a clattery conk, the engine died!

"Durn!" Renny complained, smacking the steering wheel so hard it broke.

"My new car!" howled Long Tom.

"You call this heap new!"

"I paid almost four hundred clams for this chariot!"

"Which," Renny muttered darkly, eyes on the escaping town car, "explains a lot."

"Don't just sit there! Start her up again!"

"You see the crank?" Renny grumbled, giving the starter a turn. The engine caught, pistons began knocking and slapping.

On the corner, the traffic cop blew his face red emitting shrill warning whistles.

That only made things worse. Motorists, thinking that the cop was warning of an approaching fire engine or similar emergency, tried to clear the intersection. Wheels climbed onto curbs. The sidewalks collected automobiles. Pedestrians scooted into the relative safety of doorways.

One auto bumped its grille into another. The second machine rolled backward, obstructing Long Tom's noisy sedan.

Renny and Long Tom popped into the street.

"Hey, Clancy!" Renny called. "Clear this mess! We're Doc Savage's men!"

The cop looked abject; his shout back carried an apologetic tone.

"Sorry. No special favors. Orders from Centre Street."

"You mean from that block of bone, Push 'em Down?"

"Sorry," the cop said again, wading into the knot of impatient machines and simultaneously waving his arms and blowing on his attention-getting whistle.

By the time the boulevard had been cleared, the white town car had long departed the scene. Drive as they might, the electroscope failed to buzz.

"Lost him," Long Tom said sourly. "He musta left the island."

"Maybe not," Renny said.

"What do you mean?" Long Tom asked hopefully.

"Could be a bad tube in there," Renny said.

Horror coming over the pallid electrical wizard's face, he began swapping tubes with wild abandon as Renny grimly drove about lower Manhattan.

The net result was that no sign of the elusive chauffeur, Elvern D. Kastellantz, or the dazzling white town car, was brought to light.

Renny summed it up this way: "Any way you slice it, that's the second time your durn nickel-squeezing has cost us."

They contacted Doc Savage by short-wave radio. Johnny answered.

"Salutations," he said.

"Doc there?" Renny asked, not in the mood for Johnny's words.

"He is in the reception room, working on the ceiling," Johnny reported, evidently sensing the big-fisted engineer's mood.

"He what?"

"I will be glad to convey any message."

"Tell him we spotted that Elvern D. Kastellantz. He's in New York!"

"Supermalagorgeous!"

"But we lost him," Renny added glumly.

"One moment." Johnny came back a moment later, saying, "Doc says to return to guarding the Goldwill offices."

"What about Kastellantz?" Long Tom wanted to know.

"Doc has asked me to endeavor to find him with the locator," Johnny said, sounding pleased with himself.

Renny switched off and said, "That long hank of bone just stole our thunder, thanks to you. A sawbuck says he finds Kastellantz, too."

Long Tom later collected on that bet. He looked almost pleased as he accepted the twenty, even though it meant that Elvern D. Kastellantz had eluded them completely, and they were no closer to solving the growing mystery than before.

"This will replace that steering wheel you broke," he told a glum Renny.

It was only after things had settled down that they started wondering what Elvern D. Kastellantz was doing in Manhattan.

It was a profound mystery.

They had no inkling that the mystery was about to take a turn that would make all that had come before seem insignificant.

# XVII

## REIGN OF TERROR

The next morning, newspapers throughout Washington began receiving an anonymous letter.

The editors were urged to send their best reporters to the U.S. Treasury and have them inquire concerning fifty million dollars' worth of government bonds, lately printed, and ready to ship to purchasers. The newspapermen were to ask to examine the bonds, and to have an expert along.

It was rather an asinine suggestion, this letter, and most of the editors put it down as the work of a crank—then wished they hadn't. Some number of journalists—still in town and lamenting their inability to drum up copy on the King Goz matter—went to the Treasury Building, and argued until the bonds were brought out.

They got their money's worth.

The government bonds—they were Liberty Bonds, Issue of 1927—were bogus. Counterfeits. Fresh ones, to boot. The ink had not quite dried.

The Treasury officials had spasms. They wondered wildly how many counterfeit bonds had been sent out as genuine. The newspapers also wondered—in their headlines.

The counterfeiting job was good, and for the life of

them, the Treasury people could not explain how bogus bonds had taken the place of the genuine certificates.

The news went out on the press wires, and the next morning hundreds of thousands of people got their government bonds out of safety-deposit boxes and showed them to bank officials and anyone else whom they thought might be an authority.

That one well-publicized incident by itself made Uncle Sam's credit a bit shaky.

That same day, counterfeit bonds were found in New York, Chicago, San Francisco, and Kansas City.

Buying of government bonds all but stopped.

A fingerprint expert went over the cases which had held the counterfeit bonds in Washington. He found a single thumb print, and compared it with a record of prints in the U.S. Bureau of Investigation files. The thumb print was found to belong to a man who, as far as anyone knew, had never been in the Treasury room where the bonds were kept.

The man whose thumb print was on the case was Laurence Kingsley Goldwill. Of this, there was no doubt. Goldwill had been thoroughly fingerprinted when booked for investigation prior to the failed indictment for robbing investors in his legal-but-detestable stock scheme.

The editors who had earlier dropped the mysterious letters into wastepaper baskets now broke out the big black type reserved for scare headlines.

"GOLDWILL BOND BUST SUSPECT!" read one streamer, in six-inch letters.

This was the most modest of the bunch.

One newspaper—not a tabloid—filled its entire front page with just three words:

FINANCIAL CALAMITY STRIKES!

Another was more succinct:

PANIC!

That was the word of the hour. Panic. Wall Street was still reeling from the black eye caused by the law's inability to indict Laurence Kingsley Goldwill. And now this. John Q. Public rushed his Liberty Bonds to redemption points. Official Washington hurried to soothe jittery nerves.

The President of the United States, on a nationwide broadcast hookup carried by both radio networks, gave a speech. It was a good speech, full of simple, well-considered words. It was designed to restore trust in financial institutions, which were only now beginning to find solid footing after the most recent panic.

The president began with a simple statement of the purpose of a government bond. He called the issuance of government bonds a loan, made by the purchaser—ordinary citizens for the most part—to the country floating the bond. Such a loan, he told the nation, supersedes all other government obligations. The faith and credit of the entire nation and all its units and peoples is pledged to honor its obligation, and taxes may be levied accordingly, without regard to the needs or sacrifices of any subordinate community or corporate body.

A national loan, therefore, is a veritable mortgage on the integrity, wealth, and taxable assets of the entire population, the president continued. And when such a loan ceases to be safe, then no other known security or investment based on any property within that nation will have any dependable market value. The default of a national obligation, he concluded, would be an absolute calamity to the entire commercial structure and credit of its people— and the currency of such a nation would become virtually worthless.

In other words, listeners understood, before Uncle Sam would welsh on his bonds, the government would go bust and collapse. No one believed that would happen.

This speech had a brief soothing effect.

On the floor of the Senate, Senator John Thomas MacPartney made a speech of his own. Senator MacPartney was in charge of the Financial Affairs Committee. He was one of the most powerful law makers in congress, and well liked by his fellows.

In a short but eloquent address, he promised to enact legislation calling for the replacement of the counterfeit bonds with sound ones, or with refunds—whichever the purchasers preferred. Inasmuch as he was a vocal opponent of the president, this made an impression.

This brought Senator John Thomas MacPartney a rare standing ovation from his colleagues on both sides of the aisle.

In the press gallery, news photographers' flashbulbs began exploding, limning of the proud legislator in his hour of courage.

Within hours those photographs were printed in the evening papers. A few editions showed up on news stands under the following headline:

PRESIDENT ASSURES NATION!
MacPartney Vows Bond Relief!

These editions were hastily recalled and replaced with nearly identical ones. Except that the main streamer now read:

MACPARTNEY ASSASSINATED!

For within hours of giving the climactic speech of a long and distinguished career, Senator John Thomas Mac-Partney was discovered in his Senate office, seated behind his desk, impaled to his chair by a gold-hilted sword encrusted with expensive jewels.

The sword had entered his mouth with sufficient force to shatter his false teeth.

There was a note, stained with blood, affixed to his necktie.

It was brief:

"I am about to force the world to embark upon the greatest experiment in human history. The United States has been selected to be the first test case.

"The end result of my legislation will be the banishing of what has been called by sages since time immemorial, the root of all evil.

"I propose to eliminate money.

"Such a momentous and fundamental change cannot be undertaken at once. My substitution of government bonds with counterfeits is but the first of many steps.

"It is up to the government to take the next step.

"If the Liberty Issue of 1927 is not declared void, I will eliminate another personage of great importance."

The note was signed: "Laurence Kingsley Goldwill."

Extras hit the streets within the hour.

"GOLDWILL BEHIND PANIC!" one screamed.

"FINANCIAL OPERATOR BLACKMAILING UNCLE SAM!" howled another.

Doc Savage turned up in Washington before the headline ink had dried.

The bronze man quietly presented himself to the Department of Justice and asked to examine two items—the thumb print found on the cases in which the first counterfeit Liberties had been discovered, and the sword used to assassinate Senator John Thomas MacPartney.

The Bureau of Investigation had possession of the cases. Doc was escorted to these with the same deference earlier shown to him. His difficulties with the New York constabulary had no bearing on his Federal standing.

The solitary mark had been brought out with fingerprint powder, which had been blown clear, leaving only a rather distinct thumb print that looked as if it had been pressed into a smudge of coal dust.

From his vest, Doc extracted a small atomizer. He jetted spray onto the black thumb print. The spray was colorless.

Federal men stood about, expectation writ large on their stolid features.

But nothing happened.

The bronze man straightened from his work, pocketing the atomizer.

Doc Savage seldom explained his actions, but he did so now.

"The reagent spray is a type which reacts to perspiration oils normally left by the human finger, causing the oily deposits to show as a visible stain."

There was no stain.

"Finger-print powder must have soaked up the oil," some one muttered.

"Possibly," Doc said, then asked to view the body of Senator John Thomas MacPartney.

The body had been taken to the same morgue that had earlier held the body of the late footman to King Egil Goz of Merida, now virtually a forgotten man amid the rush of late developments.

"It's the same sword," the coroner said as Doc Savage entered, escorted by government operatives.

"What's this?" a Federal man demanded.

"Mr. Savage inquired of the sword earlier," the coroner explained. "The one that had killed the footman to the Balkan king who disappeared. It had disappeared, too. There was no trace of it. The only thing anyone noticed was the whistling."

"Whistling?"

"It sounded just like the descriptions the papers carried of the sad whistle heard just before that king vanished."

The Federal men didn't know what to say to this. They fell to watching the bronze man work.

Doc went over to the sheeted form and removed the covering. He exposed only the agony-ridden face that was dominated by the hilt of the ceremonial sword. His active flake-gold eyes scrutinized the ornate knot of gold and brilliants.

His weird trilling came again—furious, even a little edgy.

"It's the same sword, isn't it?" the coroner gulped. "There's a scratch on the big emerald. I noticed it last time."

"It is," Doc said grimly. He had noticed the scratched emerald when he had removed the sword from the body of Caspar Prestowitz and placed the inexplicably ubiquitous blade in his office repository for—he believed—safekeeping.

But he could not tell those present that—not without having to explain the impossible.

"What do you make of it, Mr. Savage?" asked one of the G-men as they exited the building.

"Some one stole the sword and employed it to murder the senator," said Doc, stating the obvious.

"How does this hook up with the disappearance of the Balkan king? And what does the whistling mean?"

"A visit to the murder scene might be in order," Doc stated.

"What do you expect to find there?"

"Some person who might have heard more whistling."

They found a congressional page who heard a peculiar whistling, sad in its strains, right enough. But only after questioning a number of persons.

"It was haunting," said the page. "I tried following it, but when I turned a corner, there was only a blank wall. The whistling seemed to be coming from inside the wall. Then it was gone. I didn't see what made the whistling."

They were taken to the spot. It was a cul-de-sac in which the bust of a long-dead law maker stood on a plaster pedestal. The wall was solid. They stared at it a moment, in silence. The bust seemed to stare back with equal blankness.

Some of the Federal men had been present when General Graul Frontenac had been interviewed by Doc Savage.

"Sounds like the ghost of Old King Fausto is loose!" one breathed in a dumfounded tone of voice.

"Maybe we should take down this wall," suggested another who had heard the story of the entombed despot.

Doc said, "It would be simpler to see what lies on the other side."

They found the other side. It proved to be one of the many cloakrooms for which the Capitol Building is famous.

It was a dead end—in a literal as well as a figurative sense.

Outside the Capitol Building, the Federal agents were wondering where the bronze man would take them next.

He surprised them with his next statement.

"I must return to New York at once."

And he left them.

Less than two hours later, Doc Savage was back in the reception room of his 86th-floor headquarters. He had pulled a stool up to the center of the room and was standing on it.

From the ceiling, he extracted a glass plate, which proved to be attached to a motion picture camera, cunningly recessed into the modernistic ceiling.

Monk, Ham, and Renny were watching him do this. They showed no surprise as Doc brought the camera down and bore it into the laboratory. It was one of the many amazing devices that festooned the skyscraper layout.

In the laboratory, Doc ran the film through a quick-drying process of his own invention, wound it on a take-up reel, and put it in a projector in a miniature projection room in one corner of the great workshop.

Shutting the door to darken the cubicle, he turned on the projector.

On a white wall, an angled bird's-eye view of the reception room appeared, in brilliant colors. The bronze man's scientific skill had played an important part in the developing of a color process which is now being widely employed by amateur photographers.

The images ran briefly each time some one stepped into the reception room from either the corridor or the library. Monk and Ham saw themselves, and Doc, come and go.

Monk asked, "What triggers it, Doc?"

"Photoelectric cell. Timed to run for three minutes after each interception to conserve film."

Monk nodded.

There was a lot of footage and the viewing of it grew tedious, until the film came to a point showing the figure in scarlet.

"That dang whistlin' wraith!" Monk exploded.

It *was* the Whistling Wraith—as Monk had dubbed him. It literally melted through the office door and made a straight line for the safe. The Wraith passed into the big strongbox as if neither were solid.

The film ran on for its allotted span. Nothing further seemed to transpire.

During the wait, Renny made a comment: "That happened during Monk's trick at the wheel."

"I was workin' in the lab," Monk said defensively.

"Nothin' was said about stayin' in the reception room all day long."

Ham, normally quick to chime in and add to the hairy chemist's misery, said nothing. His dark eyes were on the silent safe, white showing all around.

A moment later, the scarlet figure reemerged. It still carried its gold scepter, but the heavy orb was now tucked awkwardly under its arm. That was so it could freely carry the Meridan royal sword, which seemed no more substantial than a moon beam. For it had come through the solid safe door without hanging up in any way.

The scarlet apparition passed through the reception room door as if the latter were composed of some bronze-colored light.

The film was silent. But those who had heard the regal specter's morose pipings imagined they could hear those same strains now.

"The nerve of the blamed spook!" Monk howled when Doc clicked off the projector.

"Now we know how the sword was taken from the safe," Doc said quietly as they stepped out into the suddenly too bright light of the vast laboratory.

"Gosh, Doc, I'm sorry," Monk mumbled. "I was only out of the reception room a few minutes."

"Perhaps this is for the better," Doc stated in a grim voice. "Now we know that we are up against something the likes of which we have never before encountered. It is apparently unsubstantial, yet opaque to light, for it is visible to the naked eye and the camera lense."

Renny smacked one big paw into another. "That's right! And it tripped the electric-eye traps you set, too. But what could it be?"

Monk screwed up his unlovely face in cogitation. "Say, ain't there a scientific word for what spooks are supposed to be made outta?"

"If there is," Renny muttered, "I never heard tell of it."

"Ectoplasm," said Doc quietly.

"What's that?" Renny asked, puzzled.

"A substance supposed to be disgorged by mediums or spirit guides during seances with the dead," Doc explained. "Ghosts are held by some to consist of ectoplasmic matter."

"Holy cow!" Renny gulped. "You sayin' there *is* such a critter?"

The bronze man vouchsafed no reply. Instead, he disappeared into the library, apparently to pursue some unspoken theory.

Monk and Renny noticed Ham Brooks then.

The dapper lawyer was standing in the open door of the projection room, his chiseled features as white as fresh linen.

"What's eatin' you, shyster?" Monk asked unkindly. "You look like you just seen a ghost. Haw."

The dapper lawyer, who up until this point had been a vociferous skeptic of the existence of the whistling apparition, moistened his lips repeatedly, but his mind was too busy trying to dig up a sensible explanation for what he had just seen to frame words. He separated and unseparated his sword cane in nervous hands.

"We know how you feel," big-fisted Renny put in dryly. "It floored us, too."

Ham apparently tried to think of something to do or say, but wound up shuddering.

A little while later, after Ham had regained some of his composure, Monk engaged him in brief conversation.

"You know, I sure hope Doc don't change any."

"What do you mean?" Ham asked sharply.

"We make some of the darnest bobbles and get into some of the dangest messes," Monk elaborated. "And Doc just kinda makes a guy feel he done his best and, after all, it ain't so bad. A lot of fellows would cut loose and skin a guy alive."

"Doc should do that to you," Ham snapped.

"Whatcha mean, you overdressed shyster?"

"You let that—that wraith in, didn't you?"

"I'll put you in one of your own pockets first thing you know," Monk promised.

And they fell into a loud argument which proved that the dapper lawyer had regained his nerve.

Not long after that, Doc Savage returned.

"Find anything, Doc?" asked Ham.

Doc said, "H. Startland Drago has been requested to

go to Washington and testify before Congress, according to the teletype."

"Tarnation!" Renny thundered. "Why?"

"As one of the principal investment bankers involved in selling government securities abroad, Congress would like his opinion on the advisability of declaring the Liberty Issue of 1927 void."

"Congress ain't thinking of knuckling under, are they?"

"All of Washington is jittery over the murder of Senator MacPartney and the threat letter bearing the signature of Laurence Kingsley Goldwill."

"Holy cow!" said Renny.

Doc said, "Renny, I want you to accompany Drago to Washington. Take Long Tom and Johnny with you."

"You think that Goldwill will try to bump off Drago while he's testifying?" Monk asked.

"Anything is possible," the bronze man said, returning to the seclusion of the library.

# XVIII

## TESTIMONY

The arrival of H. Startland Drago in Washington occasioned something of a press stampede.

This, despite that fact that until the Congress of the United States had requested his appearance before it, the name of H. Startland Drago was one virtually unknown to the general public. Outside of financial circles, he was a complete obscurity.

This was because international investment bankers as a class do not do business with the general public. The average man on the street would have no need to enter the staid offices of Drago & Company, and so had never heard of him.

Eager journalists descended upon Wall Street. In their

ignorance, they began asking questions of the wrong persons and received uncomprehending stares at the mention of the name of H. Startland Drago.

Some nimble legwork brought forth exactly the caliber of individual that was H. Startland Drago. The bond titan was, it came out, something of a mystery man, despite his penchant for operating in international financial circles.

The national press soon changed that.

"H. STARTLAND DRAGO TO ADVISE CONGRESS!" blared a headline, and suddenly the name Drago was on everyone's lips.

Some facts—very few—dribbled into print. H. Startland Drago was of obscure origins. It was not even clear that he was a United States citizen. No one could say, or find out for certain.

But of one thing there was no doubt: He was a rising financial power in Europe. It was Drago's financial acumen that had enabled many European countries to struggle up from the dire inflation that had buffeted the continent in the wake of the Great War. Many heads of state counted him among their advisers. Not a few kings owed him their thrones. For this reason he had acquired his impressive cognomen, the Empire Maker. He was a financial Merlin.

Some sheets took pains to point out that one head of state who enjoyed the fruits of H. Startland Drago's sage advice was the present dictator of Santa Bellanca, currently in international hot water for his conquest of a defenseless African nation.

But there were just as many European democracies which had enjoyed the benefit of Drago's wise counsel.

Some brief mention was made of the brewing trouble in the Balkans, where the leaderless and beleaguered kingdom of Merida was quaking under the threat from neighboring Carrullana, with the dictator of Santa Bellanca threatening to intervene. A few papers bothered to mention the missing monarch of Merida, Goz the First. Very few. With the financial foundation of the United States exhibiting distressing cracks, the average American could summon up little interest in events so far away.

Editorialists from coast to coast ballyhooed H. Startland Drago as the man of the hour, the man who could advise the Congress and the president of a solution to the dilemma posed by Wall Street renegade Laurence Kingsley Goldwill.

Radio commentators took up the refrain. The Empire Maker of Europe, they agreed, would point the way out of the mess, if any one could.

For his part, saturnine H. Startland Drago declined all interview offers. This only fueled the raging fires of expectation.

So when the hour for him to address Congress came, anticipation was at a fever pitch.

H. Startland Drago arrived at the Capitol Building in a bulletproof limousine, the windows curtained. The machine had been donated for the occasion by no less than the President of the United States. It was his official vehicle.

The car arrived before the Capitol steps behind another machine, this one inhabited by three of Doc Savage's men—Renny, Long Tom, and Johnny. The appearance in public by three of Doc's associates would normally have created a sensation. But they were all but ignored when the presidential machine purred to a stop and the driver got out.

The door was opened for H. Startland Drago and he ascended the steps. He wore dark glasses for the occasion. It was not the sort of thing a financial genius would normally wear, but the reason for this soon became apparent.

Flashbulbs popped and flared in his cadaverous face every step to the Capitol entrance. And there were many of those.

"Holy cow!" Renny grunted when they got Drago through the press gantlet and into the impressive Great Rotunda. "Somebody hand me a cane and tin cup!"

"A visionary Erebus!" Johnny clipped, blinking furiously.

Thunderous applause greeted the arrival of H. Startland Drago in the House chamber. The speaker of the House gaveled for silence. He gaveled a long time. Finally, H. Startland Drago lifted a long-fingered hand and silence fell until breathing sounds could be heard plainly.

H. Startland Drago stood at the podium a long moment before speaking. He had removed his dark glasses. His intensely black eyes, like drill points, seemed to pierce each member of Congress as they swept along the aisles.

"None of you here know me personally," began H. Startland Drago, his voice repeated by loud-speakers stationed throughout the gallery. "But you all know my reputation.

"Yesterday, the President of the United States made a fine speech. He spoke of the importance of a government honoring its financial obligations. He spoke of the flotation of the Liberty Bond as a loan from the people to its government. He made his points very clearly, so that all understood his meaning: The United States would never renege on its lawful obligations."

A pause came. Brows were wiped. It was a nervous moment.

"But he left out one significant item," Drago went on in his cold, even voice. "That the good people of the United States are not the only purchasers of U.S. bonds. In fact, they are not even the majority purchasers of these instruments. Foreign governments are."

He paused again. Heads inclined forward. Bodies leaned toward him, as if to catch his every word. And the Empire Maker resumed his discourse.

"Through my bond house, Drago & Company, I sell Liberty Bonds. They are considered the finest such bonds issued in the world. The financial instability created by the discovery that many of these bonds are false is grave. To call these bonds will not erase or undo the damage already done. In foreign capitals, the credit of the United States is now regarded as unsound. Thus, I must undertake the extraordinary step of offering to exchange any Liberty Bonds Drago & Company have sold abroad for equivalent instruments. No questions asked."

A gasp, large and singular, floated over the vast chamber.

"I have done this for two reasons," H. Startland Drago continued gravely. "First, because the reputation of Drago & Company is precious to me. More precious even than its solvency—for an offer such as I have just made could very well bankrupt the firm. And the second reason is that knowing the criminal mind behind this, I believe that this reasonable body will soon have no choice but to capitulate to his mad demands and declare the Liberty Issue of 1927 void and worthless."

A gasp came.

"Indeed, that is my recommendation to you to-day."

That final sentence, the climax of the speech, went virtually unheard. Pandemonium had already seized the halls of Congress.

Law makers jumped from their chairs. They turned to one another in consternation. The speaker of the House rushed to call the President of the United States. Reporters rushed to call rewrite men.

In the chaos following H. Startland Drago's dramatic statement, the Empire Maker was all but forgotten.

Renny, Long Tom,, and Johnny rushed him out a side door and to his waiting limousine. They were nearly trampled in the ensuing panic.

"It is best that I return to New York at once," Drago said, tight-voiced. "I must prepare my staff for to-morrow's workday. I only pray that Drago & Company will survive this terrible time."

"Holy cow!" Renny gulped. "Do you know what you just did!?"

H. Startland Drago said firmly, "I know Laurence Kingsley Goldwill as well as any one. He will stop at nothing. Congress has no choice!"

"Not anymore," Long Tom said sourly.

"Our plane is waiting," Renny added.

The limousine got rolling. Renny's machine fell in behind it.

In the back seats, Johnny and Long Tom were grimly silent.

"A conundrum of labyrinthine unintelligibility," Johnny muttered thickly.

"I'll second that," Renny muttered.

"This is bad," Long Tom said. "This is damn bad."

"The Congress won't vote to void the issue," Renny said firmly.

No one seconded that. They knew the mood in Congress. It was uncertain. Anything was possible.

The trip to the airport was of short duration and tortuous. They stayed close behind the limousine carrying H. Startland Drago every foot of the way, until it stopped before the hangar which housed their speed plane.

The chauffeur—it was Drago's personal butler, bow-legged Seymour Holman—stepped out and went to open the door for his master.

He was still holding it open, knobby knees knocking together, when Renny and the others trotted up.

"What's the hold-up?" Long Tom demanded.

Holman's natural color was sagebrush. Now, he blanched. His eyes were dazed, his face slack. He tried pointing into the machine, but his stabbing finger shook too much.

No stir came from the curtained rear of the limousine, so they peered within. And their hair stood on end.

The hair erection did not occur immediately. It came some moments later, when the true significance of what they were seeing—or not seeing—dawned on the trio.

"Holy cow!" Renny thundered. Later, the others agreed it was the most explosive such ejaculation the big-fisted engineer had ever authored. For their own part, Long Tom and Johnny were struck dumb.

For the limousine—the limousine that they had followed closely all during the trip to the airport—had somehow lost its passenger.

Of H. Startland Drago, there was no sign. Renny spanked a big hand on the seat cushions. They were still warm.

"Holy cow!" he repeated. This time, the words sounded very small.

They accosted the chauffeur, whose wobbly legs seemed ready to collapse.

"You didn't see nothing!" Renny demanded ungrammatically.

"No!"

"And you didn't hear anything?" Long Tom prodded.

"Hear?"

"A manifestation of a sorrowful minuet," Johnny interposed.

Seymour Holman looked dubious.

Renny asked, "Hear a goshawful sad whistling?"

Seymour Holman got some clarity into his eyes. He cocked his head to one side. "Yeah, I did," he said slowly. "Back at that last stop sign. It made me feel like busting down crying, it was so sorry-sounding."

The Drago butler then attempted to duplicate the sound he had claimed to hear in a noticeably off-key tremolo.

The three Doc Savage men felt as if something with tiny ice feet were walking down their spines. They had heard that doleful melody once before. In a dark Virginia forest. And they had seen with their own eyes the uncanny untouchable apparition which had been its author.

"And you didn't stop?" Long Tom asked in exasperation.

"Why would I stop?" Holman returned defensively. "I thought it was coming from the truck behind me."

They all remembered the truck then. It had pulled up behind the limousine at the stop sign. None of them had thought anything of it and still weren't certain that they should. It had been an ordinary truck.

They backtracked to the intersection, taking trembling Seymour Holman with them.

They made a search of the intersection. And discovered nothing out of the ordinary.

A call to the concern that owned the truck—it was a moving concern—produced the information that a truck fitting the description they gave had been indeed trundling through the area, filled with the household belongings of a family relocating to Baltimore.

It had no connection with the inexplicable disappearance of H. Startland Drago.

"This sound," Long Tom queried Holman, "could it have come from in back of your machine?"

Holman made thinking faces. He rubbed his sharp nose.

"Now that you bring it up," he said, "it could have, sure. But the partition was closed tight, so it would have had to be pretty loud to get through."

"There's gotta be a sensible solution to this," Long Tom said fiercely. So they returned to the airport hangar and searched the limousine. They took pains with it because it belonged to the president, but by the time they were done, it was clear that there was no trace of the missing international investment banker in the car, nor was there evidence of any machine or thing which could have authored the whistling dirge.

Renny gave the tonneau roof a frustrated pound. "Damn! Just like King Goz."

"That ain't the king I'm thinking of," Long Tom grumbled. "Remember Old King Fausto? Sounds like his spook is loose again."

Dejectedly, they repaired to the waiting speed plane and its short-wave transmitter to break the news to Doc Savage.

After Renny's mournful recital, Doc Savage's melodious trilling permeated the cabin interior. The tonal reproduction was so true it gave the three chastened aids a creepy feeling, as if the bronze man were present in the cabin, somehow invisible and all-seeing.

After it had trailed off, Renny muttered, "Doc, do you—do you suppose you should check the safe?"

The safe was checked. Doc's voice came again.

"The safe," he said, "is empty of cadavers."

They all breathed a long sigh of relief over that. But none of them could explain what had happened—any of it.

Then they remembered the other matter.

Renny said, "Doc! Did you hear? Drago told Congress they should void that bond issue!"

"It just came in over the teletype," Doc said.

"What does it mean?"

Doc Savage's voice was grim. "It means," he said, "that great mistakes have been made in the investigation of this affair. And I have only myself to blame."

The three aids were speechless. Over a long association, going back to the halcyon days when they had first met in the Great War, they had come to see their bronze chief as infallible. It was not the case, and in their hearts they understood this. Still, the admission was a rare one.

Renny asked, "What do you want us to do, Doc?"

"Return to headquarters. We will need every man for the task before us."

"Pat, too?"

"Why do you ask?"

"Because when I went to collect Long Tom and Johnny at Drago's place, she breezed in and hornswoggled us into letting her guard that Joan Manville while we're down here."

"Pat is back in this?"

"We kinda made her a promise earlier, and she twisted our arms," Renny admitted gloomily.

The big-fisted engineer might have expected a rebuke from the bronze man, but he did not receive one. Instead, Doc said, "Bring Holman with you," and cut the microphone out of circuit.

But when they stepped out of the hangar to collect the bowlegged butler, he, too, had vanished!


# XIX

# VOID!


The disappearance of H. Startland Drago did not make the afternoon editions. It was not even reported. If it had been, it might have made page 3—page 2 at best. Things were happening.

The first extra to hit the streets proclaimed, "DRAGO RECOMMENDS VOIDING LIBERTY ISSUE!"

The story was dropped to the lower front page of the next edition, which read on top, "PRESIDENT ESCAPES ASSASSINATION!"

Then: "CONGRESS VOTES IN EMERGENCY SESSION!"

By this time, the headlines were in blood-red ink. Newsboys cried themselves hoarse, trying to keep up. Papers were snapped up by pedestrians, only to be tossed aside, partially read, as new editions hit the streets.

People gave up buying newspapers and huddled

around their radios. The wire services were getting the latest bulletins out much faster, anyway.

The sequence of events ran like this: News of the Drago recommendation that Congress void the tainted Liberty Issue hit Wall Street like a ton of TNT. Stocks would surely have plunged, except that it was Sunday and the market was not open. That did not mean the financial titans of the Street were not hard at work, preparing for the Monday morning opening bell. There was panic in the air—panic on a scale never before witnessed. Something had to be done.

The President of the United States happened to be cruising the Potomac River in his yacht. It was no pleasure cruise. His famous brain trust was with him. They faced a momentous decision and they wished to argue and shout and argue some more the pros and cons of the matter without fear of being overheard.

A bullet from a high-powered rifle whistled in the direction of the presidential yacht. It split the skull of a Secret Service guard who happened to move in front of the chief executive at an unfortunate moment. Unfortunate for the Secret Service man, that is: The move undoubtedly and unwittingly preserved the president's life.

Churning water, the yacht hastily betook itself away. A search was made of the segment of river bank from which the shot had come.

They found nothing. No footprints, no other sign, no empty shell casing.

The papers laid the blame for this heinous crime on the financial sharper, Laurence Kingsley Goldwill.

It was in that atmosphere that Congress convened to vote on a hastily written bill calling for the voiding of the Liberty Issue of 1927.

The session—a rare joint emergency one held in the commodious House chamber—was hectic, contentious, and rambunctious; in short, it was not different from many such past sessions. Except that more than pork and politics were at stake. The members of Congress knew that the perpetrator of this audacious scheme—possibly the most fantastic extortion plot of all time—had made one attempt on the president's life. Had, in fact, successfully assassinated one of their most powerful colleagues.

None of them felt safe. And any of them could be next.

Much has been said about the moral backbone—or absence thereof—of Congress as a legislative body. Some of it undoubtedly is truth.

Arguments were propounded on both sides. The speechifying was furious. There were threats to filibuster. Invitations to step into corridors for old-fashioned fisticuffs. None came to pass.

At many points during the loud debate, the name of H. Startland Drago, all but unknown less than twenty-four hours ago, was invoked in thunderous tones.

A speech from the president—an earnest plea for reason and a recess—was read into the record, and then ignored.

What the Congress of the United States might have voted under less fearsome circumstances, no one would ever know.

What they did vote, 289 to 42, with numerous abstentions, was to declare null and void, now and forever, the Liberty Bond Issue of 1927.

"The yeas have it," the speaker of the House choked out, gaveling the feverish session to a close. "The bill is passed." Then he sat down in his speaker's chair and trembled uncontrollably for the better part of fifteen minutes.

It was done. No one gave a thought to the consequences of their vote, or how to deal with the next promised escalation of the mad scheme of Laurence Kingsley Goldwill.

The only hope of a reprieve for millions of citizens and institutional investors was that the president would veto the legislation when it reached his desk.

No one knew what the president would do. Or what would be the reaction of Wall Street when it opened the next day.

The nation held its breath.

When Renny, Johnny, and Long Tom arrived at Doc Savage's 86th-floor New York headquarters, the bronze man was in the laboratory, working on a piece of equipment that was familiar to them all.

It was Doc's locator device, which had failed to find the elusive Elvern D. Kastellantz anywhere in the District of Columbia three days before.

Without looking up from his toil, Doc made an announcement that was startling despite his low tone of voice.

"I have been in touch with the District of Columbia coroner," he said. "The sword employed to assassinate Senator John Thomas MacPartney has vanished from a locked safe."

Immediately, they began looking over their shoulders, as if expecting a visitation from the soul of death.

Doc resumed speaking.

"From the beginning of this affair—and the beginning would seem to have been the disappearance of King Goz of Merida—one thread has been running through all the trouble."

Johnny offered, "Laurence Kingsley Goldwill?"

Doc shook his head. "Elvern D. Kastellantz."

Monk piped up. "You sayin' that Kastellantz is back of this mess?"

"Not quite. But he *is* the key."

The five aids exchanged blank looks.

Ham opened his mobile mouth to put forth a question when a buzzer announced some one at the reception room door.

"If that's that Push 'em Down," Monk growled, "I'm in no mood for him and his court orders. The guy's worse than a pack of lawyers."

But it was not the gruff police inspector.

Monk came back with Pat Savage and presentable Joan Manville in tow.

"Miss me, any one?" she asked cheerfully.

When no one answered, Pat snapped open a newspaper she had brought along. "The latest edition," she said, slapping the paper on the workbench for all to read. "Have a look, gentlemen."

The scareheads were stark:

**PRESIDENT TO DECIDE TONIGHT!**
**WALL STREET SLEEPLESS!**

Doc ignored the paper set beside his locator and turned his golden eyes on Joan Manville.

"I asked my cousin to bring you here so that you may answer some questions," he stated.

"I am afraid I can tell you nothing of my uncle's disappearance," said Joan Manville in a contained voice. "Really, it is as much a mystery to me as it is to you. I only know that Uncle Startland showed both great bravery and generosity in offering to replace any Liberty Bonds his house sold. For such a move is certain to plunge Drago & Company into bankruptcy."

Doc cut the woman off with a single no-nonsense statement. "You may begin by telling us your true name."

"Hah!" Pat crowed. "I knew it!"

A queer look came over Joan Manville's features. She hesitated. "I—I do not know what you mean," she stammered.

"I have made inquiries into the background of H. Startland Drago," the bronze man told her. "He has no known relatives. Therefore, you cannot be his niece."

Joan Manville might have been an accomplished stage actress for all the outward reaction she evinced after the bronze man's flat assertion. She did not deny it, however.

"Holy cow!" Renny rumbled. "Don't tell me she's really Barbara Bland after all!"

"There is no such person," Doc said. "Any more than there is a Joan Manville."

Doc's arresting golden eyes bored into the woman's own for a long moment. They seemed to whirl faster, as if the fine gold flakes suspended within were coming to a boil.

She turned her head abruptly.

"I will not be hypnotized," she said jerkily.

"Want me to get the truth serum?" Monk asked. "The latest batch is guaranteed to make a monkey sing 'The Star-Spangled Banner.' I should know. I mixed it myself."

"You should know," Ham inserted archly, "being an authority on monkeys."

"That might be a good idea," Doc told Monk quietly.

Monk Mayfair was destined never to get the truth serum.

Suddenly, in the room, all around them, the air was suffused with a low, mournful melody.

They all heard it, faint as it was.

They were looking about the room. Supermachine pistols came out. Pat hoisted her six-shooter from her hand bag and pointed it in the direction of Joan Manville, saying, "I have six western settlers in here—that's shells to you—and if there's going to be a shooting bee, count on collecting your rightful share."

"Holy cow, Pat!" Renny rumbled, looking around warily. "You wouldn't shoot a female, would you?"

Pat cocked her weapon. "You can never tell about a woman," she said tightly.

The depressing whistling grew louder. A new sound came then. Musical, but without tune. Rising, inspiring, it was the awesome sound of Doc Savage!

The two strains merged and blended as if fighting for supremacy. Both seemed to come from everywhere and nowhere at once. It was eerie, uncanny, fantastic, the way the vast white-walled room filled with voiceless song.

Then—the Whistling Wraith entered the room!

He came through the door. It was closed. Shut tight. But the white-bearded entity passed through it as if composed of some hard-looking substance that defied natural law.

The bejeweled scepter of gold emerged first. It extended itself, seeming to pull a disembodied arm with it. Then the golden orb broke the door's undisturbed surface. Finally, the dried, bearded face and body broke through.

Before the door, the apparition paused. Its robes were scarlet, as was its ermine-rimmed cloak. The golden crown on its head was preposterous with gems, and the weight of it seemed to make the regal head supporting it sway ungently.

Its mouth was a dried knot of a hole surrounded by snowy hair, and from it was coming the whistling that made them think of a funeral procession.

"Old King Fausto!" Monk howled.

"I hope," Pat said, "everybody has a good look at the old geezer now!"

Ham, the most quick-witted of the group, unsheathed his sword cane and, striking a fencer's pose, lunged forward in an attempt to run the taunting apparition through. The tip of his blade was coated with a sticky anæsthetic chemical designed to drop opponents in their tracks.

The tip of the blade pierced the scarlet silk of the Whistling Wraith's robes. Quickly, Ham withdrew it and stepped aside to let the figure fall.

The Wraith merely stood there whistling. Its dark eyes held a merry light in contrast to its sad dirge of a song.

The dapper lawyer became very round of eye.

Then, Monk opened up with his superfirer.

The others quickly joined in, Pat fanning the spur of her six-shooter with grim-faced rapidity.

The racket split the air all around them. Joan Manville clapped hands over her ears and squeezed her gray eyes shut.

The wall behind the apparition quickly became moist with the colorless chemical as the hollow shells broke open, and an incredible quantity of brass littered the tiled floor.

Soon, the amazing weapons ran empty; they consumed ammunition in amazing gulps.

Renny and the others fished spare drums from their clothing.

Roaring, Monk threw his at the apparition. When it passed harmlessly through the long Father Christmas beard, the hairy chemist beat his chest like a bull ape as if to frighten the taunting figure in scarlet.

Doc Savage, golden eyes absorbing every moment of the tableau, moved then. His trilling had not ceased, nor did it now. But there was a quality of excitement and vibrance that was new to the sound. The changed quality of the piping melody gave the others in the room a shock as from an electric wire.

He flashed across the room, got in front of Monk, and drove a metallic fist in the direction of the Whistling Wraith.

The fist passed harmlessly through. No expression crossed the bronze man's features. Circling his opponent, Doc used his hands. Bronze fingers dipped into seemingly solid scarlet silk that might have been some fantastic intangible form of water. The tips disappeared from sight, seemingly sliced off.

When he withdrew them, they were whole again.

Joan Manville screamed out, "Don't touch it! You can't hurt it!"

Doc, his strained trillation still permeating the air, used both hands to make shooing motions. He might have been trying to dissipate a dense scarlet fog become human form.

Nothing happened—except that the whistling swelled, overwhelming Doc's eerie strains.

Off to one side, Monk was jumping up and down and howling, "Let me at 'im! Let me at 'im!" Plainly, the apish chemist wanted something to punch, and the bronze man was proving there was nothing substantial to attack.

The Whistling Wraith then manipulated its scepter. It seemed only to raise it, tilting it this way and that, as if the bedizened rod were some heavy conjuror's wand.

No visible result seemed to be accomplished by this cabalistic gesture.

Then Doc Savage plunged a bronze hand into the chest and could not remove it again.

His trilling stopped. Abruptly, as if frightened into silence. Such a phenomenon had never before happened—and it made those who knew the bronze man run cold in the blood.

Mighty muscles bunching along his back, Doc Savage attempted to extract his hand.

It might have been encased in ice formed of congealed human blood. Perspiration popped out on his high metallic brow. His flake-gold eyes whirled with agitation.

Muscular exercises adhered to faithfully over a period of years had given the bronze man strength which often struck strangers as being superhuman. The thing which held his hand seemed to have clutched no more than fingers. Doc probably could have wrenched, and with his own strength alone, torn the fingers off. That, of course, would have been foolish, unless essential to save his life. And the thing he had contacted did not seem to be striking any blows. It just held him. And awful agony came from his captured hand.

Then the Whistling Wraith lifted its scepter and, as the others watched helpless, touched the bronze man's shoulder.

Doc Savage jerked as if from contact with a high-voltage line. Barely three seconds of time elapsed, but it seemed an eternity. The bronze man was helpless.

Monk Mayfair charged, howling.

Then, the Whistling Wraith lifted the scepter and Doc Savage collapsed to the floor. Only the feeble twitching of his fingers told that he had managed to hold on to consciousness—and life.

"I told you not to touch it!" Joan Manville screamed. "It is the ghost of Old King Fausto! H. Startland Drago told me all about it! He believes it to be a soul encased in an indestructible body, because its purpose seems to be punishing the evil!"

The Whistling Wraith moved past the prostrate form of Doc Savage, its black boots actually passing through it as if it were a mirage.

Monk, coming on, tried to gather up the phantasm in his great hairy arms. His headlong charge proved to be his undoing. He passed through it and landed on his barrel chest. Breath exploded out of him with a gusty, "*Whoof!*"

The others, more chary, kept their distance.

Renny went to assist Doc Savage, but the bronze man was already coming to his feet, metallic features strange.

The Whistling Wraith took up a position in the center of the room. It made more queer gestures with its scepter. It might have been a wizard of old weaving a spell of black magic.

It suddenly tucked the scepter under one arm and transferred the weighty orb to the other. With its free hand, it took hold of the ornate adornment atop the orb, which was remindful of a dungeon key's filigreed handle.

It began twisting this, as if winding a clock.

Faint noise of a mainspring and gearing came to their ears.

"What's he doing?" Long Tom wondered.

The answer came when the Whistling Wraith calmly placed the heavy object at its booted feet and stepped back.

All eyes went to the golden object.

Then the keylike handle began to twirl in the reverse direction it had been wound.

From under the golden orb rose tendrils of scarlet smoke. Then eddies. Billows. And with a mushy *whoom!*, a great cloud of the blood-colored stuff filled the immediate area. It smelled of garlic and toadstools, of all things.

They were soon in a blinding world of crimson that smarted their eyes.

"Holy cow!"

"A lachrymator!" Johnny complained.

"Some infernal exhalation!" Ham howled, swatting at the vile concoction with his unsheathed cane.

They all carried compact gas masks, consisting of goggles, nose clips, and mouth filters. These came out of pockets in time to save their vision. But seeing through the dense cloud was another matter. Soon, they were bumping into one another and cursing. Ham employed his cane to trip a moving figure and Long Tom, in response, kicked out at his shin.

They might, in their floundering about, have passed through the ethereal entity that was the Whistling Wraith, so-called.

They never knew.

Moments later, a steady humming filled the room and the great ceiling vent began ingesting the scarlet swirls.

As the room cleared, they began to see objects again. They removed their masks, coughed their vapor-stung lungs clear.

The first thing they saw was that Joan Manville was no longer present.

Doc pitched for the library, raced to the reception room before the others could get organized. He flung himself out into the corridor and around the corner to his speed elevator.

It was already engaged. The whine of its descent was not loud.

Three other elevators also serviced this floor. Doc pitched toward those. He was in luck. One came almost at once.

"Down!" Doc ordered the operator.

The boy obeyed. With a whine like an unhappy pup's, the cage dropped.

Out in the lobby, Doc encountered confusion. Faces reflected disbelief. People stood about, faces white.

"It wasn't human!" a man kept mumbling.

The cigar stand operator told it succinctly enough.

"Guy like a fairy-tale king went through the door—and brother, I mean *through*!"

"Girl with him?"

"Yeah. She didn't look happy about it, either. She was as much a ghost as the other one."

Doc was out in the street a moment later.

He followed a clear trail of amazed and shocked-white faces around a corner where a knot of passers-by were pointing into an alleyway.

As Doc approached, one of the knot—a woman—simply fainted where she stood. He put on speed, whipped into the alley.

Each day since he was a youth, Doc Savage had performed a regimen of exercises responsible for his greater-than-normal physical development. It was the secret of his unbelievable prowess. No discipline was excluded, but strength, muscular coordination, speed, and reflexes were emphasized overall.

The bronze man showed what he was capable of then.

He plunged into the alley. His flake-gold eyes picked out a fragment of black leather against the brick of the alley wall. It was the back of a booted heel. And it was melting into the solid brick!

Doc lunged for the weirdly disembodied heel, realized the folly of trying to arrest it, shifted abruptly, and drove his hard metallic body against a steel door.

The door lost a hinge pin, caved, and Doc went through into darkness.

His flash came up, roved like a finger of fire.

It speared two silent figures! The Whistling Wraith and Joan Manville. The girl turned, blinked eyes in Doc's direction.

The Wraith had been holding the girl by one hand. It tugged.

The bronze man did not directly answer. "Your radioactive token, please," he said. "Yours too, Monk."

Ham extracted his from the watch pocket of his vest. Monk's was produced from a pants pocket. They were standing before the bronze-colored reception room door.

Then the bronze man brought the coinlike disks up to the panel. It opened and they stepped through. They noticed that Doc's movements lacked his usual sure grace.

"You O.K., Doc?" Monk asked plaintively.

The bronze man did not reply. But he absently felt of the spot on his shoulder where the incredible Whistling Wraith's scepter had touched. The spot ached. And the skin was puffing up in strange little white mounds.

The others, seeing this strangeness, licked suddenly dry lips and felt their skin bunch and creep unpleasantly.

Doc Savage began speaking.

"To understand the uncanny phenomenon we have witnessed," he said thoughtfully, "it is important to review a proven but difficult-to-comprehend fact of physics. Namely, that solid matter, as we understand it, is not truly solid."

"Sure, everybody knows that," Monk said.

Ham looked puzzled. "Are you referring to the atomic nature of—"

The warning chime sounded, and Monk flung himself to the inlaid table, engaging the telephoto device that reflected the corridor approach. The apish chemist's tiny eyes bugged out.

"Old Push 'em Down again!" he squawled.

Moving with eye-defying speed, Doc Savage attacked the big safe. His features were dark with exertion as he tapped out the combination. The door jumped open in one metallic hand as if made of balsa.

There was a body lying on the floor of the safe, lying on a swath of oilskin. A tarpaulin. Waterproof.

Because of the way the body lay, and the obstruction of the sword hilt protruding from the dead man's yawning mouth, his face was obscured from view.

"Who in blazes is that!" Monk roared angrily.

"No time," Doc rapped, gathering up the tarpaulin so that pooled blood would not drip onto the floor. Obviously the bronze man had foreseen such an eventuality as this, incredible as it was.

Ham pushed the safe shut.

The doorbell buzzed insistently.

"Stall, Monk," Doc clipped, heading for the library.

"Hold your dang horses," Monk called to the door. "I'm talkin' on the telephone!"

The buzzing began sounding like a bumblebee trapped in a box.

By that time, Doc Savage had carried his burden through the library and into the laboratory, where he moved directly to one wall of the room. He carefully altered the positions of glasses on a certain shelf. The glasses were of varied weights. And, although there was nothing outwardly suspicious about the shelf, it held a combination mechanism, which the weighted glasses operated if placed properly.

A section of apparently solid wall opened. Doc Savage stepped through with the one he carried. His movements were rapid.

Before him was a heavy metal pipe, some feet in diameter. It ran downward chimney fashion through the masonry of the great building. An open hatch in its side admitted to the upholstered interior of a car, which had a shape reminiscent of a big, double-ended bullet.

Doc Savage got in with his burden, closed the hatches, grasped a lever not unlike the control on an ordinary elevator, and moved it.

A terrific windstorm seemed to spring up outside. Close observance would have shown that Doc Savage's feet completely left the floor for a time. The bullet car was descending with tremendous speed. A moment later it changed its course rapidly. In expectation of this, Doc Savage had braced himself against large cushions, which were plainly there for that specific purpose.

The scream of the bullet's progress increased. An engineer listening could have told that compressed air played an important part in the propulsion of the thing.

This conveyance was a comparatively recent addition to Doc Savage's menage of mechanical devices. It had been constructed—the secrecy of this installation had added no little to the tremendous expense—as a means of passing between Doc Savage's skyscraper headquarters and his combination aircraft hangar and boathouse on the Hudson River.

The bullet car began to slow, braking devices whizzing. It stopped. Doc Savage flung the hatch open and climbed out with his burden.

Doc bore the oilskin-enwrapped victim to a device rather like a large steel tank studded with valves and gauges.

It was a so-called "iron doctor," a device used by deep-sea divers to decompress after exposure to the often-crushing pressures of their work and to prevent fatal air bubbles from forming in the blood. It would hardly do the impaled man much good, but it was the perfect place in which to store an inconvenient body.

Opening a hatch at one end, Doc deposited the body inside. Without stopping to examine the man's features, he sealed the thing. Inasmuch as the vaultlike hangar was generally unknown, it was unlikely that the corpse would be discovered.

Doc went to a wall panel, opened it, and snapped a switch. Instantly, a violent exchange was reproduced by a nearby loud-speaker.

"And I'm tellin' you," Monk was bellowing, "Doc ain't here! You looked around. Ain't the evidence of your own eyes good enough?"

A froglike voice slammed back, "I have a dozen witnesses who swear Savage was seen coming into this building. He ain't come out. That means he's here. And I have a court order to open that box."

"So open it," Monk said casually. "See if I care."

"I will. After I find where that bad smell is coming from."

Doc snapped off the device, an ingenious intercommunications system. Monk, knowing that his bronze chief could only have been headed for the secret pneumatic escape tube, had obviously thumbed a table inlay, cutting in a concealed pickup microphone installed in the reception room.

A number of vehicles were kept garaged in the warehouse setup. Doc selected a coupe and drove to his skyscraper headquarters in short order.

He strode into the big laboratory as Saul "Push 'em Down" Sampson was complaining, "Don't tell me I don't smell a body here, because I do! I've been in this game long enough to recognize corpse stink when it tickles my nostrils!"

"Perhaps," Doc's calm voice interposed, "I might be of assistance."

Saul Sampson turned, a human pile of building blocks.

"Where'd you come from?" he exploded.

"I just arrived."

Sampson's square face turned the hue of a freshly baked brick. "There a back way out of here I should know about?"

Doc ignored the query. "Something was said about an odor."

"Got a call we could find a body," Sampson bellowed. "A very *interesting* body."

Doc went to a refrigeration case and extracted a box.

"Perhaps this might explain the smell," he said, offering it.

Push 'em Down Sampson yanked off the lid and peered within. His square face contorted.

"Ugh! Fish!"

"Salmon," Doc elaborated. "Caught by my cousin and expressed as a present. The shipping label is on the side of the box. There will be a record at the express office, if you care to check."

"I think," Sampson said sourly, returning the odoriferous box, "you waited too long. They don't look good to eat."

"We have been preoccupied with other matters," said Doc, returning the box to the refrigeration case.

"I'll bet."

Doc asked, "Would you like to examine my safe? I understand you have a court order."

Sampson slapped a folded length of paper against the bronze man's chest. "Yeah. One that will stick, too. It's proof against fancy-pants lawyers."

Ham opened his mouth to speak, but Doc quieted him with a gesture.

They went to the reception room. The safe door lay open. Doc had opened it on the way in.

Saul Sampson took one look at the open depository and said in a suspicious voice, "I thought you said it couldn't be opened."

"I explained that it had not been opened in some time," Doc related, truthfully enough. "That problem has since been remedied."

Saul Sampson looked into the great safe. He had a flashlight and used it liberally to examine such shelves and drawers as he found.

"Smells funny in here," he muttered.

"My good man, what do you expect?" Ham drawled. "It is a very old safe."

"It don't smell old. It smells like a dead wagon."

"Try sneezing," Monk suggested.

"Huh?"

"Might blow the fish stink out of your long nose."

"Bah!" snorted Push 'em Down, stepping out. He stamped over to the bronze man and began waving his court order under his nose.

"Don't think I don't know about the way your boys barged in and took that Drago fellow down to Washington, practically out from under the noses of my men," he grated.

"H. Startland Drago preferred it that way," Doc stated.

"And then he up and makes a speech that practically turns Washington on its ear."

"What are you trying to imply?" Ham put in.

"I smell something fishy, and it ain't fish. You get me, Savage? You're up to no good. I got a nose for such things."

"Haw!" Monk snorted loudly. "Go peddle your papers, copper."

"And another thing," Sampson blustered. "Didn't you go down to Washington to look into that business of the king who vanished into thin air?"

"I did," Doc admitted.

Saul Sampson thrust big hands into pockets too small for them. He rocked back on his heels. "Find him?"

"Not as yet."

Sampson made a face. "Funny."

"What do you mean?" the bronze man said.

"They say you have a lot on the ball, Savage. Usually get what you're after, don't you?"

When Doc declined to fill the silence that followed, Sampson offered, "I read where the only clue they had to that king disappearing was a funny kind of whistle. Ain't that a trademark of yours? A funny whistle? Makes an old harness bull like me stop and wonder."

"Idle suspicions!" Ham inserted hotly. "You have no grounds to charge Doc, and you know it!"

Saul Sampson only glowered at the bronze man.

Doc said, "If you have no intentions of formally charging me or my assistants, we have matters to attend to."

"You birds ain't heard the last of me!" Sampson vowed, abruptly turning on his heel and storming from the room. The door closed after him.

"That guy keeps it up," Monk said grimly, "we're going to be in Dutch one of these days."

Ham said, "As much as I detest agreeing with this lop-eared miscreant, Monk is correct. It is only a matter of time before this infernal Whistling Wraith succeeds in framing us. What can we do?"

"First," Doc Savage said purposefully, "we must locate Elvern D. Kastellantz."

# XXI

## SKY SEARCH

Minutes later, Doc, Monk, and Ham were in their laboratory, crating the big locator for transport to the Hidalgo warehouse, where it would be restored to its swivel mounting.

"Hey!" Monk said suddenly. "I just thought of somethin'."

"Even an ostrich egg will hatch if one waits long enough," Ham said without much sharpness. It was clear that his encounter with the Whistling Wraith had knocked the wind out of his shirty sails.

Doc said, "Yes?"

"That fancy orb of a thing—where is it?"

"You *did* have a thought," Ham said, as if the very notion astonished him. They craned necks, hunting with their eyes.

Monk spied the orb first and went to it. Bending down, he lifted it up to his homely face. His unlovely features mirrored ludicrously monkeylike curiosity as he turned the heavy sphere about in his hands. On impulse, he gave the keylike ornament a hard bite.

"*Yeow!*" Monk howled, nearly dropping the object.

"What is it?" Ham demanded.

"I dunno," Monk muttered, "but it ain't gold. It don't take teeth marks."

Then the sphere separated in his hairy hands. Inside, was revealed a kind of generator mechanism designed to expel gas.

Monk sniffed. "This smells awful familiar," he said, wincing.

Doc said, "Johnny called it a lachrymator."

The hairy chemist looked up. "Tear gas!" he exploded. "That red stuff was tear gas mixed in with other things to make it smell spooky." He frowned like a monkey who had peeled a banana only to find a carrot. "Whoever heard of a spook that used tear gas?"

A light of understanding came into dapper Ham's dark eyes.

"Perhaps," he said slowly, "the gaudy entity is not a spirit after all."

"You saw it do what it did," Monk snapped. "If it ain't a ghost, what is it then?"

Their eyes went to Doc Savage, who had finished packing excelsior around the crated locator device.

"We will drive this to our Hudson River place," Doc said grimly.

"We'd better shake a leg, too," Monk muttered. "No tellin' when that spook might turn up again."

"It is not a spook," Ham insisted firmly.

"Says you."

They took the speed elevator to the sub-basement garage, where Doc maintained a small fleet of automobiles. They placed the locator in the back of a delivery truck they used because of its unobtrusive ability to blend in with ordinary traffic. The pneumatic tube to the Hidalgo Trading Company would have been too strenuous for the locator to survive intact.

The ride was short, and soon they had the device in place.

"Think it will work O.K.?" Monk asked when they were done. "I mean, did you finish workin' on it all right?"

"It will have to be tested. You have your superfirers?"

"Sure as tootin'," Monk said, enthusiastically producing his.

His broad, ear-threatening grin collapsed when Doc wordlessly collected his weapon and a second from Ham and placed them in a lead box, along with the two radioactive tokens earlier confiscated, and his own.

"So they do not confuse the locator," Doc explained.

Monk snapped furry fingers.

"Hey! In all the excitement, I keep forgettin' to ask—Who is this second guy the spook left in our safe?"

"Simpleton!" Ham snapped. "The answer to that is obvious: H. Startland Drago."

"Why him?"

"The Wraith kidnaped him, did he not?"

"Maybe," the hairy chemist allowed. "But the same thing happened to King Goz, and *he* didn't end up in our safe, did he?"

Doc interrupted. "The body is in the iron doctor. You might take a look."

Monk and Ham piled out of the plane and threw open the hatch on the steel tank.

Together, they peered into the iron doctor, and were astonished to discover *two* bodies inside the dark chamber.

"Is that Prestowitz I see?" Ham asked.

Doc's voice carried from the plane. "It was more logical to store him here until we have matters under control," he said.

"Good thinkin'," Monk muttered, pinching his nose. "He smells worse than the dang fish."

The apish chemist reached a long arm in and took hold of the second corpse's hair, unceremoniously dragging it into the light.

Monk and Ham saw a rather florid face that seemed familiar to them.

Ham frowned. "That is not Drago."

Monk scratched his bristled hair. "Danged if I place this guy, Doc? Who is he?"

The hairy chemist probably did not expect Doc to answer. Late events had been too headlong to allow for much investigation. But the bronze man surprised them.

"That," Doc said, "is Laurence Kingsley Goldwill."

Monk's gimlet eyes all but bugged out of his head.

"But he's the guy back of this bond extortion!" he howled.

Doc imparted, "At no time has Laurence Kingsley Goldwill been the brains behind this incredible affair."

Ham jointed and unjointed his cane. "Then who is?" he demanded. The bronze man seemed not to hear. He finished making connections and snapped on a switch. Visible tubes in inspection ports along the locator device warmed up.

"We need to move swiftly," Doc rapped. "We may have much ground to cover."

Monk and Ham clambered aboard.

Moments later, the big trimotored speed plane was rolling down the inclined apron under power. It was an amphibian, at home on land or water. Doc raced the throttles. The engines roared.

In a short time, the speed plane was on step and vaulting into the lowering sky. Night was coming. The next day promised dire happenings.

High over the turreted masonry metropolis that was Manhattan, they circled. Doc had the robot pilot on. The device, designed to guide the ship without the need for a human hand at the controls, was functioning perfectly. The speed plane traveled with a muted hissing sound, thanks to efficient engine silencers. Unless a person happened to look up, it could buzz the city without stirring interest.

Monk pointed at the box holding their own superfirers. "You said you were going to test this thing, Doc. Want me to throw the lid open?"

"We will fly over Drago's home and see how the presence of Renny and the others registers," Doc replied.

The bronze man disconnected the robot pilot. Under his skilled hand, the speed plane swooped upon the city.

Monk and Ham maintained silence. Both gazed at the intricate mechanism in the plane cabin.

Outwardly, it seemed no different than before. But they understood that their bronze chief's great inventive genius had been brought to bear with an eye toward improving the range and sensitivity of the bulky device.

At a low altitude, Doc flew over the district which held Drago's place. The new apparatus was switched on by Monk.

There was no expression on the bronze features, no expectancy. Doc rarely showed emotion. But he had expected some response from his device. This was demonstrated by the abruptness with which he banked the plane back for a second try.

"Ham, take the controls," he directed.

Ham complied. All of Doc's aides were accomplished airmen.

Doc maneuvered the locator mechanism from side to side on its swivel mounting. From the loud-speaker came only a loud hissing. This indicated only that the amplifier was functioning.

The Man of Bronze leaned over and opened the metal case which held the superfirers. Instantly, a shrill howl came from the loud-speaker. It stopped when Doc closed the case. This test proved that the apparatus was functioning.

Ham sent the plane back. Once more, Doc Savage sought to detect the presence of radium-salted supermachine pistols in the neighborhood of Drago's palatial home.

He said nothing when he was unsuccessful, but the

weird sound that was Doc's uncanny trilling seemed suddenly to fill the plane cabin, communicating to Monk and Ham that the bronze man was perturbed.

"Our friends are not down there," Doc stated. The very quietness of his tone was ominous.

Binoculars, the most powerful type available, were in cases affixed to the cabin walls. Doc used a pair of these. Monk did likewise.

"There's Long Tom's clunker of a coupe," Monk muttered. "And one of our sedans is parked near it. Guess Johnny and Long Tom came in that machine. If they lit out for somewheres, they must have been in a powerful hurry to leave them behind like that."

Saying nothing, Doc cased the binoculars. Clipped to the ceiling were parachute packs. These were fitted with quick-snap-on harnesses.

Doc Savage wrenched one of the packs loose and began donning it. His intentions were obvious.

"The air currents among them buildings are bad," Monk muttered uneasily. "Going down by chute is dangerous."

"Circle over the place," Doc instructed. "I'll signal you after making an inspection."

"What about Kastellantz?" Ham asked.

"We will get around to him."

The bronze man opened the plane door and took a step out into space.

Ham climbed the plane immediately, but it was still low altitude for a jump. Almost immediately, Doc pulled the rip-cord ring.

Silken chute folds spurted like smoke from the pack. There was a sound remindful of a blanket being shaken, a jar, and the lobe blossomed to its fullest. Tall buildings came up. They might have been blunt, hungry fangs.

Easing the shroud on one side, Doc tugged and the chute skidded, air spilling under one edge. Thus the bronze man guided his descent to a degree.

Rooftops in the neighborhood of H. Startland Drago's home were flat. Doc desired to reach one of these, in preference to dropping into traffic.

That desire evaporated abruptly.

An unseen, high-pitched tuning fork seemed to pass close to Doc's ears. There was another sound, as if a hand had clapped hard against the chute top. The two noises were so close as to blend.

Doc's flake-gold eyes flicked upward. The chute lobe had acquired a tiny puncture. Even as he stared, the combination of noises was repeated. Another small hole appeared.

He was being shot at!

Gathering in shroud line with both corded hands, the bronze man gave a tremendous yank. The chute all but collapsed. He plummeted downward at greatly increased speed.

His gaze switched over rooftops. The bronze man possessed a remarkable knowledge of the layout of New York City. He had trained his memory to retain such facts.

From the air, he was able to locate with approximate correctness the house of H. Startland Drago.

On a nearby apartment house rooftop, two figures crouched. One, a tall man, had his face upturned. His hair was black. Only that much could Doc Savage see clearly.

The black-haired one crouched close to a roof hatchway. His posture, even from Doc's height, showed care.

The second man was doing the shooting. This fellow wore an overcoat, collar upturned. A dark hat was down on his ears. In addition, he had his left arm across his face, concealing it.

He fired again! Doc could see the recoil of the fellow's heavy automatic jar his hand. The bullet made tuning-fork noise somewhere near.

Doc released the chute shrouds. The lobe filled. It pitched about in the air current breathed upward by the street.

He landed heavily. But the shock was absorbed by his tremendous leg muscles.

Pedestrians gawked slack-jawed at the giant Man of Bronze. Some recognized him.

"It's Doc Savage!" a truck driver shouted excitedly, and quitted his vehicle in such haste that he fell headlong. The driver hoped to see the remarkable Man of Bronze perform some of the feats of which he read in newspapers. Doc freed himself of the parachute harness and was gone with a suddenness little short of uncanny.

Doc had landed two blocks from the apartment house. He sprinted the distance in time which would have astonished a professional runner.

Gaining the roof, he found exactly what he had expected. The birds had flown.

From the rooftop, he heard an engine rumble to life. The sound came from the rear. Doc raced the length of the roof, one hand plunging into his equipment vest.

He reached the parapet in time to spy a dark sedan race away. He gave the object he had extracted from his vest a hard throw.

Wind and the lack of preparation were against him. Too, the object he hurled had insufficient weight to impart velocity.

It was a tribute to the bronze man's skill that the object struck the sedan roof squarely. It broke. Nothing else happened, however. There was no explosion, nor release of gas. Just a tinkling—and the sedan lost itself in the gathering dusk.

Doc Savage watched it depart. No disappointment was inscribed on his cast-in-bronze lineaments. No expression of any kind roosted there.

Then, he turned on his heel and floated away.


## XXII

## DEAD MAN DYING


A policeman, standing on the street before the apartment house, a bewildered expression on his red face, greeted Doc as he emerged from the apartment building.

The bronze man pointed at the apartment house entrance. "Happen to see who came out of there a moment ago?" he asked.

"Two guys," said the cop. "They dived into a car and drove off."

"Describe them."

"One was black-haired. Didn't see the other bird's face. He was all bundled up."

The patrolman looked at Doc and shifted uncomfortably. He had recognized the bronze man. Not only did he know Doc's reputation, but he was also aware of an order posted in the precinct station, signed by the police commissioner himself. It directed that Doc Savage was to receive no further official police cooperation—and no exceptions.

It became clear that the patrolman had no sympathy for the change in policy.

"Sure sorry I didn't get a look at him, Mr. Savage," mumbled the cop contritely. "They were gone before I could do a thing. You see, I heard some shots, and was coming down the street to investigate."

Doc Savage glanced upward. The speed plane was not directly above. It was spiraling slowly, and moving across town as it did so. The antics of the trimotored craft were meaningful.

Monk and Ham were following the fleeing criminals.

The cop began again, "I'm sure sorry—"

"Phone your precinct station," Doc directed. "Have a general pickup order issued for a man named Elvern D. Kastellantz. He is wanted by the Washington, D.C. police for involvement in the disappearance of King Goz of Merida."

Doc gave a rapid, accurate description of Kastellantz—a complete word picture which would have astounded Kastellantz, who had encountered the bronze man but once, and then only briefly.

"Also have a general search started for my men— Renny, Long Tom, and Johnny," Doc instructed.

"What do they look like?"

"Your superior officer will have their descriptions."

"I'll do my best." The policeman departed at a run for the nearest departmental phone. He would have preferred to remain, having heard much of the remarkable detective ability attributed to this bronze man.

Had the cop looked on, he would not have been disappointed.

Moving swiftly, Doc entered the old heirloom of a mansion. The front door was not locked. In fact, there were signs the lock had been jimmied rather clumsily.

Inside, further indications of burglary were in evidence. The searching had been careless and hasty. It was not the work of his own men, Doc decided.

As he expected, there were no other signs of Renny, Long Tom, or Johnny. The locator had told him that.

He had instructed them to search this house and report back. Only some emergency or dire calamity over which they had no control could have moved them to vacate the premises before they had carried out his orders to the letter.

Signs of violence were absent. Doc had searched the house once before, during his first visit. But that had been in the company of the mystery woman who had first called herself Barbara Bland and was now claiming—falsely—to be Joan Manville, niece of H. Startland Drago. Now, he had free rein.

As he floated through the rooms, golden eyes animated with aureate life, he seemed to only glance about. He spent but seconds in each room, until finally he stood at the foot of a short flight of steps that led to a padlocked door and presumably an attic beyond.

Intermittent creaking came from the other side. Doc had heard the sounds on his earlier visit. Now they were quite loud and as unsettling to the nerves as a penny nail scraping along old slate.

The bronze man eased up the old stairs and paused at the door.

It was very difficult for persons with everyday senses of smell, hearing, and sight to credit that Doc Savage, with faculties trained from childhood, could nearly duplicate the feats of some animals. Had a trained bloodhound, for instance, come to the door and, by testing the air, ascertained that the attic held no one, it would not only not have attracted undue notice, but almost any one would have agreed it was to be expected. When Doc Savage did something similar, it was called impossible, superhuman. It was nothing of the sort. It was training, and practice.

Doc hesitated only a moment, but that was enough for his remarkable hearing and trained nostrils to impart to him that the attic was untenanted. He took a firm grip on the padlock with one tendon-wrapped hand, gave a quick wrench.

The padlock held. But the screws holding the hasp arrangement groaned torturously as they came out of the wood. Doc flung the whole setup aside, and entered.

Immediately, the strong scent of must entered his nostrils.

Doc produced his generator flashlight and thumbed it on. The place sprang alive with light.

The attic consisted of a single paneled space. The long room was tall, arched, and hung with armor and weapons. It was dark. Evidently there were no electric lights in the attic, not even gas fixtures. Only candles in wall sconces. It was probably part of the atmosphere of the place, which had less the aspect of a storage area than a private museum of some sort.

Glancing about, Doc decided the place stood a good chance of being soundproof. The walls certainly appeared thick enough.

He crept forward.

The bronze man had seen such contraptions as stood about the place. Pictures of them had been in his history books when he was a youth. A windlass affair for stretching a man's arms and legs, and finally pulling them off, if it went that far. A forge, caldron, bars of lead. A quaint little funnel used for pouring the molten lead into a victim's ear. And a coffinful of spikes, known as the iron maiden.

It was plain that H. Startland Drago was something of a collector of antique weapons and related oddities.

Over in one corner was a round vat, containing acid. But this was no medieval implement for inflicting torment. Redeemed bonds are usually destroyed in acid baths, Doc knew. Although the vat could have other uses, of course.

He hunted for signs of such use. He found only a whitish, pasty residue at the bottom of the vat. It was difficult to disclose what it might be. He moved on.

There was a contraption of iron in one corner, Doc discovered next. No machine of pain, however; it was a crude but quite serviceable printing press. Doc engaged the lever that separated the sandwich arrangement which ordinarily contained the printing plates in facing receptacles. They were empty.

A safe stood nearby. It, too, bore signs of age. Placing an ear to the door, he worked the tumblers. Some moments dragged. Concentration was written on the bronze man's features. One who knew him well might have guessed that he was attempting to crack the depository in greater haste than he would have preferred.

The door came open in short order.

There were no shelves or cubbies inside. Just four sides and a back wall crammed with piles of official-looking paper.

Doc extracted a sheaf of them. Liberty Bonds. Issue of 1927. He fanned the stack, his eyes memorizing serial numbers. His trilling came momentarily, an appropriately hollow sound in the musty, dungeonlike confines.

He moved away, leaving the safe open.

Doc found the hidden door after a cursory examination. It was cunningly done, but like every artifice, left telltale signs of use. In this case, dusty cobwebs hung limp where a tiny spider was busily spinning a fresh web, indicating recent disturbance.

Doc got the hatch open. A simple catch sprung it. The opening faced the rear of the grounds, was large enough to admit a man, and was within easy reach of the spreading oak tree which had been allowed to grow uncomfortably close to the great house—and which was the source of the unnerving creaking sounds.

Under proper conditions, a nimble person could easily exit the home, crawling along the thick branches to the ground, and slip away undetected.

Doc restored the hatch.

Pocketing a sample bond, he glided from the attic and down to the lower floors.

His metallic features held the grimness of cast bronze.

Going outside, Doc Savage made an unpleasant discovery.

The speed plane was back, circling overhead. It was

flying low. Monk, astonishingly gorillalike viewed from below, leaned half out of a window.

With his arms, Monk transmitted semaphore signals.

"G-o-t a-w-a-y," he gestured.

Doc flung his own arms at various angles, semaphoring.

"H-o-w?"

"S-u-b-w-a-y."

"M-e-e-t y-o-u a-t r-i-v-e-r," Doc signaled.

The bronze man took a taxi to the river front. The speed plane was waiting for him, wallowing at the foot of the seaplane ramp. Soon, it was again in the air.

"I watched their car with binoculars the whole time," Monk explained as they droned along. "The darn mugs were smart. They left their car and dived into a subway. They'd have been gone before one of us could even have gotten down by parachute."

"See their faces?"

"Only one. Black-haired guy. The other guy kept his hand up to his phizz."

"The black-haired one was a member of King Goz's retinue," Doc informed them. "A courtier. I recognized him."

"Blazes!" Monk squeaked. "What was he doin' hangin' around Drago's joint for?"

Doc told what he had found in Drago's home.

"Renny and the others were either kidnaped or lured away, after coming upon a person or persons in the act of ransacking Drago's home," he explained.

"That's bad," Ham groaned, twisting his sword cane uneasily.

"I also found a safeful of Liberty Bonds, and evidence of a counterfeiting setup."

Monk and Ham took the bond Doc produced.

"A phony?" Monk breathed.

"Real," Doc said.

"You mean to tell me that Drago had a safeful of these and yet recommended that Congress void the issue?" Ham asked.

"Puzzling, isn't it?"

"Baffling," Ham returned. "Everything about this Whistling Wraith business defies logic."

"What d'you reckon happened to the girl the Wraith grabbed?" Monk pondered.

"That's you," Ham told Monk sourly. "Shake a skirt in front of you and you forget everything else!"

"One more remark out of you, shyster," Monk promised, "and I'll give you debutante teeth."

"Huh?"

"Coming out."

Doc took over the plane controls. "We have one chance of finding them—the locator device."

He indicated the mechanism, newly installed in the plane.

Monk eyed the maze of wires, coils, and amplifier tubes. "Over what distance is that thing effective now? I mean, if they're fifteen miles away, and we point that trap at them, will it squeal?"

"No," Doc said. "It is just about as sensitive as it can be made, but it won't work over nearly that distance."

"Then what'll we do?"

"Just hunt."

Manhattan, the heart of New York City, is an island, rather long and not wide. Doc swung the speed ship up one side of Manhattan, and down the other.

Only a soft operation-hiss came from the locator.

"They are not on the island," the bronze man decided. "We will try Long Island next."

"Why there?" Ham queried.

"The town car Kastellantz was driving when Johnny attempted to locate him the other day was in lower Manhattan, on the East Side. Johnny found no trace of it. It stands to reason that the machine left the island. Johnny was in the air too quickly for Kastellantz to have gone west, into the Jersey area, without detection."

"But what does that have to do with any of this?" Ham blustered.

"This will come out in time," was the bronze man's only reply.

Queensboro Bridge was very near the section where

the Kastellantz machine had last been seen. This bridge led to Long Island.

Two arterial highways feed the Long Island end of the bridge. One, Queens Boulevard, passes for ten miles through a thickly populated district.

The other thoroughfare, Northern Boulevard, has adjacent to it certain sections which for some reason are thinly settled. Doc chose the latter road.

The speed plane swooped over Long Island City, passed the industrial section of Long Island, volleying toward Sunnyside.

"Listen!" Monk yelled.

From the locator speaker was emanating a faint sound. It rose in volume steadily, was soon a steady wail.

Doc gave Ham control of the ship and came back to manipulate the device. He swung it to the right, and the wail decreased. He angled it left, and the sound swelled.

"Left!" he called to Ham.

They banked away from Northern Boulevard, along which cars wound their way eastward. It being Sunday, traffic was sparse.

They flew southeast for some time and the loudening wail swelled.

"We're gettin' closer," Monk enthused.

Then, all at once, the wail began to die.

"Which direction, Doc?" Ham called back.

"Try due south."

Ham banked the plane again. Almost at once, the wail grew in volume. A road lay below. It pointed south.

Darkness had clamped down upon the world. Their binoculars were useless now.

Doc and Monk employed an infra-light projector mounted on the ship's nose and goggles whose lenses were as large as condensed milk cans to "read" the invisible light.

It disclosed a solitary machine, running with lights doused. It was as white as polished ivory.

"I think I recognize that car!" Monk howled. "Ain't it the machine Renny and the others said that Kastellantz was drivin'?"

"It is," Doc agreed. "The make is popularly known as a Ten Thousand."

"He must still be packin' one of our superfirers!" the hairy chemist said. "What say I break out one of our own and use it to discourage him?"

Doc nodded. "Endeavor to run him off the road. But be careful. We want no injuries."

"You betcha!" Monk said.

From the cockpit, Ham called back, "Where do you think Kastellantz is headed, Doc?"

"This road leads to Brooklyn and environs," the bronze man said, continuing to track the fleeing machine.

Monk went to a window and shoved it open. He had taken a supermachine pistol from the lead box, after first switching off the locator—which had accomplished its difficult task—and changed ammunition drums. This one was daubed in red. The other had been painted blue.

Latching the pistol to single-shot operation, Monk aimed carefully, his tongue clamped between large teeth, and fired once.

The superfirer made the sound of a pencil snapping in two, thanks to a cunning arrangement of baffles and silencers.

But the bullet, striking a roadside boulder ahead of the car, crashed like a thunderbolt. A demolition shell.

The racing machine veered, swerved, but the driver had skill. He regained the road after running along a shoulder rut for a brief time.

"This guy's either stubborn or scared," muttered Monk. He poked his head out for another try.

A great bronze hand clamped down over his shoulder.

"Wait," said Doc.

"Huh?"

"There is another car coming up from behind."

Monk craned his bullet head around for a look. In the stark infra-ray light, it seemed to be a dark sedan.

"Don't recognize it," he said. "It's not one of our special jobs, so it ain't Renny or one of the others."

"Unless I miss my guess," Doc said, "Renny and the other two are in that lead car."

"What!" Ham exploded.

"The locator sound has been newly calibrated to register the quantity of radium it detects," Doc explained. "According to the indicator, more than one superfirer is in that lead car."

"But Kastellantz *stole* more than one, didn't he?" Monk demanded.

"There are at least four down there. Kastellantz had three. One was found destroyed at the Washington hotel amid the Thermit bomb damage."

"Great Scott!" Ham said. "It must have been Kastellantz who ambushed Renny and the others at the Drago mansion!"

Doc nodded grimly. "It is reasonable to think so."

"So who is the bird trailing Kastellantz?" Monk wondered aloud.

Doc did not reply directly. He asked, "Do your infraray goggles show a luminous splash on the sedan's roof?"

"They do," Ham reported.

"I believe the King Goz courtier and his mysterious companion are in the pursuing machine," Doc stated. "I managed to mark their roof with a capsule containing a chemical which fluoresces under infra-light. They must have doubled back for the machine after escaping into the subway."

"Think they're out to get Kastellantz for killing that footman and makin' off with their king?" asked Monk, who tended to be bloody-minded.

Doc seemed about to say something, but at that juncture, the dark sedan overhauled the white town car. It came abreast. The two machines paced one another.

"We'll see some fireworks now!" Monk predicted.

The hairy chemist was correct.

Ham dropped the plane in an effort to forestall violence. If Renny and the others were in the Kastellantz machine, as Doc believed, any gunfire directed toward it might bring them to harm. The great bulletproof plane might collect any vented wrath instead.

That was not the way it happened.

A hand emerged from the driver's side of the town car. It was not empty. A saffron tongue of flame flared. And the bullfiddle moan of a supermachine pistol came briefly.

Abruptly, the sedan lost the road, sideswiped a telephone pole, and piled into another some yards ahead.

The town car roared on.

"Did you see that?" Monk howled. "That Kastellantz up and shot the other guy with one of our superfirers! And now he's gettin' away!"

Ham called back, "Doc! There's no place to land!"

For the briefest of moments, the bronze man hesitated. His silence told his aides that he was torn between following the machine in which his missing assistants were undoubtedly captives, and going to the rescue of the second driver.

Doc Savage had long ago sworn to hold all life sacred. And to parachute down would be to invite further gunfire, some of which might be mortal lead.

"Land!" he rapped.

Grimly, the dapper lawyer sent the great airplane higher, scouting for an adequate landing spot. He found one moments later.

It was an old disused field, overgrown with scrub but long enough for the purpose.

Dropping the wheels, Ham brought the plane down. It bumped along ruts until it rolled to a slow stop.

Doc was the first out, Monk bounced after him.

Ham remained behind to secure the plane.

A dozen minutes of hard running brought the bronze man to the wreck. It was on fire. There was a figure behind the wheel, a silhouette in the flame. It slumped with a creepy slowness which told that the greedy flames were consuming one no longer living.

Doc swept about the flaming tangle, golden eyes bleak.

He found the broken thing that had been the passenger lying in a ditch where the impact had thrown him clear of his mangled machine.

A low groan came from the man. He was on his stomach, half in a ditch, his chin up on the macadam, one hand clutching the edge of the road.

In the glow of Doc's flash, there was a great deal of crimson. Crimson on the man's hands, crimson on the roadside—and crimson was hue of the hair on his head.

Doc knelt at the figure, touched the shoulder gently. This brought a sharp groan.

"I am Doc Savage," Doc said quietly.

"And—I am—finished," the victim rattled.

Doc did not contradict him. It was the truth.

Instead, he said, "You have been betrayed, and you have little time left. Some truth might be in order."

"I—I lied about—the—sword," the other managed.

"I know," Doc said. "It was not in King Goz's possession when he entered his limousine. The newspaper photographs showed as much. In fact, I have known from the first how the king effected his mysterious disappearance."

"How—?"

"Not important," Doc clipped. "Where will I find the king?"

The man began to speak. His words choked off, turned into a liquid gurgle, and he began to heave and twist. Blood came out of his mouth in a rush.

Doc reached for the dying man's neck, found the nerve centers that could cause paralysis and unconsciousness, and manipulated them swiftly. This time, his touch produced a pain-deadening effect.

It was not enough to save the dying man, or to restore speech. But there was time enough for the unfortunate to dip a forefinger into his own blood and hastily scrawl two words on the smooth black macadam.

Then, he died.

Doc Savage was examining the dying message under the glow of his flash when Monk Mayfair ambled up, his barrel chest heaving from a strenuous run.

"Croaked?" Monk wondered, long arms dangling helplessly.

Doc nodded.

"Who is he?" Monk asked, and when the bronze man did not reply, the apish chemist rather callously gave the body a nudge. The face came up to the backglow.

At first, Monk Mayfair failed to recognize the man. He had never seen him before. But his likeness had appeared in newspapers in the wake of the disappearance of Goz the First, King of Merida.

The dead man lacked his braided crimson uniform and

monocle, and his formerly snow-white hair was a cloud of gore, but the profile was unmistakable.

"General Frontenac!" Monk yelled. "But he died in that hotel. We found his bones!"

"Faked his death," Doc explained. "No doubt a courtier or some other functionary was left to die in his stead."

"Why?"

"Part of the scheme."

"What scheme? Is he hooked up with Goldwill and the Whistlin' Wraith?"

"It all ties in together," Doc said. "But not in a way you might imagine."

Monk noticed the message in blood then.

"What's this he was writin'?" he asked, squinting.

The words were difficult to read. Fortunately, they were short, so recognition was a matter of a moment or two.

The message was:

## GRIM SEAS

"Guess he didn't get to finish what he wanted to say," Monk muttered.

"The contrary," Doc told him. "He has communicated the present whereabouts of King Egil Goz."

Monk made a perplexed face. "What's it mean?"

Before the bronze man could offer further explanation, the banshee howl of approaching police sirens came.

"Maybe we shouldn't stick around, considerin' all that's happened," Monk said uneasily.

"An idea," said Doc. They melted into the darkness at the side of the road and made fair time back to the plane.

They met Ham on the way and made short explanations while getting the speed plane back into the air. The pained expression on the dapper lawyer's chiseled face told that he was growing more, not less, perplexed.

Doc was at the controls. To Monk and Ham's surprise, he did not bank the plane southward in pursuit of the Kastellantz machine, but winged back toward Manhattan.

Monk wondered, "Ain't we gonna follow that tricky Kastellantz?"

Doc said, "I know where he is going."

"You do?"

"To Staten Island, by Brooklyn ferry. And stealth will be needed if we are to rescue our friends Renny, Long Tom, and Johnny from harm."

Monk and Ham swapped uncomprehending looks. They could not imagine how the bronze man had deduced all this from two cryptic words.

## XXIII

## HARRIED

Doc Savage was a man of precautions. It was rare that he was caught flat-footed. But throughout the affair of the Whistling Wraith, by his own admission, he had been hoodwinked more than once.

He began restoring his reputation for foresightedness as he dragged the Hudson River prior to setting down.

Abruptly, the bronze man pulled back on the control wheel and the big ship clawed for altitude.

"Something wrong?" Ham wondered, crowding forward.

"Examine the warehouse roof."

Monk and Ham went to a window and made faces as they tried to squint through the darkness.

There was no need for them to strain their optics, as it turned out.

The reason for the bronze man's abrupt change in plan was plain to see. It was a red angry eye visible at one end of the long warehouse roof.

"Hey!" Monk yelled. "That's our warnin' light! It means some one busted into the joint. But who?"

"A reasonable guess would be the authorities," Doc stated calmly.

Monk said, "The cops! But they don't know about the warehouse. It's a dang secret!"

"You forget that Joan Manville once visited the place, with Pat."

"You think Joan Manville tipped off the police?" Ham demanded of Doc. "But she's a prisoner of the Whistling Wraith!"

"Joan Manville," corrected Doc Savage, "is in league with the Whistling Wraith."

This sunk in. Ham's doubtful expression worsened.

Monk asked, "So what do we do?"

Doc seemed to have already made up his mind.

"We land."

Doc dropped the big amphibian onto the Hudson. The ship bumped along, slowed, settled, and he jockeyed the craft toward the sloping ramp that gave access to the cavernous place.

Monk and Ham, mechanical goggles over their eyes, were examining the long, gloomy structure by the aid of the infra-light ray.

"Seems quiet," Monk muttered. "We take a chance and go in?"

"We do," Doc said, snapping a switch that transmitted a radio signal. At the river end, ponderous doors opened.

Doc Savage sent the great aerial steed, still under power, lunging up the ramp. He killed the ship's hammering engines after they were parked inside and the great doors were closing.

Monk and Ham peered out from every available window and port before the hairy chemist offered, "Coast looks clear."

"Be prepared," Doc admonished, going to the hatch and flinging it open.

They stepped out, caution in their movements.

Abruptly, a bullfrog voice resounded through the great vault of a place.

"Reach for a rafter, Savage! The jig is finally up!"

"Push 'em Down!" Monk howled, reaching into his coat for a superfirer.

"Easy," Doc warned. Monk subsided. Following the

bronze man's example, Monk and Ham raised their hands high. They looked none too happy about it.

Out from behind a nest of cranes, fuel drums, and great ammunition cases stepped assorted bluecoats, cradling riot guns.

In the lead, brandishing a regulation Police Positive, was the human building block that was Inspector Saul Sampson. He was wearing a grin that, while not square, had its rectangular aspects.

"You are all under arrest," he said exuberantly. "And won't the new commissioner be pleased as punch!"

"On what charge?" Doc asked.

"Well, let's see," said Sampson, waving his pistol barrel carelessly about the air. "From that steel coffin back there, we pulled two stiffs. One guy I don't know, but the other dead one was an interesting specimen. He looked kinda like Laurence Kingsley Goldwill to me. And with that sword they keep finding in dead people down in Washington jammed clear into his gullet."

"There is an explanation for that," Ham retorted.

"I know there is," Push 'em Down snapped back. "It means that this whole bond scare, the fact that suddenly no one can find hide nor hair of H. Startland Drago, and maybe even the murder of Senator MacPartney, the attempt on the president's life, and that missing king business, show your fine hand, Savage."

To make his point, Saul Sampson whistled loudly. It sounded neither sad, like the Whistling Wraith's tune, nor mysterious, like Doc's trilling. But his meaning was clear.

"Absurd!" Ham said indignantly. "I shall have your badge."

"We got the evidence," Sampson said flatly.

"Who tipped you off, short and hoarse?"' Monk asked derisively.

"That Drago's niece, Joan Manville. She called to complain that her uncle never came back from Washington after your men took him away. Said we might start looking for him in this place."

"The Whistling Wraith must have been prowling here," Ham murmured. "That Manville woman could not have known those bodies would be found on these premises."

Sampson looked doubtful. "The which?"

"You," Doc Savage stated in an unperturbed tone, "have been duped. We are innocent of these charges."

Sampson made a derisive noise. "They all say that. But you can tell it down at the station house." Sampson wagged his gun muzzle upward. "Now keep them hands up there while I slap some bracelets on well-deserved wrists."

Doc seemed to clear his throat. Monk and Ham stiffened.

Then, without any preliminary warning, Saul Sampson and his bluecoats simply dropped to the floor and lay there. Sampson gave a single ripping snore and his breathing settled into a whistling rhythm.

Doc, Monk, and Ham lowered their hands and stood about unconcernedly. They seemed to be waiting for something.

At length, Monk exploded, "Good goin', Doc! They're sleepin' like babies!"

Doc Savage took off his coat, reached in, and pulled the linings of several hidden pockets inside out. Tiny sprinkles of glass collected on the floor. The explanation was quite simple.

Doc often carried in pockets hidden about his person, tiny thin-walled glass capsules containing the colorless, odorless anæsthetic gas that vaporized within less than a minute. Simply by expanding his bicep muscles, Doc had broken the globules, releasing the contents unnoticed.

Doc, Monk, and Ham had all held their breaths until the potent stuff had mixed with the air, rendering it harmless—Monk and Ham because Doc had warned them in the Mayan tongue. That had been the sound like throat-clearing.

"Well, we're framed, but good," Monk said as he collected riot guns from insensate fingers. "If they make those charges stick, we'll all be sitting on the hot seat pretty dang soon."

"Can't you think more pleasant prospects?" complained Ham, who understood that the law sometimes convicts innocent persons.

Meanwhile, Doc was at a periscope device that allowed him to examine the landward entrance to the great warehouse hangar.

"There are police machines parked outside," he said. "But no persons in them. We must move swiftly."

Doc Savage strode to the side of the boathouse end of the great structure, where various speedy craft lay in dry dock. He selected a low-slung racing boat, a streamlined gem of mahogany and chrome trim.

"A boat!" Monk grunted. "How come, Doc?"

"Give a hand," Doc directed. There was a wheeled cradle which could be used to hoist sea craft out of their dry dock and run them to the water. Doc was getting this into position.

"Ham," he said, "you might check on Pat's present whereabouts."

"You don't think she's mixed into this again?"

"We may have need of her before the night is over," Doc returned in a somber voice.

Monk lifted his eyebrows until they merged almost perfectly with his rust-red hair. He vented a low whistle, denoting surprise.

"Hope she don't faint when she gets the word," he grinned.

While Doc and hairy Monk prepared the speedboat for transport into the river, Ham used the telephone.

Pat Savage maintained an apartment in the Park Avenue building that contained her beauty establishment. Ham skipped the latter because of the late hour, and tried the apartment.

After a wait, he shouted, "Not there."

"Try our headquarters."

A moment later, Ham yelled, "Doc! Pat's holed up in our headquarters! Says the authorities tried to haul her in for questioning and she skedaddled for headquarters, thinking she'd be safer there. Now the place is crawling with cops!"

Doc left off what he was doing and snapped up the phone.

"Pat, there is a secret way to the floor below."

"The hidden stair in the lab?" Pat said. She sounded as if she were enjoying herself, after a breathless fashion.

"Right. Go to Drago's place. In the attic you will find an unlocked safe containing Liberty Bonds. Take them. Stash them in a secure place and wait until you hear from me."

"That's all? Nursemaid some paper?"

"Or you can remain where you are until the police blunder their way in," the bronze man said.

"Oh, all right. But this better not be a wild-goose chase because of that harmless fish prank I pulled."

Pat hung up.

Monk, steadying the speedboat in its cradle, grinned broadly.

"Maybe this once," he said, "Pat is gonna get her share."

Then, sirens made a bedlam. They were close. And coming closer.

Doc whipped to the periscope.

"What's going on?" Ham asked anxiously. "Those cars cannot be coming here."

"They are," said Doc.

"But how?"

"Wire tap."

"The cops tapped our phone!" Ham bleated, aghast.

"Evidently."

Hearing this, Monk rushed to an identical periscope at the river end.

"Harbor police!" he yelled. "Three boats. We ain't gettin' out this way, either."

The bronze man was moving toward the section housing automobiles.

"We have one chance," he said grimly. "We will have to drive through."

"This ain't gonna be no tea party," Monk said as they climbed aboard an auto. "Sounds like they mustered half the force."

"What about the speedboat?" Ham asked anxiously.

"We will have to find another method of reaching our destination," the bronze man said grimly.

Doc got the engine going, hit the dash switch that

opened the landward doors, and the car lunged for the opening.

They had their first piece of luck in some time. The police had tripped their sirens prematurely, thinking perhaps that they were converging in such numbers that escape was impossible.

It was very nearly the case.

But the bronze man had selected a taxi cab, one that was painted the horrible blue to which certain New York cabs are addicted. It was an otherwise unprepossessing machine, and such a common sight that he was able to scoot down a side street in full view of the oncoming radio squad cars, and not attract suspicion.

"Whew!" Monk breathed, as they drove north. "Made it!"

"We are not in the clear as yet," Doc warned.

Doc drove without haste. Traffic was thick. It had rained briefly earlier in the day, and the streets were still damp. The sky was clear now, and as dark as lampblack. Whistles of traffic cops were the loudest noises on the streets.

Almost casually, a squad car, the gold letters "P.D." on its doors, fell in behind them. Most of Doc's machines boasted low-number plates, but not this one. It was registered to a hack concern in which Doc owned a small interest.

In the back, apish Monk ducked from sight. Ham pretended to be a passenger.

The prowl car seemed to be doing just that—prowling. The driver made no attempt to pull them over.

Up ahead, a motor cycle cop swung around the ponderous structure of Grant's Tomb, and approached. His shield and polished Sam Browne belt glittered in the glow of the machine's headlights.

There was no avoiding what came next. There had been no time for Doc Savage to disguise his remarkable features.

The motor cycle cop spied Doc's metallic face in the headlight glare. His steed popping, he swung it about and fell in behind, while waving a gloved hand to the radio car.

"We're in for it now!" Monk grumbled, coming up in his seat.

Doc floored the gas, and began making evasive turns.

A second motor cycle patrolman joined the pursuit.

Sirens set up a wailing that brought heads out of windows and curious citizens out of entries. The taxi speedometer rotor shook itself slowly past seventy. Buildings, doorways, alleys, parked cars blurred past, and the car took great leaps at intersections where the pavement was higher.

Showing expert skill, the bronze man sent the taxi west, then east, and then south, often beating caterwauling prowl cars to busy intersections just as traffic signals changed. Numerous pursuers were foiled by Doc's lightning reflexes at the wheel. Although the taxi did not boast the bulletproof body or tires of Doc's regular machines, the engine under the hood was supercharged. It could make the hack do miraculous things.

"We're not shaking them!" Ham howled, glancing out the rear window.

Doc called back to Monk. "Monk, can you put a penetration bullet in your machine pistol and hit one of the tires, shooting from inside the car?"

"Hey!" Monk yelled. "What'd you say?"

"Can you?" Doc asked.

"Sure I can! But can you keep the blow-out from wrecking the car? And what's the idea?"

"Go ahead," Doc said.

Monk, strain all over his homely face, fitted the penetration cartridge—bigger powder load and copalloy over a special steel bullet—in the breech of the machine pistol. It was pretty much guesswork shooting for the tire on the left side.

The supermachine pistol made no great noise. But air leaving the tire did. It was as if a big piece of some hard-woven cloth was being torn with short jerks. The cab only skipped about at first. Then it did just about everything but swap ends. There was a robe rail. Monk hung on to that.

The cab did not go over. Within a block and a half, its speed was down to twenty. They were in the vicinity of the Battery now, on the East Side of lower Manhattan.

The motor cycles swerved in. The squad car came up close behind. The men in blue looked strange. They had their hands close to holstered guns.

"Blow-out!" Doc called. "We're pulling over."

The bluecoats looked relieved. They swerved away from the swaying car.

"Get set," Doc told Monk and Ham.

He did not sound excited.

The car bumped up onto the sidewalk. Brakes took hold. The brakes were good. The car skidded just enough, straightened at the crucial instant, and came to a rest with its nose half in a store front. The door, knocked off its hinges by the impact, wobbled briefly, then fell over with a bang, stirring up quantities of dust.

The pursuing vehicles, caught unawares, traveled on a short distance. Shouting, the motor cycle police struggled to get turned around without forking their front wheels.

"Into the store!" Doc rapped.

His voice, without being lifted or excited, was as effective as an explosion. Monk dived out; Ham a step behind.

The dapper lawyer, dazed by things happening too fast, yelled, "But what good will—"

Monk, showing a cooler head for once, reached out, took hold of Ham's ever-present cane, and yanked it along. Since the dapper lawyer would sooner part with his right arm than relinquish the affectation, he went with the stick.

The store was empty, its front windows soaped over. Some one had broken into the place, moved out, and left a scuffed counter, some shelves, old boxes, and a lot of trash. Rear windows were boarded. There was no glass in the door.

They ran out the back, stopped dead.

Ham gave a low groan.

"They've got us!" he shrilled.

The reason for the dapper lawyer's expression of defeat was plain.

Back of the store was a vast vacant lot. There was a very good reason for the absence of buildings: It was marshland. It had been made a trash dump until filled in, and the litter had been leveled off. Even a rabbit would have needed luck to get across it, with men and guns in on the hunt.

"Come on!" Doc rapped, urging Monk and Ham along with hard shoves of his great arms. He got them moving along in the lee of the building.

As was the style in New York's eyesore suburbs, the store was only one cell in a two-story, block-long string of buildings which might have been one long building, since each cell was alike.

The second door to the left was open. Monk and Ham raced for the open door, piled in.

Only then did they realize the bronze man was no longer behind them.

Doc Savage sprinted along the rear of the buildings in the direction opposite that taken by Monk and Ham. He did more than one thing at once, a practice at which he was good. He watched for open doors or windows. He watched for the first pursuer to appear. His right hand got a metallic object out of his clothing. And he kept a lookout for junk on the ground which might trip him.

There did not seem to be a window or a door that was not boarded or locked. Virtually all of the block, in fact, was empty.

At the farthest cell in the block, Doc stopped, rammed an elbow against a boarded-up window, and made an opening. One glance told him that the space was no longer in use.

He gave a twist to the object in his hand. It was one of his explosive grenades, which were enormously powerful for their tiny size. Its discharge could be delayed for almost as long an interval as could be desired.

Doc tossed the violent little thing inside, and abruptly reversed direction.

The explosion sent brick and board vomiting from all directions. The noise was enough to startle the converging police into exchanging worried shouts.

"They're down at the other end!" one called. And immediately there was a stampede of footsteps audible on the other side of the block, and coming closer.

Doc put on speed. Timing would be everything, if the diversion was to work.

He gained the door through which he had sent Monk and Ham, bounded in.

They were no longer there!

A hastily wrenched-free board off an opposite window told the tale. Doc rushed to it, took a chance and stuck out his bronze head.

Monk and Ham were pulling at the squad car doors. The hairy chemist spotted the bronze man, grinned, and waved one furry beam of an arm for Doc to join them.

If his aids had read his mind, Doc Savage realized, it could not have worked out more perfectly.

He stepped out through the open aperture.

Then, everything blew up!

Not literally. There was no explosion. What there was was a flurry of blue uniformed figures coming at a dead run from the far end of the block, where they had gone to investigate the explosion. They had guns out.

Monk bellowed, "Doc! Hurry!"

The bronze man put on speed. Monk was behind the wheel now. He got the motor going.

And a riot gun opened up. It shredded both tires on the far side of the police machine. The auto listed, rubber hissing.

Monk, a horrified expression on his face, waved the bronze man away.

"Nix! Nix! We're cooked! Don't let 'em get you, too!"

Doc skidded to a stop, hesitated. His hands became fists—but he knew the hairy chemist had the right idea.

The car was now useless. The police were coming hard, their weapons up and ready for use.

One of the police motor cycles sat on its stand near the curb. Veering, Doc mounted it in a blur of motion, kicked the stand up, and the engine to life.

A cop yelled, "Savage's stealing my mount. Get him!"

Bullets would have sought him, possibly with success, had Doc Savage tried to get the machine turned around. He did not. Instead, the bronze man sent the motor cycle lurching up onto the sidewalk, through a door that gave before him, and out the back of the block.

By the time the police got to the rear, he was a popping in the night distance.

## XXIV

### "GRIM SEAS"

Doc Savage's abandoning of his beleaguered aides might have seemed uncaring, disloyal. Actually, it showed clear thinking in the face of insurmountable odds.

It was not unusual for him to go into action without his aids. For all their skill, the bronze man was something of a lone wolf at times.

Not that Doc did not need his assistants. He did. They gathered information, made many indispensable moves. But when a climax came, when there was a situation demanding the extreme, the unusual, Doc Savage had a habit of acting alone, telling no one his plans, asking no help.

This was one such situation.

Monk and Ham possessed sense enough not to give the police cause to harm them, so Doc had left the pair to surrender peaceably.

Greater matters were at stake now, the bronze man knew. Come the morrow, the stock market would open, and all the nervousness engendered by the events of the past twenty-four hours would be certain to result in a panic the likes of which the nation, just struggling out of a long business slump, had never before seen.

Doc Savage had but hours to accomplish his goals.

Like some ultramodern knight, the bronze man piloted his gleaming steed south to the lower end of Manhattan, where he prowled the docks, making inquiries about renting a motor boat. He found one rental concern open, but the only thing available was a tiny dory fitted with an outboard motor. The owner demanded the full value of the craft as a deposit and Doc put up the money without objection, at the same time agreeing to an exorbitant rental.

Doc climbed into the dory, got the outboard going, and *put-putted* out into New York Harbor. A liner was coming up through the mouth of the bay, and a searchlight playing from the deck of the vessel splashed the up-flung arm of the Statue of Liberty on Bedloe's Island with light.

The bronze man set a course down the center of the bay, heading to the right of the statue. He seemed to have a definite goal in mind. The night air was warmish and the salt tang not unpleasant in the nostrils.

The dory made good speed under the kicking of the outboard. But the little craft was none too seaworthy, as Doc discovered when the wave thrown out by the bow of a passing tugboat almost capsized him. After that near disaster, he watched for the waves and turned the dory into them, bow-on.

It soon became clear that his goal was the Borough of Staten Island.

The distance to Staten Island was approximately five miles, Doc knew, and it usually took him twenty minutes to make the crossing, all told.

Avoiding a night-prowling tugboat, he cupped hands before his mouth and shouted an inquiry.

"Ahoy! Know the *Grim Seas*?"

"Sure, an' I've seen the scow," the captain replied. "Part of that ghost fleet."

"Where is she anchored?" Doc asked.

"Begorra, I'm not too sure," said the tug skipper, and proceeded to describe the spot where the *Grim Seas* might lie. " 'Tis a four-master, with a steel hull," he finished. "And a stinkin' pile o' rust, she be."

Doc thanked him and pulled away.

Doc located the *Grim Seas*, anchored close inshore, a darker smudge against the shadow of Staten Island hills.

Whoever had named her might have been a prophet. Corrosive effects of the salt air had sanded her hull with a thick layer of rust. The sullen hulk rode her anchor like a forlorn, forgotten thing.

Doc reviewed what knowledge he possessed of the so-called ghost fleet as he stared at the looming hulk. The ships had been built during the war—some by profiteers—and put together with a speed that did not permit safe workmanship. After the cessation of hostilities, the government had found the ships to be a string of white elephants; they were not seaworthy, so nobody wanted them. The derelicts, condemned and representing many millions in public money, were quietly tied up by the hundreds in out-of-the-way spots.

By far, the greater number had been anchored in the Hudson. Of these, a few were later found to be worth refitting to make them seaworthy, and others were sold for junk. The derelict fleet had dwindled gradually until now only a few remained.

Doc recalled a newspaper story which reported that the fleet of dead ships had been moved from the Hudson and anchored off Staten Island. The story had also carried the information that a skeleton crew had been kept aboard the vessels to make sure they remained afloat.

His amazingly retentive memory had immediately identified the meaning of the cryptic message, "Grim Seas," which General Frontenac had scrawled in his own life's blood. The bronze man had not apprised his aids of the phrase's meaning as a precaution against their possible capture—very wise in light of their subsequent apprehension by the police.

Even in the gloom of the harbor darkness, the *Grim Seas* looked like a derelict. The foremast was lightly a-cant, and strings of rigging drooped like cobwebs.

Doc could discern no light aboard the craft. With a canny eye, he gauged the distance of the vessel from shore, then turned the dory toward land.

Doc Savage beached the dory on a sloping mud beach fully two hundred yards distant from the anchorage of the *Grim Seas*. Standing in the craft, he stripped to the jersey shorts he habitually wore and which doubled as swimming trunks, folding his clothes carefully and placing them in the stern.

He retained his padded, many-pocketed vest, which, in addition to being an arsenal of no small formidableness, was bulletproof.

The water was not excessively cold. Doc waded until it came to his shoulders, then struck out with an overhand stroke, keeping his head well above the surface. Water striking his smooth bronze hair seemed to bead up and roll away. It was a peculiarity of the bronze man's skin and hair that they shed water like the proverbial duck's back.

As he drew near the old hulk, he slipped underwater. Weight of the vest was enough to keep him under the surface, but not so heavy that he could not swim with it.

He emerged alongside the hull, perhaps a hundred feet back from the bow. Monster rust scabs clung to the steel plates, some of which, he discovered, were large enough to support his head above the surface. He treaded water for some minutes, listening, then released his grip and stroked for the bow anchor chain.

The links of the chain, rust-encrusted, were as thick as his wrists. Grasping one, he pulled his bronzed body half out of the bay and waited for the water to drain down his muscular legs. Then he climbed the links like a ladder. Rust scales scraped his skin. Some broke off and clung to his flesh.

Doc Savage silently gained the hawsehole and paused with an arm thrust inside. The lifting of his body until his fingers hooked the rail, he accomplished by an intricate feat of balancing. He slid over the rail, and rust crunched softly under his bare feet as he planted them on deck. It was practically the first perceptible sound he had made.

There was life aboard the hulk, *Grim Seas*. His sensitive hearing detected the mutter of voices somewhere near. The words were indistinguishable.

A match flared amidships as it was applied to a cigarette. Doc froze, seeming to become part of the surrounding rust.

The flame disclosed a swarthy face and thin lips. Obviously a guard.

Doc slipped silently into the lee of the low steel bulwark. Should a flashlight beam be thrown in his direction, the bronze man knew, he would be in plain sight, but no chance splash from the searchlight of a harbor craft would betray him.

Doc approached the loitering guard. As he drew near

the man, he increased caution. He went momentarily rigid as metal as the fellow walked to the rail and spat overside, then stood staring out over the harbor.

Exploring about, Doc located a heavy rivet head. It was frozen to the deck by rust, but when the guard hawked loudly, clearing his throat, corded bronze fingers wrenched the rivet head free under cover of the unpleasant sound.

Doc waited a moment, then tossed the rusty object overboard.

Hearing it, the guard bent forward to peer in the direction of the splash.

Doc sprang to his feet and clamped metallic fingers on the back of the man's neck. No outcry was given. The guard quivered, but kept his feet. A leaky sigh escaped his lips and his eyes rolled up in his head. He sagged at the knees, and Doc eased the unconscious figure gently to the deck.

Coils of rotted rope and other waste created a serviceable covering for the conquered crewman.

That done, Doc moved on, a metal giant in a fantastic realm of rust and corrosion.

The murmur of voices continued coming from a spot back by the stern. Doc floated toward the sounds.

He found a companionway, hesitated. The voices were more distinct now, but to the ear, not readily audible. This phenomenon became more understandable as Doc eased down the companion.

The voices were speaking in a foreign tongue.

At the bottom of the companion stairs, Doc found an open cabin. Whatever it had been intended for originally, it had since been converted into a storeroom of sorts. Coiled hawsers, piles of chain, and unwieldly machinery littered the floor. Going through it barefoot would have been a task in daylight; in the darkness, it was agony.

The undertone of voices grew louder. Doc eased himself into another cabin and beyond it into a passage. The place was pale with light, which came from the slash of a partially opened door.

Doc faded back swiftly as the slash widened, accompanied by a squeaking of rust-cankered hinges.

Three figures stepped through.

"Frontenac has failed," one said in thickly-accented English. "It is up to you two to locate and dispose of Drago. He must die for what he has done."

The second voice spoke distinctly American English.

"What good will that do? It ain't gonna change Congress's mind. They already voted."

"We will deal with that later," snapped the first voice. "The president has yet to sign the bond bill into law."

"What about Doc Savage's boys?" asked a third voice, also American.

"Where they are, there is no need to do anything to them one way or other," the owner of the first voice said.

"You mean—just let them rot?"

"Rot? Ah, how appropriate a choice of words. Yes, let them rot."

The trio passed to the other end of the cabin, through a zone of faint light, and their faces showed briefly.

Two were hoodlums of the American variety. But the third possessed a face Doc Savage had seen before. Not that he needed to see him in the light. Doc had already placed the man by his distinctive voice.

Elvern D. Kastellantz!

Doc waited until the trio had mounted topside—the monotonous crunching of their shoe soles on rusty steps going away—before he detached himself from a shadowy corner, like a fragment of metal come to life.

Back out in the corridor, Doc felt his way along. His hands and elbows, accidentally scraping rusty walls, brought pain. None of it was reflected in his inscrutable features.

At one point, he paused to smear his gleaming body with rust collected from bulkheads. When he resumed his course, he appeared all but invisible.

As when so many highly skilled feats are observed, there seemed nothing unusual about his progress. He just walked forward. But he always seemed in shadow and he made no noise whatever.

Doc traveled down a corridor, took a chance and employed his flash beam, twisting the lense until it stabbed a thin bar of radiance ahead of him, and found a narrow steel companion of metal. He went down this. Flakes of rust made brittle crunching sounds and lacerated his bare soles, which left tiny specks of blood as they rose and fell.

The companion gave into an engine room where the bronze man wedged past the gutted remnants of internal-combustion engines, apparently of a power rather small for a vessel the size of the *Grim Seas*.

Beyond, near a bulkhead, was a steel wall panel. It gave inward with a complaining screech from the hinges.

Doc played his flash ray inside. He saw, in a cramped space, a table improvised out of a box. More boxes had been placed side by side and covered with burlap bags to form a bench. One draping of burlap, affixed to a wall, seemed intended to pass as a rude tapestry.

This was a part of the hold of the condemned rust bucket, Doc knew. The stench of foul bilge water was nauseating.

Still, Doc pocketed the flash and squeezed through the aperture.

His beam out again, he lifted the sacks, confirmed that boxes supported them, and went to the one attached to the wall.

The lifted burlap revealed a wall safe, small, old, but not in the least rusty, owing to the high quality of the steel of its construction. The ship's safe.

Doc restored the burlap as it had been and passed on to a stout door on the opposite side of the hold compartment.

It was secured with a rust-eaten lever arrangement which had originally been intended to draw it sufficiently tight against a rubber batten to make it waterproof. Doc wrenched the steel panel open and stepped through.

He had his flash out, but had doused it.

From the darkness of the malodorous area, came sounds. Buzzings. Like frustrated bumble bees in search of honey.

Doc thumbed on the light and the bumble bee sounds ceased, becoming something else. Muffled grunts.

For the light had disclosed the bound-and-gagged forms of his three missing aides, Renny, Long Tom, and Johnny! They had been trying to speak past their gags and, that failing, had hummed through their noses to attract attention to their plight.

Reaching back, Doc shut the door and threw the inside lever, securing the door.

Doc went to them, undoing their gags.

Renny's hoarse "Holy cow!" echoed tinnily in the murky, unpleasant confines. "It happened to us again!"

Long Tom explained, "We were bushwhacked by that Kastellantz. He was going through Drago's place when we barged in."

"Kastellantz got the drop on us with one of our own mercy guns, and the minute we put our hands up, he cut loose," Renny added.

"A lamentable repetition of concurrence," Johnny said unhappily.

"When we came to," Renny said, "Kastellantz tried to get us to tell where Drago was. Seems he's got it in for Drago something bad. But when we told him the truth, he refused to believe it. Not that I blame him."

"Know where you are?" Doc inquired.

Renny nodded his gloomy head. "Ship somewheres, by the smell," he rumbled.

"A ghost ship," Doc supplied. "Talk of leaving you to rot gave me a fair idea of your situation."

Bonds off, Renny raised his monster fists. They were liver-hued from scrapes and cuts made by the tiny mercy shells, which included a cauterizing chemical that prevented infections from taking hold.

The three Doc Savage aides climbed to their feet, started stamping the floor and flexing their wrists in an effort to restore normal blood flow.

"Holy cow!" Renny said gloomily. "First blisters and now this. My left foot's asleep!"

Then the grinding of rust told them that some one had stepped into the compartment on the other side of the closed door.

Doc motioned for silence and doused his light.

Darkness clamped down. They held their breaths. A good idea in the close air anyway.

And Doc Savage set one muscle-cabled hand on the locking lever.

Grinding sounds continued, slow, tentative. They grew near. Stopped.

Doc felt the lever on his side of the door quiver. He tightened his grip.

Fortunately, the levers on both sides worked off the same mechanism. The person on the other side could not budge his.

In the darkness, a silent struggle was waged. Doc Savage, possessed of muscles gained over a lifetime of rigorous exercise, was certain to win the contest of thews, his three assistants knew. But to fool the prowler into believing the rust-fouled mechanism was simply jammed was another matter.

Then, a shout!

"Hey! This lever won't budge! Maybe there *is* somebody creeping around down here, after all!"

"Throw a slug through it and see!" suggested another hard voice.

Instantly, Doc and his men sank to their knees.

"Will that door turn slugs?" Long Tom undertoned.

Doc shook his head in the negative.

The truth of this was demonstrated a moment later when a bullet smashed through the panel, leaving a hole with outcurled edges.

It spanked harmlessly into the back of the smelly hold.

The gunman called out, "I got a hole!"

"Put your eye to it!" a second voice said.

"You nuts?"

"Just checking your horse sense," the other offered dryly. "Hold the fort. I'll go get the poison gas. That should solve the problem."

Poison gas! They would be helpless!

Doc Savage came up from the floor like a thunderbolt. He wrenched the lever upward, yanked hard.

The gunman on the other side was so surprised, he only got off one shot.

It struck the oncoming bronze man square in the chest, hindering him only a little, thanks to the bulletproof qualities of his special vest.

Doc Savage sent one bronze block of a fist sweeping

up from his hip. It connected, broke a jaw, lifted both feet, and put the gunman on his back and out cold.

On his way out, Renny grabbed the man's gun, a blue automatic, and rumbled, "Lead the way, Doc."

They got as far as the panel on the other side of the hold. The ugly snout of a submachine gun poked out and a voice growled, "I *thought* that talk about gas would bring some results."

"Holy cow!" Renny thumped, hopping on his one functioning foot.

## XXV

## MONARCH OF MYSTIFICATION

If Renny Renwick had not had one monster paw filled with the blue automatic, he might have made a grab for the threatening Tommy gun. For all his bulk, he was fast and in a good position to do so successfully.

He was also in an excellent position to collect a belly-ful of .45-caliber slugs. For that was where the rapid-firer muzzle was directed.

The big-fisted engineer looked questioningly to the bronze man. "Doc?"

"Surrender." And Doc Savage threw up his hands.

The others did likewise. Renny held on to the blue automatic, not wishing to startle the gunman by dropping it suddenly.

"One at a time," the Tommy jockey warned, "step out." The muzzle nudged toward Renny. "You first, big fists. And heave the roscoe ahead of you, while you're at it."

Renny complied. He had to struggle through the aperture. The gloomy engineer lost some hide, especially on his already-damaged fists.

One by one, the others passed through. Doc Savage came last.

Others had joined the gunman with the Tommy gun. They relieved Doc Savage of his equipment vest.

Not a few eyes bugged out at sight of the bronze man's exposed musculature. It was tremendously daunting, even powdered by rust collected during his foray below.

The man with the chopper snapped, "O.K. Up we go. Topside."

Reluctantly, they went.

More men with guns showed themselves along the way. They were carrying shaded lanterns that made the rusty steel walls seem as if they were caked with gore.

These new arrivals were of a different character from the others, who appeared to be hired guns of the domestic variety. The new ones had faces of foreign cast, many decorated by prissy little trick mustaches, and there was nothing of the ordinary ruffian about them.

The man with the Tommy gun offered a curt explanation for the untimely discovery of Doc and the others.

"We heard you open that panel, smart guy," he told Doc. "Every hunk of this tub creaks and groans. It's the best burglar system you could have."

"Don't count your chickens," Long Tom warned, "until they come home to roost."

"An ornithological inevitability," Johnny chimed in.

Among their captors, strange expressions were exchanged between those who doubted that the big-worded archæologist's observation had been couched in English and those who questioned it was language at all.

Eventually, they emerged on deck, where other foreign-looking men were waiting.

Words were exchanged. The language was not English. One of the speakers went to get some one.

A moment later, he returned—with no less than Elvern D. Kastellantz.

Kastellantz, very grim of face, strode up to Doc Savage and said, "You are very clever. But then, that is your reputation."

Doc held silence.

"Still, it behooves me to ask: How were you able to locate my carefully chosen hideout?"

"General Frontenac."

"He betrayed me!"

"You betrayed *him*."

\* \* \*

Elvern D. Kastellantz's mouth became a thin line. There was a faint shadow on his upper lip, as if he had begun a mustache.

"You mean Kastellantz and Frontenac were in cahoots!" Renny exploded.

"From the beginning," Doc stated, not taking his eyes off the smooth, powdered face of Elvern D. Kastellantz, whose hair was once more its natural coppery-red.

"I don't get it, Doc," Long Tom added. "What is this—a coup?"

"No. You might say it is the opposite of a coup."

Johnny Littlejohn snapped thin fingers over his shaggy head. "An abdication!" he exclaimed.

"But Kastellantz *did* make King Goz vanish, didn't he?" Renny demanded.

"He did," Doc stated.

"When we first encountered one another," Kastellantz said slowly, matching the bronze man's steady regard, "you claimed to know how King Goz disappeared. You made similar representations to General Frontenac. I did not believe these statements, but I am willing to entertain the possibility."

"In other words," Doc said, "you would like me to explain my theory?"

"It might be amusing."

Doc Savage considered briefly. Only a flickering of his golden eyes betrayed the thoughts behind them. Then, perhaps concluding that talk would forestall any planned violence, he launched into a crisp recitation of the known facts.

"Several witnesses saw King Goz enter his limousine outside Blair House," he declared. "A few journalists hoping to get the jump on a story, the usual tourists and sightseers, and the king's own retinue. No photographs were taken at that time. These people witnessed the king enter his machine, and his departure. The king's retinue, including General Frontenac, followed the limousine in their own cars. Some journalists took up the rear of the motorcade, which took a circuitous route to the White House, ostensibly to enable the press to prepare themselves. It was the testimony of all that the official machine stopped only once and that no person at any time left the automobile."

A smile quirked Elvern D. Kastellantz's mouth. His dark eyes shone.

"You doubt this?"

"The king *did* leave his auto," Doc said carefully. "The whole world, almost, saw him do so. That event was recorded by a newsreel camera at his destination, at the White House door."

Renny grunted. "Huh?"

"I don't get it," Long Tom chimed in.

"It is deceptively simple," Doc related. "King Egil Goz, dressed in his military-style uniform, entered the limousine. The footman closed the door behind him and took his proper place in the driver's compartment, beside the chauffeur's seat. At this point, the journalists naturally rushed to their cars in order to follow the motorcade. If any had tarried, they would have witnessed the limousine leave with the chauffeur plainly visible in the driver's compartment, and the king, presumably, seated in the curtained tonneau. Which he was."

Doc paused. Somewhere, a bell buoy clanged like a forlorn cowbell.

"The king's so-called disappearance occurred at a traffic signal en route," Doc continued. "It was all accomplished in a manner so deceptively simple that if the true facts were not known, it would baffle the imagination."

All attention was on Doc Savage now. His voice, normally pleasant and well-modulated, gripped them strangely.

"While the limousine was stopped, the king simply rolled down the partition between the tonneau and the driver's compartment, exchanged coat and cap with the man behind the wheel, and climbed forward, taking his place. Then he drove on."

Renny's jaw was slowly going slack. He snapped it up and asked, "Where did the footman go?"

"The murdered footman had been behind the wheel up to this point," Doc stated quietly.

Long Tom exploded, "But Kastellantz was the chauffeur!"

"Not true. After the footman first entered the driver's

compartment, he simply donned a chauffeur's cap and liveried jacket and slid behind the wheel. In the excitement of the moment, no one noticed that there had been no chauffeur seated behind the wheel until the footman took it."

Johnny murmured, "Where does Kastellantz come in?"

"Elvern D. Kastellantz seems to be a nonexistent person," Doc explained. "At best, his was a borrowed identity. At no time did anyone other than the king and the footman enter the limousine. General Frontenac's story that he did was given to cover one of the greatest sleights of hand in modern times."

An inkling of the truth dawned on Doc Savage's men. Fact by fact, he had been leading them to the truth. But a look came over the powdered face of Elvern D. Kastellantz then. A wise and knowing look, almost crafty.

Doc said it a moment ahead of their collective gasps of recognition.

*"The man standing before us is King Egil Goz of Merida."*

No one said a word. All eyes were on the copper-haired man whom they had come to know as Elvern D. Kastellantz, royal chauffeur. Then he spoke.

"You are everything they say you are, Savage," King Goz the First said with what seemed grudging suaveness.

Doc went on. "Your uniform and that of the footman driver were similar enough in appearance that the exchange of cap and jacket was all that was necessary to effect the switch. Of course, you had to shave off your mustache. Some of the hairs fell to the limousine floorboards, where I discovered them. I recognized from their length and thickness they were mustache, not head, hairs."

"So what's it all about?" Renny muttered.

"Johnny said it a moment ago. It was a bizarre abdication—coupled with a nearly perfect scheme to abscond with the wealth of the Meridan people."

"Abscond?" Long Tom gulped.

"But too many knew about it," Doc continued. "The footman, for one. When I arrived at the Washington hotel to question him, King Goz was in seclusion, passing as his own chauffeur. It was he who slew the footman, out of fear I would wrest the truth from him."

"That is a rank guess!" sniffed the revealed King of Merida.

"The footman was discovered in a kneeling position," Doc countered. "That suggested he had been murdered by his liege, who commanded him to kneel and then drove his personal sword into the victim's mouth."

"You mean the Whistling Wraith didn't kill the footman?" Renny rumbled.

Doc nodded. "General Frontenac, as he admitted to me, lied about the sword. It was not in King Goz's possession when he entered the machine. It was a fabrication to further confuse the issue, just as was the claim by the disguised king, and repeated by the footman, that at the time of the king's disappearance, the mysterious whistling was heard. There was no whistling."

"But there was!" King Goz insisted. "I heard it in my very castle. And I saw the shade of Old King Fausto whistling down the stone corridors. I flung a dagger into its back, and it walked on completely unaware. For the dagger had passed through its unsubstantial form."

"I'm not following this," Renny rumbled. "Does that mean the Whistling Wraith didn't have anything to do with the king's disappearance?"

"He did not," Doc said.

"So who made Drago disappear from the president's limousine?" Long Tom wondered. "We know he didn't change places with that butler, Holman. Although he vanished, too."

"Unless I miss my guess," Doc said, "the so-called Whistling Wraith was involved in H. Startland Drago's mysterious vanishing act."

"It is true, then?" demanded King Goz. "Drago has vanished, as your men have told me?"

"Yes."

King Goz broke into a broad smile.

"*Ma bucar!* Good! Then my enemy is no more. Perhaps Old Fausto will be satisfied with his soul and leave me alone."

"I fail to understand," Johnny chimed in. "Drago was your personal banker. How did he become your enemy?"

"These things do not matter," Goz snapped. "All that is important is that the vexing persons who could ruin my perfect plan disappear so that I may enjoy my wealth in peace and comfort." His voice turned sad. "I am sorry it is to be this way. Had you remained out of my affairs, *Domnule* Savage, none of these unpleasantries would be necessary."

The king's words were so smooth and unthreatening that for a moment their true meaning escaped them.

Renny said it. "Doc! They're gonna kill us!"

The moment of shocked silence which followed was just that—a moment. Not long.

Then the warm sea air around then turned sad with whistling notes they all knew too well.

"He is here!" Goz shouted, looking about wildly. "How can this be?"

Guns which had been pointed unwaveringly at Doc Savage and his three men now swept about warily. Uneasy eyes raked stanchions, bulkheads, and the leaning masts of the rust-scarred old hulk.

And out from behind a darksome mast, clutching the ubiquitous sword of Merida, stepped a fantastic figure in scarlet.

The Whistling Wraith!

His long, snowy beard swayed as he came forward. The approach was more of a floating, it seemed. It was not silent. The mournful air emerging from the knothole in his gnarled face dispelled all quietude.

Whistling, he lifted his bejeweled scepter, as if to menace them with it.

"Slay him!" King Goz howled, backing away.

And the guns swiveled and began vomiting lead and noise!

The superannuated specter was standing before a rusty bulkhead. The bulkhead wall visible around him began to hammer and give up little puffs like rusty ghosts where the bullets struck. Shiny spots suddenly peppered the red corrosion.

Most passed through the Whistling Wraith, who too. no notice of the leaden onslaught.

Once, he ceased his infernal whistling long enough to smile mockingly, his black eyes bright with humor.

The gunmen were stubborn. The figure in scarlet looked solid to the eye. There was nothing of the ethereal about him. So they kept firing.

It was not long before they ran out of bullets. Doc waited until the defiant reports had turned to futile clickings before he acted.

The bronze man swept forward, picked up the shocked figure of King Goz, and retreated.

Some of the gunmen took notice. They whirled, bringing their smoking gun muzzles around.

Renny, Long Tom, and Johnny got between Doc's retreating figure and those worthies.

Fists cracked. Renny grabbed two men by their opposite ears and rammed heads together, flung the victims in either direction. He reclaimed the blue automatic earlier surrendered.

The Whistling Wraith started forward then.

And for the first time, he spoke!

"I have come for King Goz," he announced in a tone that brought to mind electric sparks. "He must sit upon the Meridan throne, where I may bedevil him at my will."

"Nothing doing," Renny rumbled. "I've been wanting a crack at you for a while now!"

The big-fisted engineer swept in.

Doc Savage's voice was a crash. "Renny! Back away! Do not close with it!"

Renny probably heard. But his ire was aroused. He wanted a shot at the mocking figure. He got it.

The great sword swept around as if to decapitate Renny. The big-fisted engineer ignored it. The blade sliced through his neck. Men turned away from the sight, expecting to see the head separate from the fast-moving body.

But both blade and man showed no effect of their flashing encounter.

"You had your chance!" Renny boomed.

One hamlike fist rammed into the whistling face. And kept going, taking Renny with it.

Turning, the Wraith made a pass in his direction with the bejeweled scepter. It connected.

This time things were different.

Renny jumped a foot, came down in an awkward pile of angular limbs that twitched on and on.

The fantastic figure passed over and through him. Men gave before it. It was not the weird confidence stamped on its wrinkled visage so much as the way it progressed. There were things in the way. Objects. Projections. The Whistling Wraith paid them no heed. It simply passed through them where it would.

It was enough to unman the hardiest of souls, and not a few of the gunmen simply took the simplest way off the hulk, and jumped overboard.

Retreating, the King of Merida slung over one broad shoulder, Doc Savage led Long Tom and Johnny to a bulkhead door. It was locked.

It took them a moment to get the lock open. Doc Savage solved this problem by crashing a metal bar, heaving it up from the floor, against the lock. He shoved the door open. They piled through.

Long Tom stopped to shut the door behind him. It was a natural reflex. But absurd under present circumstances.

The scarlet figure's hands started coming through the shut door as if neither were quite real.

Once through, it floated down the stairs. His boots, lacking substance, seemed unable to find proper footing. They melted into the rust-caked runners. But some species of momentum carried the apparition forward, so that it did not sink entirely into the companionway, but glided, its boots passing in and out of view with each step.

It reached the corridor, seemingly gliding along on the stumps of its booted ankles.

"What is that thing!" Long Tom said hoarsely, catching up.

"Keep moving!" Doc warned.

They pelted down twisting corridors, seeking sanctuary.

Johnny stopped at a porthole. But it was blocked by a steel cover, apparently bolted to the outside hull of the *Grim Seas*. There was no quick dislodging of it.

They moved on. Seemed to gain headway.

Coming around a sharply angled corner, they were unceremoniously brought up short.

For there, standing before them, was the Whistling Wraith!

"How?" Johnny gulped.

"Cut through the solid walls," Doc explained.

"Talk about a shortcut," Long Tom breathed.

And suddenly Doc was passing the king to the puny electrical wizard's hands. The king, once loose of the bronze giant's inexorable grip, put up a fight. Long Tom socked him once. Once was enough. Goz slumped.

"Retreat," Doc urged.

Johnny and Long Tom obeyed.

Doc held his ground. He was bereft of weapons. The look in his eyes was wary. The bronze man might have been recalling his last brush with the unstoppable being.

The expression on the Whistling Wraith's withered countenance was confident, thinly amused.

Doc threw a punch. The Wraith blinked. Doc's fist passed through its jaw, unresisting.

The sword that had slain so many sought Doc in a backhanded swipe that was unsettling in its utter soundlessness. It bisected the bronze man's left arm at the elbow.

Doc faded back, his arm whole. There had been no pain. He swatted at the face again. And again, he got the very human blinking reaction. But no other. The Wraith came on.

Doc Savage next used one hand to swipe a layer of rust off a wall and dash it into the Wraith's face. The action scraped bronze skin raw. It made the Wraith flinch satisfyingly, gaining time for the others.

Suddenly sheathing the sword in a long belt scabbard, the goat-bearded apparition began to weave the murky air with the scepter, making passes and circles that threatened the bronze man with terrible punishment.

Slowly, Doc was backed around a corner. He stopped. The Wraith faded back, as if suddenly afraid. Its whistling abruptly ceased. Doc eased forward, peering around the turn.

The Whistling Wraith was no longer in the corridor!

Some intuition must have seized the bronze man then. There was no warning sound, no hint of danger, but Doc whirled.

And the bejeweled scepter was plunged into his chest!

Instantly, agony flooded him. Before, when it had merely touched him, he had been blinded, his whole muscle-cabled body shot with pain. It was worse now.

Blackness in his eyes, thunder in his ears, an awful clutch at his heart!

And as a coldness unlike any Doc Savage had ever known swallowed his brain, he could hear a distant bullfrog voice shouting.

*"Grab the rails, everybody! This is a police raid!"*

And guns began crashing!

## XXVI

## DOWNFALL

The finger of death is probably the most stimulating touch in life. Nothing else will stir a living being to greater activity. It is a natural instinct, this effort to go on living, and not something that is dictated by the conscious mind.

The pain wracking Doc Savage's body was radiating from the golden scepter that had been thrust into his chest. His great body trembled. Perspiration popped out along his metallic skin, sending rivulets of rust flowing down his legs. As before, he was helpless against it.

But this time, he found the will to wrench himself free of this agonizing power.

Blindly reaching out, Doc took hold of something—he never knew what—and, with an arm whose musculature resembled piano wire bundles coated in bronze lacquer, jerked his convulsing body hard, away from the impalpable death touch.

Instantly, the spasming of his pain-knotted body ebbed. Vision restored, Doc took stock.

The Wraith, surprise on his graybeard contenence, seemed to waver. He whistled once, an eerie questioning sound that made him seem human for once.

Doc was leaning against a corridor wall for support. He shook his head twice, as if to shrug off some spell that had seized his brain. His legs were bent at the knees, seemingly averse to supporting him.

"It is folly to resist Fausto the Deathless," the specter said in his crackling tone. "I shall make an example of you, Man of Bronze."

Grinning, the Whistling Wraith started toward the bronze man. His mouth pursed, began emitting that doleful funeral march.

Doc Savage knew there was no resisting the apparition. Nor could he fight it. Even had it been an ordinary foe, he was not up to a battle with the materialization—vision, haunt, shade, or whatever it was. All strength had been sapped in the brief interval of agony.

The Whistling Wraith knew this. Extending his punishing, pain-giving scepter, it came on.

"The touch of Fausto," he intoned, "is death to all mortals."

So it seemed. The bronze man made no move to escape. His flake-gold eyes were queerly still, as if they had died. He might have been on his last legs.

The scepter inched closer, its gems like spiders' eyes.

Doc Savage, doing the unexpected, simply threw himself toward his foe, one hand flinging a cloud of rusty scrapings before him.

Caught by surprise, the Wraith recoiled. The hand clutching the scepter lifted to protect the eyes. The bronze man ducked under the deadly thing of gold and jewels.

And Doc passed through the startled apparition as if it were not there!

He stumbled briefly, then kept going, not looking back, not concerning himself with his eerie foe at all.

The bronze man was intent upon getting topside.

He emerged into warm moonlight like a statue of antiquity that had shaken off the rust of ages.

The decks were a pandemonium of men, most seeking companions, or sheltering objects.

The brief flurry of bullets had abated. Holes had been punched everywhere, snapping stays and perforating thinned-by-corrosion bulkheads.

Out in the bay, harbor police boats hung off, their searchlights raking the rusty hulk in great blinding funnels.

A familiar frog's voice called out, "I said this is a police raid! Nobody do anything that might get them drilled!"

Push 'em Down Sampson! Doc spotted the boxy police inspector in the bow of one of the harbor boats. Near him, looking very forlorn, were Monk, Ham, and Pat Savage—prisoners.

One of the dark figures scuttling along the deck of the *Grim Seas* crept up to the rail, angled a long pistol barrel over the edge, and snapped off a single shot.

That ignited everything.

Police riot guns, submachine guns, and assorted revolvers returned fire. Bullets again began gnashing at the hull, the masts—everything in sight. Clouds of rust commenced percolating.

Moving low, Doc Savage glided through this fall of bitter snow. The searchlights helped him. His equipment vest was visible on a coil of rope. He made for it, pulled it on.

From a vest pocket, he extracted one cartridge. He snapped something, tossed the thing. It rolled into a corner and, hissing furiously, uncoiled a long worm of black smoke.

"We musta hit something!" a voice from across the water yelled. "The old hulk's caught fire!"

Huddled under the rail, Doc fixed the voice. Another cartridge came up. He gave it a snap and threw it high and over the rail.

"Hey! They're throwing smoke at us!"

And Doc knew he had struck one police boat with his smoke grenade. The spreading pall was soon picked up by a steady breeze and distributed over the decks of the other harbor police craft in a sooty haze. The shooting died. There was a lull.

In Mayan, he rapped out guttural words.

A dazed answer came from nearby. Renny. Doc made for the sound. The smoke was still uncoiling on deck, so it was possible to locate the big-fisted engineer.

"Long Tom and Johnny," Doc rasped. "Where are they?"

"Holy cow! How should I know! I just came to. Is that Sampson out there?"

Doc nodded, asked, "Up for a swim?"

"Reckon so."

"Try to get Monk and Ham free. We may need them."

"O.K." The gloomy engineer hunkered down, made his way to the bow, and clambered down the chain. Thanks to the prodigious scooping qualities of his gargantuan hands, he was an excellent swimmer.

Meanwhile, the bronze man was making his way to the main companion. He encountered various gunmen along the way. Some, recognizing him, attempted to impede his progress.

Doc seized wrists, tripped ankles, slammed heads, broke bones, a metallic juggernaut of vengeance.

At intervals, he cast his golden eyes toward the bulkhead from which he had emerged, the Whistling Wraith in close pursuit.

Of the apparition, there was no sign. Nor any sound. It was quiet enough for its unutterably sad whistling notes to be heard. But the Wraith did not always whistle, as Doc had come to understand.

Doc gained the companion. Voices were busy below.

He started down.

Came a shrill whistle, a *ping! crack!* as a bullet snarled up at him.

Doc withdrew. He gobbled a sentence in Mayan.

From below, Johnny's returning gobble was cut off in mid-sentence. The gaunt archæologist got out enough to inform Doc that he and Long Tom, driven by the furious storm of police lead, had taken shelter below, along with King Goz's minions.

Doc listened.

Angry voices were volleying back and forth.

"I'm strictly hired talent," one was saying. "I got no stake in this beyond my cut."

"Yeah. And if the president signs that damn bill, our share goes up in smoke."

A foreign-sounding voice snarled back, "*Caineles!* Dogs! You have no vote here."

"Says you."

"With the king unconscious, I am in charge."

"Yeah? Well, it looks like he's coming around now."

Out on the water, Doc detected splashings. He crept to the rail. Peering through a rusty rivet hole, he spied four figures beating toward the *Grim Seas*. Renny, Monk, Ham, and Pat!

A froggy voice cried, "Stop them! Who let them get away!?"

Doc lifted his voice.

"Sampson! Let my friends get clear! It is in your best interest! Matters are coming to a head!"

"Nothing doing! They're escaping police prisoners! Ripe for shooting!"

Doc had expected the ripping reply. He got out a small tear gas grenade, set the charge, and gave an overhead toss.

It landed, not by chance, at Saul Sampson's square feet, and let go with a mushy *whump!*

Bawling, Sampson stormed about, his words incoherent.

That settled any notions of shooting at Renny and the others.

Doc went to meet them at the anchor chain.

Monk ambled over first. He wore a big grin as he wrung water out of sleeves.

"What's the score, Doc?"

"Long Tom and Johnny are below. A battle is brewing between Goz's retinue and some hired gunmen."

"We gotta haul them two outta there," the hairy chemist said with enthusiasm.

Ham, drooping and bedraggled, was assisting Pat Savage over the rail.

"Am I steamed!" Pat hissed, looking somewhat like a

half-drowned kitten. "Here I am in the thick of it at last and I don't have my trusty hogleg!"

"Later," Doc rapped. "Follow me."

Moving low, they reached the companion. They kept out of shooting range. Bay water was puddling about their bare feet.

Renny thumped, "Where'd that spook get to?"

"Hasn't emerged from below," Doc advised.

"You defeat it?"

Doc shook his head grimly.

"The way that thing can go through walls," Monk said warily, "it could be anywhere on this tub."

Doc motioned for silence.

From below, a voice was speaking groggily.

"We must escape these American police. I must not be captured."

"Who's that?" Ham hissed.

"King Goz the First," Doc supplied.

"Huh?"

The voice continued. "Nothing matters but my escape. I will not return to Merida. I will be a puppet no longer."

Pat wondered, "What is he talking about—puppet?"

Then they heard the whistling.

It filtered up from the rust-fouled innards of the ship.

"What are we waiting on?" Renny boomed.

"Sharpshooter below," Doc advised.

"That so? I'll fix him."

And the big-fisted engineer produced the blue automatic he had earlier taken from a gunman. It looked like a toy in his gargantuan fist. He pointed it downward, and with his smallest finger—the only one that would fit inside the trigger guard—fired.

The echoes were deafening. But a groan came back.

Doc pitched down, vaulting over a writhing body. The others pounded after him.

Doc called back, "Get that man on deck."

Pat and the others fell to that task.

The bronze man followed the whistling. There was shouting now. A gun banged. A man screamed. Doc pitched forward.

In the litter-strewn stateroom, men were backing away from a rust-red wall.

For coming through the rusty surface was the Whistling Wraith!

It paused, as if to allow lesser mortals to drink in their own stupefaction.

Then it spoke: "King Goz of Merida: Hear my curse. You have no wealth, no refuge, no escape. Throw yourself on the mercy of the American police and be returned to your country and your people. This is the decree of Fausto."

A frightened voice—not the king's—cried, "Fausto is dead! Long dead!"

"*I* am Fausto! And I have followed you all to this strange land to undo your wicked schemes."

"I will not go back!" Egil Goz screamed.

And the Wraith advanced.

"Stop him!" Goz shrieked.

The gunmen ignored the command; they kept firing. But the retinue of Meridan courtiers were used to obeying their monarch.

"Throw yourself at him!" Goz shouted. "You are my servants. It is your duty!"

Doc lifted his voice then.

"Enough have died because of one man. It must stop here."

It was rare that the bronze man's voice had no effect. But the room was charged with emotion. All eyes were on the Whistling Wraith.

Cowering, King Goz began shoving reluctant courtiers toward the oncoming figure. One tried to brain it with the butt of his gun. The scepter snaked out and the man fell twitching to the rusty floor.

King Goz grabbed a man. "You! Your turn!"

It was too much. The figure coming through the walls. The inability of mortal lead to stop it. The police outside.

The courtier who had been grabbed turned savagely on his monarch. Lifting the barrel of his gun, he shot the king from temple to temple, crying, "My brother died protecting your cowardly life!"

From the Wraith, came a long, astonished howl of anger.

Like a scarlet bat, he surged forward, descended upon the man who had murdered his own king, felling him.

There was a mad rush for the exit. Doc got out of the way. He was all but ignored as the men charged out.

The Wraith started after them, eyes cold and venomous. Then, as if changing his mind, he stopped, and walked back into the wall from which he had materialized.

Doc pitched deeper into the ship and collected Long Tom and Johnny, who had taken refuge in the engine room.

"Come on!"

They worked their way back, rejoining Renny and the others, who had returned after taking care of the wounded man.

Monk demanded, "Where did the dang Wraith go?"

"No time!" Doc rapped. "Make for the deck!"

"What about the Wraith?"

"The Wraith is up to something."

"What?"

"Something was said about poison gas earlier."

Renny thumped, "A bluff, right?"

"Maybe not."

The bronze man swept them up the complaining steps.

Deep in the innards of the rust bucket that was the *Grim Seas*, an extended hissing began.

And like the breath of a cave-dwelling dragon, a yellowish cloud rolled along the rusty corridor.

"Move!"

Doc had recognized the stuff. He knew the gas type, could duplicate it, in fact had. So he knew that without completely enveloping gasproof suits, they were helpless.

The stuff settled, therefore would be thicker in the hold, in the boiler room. But it was already sending creeping, sinuous yellow fingers up the companion. To remain would be inviting disaster.

They mounted the steps and ran smack into a young war.

The deck had cleared of Doc's smoke screen. The police below were shooting upward—shooting at anything that moved.

On deck, the gunmen were returning fire! They had the advantage of height but they were ineffective, their fire ragged. Too, they were not well-armed. Only one Tommy gun was racketing.

Bullets snapped at the companion entrance, whined away.

"Trapped!" Renny boomed. "What do we do?"

The bronze man felt of his many-pocketed vest. His fingers came out empty. He had exhausted much of his bag of tricks. His golden eyes, little fires in them, went back to the yellow seepage collecting in the bowels of the hulk. The gas was mounting the rusty steps like a silent, voracious beast.

Doc turned to the dapper Ham. "Still carry that cigarette lighter?"

"Of course."

"Give it here."

"But why—?"

"*Now!*"

Ham surrendered the lighter. It was a jeweled thing of platinum, an affectation, for the dapper lawyer did not smoke.

Doc thumbed the trinket to flame.

"Get set to go over the rail," he warned, running backward.

Monk, the chemist, catching on, gulped, "Blazes!"

"Exactly," Doc said, tossing the lighter down.

They were taking a big chance. They all knew it. If the flame went out before reaching the gas, they would be running through a thick fusillade of bullets.

On the other hand, to delay would be to risk catching the consequences of Doc's action.

They were over the side when the condemned hulk shuddered from stem to rudder like a stricken thing.

It was not an explosion. Not as such. The sound was more a *whuff!* than a *boom!* But the bolted-over portholes here and there violently ejected their steel plates. Fire vomited out from chinks, empty rivet holes, companions, and vents along deck and rust-scabbed hull.

Doc Savage, his aids, and Pat Savage were dropping into the water by that time. They were forced to leap from the bay side of the ship, the other being too shallow. They had luck. The shock of the fiery gases coming out of every seam and rent in the rusty old hulk had quelled police firing.

They bobbed to the surface, struck out for the harbor boats.

"Hold your fire!" Doc called.

"Why should we?" Saul Sampson shouted back.

"Because we surrender."

The police held their fire.

But that was not the end of it. The gunmen along the deck were trying to get out of the flame-licked ship, too. They fought for the privilege of clambering down the anchor chain. Some jumped. Others ran around searching for a safe hiding place.

Then the Wraith showed himself once more.

In the water, Doc and the others learned this when a hoarse, foreign-sounding voice cried, "It is the ghost of Fausto! It has emerged from the flames to punish us for Goz's perfidy!"

They stopped their swimming, and began treading water.

And saw the Whistling Wraith come out of a wall of fire that blocked a companion!

"Blazes!" Monk squeaked. "Even fire don't hurt it none!"

The scarlet apparition floated along the deck in full view. It was moving along the near rail, its face satyrlike in the hellish light.

A police sharpshooter took a shot at it. In the dark, he was never sure if he struck it or not. It kept going.

"Somebody put a light on that thing!" Sampson called out.

A searchlight swung into play. It had been spotlighting the bow. Now it swept back.

The beam, crossing the wizened face of the Whistling Wraith, struck it full in the eyes.

The Wraith showed its one human characteristic then. It threw a hand before its black orbs to shield them from the glare. Atop its head, the great oversized crown wobbled. The Wraith reached up with both hands to steady the ungainly object—and a second beam of light caught it full in the face!

The light—of enormous candlepower—must have been painful to the optic nerves. The Wraith, off balance, brought protective hands down again. It swayed. And the precariously balanced crown tumbled off its head!

A simple thing. But the Wraith was suddenly galvanized, as if some momentous fright had seized it. It lashed out to recapture its splendid crown.

Gnarled hands snatched and fumbled.

Whether it would have been successful, no one was ever to know.

A strange, inhuman cry came from the specter's lips.

For the Whistling Wraith, leaning out, seemed to forget it was no more corporeal than mist. It passed through the unresisting rusty rail of the *Grim Seas*—and floated down!

Like a scarlet feather, almost weightless, it sank toward the water. Uncanny sight. Crown tumbling ahead of it, kicking legs passing in and out of the rusty hull in ghostly fashion, it was madly clutching for the lost symbol of royalty.

And when it struck the water, there was no splash— just the heaving black water swallowing a fragment of red silk.

Without warning, Doc Savage plunged beneath the surface, eyes wild.

The others, swapping looks, dived after him.

It was dark below. Police searchlights, crossing and uncrossing, sent out long, questing fingers of illumination.

They could see then.

The bronze man was swimming furiously—swimming toward the Whistling Wraith, who was continuing its slow downward fall. The water seemed not to support it. Its mouth was open and gulping like a fish. No bubbles of air emerged.

It was still scrambling for its crown. And its scepter. To no avail.

Doc came up on the thing. Tried to capture it. He might as well have been attempting to lay hands on a streak of red sunlight. Bronzed fingers clenched, snapped, and clenched some more. Each time, the Whistling Wraith defied his touch.

But this time, the apparition no longer reveled in its awesome power to defy capture. Seeing the bronze man, it reached back, as if grasping at a straw—a straw with no more substance than itself.

Soon, it floated to the silty harbor bottom—*and kept going!*

Like a man drowning in quicksand, the Whistling Wraith struggled, floundered, all to no avail.

Enervated by the urgency of the situation, Doc Savage attempted to scoop up handfuls of silt to keep the specter from dropping from sight completely. But the situation was hopeless.

The silt swallowed him from sight. The last glimpse they had of the Whistling Wraith was its head, black eyes stark, unbelieving. They held a doomed, mournful light.

The others pitched in then. Frantic fingers dug into the bottom of the bay, but all they accomplished was to stir up cloudy murk through which police searchlights prowled silently.

Then their air ran out. They swam back to the surface.

They only noticed the presence of Inspector Saul Sampson in the water then. His eyes were wide and unbelieving, like skinned grapes. He followed them up.

Doc Savage, with the power to hold his breath for prodigious lengths of time—a skill learned from the pearl divers of the South Seas—remained below.

After they got air back into their lungs, Monk, Ham, Pat, and the others returned to the bottom of the bay.

The silt had settled some. Doc Savage was swimming about, searching, his bronze fingers feeling under the silt. In vain, they knew.

Monk Mayfair got the bronze man's attention and, using the deaf-and-dumb sign language they all knew, signaled that it was hopeless.

The wild urgency went out of Doc's eyes. He signed back.

"O.-K."

Together, they returned to the surface.

## XXVII

## CROWN OF GUILT

"Don't anyone ever tell ghost stories around me again," Pat Savage said after Doc Savage's head broke the surface. "*Brrr!* I never believed in such things, but after tonight—"

"It was no ghost," Doc said quietly.

"My foot! I saw it. You saw it. We all saw it."

"Yes. But it can be explained."

"Fine," bellowed the bullfrog voice of Push 'em Down Sampson, bobbing not far distant. "I'm going to want to hear all about it."

A searchlight swept across the dark water, blinding them.

Shielding his eyes, Doc said, "The fire should have burned out the poison gas. Much can be explained aboard the ship."

"I can hardly wait!" Sampson said fiercely.

They allowed themselves to be helped out of the water and onto the police boats, where they set about the arduous task of wringing water out of such sopping clothes as they had managed to retain through the hectic events of the last several hours.

The police had already collected most of the gunmen and the remnants of King Goz's retinue. The fight was out of them. They looked dazed, spiritless. They stood about under heavy guard.

"You," Sampson told Doc, "are under arrest. The charges are counterfeiting, assassination of a high government official—"

Doc lifted a palm that was scraped raw by numerous rusty encounters.

"If you will allow us some leeway, we can explain everything."

"Including that fright show I just saw?"

"You mean the Wraith?"

"That," Sampson said, "is a better name for it than I had thought up. And politer, too," he added, eying Pat Savage.

"The Wraith can be explained."

"And so can the counterfeiting charge," Pat added. To Doc, she said, "Inspector Bullfrog here descended on me when I was trying to get those bonds out of Drago's place."

"Caught red-handed," Push 'em Down retorted. "Along with the counterfeiting setup that printed them."

"The bonds are real," Doc said.

"Hah!"

"If you check, you will find the serial numbers match the bogus bonds found in the U.S. Treasury. And others which ended up in investor hands."

"If you know that much, it makes you an accomplice with Goldwill, and whoever else is involved in this extortion."

"That reminds me," Doc said. "Where is Joan Manville?"

Pat answered that.

"She showed up at Drago's before Sampson did. Alone. I spilled the beans, Doc. I told her about Prestowitz's death. I figured it would jar some truth out of her."

Sampson demanded, "Who's Prestowitz?"

"She took it hard," Pat continued, ignoring the squat police inspector. "When the police came, they had to take her away."

Doc turned to Inspector Sampson. "You might," he said, "have Miss Manville brought here."

Elaborately, Saul Sampson expectorated on the deck, and considered the bronze man's request at some length. Finally, he nodded to a patrolman, who went to the ship's radio. Then Sampson addressed the others.

"Somebody want to tell me who this Prestowitz is?

And while you're at it, identify the bodies found in Long Island." He gave Doc the eye. "You should have erased that message, Savage. The one that said, 'Grim Seas.' I used to pound a beat at Gravesend, you know. The name meant something to me when I heard about it."

"Precisely why I did not obliterate it," Doc stated quietly.

"Tall talk," Sampson snorted.

"As for Caspar Prestowitz," Doc said, "Miss Manville can explain him. But his was one of the bodies found in my warehouse place."

"And the two found at the Long Island wreck?"

"General Graul Frontenac of Merida and a countryman."

Sampson arched a squarish eyebrow. "The general that lost the king?"

"The very same."

"So this mess *does* hook in with the hullabaloo down in Washington!"

"It does."

"Hell's fire!" Sampson roared. "That does it! You're all going to the hold-over for questioning."

Monk put in, "You want explanations, maybe you should listen and not shoot off your yap so much."

Inspector Sampson gave the hairy chemist an appraising look. "I think I met your brother one time, at the Bronx zoo. He peeled a mean banana."

Ham tittered mirth at that.

The bronze man offered, "This derelict ship was a temporary hideout for the retinue of King Goz. It is here they were guarding something important."

"The king?"

"And more—if you care to see for yourself."

"O.K.," Sampson relented. "Let's investigate that hooker."

The police boats warped alongside the *Grim Seas*. Lines were made fast. And under police guns, Doc and his party were allowed to mount the deck.

Gingerly, they went down the main companion. The air was acrid with smoke stink. It was pungent, but not harmful to inhale. The poison gas had been highly flammable. One match had consumed it.

Doc Savage first took them to the litter-strewn storage room. The body of King Goz of Merida lay there. Dead. The quantity of brain matter that had been splashed about made further examination unnecessary.

"Who's the stiff?" Sampson asked callously.

"The missing king," Doc explained.

"Who croaked him? You?"

"His own people."

"That wasn't the missing king we saw fall into the"— the queer look came into Sampson's eyes again—"the water?"

"No. It might have been reasonable to connect King Goz with the Whistling Wraith, but it was clear to me from the first time I beheld the latter, that they could not be one and the same."

"Why not? White whiskers make a good disguise."

"The Wraith wore silk and ermine," Doc pointed out. "King Goz was a Mohammedan, to whom the wearing of such animal products is forbidden."

Sampson grunted. Doc next led them to the panel leading into the hold. Here the gas had been thickest. The rusty walls were now scorched to a black, gritty finish resembling burnt toast.

"I ain't crawling through that rat hole," Sampson said of the aperture.

Fire axes were brought. Police made short work of the wall, widening it enough that they could step into the hold.

The burlap bags draped over boxes were singed and blackened. The one that had been hanging on the wall had fallen in a formless pile, revealing the combination dial and handle of the old hulk's safe.

"If you will allow me," Doc said.

Sampson grunted his assent.

Doc worked the dial. It complained. A little of the rust that permeated the rotting derelict must have gotten into the mechanism, but it surrendered soon enough.

The door came open.

Sampson shoved his head in. The others crowded forward. By their expressions, most half expected to find a body.

Instead, they saw stacks and stacks of wealth. Some of it was gold in small ingots, others represented cash of various nations. There were bonds, too. British Consuls and French Rentes. But by far the greatest quantities of printed matter were Liberty Bonds.

Saul Sampson cocked a thumb. "These the counterfeits?"

"Real," Doc said.

"Not more of the missing ones?"

"No. They have nothing to do with the cache found at Drago's home. These represent, in large measure, the stolen wealth of the people of Merida."

"Yeah? Who stole them?"

"King Goz."

Sampson's blocky jaw dropped.

"You trying to tell me that Goz pulled his own disappearing act?"

Doc nodded. "The king was absconding with his nation's wealth."

"But why? He was the king, for hell's sake! Why would he need to do that?"

Just then a voice called down, "Inspector! That dame is here!"

Doc advised, "Miss Manville will be able to explain the rest."

"This," Sampson gritted, tossing the bonds back into the safe, "had better be one heck of an explanation, or the lot of you are going to be making little ones out of big ones till hell's fire freezes solid."

They repaired to the rusty deck of the *Grim Seas*. The breathing was better there, anyway.

Joan Manville had not been handcuffed. She looked the picture of defeat. Her natural beauty, which could be enhanced by make-up or washed out to deceptive plainness, was absent. She was pale, withdrawn, her gray eyes downcast.

"My actual name," she said without preamble, "is Jone

Vernelle. And I am—or was—a secret agent in the service of Santa Bellanca."

"Holy cow!" Renny boomed.

Sampson snapped, "Shut up, you! Let her tell it!"

Jone Vernelle moistened colorless lips.

"I have lied from the first. But one thing was truth: Caspar Prestowitz is—was—my fiancé."

"I keep hearing that name," Sampson growled, "but not who he is."

"Caspar Prestowitz is one of the great inventors of our time," Jone Vernelle elaborated. "He invented a device which he realized could make him a fortune if he sold it to certain unscrupulous countries. He had no interest in doing so. Instead, he decided to hire out himself and the device to the highest bidder. The first country he approached was Carrullana, which desired information about its Balkan rival, Merida.

"Using this device, Caspar spied on the King of Merida and learned that he was planning to abscond with his nation's wealth. You might wonder why a king should do that."

"It had crossed my mind," Sampson allowed dryly.

"It is well-known that in recent years the king was forced to turn to its European neighbor, Santa Bellanca, for protection against territorial encroachment. But there was a price attached. Officers of the Federal Army of Santa Bellanca assumed command of key Meridan military units. Santa Bellancan banks and financial advisers grew in power until their influence rivaled that of the king's. In time, this arrangement grew chafing. The king was reduced to being a puppet of the leader of Santa Bellanca, and having seen what happened to a defenseless African nation Santa Bellanca coveted, feared for the absorption of his nation into the other."

"I begin to see where this leads," Johnny murmured.

"Hush!" Pat snapped. "I want to hear this from the mare's own mouth."

Jone Vernelle continued in a hollow, drained voice.

"King Goz decided to vanish, taking with him the wealth of his people, much of it invested in Liberty Bonds. He told only certain trusted aides, men who were sworn to secrecy, and who would participate in the faking of his disappearance. Caspar learned of this and realized—greed had possessed him by now—that this information was worth more to the dictator of Santa Bellanca than it would be to Carrullana's president. But he could not learn of the time, place, or method of the planned vanishing. By this time it was too late to influence the king to abandon his plan. So Caspar agreed to assist in the dictator's scheme to force the king to return to his throne, an obedient puppet of Santa Bellanca once more."

Jone Vernelle drew in a long, sad breath of contrition.

"I was a part of that scheme, first playing the part of Barbara Bland in an effort to learn where the king had disappeared to. Caspar was pretending to be a financial agent for H. Startland Drago. In fact, it was Caspar who planted the counterfeit bonds in the U.S. Treasury, a scheme that was already under way, in anticipation of the king's evanishment."

"Wait a minute!" Monk exploded. "Laurence Kingsley Goldwill's thumb print was found on them counterfeit bonds."

"A fake," Doc said. "An impression was made of the thumb in wax and carefully planted."

"How did you know?" Jone wondered.

"Telltale perspiration oils did not come to light under a chemical test. That meant the print was not made by human skin."

Jone Vernelle nodded somberly.

"Somebody tell me how this Caspar fellow got in and out of the Treasury," Sampson demanded. "That place is a fortress."

"Caspar Prestowitz," Jone Vernelle stated, "was the person many mistook for Old King Fausto."

"He was!" Sampson's voice was a deep, astonished croak.

"The device he invented enabled him to pass through solid objects. It consisted of a helmet and a control wand. Knowing of the legend of the shade of Fausto, he rebuilt them to create the imposture so that if he were seen moving about the royal castle, it would be dismissed as superstition—or explained away as a haunting by those credulous enough to believe in such things."

"Us? Believe in haunts?" Pat scoffed. "Never."

"The crown was the helmet and the scepter the control wand," Jone Vernelle explained further. "Vacuum tubes were sewn into his thick cloak, and connected to the other elements by insulated wires. You see, the crown functioned as a kind of generator, creating an electromagnetic-field effect. In the event of an electrical problem, he carried a hollowed orb housing a tear gas generator so he could escape difficulty under smoke screen cover. The scepter, which was tipped with an exposed electrode, could also be used as a frightening weapon, for it contained a powerful dry-cell battery which supplied the generator crown with current."

Renny rumbled, "So that's what laid me out that time! That rod sure packed a jolt!"

"It nearly finished me," Doc related grimly, "the second time I encountered its effects."

Saul Sampson, who had been listening to all this with an increasingly loose-jawed expression, now exploded.

"I don't believe in ghosts! Everybody understand that! But I don't buy no gimmick that would make a man so he could walk through walls, either! That's bunk."

"Not bunk," Doc Savage said. "But the application of one of the more fundamental rules of atomic matter."

"Which is?"

"That matter is not solid. It only appears to be."

Sampson pounded a square fist on a stanchion. It came away redder than before.

"You can't tell me that ain't solid!"

"Matter," Doc related calmly, "as we understand it, is composed of molecules, which in turn are collections of atoms—the smallest particles known to man. As every schoolboy knows, each atom is made up of a central nucleus and electrons, all whirling in orbits. The model of a solar system with planets orbiting a sun—or the nucleus— is a perfect illustration. These planetlike electrons orbit at incredible speeds, creating the illusion of a solid shell, just as a whirling airplane propeller appears to be a solid disk to the casual eye."

"Sure," Monk said. "It's the positive electric charge of the nucleus that keeps the electrons in line, so to speak."

"On the atomic level, there are great spaces between nuclei and their electrons," Doc continued. "Most of the atom is, in fact, composed of empty space. Just as you cannot insert your hand between the blades of a spinning prop, electrons repel other electrons. If it were possible to manipulate the atomic constituent of an object so the tiny nucleus and its always-moving electrons filter between the atomic components of other matter instead of colliding, it is conceivable that an object thus treated will pass safely through another, seemingly solid, object without harm to either."

"Or a person," Jone Vernelle inserted. "Oh, I do not understand the theory perfectly, but it is much as Mr. Savage has said. Wearing the electric crown and control wand, Caspar could enter any room, pass through any object, immune from harm, for his atoms were charged so that they repelled the electrons and nuclei of any object he encountered when in the intangible state. Any person or object carried within the field was similarly intangible."

Johnny ran bony fingers through his longish hair. "Now we know how he got the fake bonds into the Treasury and the real ones out again, as well as repeatedly stealing that sword to confound us."

"Caspar found by experimenting," Jone added, "that it was sometimes necessary to adjust the field so that he was *semi*solid. When climbing stairs or riding elevators, for example."

"Explains how the Wraith was able to ride our elevator down," Ham said slowly, "but when Monk tried to take him back up, his atoms went through the cage floor like sand through a sieve."

"And how I could thrust my hand into the Wraith's apparently ghostly body, yet be unable to withdraw it," Doc added. "By manipulation of the wand, he effected a subtle change in his atomic state, making it more akin to a colloid than a gas or a liquid, his preferred state."

"Something don't add up here," Monk growled.

Jone Vernelle looked faintly curious. "Yes?"

"You say Prestowitz was the Wraith. But we saw the Wraith after Prestowitz turned up in our safe croaked."

Jone Vernelle paled visibly. She wavered on her feet. Oddly enough, Long Tom Roberts came to her aid. He held her cool hand until she had recovered.

"Thank you," she said meekly.

Then he withdrew, looking thoughtfully at his shoes.

"Caspar was the *first* 'Wraith,' as you call it," she related, her voice itself a ghost. "There were two."

Pat Savage turned to Monk Mayfair. "So that's why I saw a blue-eyed spook and yours was black-eyed. They weren't the same person!"

"I'll be danged!" the apish chemist shouted. "Makes sense to me!"

Johnny asked, "So who was the second specter?"

"It should be obvious by now," Doc Savage said. "The man who masterminded the financial scheme to compel King Goz to return to his throne, was the only man with the inside knowledge of the king's financial affairs and the power and influence to carry out the plot. A man who had close ties to the Santa Bellanca dictator and did not care if he wrecked the American economy in the pursuit of his aims. Or his own business enterprise."

"Yes," Jone Vernelle intoned. "H. Startland Drago is the Wraith. The evil Wraith. Caspar murdered no one. It was not in him to do so."

"I hope somebody is writing all this down," Saul Sampson muttered to no one in particular. "I ain't got the gray matter to hold all this."

Jone Vernelle went on in a faint voice.

"When H. Startland Drago learned that the Meridan footman had been murdered with the royal sword, he reasoned that it was the work of King Goz, who was attempting to lay the blame on the spirit of King Fausto, in whom he implicitly believed, having happened upon him in his own castle."

"And Drago hit upon the idea of stealing the sword, using it as a way to further confuse the issue," Doc stated.

Jone Vernelle nodded. "We had been making no progress in our search for the king, when the appearance of Doc Savage in Washington changed matters. H. Startland Drago ordered me to make contact with Mr. Savage in the hope that would lead me to King Goz. While I was pretending to be Barbara Bland, Caspar had gone to Mr. Savage's headquarters, hoping to learn what he could of any progress by eavesdropping."

"That's when I spotted him," Pat said. "Prestowitz waylaid me right after. I should have connected the two, but I didn't."

"As I understand it," Jone Vernelle went on, "Caspar was forced to assume his Fausto disguise in order to escape from Doc Savage's men in Virginia. He had already been instructed to steal the sword of Merida from the morgue and bring it to Drago. Drago, I now know, coveted the Wraith device. He knew if forced to embark on his scheme to void the Liberty Bond issue, Drago & Company would be no more. And Caspar's failed abduction of Miss Savage could not be adequately explained. Drago decided that Caspar had to die. I imagine they fought. Or I hope they did." She shuddered. "I would hate to think Drago murdered him in cold blood without a fight."

"From then on, his face aged by make-up, the Whistling Wraith was H. Startland Drago," Doc stated.

Jone Vernelle nodded. "Unable to locate the king, he embarked upon his great plan. The press was tipped off to the counterfeit bonds, igniting a panic. Drago knew he would be summoned to testify before Congress. But to pull off his scheme, he needed a scapegoat, some one to take the blame."

"Laurence Kingsley Goldwill!" This from Saul Sampson.

"He was perfect. Under indictment, reviled, he could never clear himself. Certainly not after Drago sent out all those demand letters in his name, implicating him in a fictitious plot to force America to abandon money. He was then murdered and planted in Doc Savage's office safe, to close the books on him and remove Mr. Savage from the picture."

"A double frame!" Sampson breathed.

"And you fell for it, flatfoot," Monk muttered. "Hook, line, and sinker."

Sampson glowered.

"Let her finish. This is interesting."

"If you like ghost stories," Monk snorted.

"Where was Goldwill all this time?" Sampson prompted.

"A prisoner in Drago's attic. That had been planned from the start. To make it look good, Seymour Holman had tied Drago up in Goldwill's apartment, to make it appear as if Drago had been kidnaped by Goldwill."

"It was a clever scheme," Doc said. "I was hoodwinked into opening the Drago safe and picking up the false trail to Goldwill's, where I found Drago, a seeming prisoner."

Renny, a tower of bone and gloom in the night, blurted, "Wait a minute! Drago was under police guard. How'd he come and go so easy?"

"A secret exit from the attic," Doc explained. "It was easy enough to climb down a great oak and slip away without attracting police notice. Drago did this while we were guarding him, too. His penchant for seclusion made his absences go virtually unnoticed."

"So when I left him with Ham that time," Monk exploded, "he just slipped out the back and beat me to our headquarters, where he planted Prestowitz in our safe!"

"Exactly."

Monk turned to Ham Brooks. "Some watchdog you turned out to be, shyster!"

Jone Vernelle said, "That was my fault. I kept Mr. Brooks entertained the entire time, distracting him."

Ham colored. "I could not let this knuckle-dragging gorilla get away with telling fibs about my matrimonial situation," he snapped. "I had to clear my good name."

Doc picked up the explanations from there. "Once Drago persuaded Congress to void the Liberty issue, it was necessary for him to disappear. He did this when his limousine was blocked by a truck. He simply donned the Fausto disguise and slipped from the solid car, unseen."

Renny grunted. "I remember that Holman cut the car in front of that moving truck."

"Where is that little clunk, anyways?" Monk wanted to know.

"Forgot to tell you," Sampson said. "We found Holman outside your office. He didn't have a sword in him, but his throat had a sword-sized slash across it. I guess Drago was tying up all his loose ends, just like that Goz."

Jone Vernelle said, "That happened after Drago faked his disappearance. It was Seymour who, after giving Mr. Savage's men the slip, took a shot at the American president. When Miss Savage took me from the Drago home to Doc Savage headquarters, Drago, as the Whistling Wraith, came for me. To silence me, I now know. I thought I was being rescued—otherwise I would not have gone with him. But Mr. Savage shouted to me the truth about Caspar's fate. Later, Drago denied it, then forced me to call the police to tip them off to go to the warehouse. Drago was very frustrated that the police could not discover the planted bodies, and reasoned they might be there."

"So how did you get free of Drago?" Ham asked.

"I am a secret agent, as I have told you. I have some skills, and was able to fight him off and escape. I went directly to his mansion, knowing the evidence of the counterfeiting operation could be found there. The unused counterfeits had been destroyed in acid, along with the plates, but there was enough evidence to take to the authorities. I no longer cared about anything, with Caspar dead."

"That's when we collided," Pat inserted. "I thought I had cracked the whole case—that is, until the forces of the law glommed us," she added archly.

Saul Sampson ignored the jibe. "What I want to know is this: If Drago was that ghost, how'd he find out about the *Grim Seas*?"

Jone Vernelle seemed to have an answer for that.

"It must be that Drago deduced how I planned to expose him, and trailed me to his home. He could have been secreted in one of the mansion walls, listening, when Inspector Sampson learned of the *Grim Seas* clue."

"Girlie," Sampson croaked, "I think you just hit the nail on the head. Too bad you got smart too late to do you much good."

Jone Vernelle hung her head. "I am prepared to submit to any punishment the authorities of this country choose to inflict."

No one spoke for long moments.

Then Saul Sampson turned to Doc Savage. "Guess I was wrong about you, Savage."

"We all make mistakes," the bronze man said without rancor. "I am not without blame. Although I quickly determined how King Goz had managed his vanishing act, and exposed myself to danger in the hope of panicking those responsible into making an attempt on my life, I did not at first suspect that two opposing forces—the Goz group and the Drago group—were at war with one another. It was not until H. Startland Drago testified before Congress that the true picture began taking shape. By then, it was nearly too late. King Goz, realizing that Drago—who had unwittingly helped him convert the stolen Meridan wealth into his Liberty Bonds—was now attempting to bankrupt him, took steps to capture the banker at his home."

"Yeah," Renny rumbled. "Capturing us instead. Holy cow, but there's sure enough facial egg to go around, if you ask me."

"This ain't over yet," Sampson said, indicating a hint of orange creeping up over the Staten Island hills. "Somebody's got to get word to Washington that the real bonds have turned up."

Doc cast his steady gaze upon Inspector Push 'em Down Sampson. "I think you should do that."

"Why me?"

"My aides and I do not care for publicity."

Sampson made a skeptical noise deep in his throat.

"It's true," Pat said firmly. "But we *do* like a little action now and again," she added archly, looking toward her cousin.

"Well, you got it to-night."

"Speak for yourself," Pat snapped. "All I got, was wet."

"Tell that to the ones who got dead," Sampson shot back.

Pat Savage made shapes with her pretty mouth, brows, and eyes while her brain tried to come up with a suitable retort.

In the end, she lost a few shades of tan and said nothing.

* * *

Matters were wrapped up rather quickly after that.

Inspector Saul Sampson got on the police radio and communicated with Headquarters. The booty in the *Grim Seas* safe was confiscated, with the intention that it be returned to its rightful owners, the people of Merida.

The safe also gave up the missing supermachine pistols, ending that particular worry. The tiny weapons were too dangerous to be floating around loose.

Doc helped with the straightening out of details. Much of this was accomplished at Police Headquarters, where he made a number of calls, most of them of a transatlantic nature.

The president was informed of the situation. The bond-voiding bill was promptly vetoed and ripped up, and he went on the radio, calming jitters and promising that all counterfeit Liberties would be replaced with perfectly sound originals, without exception.

Later, a few enterprising criminals would attempt to pawn off their own versions, but these were easily detected by comparing serial numbers with the recovered bonds.

Wall Street threw its collective hat into the air at the good news. The Curb had a memorable day, gaining a substantial number of points.

In the Balkans, the encroaching legions of Carrullana withdrew from the disputed border. No one knew why. No one suspected that Doc Savage had let the government of that nation know, in no uncertain terms, that he would take a personal interest in any land grab.

The dictator of Santa Bellanca made public noises, but they were uncharacteristically muted. Not wishing to further annoy the League of Nations was his stated reason. Fear of Doc Savage was the real explanation.

By evening, the truth had come out. Not all of it. Enough to explain what had to be explained, and no more.

Doc Savage and his aides, in a manner little short of miraculous, had managed to fade into the background. Doc did his best to escape the credit for solving the affair. He succeeded to a degree. Some newspapers even came out with editorials stating that the famous Man of Bronze, Doc Savage, was probably overrated.

Going over the final details in the seclusion of his vast library, the bronze man's attitude was not especially intense. He seemed, indeed, a little tired. It was a hectic life, this one which he led, with excitement following excitement, and his life almost perpetually in peril.

Ham, who was now acting as a legal representative—at a hefty fee—to the lawful Meridan government, hung up the telephone after a lengthy consultation with the Washington authorities, and made an announcement.

"The king's retinue have all confessed. Looks like they are to be deported for the unhung rascals that they are."

"Betcha they don't stay unhung long," Monk observed.

"One of them told an interesting story," Ham added. "He was the man who shot the king. Seems he was the brother of Elvern D. Kastellantz."

Renny popped one fist into the other. "There was a real Kastellantz?"

"The king's official chauffeur," Ham elaborated. "It was his bones that were mistaken for General Frontenac's after the Thermit bomb failed to take Doc's life. Frontenac murdered him to cover his own tracks so he could join the king in hiding. The brother had been steamed about it for days."

"Steamed, huh?" Monk observed. "Guess you could say he just blew a gasket in the end."

That evening, Inspector Saul Sampson showed up at Doc Savage headquarters unannounced.

He entered without his usual belligerent demeanor, his hat in fidgety hands.

"I was just talking with the commissioner," he began.

"Yes?"

"He's restoring your special commission," Sampson beamed. "I wanted to be the guy that broke the good news."

They shook hands.

"A favor in return?" Doc asked.

"Name it."

"Jone Vernelle. A more humane disposing of her case might be in order."

Sampson rubbed his square jaw. "She ended up being as much a victim as any of them, I guess. Got anything special in mind?"

"You will have to trust me."

Sampson shrugged. "If anybody rated the trust, you do. I'll have her brought over."

After Sampson had taken his departure, the others crowded around. Monk and Ham had with them their queer-looking pets, big-eared, spindle-legged Habeas Corpus, and the strange monkey, Chemistry, again. The two pets were making threatening noises at one another, and their owners were likewise acting surly.

Long Tom asked, "She going to our college?"

Doc nodded. "She has a lot to forget."

"Yeah, she does," said Long Tom. He seemed satisfied.

Monk Mayfair had a thought. He expressed it to Doc Savage.

"Say, you know how they're always saying that if you dug a hole deep enough, you'd fall straight to China?"

"Yes?"

"I kinda got a notion that's where that Greedy Gus, Drago, is headed right about now."

"The electromagnetic generator invented by Caspar Prestowitz represents a breakthrough whose loss to science is very regrettable," Doc said thoughtfully. "It might be an idea to organize an expedition, in the hope of somehow recovering it."

They were all for the idea, if for no other reason than it promised a measure of diversion.

All except Pat Savage.

When she heard about the expedition to China, Pat had a remark to make.

"I don't know about this," she said. "I seem to have the vapors, or something."

And Pat had never been known to be overawed by anything or anybody—not even Doc Savage.